I'LL BE THERE

I'LL BE THERE
Iris Rainer Dart

LITTLE, BROWN AND COMPANY
Boston   Toronto   London

As long as there's the two of us
We've got the world and all its charms
And when the world is through with us
We've got each other's arms.

from "The Glory of Love"
by Billy Hill

"Making a living is getting.
Making a life is giving."

from a magnet on my
Aunt Sylvia's refrigerator.

This book is dedicated to every member of my beloved, crazy, brilliant, outspoken, opinionated family. With gratitude for the support, the laughs, the inspiration, and the love you each give so willingly and so well. Particularly my husband, Stephen Dart, who never fails to be there for all of us.

I.R.D.

L.T.B.

THANK YOUS

Elaine Markson
Arthur Klebanoff
Bobbi Vogel M.F.C.C.
Rabbi Scott Sperling
Meg Sivitz
Chad Saffro
Arlene Saffro
Jeff Galpin
Howard Allen
Vicki Gold Levi
Sandy Ferguson
Richard Grossman
David Steinberg
Joyce Brotman
Artie Butler
Barry Adelman
Dave McIntyre
Mary Blann
Francois R. Brenot
Sandy Cope
Andrew Fishmann
Stephen Crain
Josh Winston
Patricia Lienesch
Charlotte and Amanda Brown
Helen Lasley
Doctor Ramsey Kyriakas
Marcia, Nicole, and David Harrow
Jim and Gail Andrews
Megan
Paul Livedary
Phil Stutz
Gregory Michael Wolf
Sandi, my hero

My love, and thanks, and prayers
for the many anonymous parents and kids
who shared their stories with me.

And a special thank you to my editor
Fredrica Friedman for the faith, the confidence,
the constancy, the accessibility and
above all, the grace to make some of the
little yellow slips contain love notes.

I'LL BE THERE

LOS ANGELES, CALIFORNIA

August 1990

ONCE CEE CEE told Bertie if anyone ever wanted to torture her, they could tie her up and make her watch herself on television. Now it was Sunday night at seven thirty-eight, and while she sat watching a clip from one of her old television appearances she remembered that conversation. *60 Minutes* was using the tape as part of a feature story on Hal Lieberman, and they intercut the old shots of Cee Cee singing, with current shots of Hal talking about the days when he was her rehearsal pianist and accompanist.

There she was, singing her heart out on *The Ed Sullivan Show*, with a beehive of teased hair, eye makeup Cleopatra would kill for, and my dear, the way those voluminous bazooms were fighting their way out of that slutty little sequined dress, it was a wonder Standards and Practices hadn't called to say, "Kindly tuck in your tits."

Not to mention the fact that the chestnut of a song was about the same vintage as Ed Sullivan's tie. But the best part was the way Hal, a blurry image just behind her on the screen, wearing a tux he had obviously borrowed from a maître d' two sizes smaller, swayed along joyously, plunking away at the Steinway, grinning and mouthing the words with Cee Cee as she sang.

> Nights are long since you went away
> I think about you all through the day
> My buddy, my buddy
> Nobody quite so true

It was truly a toss-up as to which was schmaltzier, the singer or the song, but considering how nervous she used to get on those shows, she had to admit her voice sounded pretty damn good. Now they cut away to the interview they'd shot at her house last spring, where Mike Wallace was asking her to talk about her relationship with Hal, and *that* part made her sound like a Miss America Pageant reject.

"Hal Lieberman is truly the sweetest man in the world, and I love him very much." Oh please, she thought. Why in the hell when the people from *60 Minutes* called, hadn't she told them to shove it? After all the times she'd seen that show make dogmeat out of so many people, the way they could make a genius look like a bimbo just by the camera angles they used and the clips they chose, why didn't she say, "Sorry, folks," and hang up on them? Well, she should have. And if it had been for anybody but Hal, she would have.

Naturally Hal came off great in *his* interview. He was charming and bright and so funny he even made that stiff Mike Wallace laugh, which was what was supposed to happen since the segment *was* about him, not about Cee Cee. Go figure, she thought. My former rehearsal pianist, Harold J. Lieberman, has become the man being honored for saving the American musical theater from extinction. Three hit shows on Broadway in five years.

"I played in piano bars endlessly," Hal said, now in a two-shot with Mike Wallace. "Then, thanks to a friend of mine who was supposed to have the job and got sick, I started playing backup for Cee Cee Bloom, and just because she'd kill me if I did, I won't tell you what year that was . . . but one of our gigs was George Burns's bar mitzvah." Hal laughed at his own joke and Mike Wallace smiled.

"Oh, Harold, you need new writers," Cee Cee said out loud to the television. But she was laughing.

"I became her accompanist, in fact most of the time I was her whole band, and boy did we work some dives." Then as Hal let himself truly remember the past, Cee Cee saw his expression turn soft. "Of course nobody could compare to Cee Cee even then," he said. "I believe she's the greatest performer since Judy Garland."

"She really put your songs on the map, too," Mike Wallace said.

"She did. She always sang a few of my tunes in her act, which gave me confidence in the songs and myself. Then years later, when she had her own television show, she insisted they make me the musical director, and the security of that job gave me the luxury to start composing in earnest, so I'm very grateful to her."

"You're welcome," Cee Cee said, feeling a chill and hugging herself to get warm, because she knew if she went to get a sweater she'd miss the end of the interview, which sounded as if it was winding down now, and she promised herself that the second it was over she would call Hal and gush. Then, of course, she would have to tell him the news.

"And now you have three shows running on Broadway all at once," Mike Wallace said to Hal, as they cut to shots of the three marquees above the Broadway theaters where Hal's shows were playing. Then there was an extreme close-up of Hal smiling that philosophical smile of his Cee Cee knew so well. How she loved his funny dear face. The Hirschfeld drawing in the *New York Times* last month had captured it perfectly. The bushy eyebrows over the sad eyes, the too-large bumpy nose, and the pouting, wonderful mouth. "It's been a very good year," he said. "A very good life, actually. I've been very lucky." Then there was a freeze frame on him, and they cut to a commercial.

"Me too," Cee Cee said. "Me too." And she punched Hal's number into the phone, but the line was busy, so she turned down the volume on the television and watched the commercials without the sound. After a while she tried his number again, and then again a few minutes after that. By the fourth try the busy signal started to sound like a taunt. Jeezus, *60 Minutes* had been on three hours earlier in New York. You'd think by now she could get through to him.

She considered calling the operator and asking her to break in on the call, but Hal was so nuts, if an operator said the word *emergency* to him, he'd probably panic and think something had happened to his eighty-year-old mother, so instead she kept pushing the buttons and getting more and more pissed off by the minute, while she waited for him to get through with all the well-wishers and F.B.s.

F.B.s. That had been one of her jokes with Bertie. One night, when was it? A million years ago, she and Bertie were yakking on the phone and Bertie asked about a guy Cee Cee had been dating for a month or two. Maybe it was that bozo Zack. "You won't be hearing me mention *that* lowlife again, because it's all over with him," Cee Cee reported.

"Ahh, Cee, I'm sorry," Bertie had said with that sincere concern she could get in her voice. "You were so excited about a future with him. What happened?"

"I found out he was an F.B."

"Well, knowing you as I do," Bertie said, "I already know what the F stands for, so let's see. Is he an F bastard, or an F bullshitter?"

"I don't know why I let you use language like that in front of a lady like me, Bert," Cee Cee had said, putting on her most dignified voice. "All I was trying to say is that the guy turned out to be an F.B. A phony baloney." Bertie had laughed a big "Oh, Cee Cee" laugh at that, and from then on, anyone who was the least bit full of it, which applied to a lot of people they both knew, was referred to as an F.B.

Cee Cee dialed Hal again, and this time, instead of the immediate busy signal, there was a long hesitation and her heart raced, because she wondered how he would react when she told him what she was going to do, but then there was the busy signal again and she had a reprieve. A few more minutes to decide how she would say it, phrase it, break the news. For a long time she continued to sit and alternately press the buttons on the telephone and the buttons on the TV remote control, cursing the busy signal and seeing the images flash by her. A cough medicine commercial with a worried mother sitting on her little girl's bed reminded her of the first of many nights she had spent with Nina after Bertie died.

"Will you stay in my room until I fall asleep?" Nina would ask her when it was time to turn off the lights, and Cee Cee would say, "Of course I will." Then in the child's room, lit only by a night light, she would sit quietly at the foot of the bed wondering where in the hell she was ever going to get the strength to pull off raising a kid, and watching as the ruffle on the front of one of those night-before-Christmas flannel nightgowns Nina always wore rose and fell with her breathing until the little girl was in a deep sleep. Many nights Cee Cee, still drained from the past many months, would fall asleep too and wake, surprised to find herself still at the bottom of Nina's bed, in the early morning.

Hal's phone was finally ringing, and when Cee Cee glanced at the clock, she realized she'd been trying him for so long it was nine o'clock. Midnight in New York.

"Savior of the Great White Way," he said when he picked up the phone, instead of hello. It was how they had described him on *60 Minutes*.

"Harold," was all Cee Cee said.

"Cee, are you okay?"

"I'm okay," she said, "I'm just calling to add my name to the list of people who thought you were great on *Sixty Minutes*. And to thank you for thanking me in front of the entire country."

"I could have gone on about you for hours," he said so sweetly it made her want to cry. "In fact I *did* go on about you for hours when they interviewed me, but they cut most of it."

There was a long moment of only the shush of the long-distance line, the way it sounded when she put a seashell against her ear, until Cee Cee said, "Hal, I need you to come out to Los Angeles right away. It's very important to me that you be here."

"Say no more. I'm on a plane. I'll be in Los Angeles tomorrow, and you don't even have to tell me why."

"I *will* tell you why," Cee Cee said, "but you'd better sit down." Hal was already sitting, on the bench of the baby grand piano in the living room of his high-ceilinged, Art Deco Park Avenue apartment. And as Cee Cee told him why he had to drop everything and come to Los Angeles, he was so overwhelmed with emotion he sat shaking his head with his eyes closed. And when she'd finished, he promised he was on his way and would see her as soon as possible. Then he hung up the telephone, and stayed where he was for a while, picking out a few bars of "I'm Bad," because it used to be one of Nina's favorite songs in those days that seemed so long ago.

CARMEL, CALIFORNIA

August 1983

EVEN WHEN SHE wore a big hat and dark glasses because she thought they would make her look dramatically different, the disguise didn't do her any good at all, because what everyone recognized about her to begin with was her nose and her bright red hair and her funny little walk. So on those days when she was going out in public, she'd put on the hat, then the glasses, and within minutes people would still come right up to her on the street, or stop her when she and Nina were walking on the beach and ask, "Aren't you Cee Cee Bloom?"

Most of the time it was okay with her to be approached by fans, but on days when she wasn't in the mood, she could be impatient or abrupt with them, and on those days Nina would overhear the people when they walked away saying things like "What a bitch," after Cee Cee had autographed their chocolate-smeared paper napkin from Mrs. Field's Cookies, or a deposit slip from a checkbook, which was sometimes all the paper the people had with them.

Today, when Cee Cee and Nina took a long silent walk on the beach, nobody came over to talk. Maybe because it was just a day when everyone was too busy with their friends and their dogs and their kites to notice them walking arm in arm. Or it could have been that people did notice them but sensed this was a very bad time. Bertie had died exactly two weeks ago today and later this morning Cee Cee was taking Nina to the boarding school in Santa Cruz, which Bertie's tight-ass lawyer decided was the best place for the kid to be. So this was the last walk they would take together on the Carmel beach they had grown to depend on for solace over the last few months.

In an effort to make sure she was doing everything right, Cee Cee had called the lawyer a few days after Bertie's death, weighted down with a grief so heavy she could barely talk. But that didn't seem to matter to the all-business lawyer who did most of the talking anyway, while Cee Cee, trying to focus through her acute pain, only understood about half of the legal bullshit he was spouting, and during the other half she said, "Uh huh" and "Yeah" a lot so he'd think she got it all. The part she *did* get was that his law firm in Sarasota, Florida, was the "guardian of the estate," which meant they were in charge of the money Bertie had left to Nina.

"And you, Mizz Bloom," he said, putting a real buzz on the *Mizz*, the way some men did to show they'd rather say Miss, and didn't go for what they thought was some made-up feminist bullshit title, "are the guardian of the person." End of sentence, she thought, but no such luck. "Provided, of course, the guardianship isn't contested by anyone else," he had added in a snarky voice that made her clutch. Who in the hell was he talking about? Who was gonna contest it? Bertie picked *her* and that's the way it would stay. Wasn't it?

"Since Mrs. Barron's verbal nomination of you as Nina's guardian, I've made some inquiries into the school situation, and have a strong suggestion as to the most appropriate private school for Nina," was what he said next, and Cee Cee, who had been so racked with sadness watching Bertie leave this life, trying desperately through it all to hold herself and Nina together, had to admit she sure as hell hadn't thought as far as where she was going to put the kid in school.

"Isn't it summer?" she blurted out, then felt dumb when he answered.

"It's August. Long past the time to apply. School begins in two weeks."

The body ain't even cold yet, asshole, was what she wanted to say, but instead, probably because the little putz had thrown her off with that stuff about somebody contesting her right to Nina, she laid off and tried to be obliging. "Well then . . . suggest away," she said, picturing some pompous little pain-in-the-wazoo lawyer sitting in Florida deciding what was best for a kid he'd probably never even met. And it was clear as glass he wasn't just "suggesting," because then he said that as soon as Bertie told him how after she died she wanted Cee Cee to be Nina's guardian, he'd located "the perfect boarding school" for the kid, "situated conveniently in the foothills of the Santa Cruz mountains. And," he added, while Cee Cee sat there, knowing things were going very wrong but feeling unable to stop them, "I've already sent the school a deposit in order to hold a place for the child, since I was certain you'd agree."

Boarding school, she wanted to scream. Who the fuck goes to boarding school, you heartless little prick? Maybe Oliver Twist, and all those other characters from Shakespeare. Not *my* kid. Her kid. Now that's what was the hardest to believe about all this. To really get it into her head that this funny little pain-in-the-ass creature, this little lost soul of a girl, who was an amazing combination of Bertie's beauty and Michael's steel-jawed iciness, was now in the care of Cee Cee not-exactly-the-odds-on-favorite-for-Mother-of-the-Year Bloom. And here she was, already proving she was no good at it by caving like an empty beer can at a fraternity party, and by her silence, agreeing to let Nina go to boarding school.

Yeah, it was definitely because the snotty little lawyer had scared her with that stuff about contesting her right to Nina, filled her head with terrors of courtroom scenes where she had to fight Bertie's ex-husband or Bertie's aunt, two people who would jump at the chance of flinging a little mud about Cee Cee's past. And it was the vision of those two coming after her that had made her sit there on the phone with the guy like some spineless blob, never saying what she should have, afraid to challenge him, and now it was killing her.

Filling her with guilt, because she knew that implicit in her pitch to Bertie to give the kid to her was a deathbed promise to show Nina a world filled with the kind of passion and spontaneity Bertie knew only Cee Cee could provide. And now, because she'd let the lawyer walk all over her, she wouldn't even be around the kid, except during school vacations. Of course those other two phone calls she'd made during that first week hadn't exactly helped her confidence in herself either. One of them was to her agent at the William Morris office, Larry Gold, and the other one was to her business manager, Wayne Gordon.

Each of them had been real sympathetic and sweet about her friend's dying. And why wouldn't they be? Their percentage of her earnings over the many years they'd represented her would put all of their kids through college. But after the words of sympathy, each of

them had warned her in an ominous voice that her exit, in the middle
of production, from her television special a few months earlier had
damaged her career. And now that she was coming home, if she
couldn't make peace with the network, she could find herself in a
tough spot.

"They're pissed off, Cee Cee. You walked out on them, and there's
a real good chance they'll say they don't want to be in The Cee Cee
Bloom business anymore." If that was true, she'd definitely have some
big financial problems. Have to live off her savings for a while and
sell some of her stock and hustle a little to get work. And that could
mean traveling anywhere the work was happening. Maybe to make a
movie in some far-off place, or worse yet put together an act to take
on the road, which was not exactly the life for somebody raising a kid.
Which was another reason why, even though it felt so shitty, she had
agreed to let Nina go to that boarding school. At least for now.

When they had reached the southernmost end of the Carmel Beach
Cee Cee looked at her watch and already felt as if someone had kicked
her in the stomach, just thinking about having to say goodbye to this
little girl whose screaming entry into the world she had watched in
the hospital delivery room so long ago. All right, so she'd only
watched part of the time, until she realized how bloody it was going
to be, and then she'd fainted so the nurses had to peel her up off the
floor in the middle of the whole thing. But that was just a detail. The
point was that she and Nina were connected very deeply from way
back.

"I think we'd better hit the road, kiddo," Cee Cee said, hearing the
lack of conviction in her own voice. An old lady wearing faded jeans
and a fisherman's knit sweater walked by with two little dogs the size
of mice on leashes, and one of the dogs stopped, lifted its little leg,
and peed in the sand. "Good boy," the lady said, and they walked on.
Nina stood looking down at her own pretty little toes as they curled
up to scrunch bunches of sand under and between them and then
released the sand and did it again. This really is the best thing for her,
Cee Cee thought. For now this is the best thing. But it was hard to
convince herself when she looked at Nina's tiny face, because what
she really wanted to do was to zip the kid inside of her Windbreaker
and hide her there forever.

Last night they'd spent hours packing up the house Bertie had rented in Carmel. First they organized their own things and then they went through all of Bertie's. Her personal effects. "Is there any of this you want to wear now?" Cee Cee had asked Nina, sorting through some of Bertie's jewelry, while a kind of slide show of the times she remembered Bertie wearing each piece played itself out in her mind.

Nina took a bracelet of seed pearls out of the box and looked at it for a while, then handed it to Cee Cee, who opened the clasp and looped the delicate thing carefully around the girl's wrist, which she needn't have done because Nina could have easily slipped her tiny hand and wrist into the bracelet without opening it. Then both of them looked back into the box at what was clearly the most special piece of jewelry there. It was the ring Bertie had worn every day of her life since 1970, when Rosie, her own mother, died and left it to her.

It had a platinum band and a small round emerald that was such a brilliant green it always used to catch the eye of people who saw it on Bertie's long slim finger. Nina slipped the ring over her own ring finger. "Much too big," she said, disappointed.

"Nina, the ring is yours, and it's insured. It's very valuable, but if you want to wear it, I have a chain with a good safety clasp in the back, and you could wear it hanging from the chain, at least for now."

Nina thought about it and then turned the ring over and over in her hand. "I'd like that," she said.

Cee Cee found her chain, slipped the ring onto it, and had Nina hold her hair up so that she could fasten the chain around her neck.

"How do I look?" she asked Cee Cee, and stood to see herself in the oval pine mirror above the dresser. She was so much the picture of Bertie at that moment Cee Cee had to take a deep breath before she answered.

"More beautiful than anything I've ever seen."

This morning when they got back to the house and squirted the sand from their feet with the hose at the side door, Cee Cee went inside and found her car keys on the hall table, then she picked up the small suitcases they had piled up last night in the hallway near the front door and carried them out to the car, with Nina following her carrying another, her two hands wrapped around the handle as the suitcase bumped against her legs.

When the car was loaded she climbed into the passenger seat, and

Cee Cee went back to lock the front door of the house, remembering the first day she arrived, summoned by Bertie, not knowing then what the reason was for the urgency, never imagining it would be months before she would leave. With Nina and without Bertie. "Goodbye, house," she said softly. Then she got into the car, made sure Nina was belted in, fastened the seat belt around herself, and started the engine of the big Chevy she'd rented the day she arrived.

"I gotta get gas," she said, looking at the gauge on the dashboard as she pulled away from the curb, then turned the car up to Ocean Avenue, and after a while made a right turn and drove a few blocks down one of the streets of Hansel and Gretel shops, to the gas station.

"It's a good thing we're getting out of this place," Cee Cee said. "I'm about to overdose on quaint. What about you?"

Nina didn't answer. The gas station was busy and they waited in line behind a camper with the bumper sticker that said PROTECTED BY SMITH AND WESSON.

"How do I get to Santa Cruz?" Cee Cee asked the gas station attendant while he was cleaning the windshield. She had mostly used the big clunky car to take Bertie from the house down the few blocks to the Carmel Beach after the time had come during the illness when Bertie was too weak to walk that far. Now the gas station attendant had to push down hard on the scraper because the windshield was thick with a residue of salt air and leaves as a result of the car sitting unused for so long.

"You go up to Highway One, then get on it going north and you can't miss it."

"Got any maps?"

In a few minutes the man came back with a map and Cee Cee opened it, turned it and folded it, then unfolded it and muttered to herself, because she didn't have a clue how to read it. All those little blue and red lines and numbers and letters were the same blur they always were when she looked at maps.

"Where the effing hell is Santa Cruz?" she said impatiently. "The guy must have brought me the wrong map because it's not on here."

"May I help?" Nina asked, and she spotted Santa Cruz on the map before the map was even in her hands, but politely took a minute to act as if she was searching for it so Cee Cee wouldn't feel too stupid.

"Here it is," Nina said, holding the map so Cee Cee could see it.

"Oh yeah," Cee Cee said. While the gas station attendant was processing her Master Charge, she tried a couple of times to refold the map to the original size, but finally she gave up and tossed the large open piece of paper over her shoulder into the backseat and started the car. Nina wasn't saying a word, and Cee Cee knew it was up to her to say something first, something important or reassuring, but she couldn't think of anything so she drove through Carmel in silence.

Just as they reached the end of one of the long tree-lined residential streets and drove around the bend, the stone dome of the adobe Carmel Mission rose against the blue sky ahead of them. The mission was the place they had chosen a few days ago to have their own little memorial service for Bertie. Janice Carnes, the lady from the hospice, had been there and Jessica, the nurse who had been hired to take care of Bertie before Cee Cee came to take over, showed up too, and Madeline, the cleaning girl, arrived carrying a little bouquet of flowers from her garden for Nina.

As they all sat together in the mission courtyard among the pink and lavender hydrangeas, each one told a story about something nice Bertie had done for her. At the end they stood in a circle with their arms around one another and held tightly for a long time. Now Nina pressed the automatic window button, and as it opened she closed her eyes to let the clean cool air blow against her curly bangs and serious face.

You have to talk to this child, Cee Cee thought to herself as the big Chevy rumbled and rattled up the highway. *You were so busy every day trying not to lose control and to get all the details out of the way, then every night you collapsed and fell asleep, so this is your last chance to say something to her before you dump her like a hot potato. Speak up, girl.* But all she could get out was the question "You hungry?"

"No," Nina answered and sighed a deep sigh. She wasn't even looking out the window at the farms they were passing covered with neat green rows of leafy artichokes; instead she sat slumped low in the seat, and with great concentration picked at the cuticle of her right thumb with the curled index finger of her right hand. Kids. You had to be so careful with them. Their little minds were so delicate, if you did the wrong thing you could screw them up royally forever. In fact raising kids *these* days was a science. Cee Cee couldn't believe her eyes a couple of weeks ago when she noticed a whole wall of books about it in Books, Inc.

It was on one of the rare outings she'd allowed herself to take during Bertie's last days when she'd wandered numbly into the busy bookstore in the Carmel Plaza, and for a few minutes she'd stood in front of the wide rack of magazines, running her aching eyes past their splashy, glossy covers, seeing only the colors. Then, thinking she should buy one or two but too confused by all the choices, she started to leave empty-handed, until on the way out she found herself passing through the section on child care. Child care. She stopped and picked up one then another of the books whose titles intrigued her, and stood paging through them, skimming chapters that promised answers, and by the time she got to the checkout counter she was carrying a stack of books on child care.

Some of the books had titles about children and death, some had the words *positive* or *winning* in their titles, and all of them had pictures of kids on the covers. Kids whose huge smiles were obviously supposed to be evidence of their mental health. Back at the house, while Bertie slept Cee Cee had thumbed through the books, stopping to read long sections of each of them before she'd had the guts to ask Bertie to give her custody of Nina. In fact, she thought now, maybe it was reading those books that had made her think she'd be able to raise a kid. Made her wonder if it could be like following a recipe — first you do this, then you do that, and if you followed the recipe carefully, the kid would turn out just right. Like a cake. Of course she'd never baked a cake in her life.

The thing she decided she'd better read about first in those books, while she'd sat next to Bertie's bed holding her hand and listening for every breath, was how to handle kids and death.

Most children find it difficult to mourn, unless they have been raised to express their feelings freely. . . . Share with them your own feelings of unhappiness, hurt, loneliness, abandonment, and even anger and this will make it easier for them.

"Your mother was the most special person I ever knew," she said, finally breaking the silence in the car, "and she was *different* than everybody else I knew. I needed her in my life because when it came to me, she had X-ray vision. She saw through all the stuff I put on for the rest of the world, like so many different outfits from my closet."

"What do you mean?" Nina asked, looking at Cee Cee.

"Well, let's see. There was my I'm-Cee-Cee-the-Famous-Star-So-Give-Me-Whatever-I-Want outfit. Or my I-Can't-Handle-This-So-Somebody-Do-It-*for*-Me outfit. I could pull those things off with other people, but never with her. Because she wouldn't fall for it. She'd always look me in the eye and say, 'No, Cee, that's not going to work.' You get what I'm saying?" Nina nodded.

"There's a song from a great Broadway show," Cee Cee went on, "and the lyrics are 'Who else but your bosom buddy will tell you the whole stinkin' truth?' Well, your mother always told it to me. Whether I liked it or not, and I needed it to be told. Everybody does, but especially if you're famous, because then what happens is that people start telling you only what they think you want to hear."

"Why?"

"Lots of reasons. To keep you happy. To keep their jobs, if they work for you. To get you to like them so they can hang around with a star."

"Those are dumb reasons."

"So now every time it hits me that she's not going to be here to tell me the truth anymore, I get mad at her. Real mad that my one true friend is gone. Is that how *you* feel? Mad that she left you?"

Now Nina couldn't look at her. She turned her face to the passenger window, but after a moment Cee Cee heard her answer, "Yes," in a very small voice.

"I lost my mom too, a long time ago, and my husband, John . . . he left me . . . and after that I figured it was just my fate to get left by anyone I loved," Cee Cee said. "Matter of fact, once when I lived in New York I had this cat named Tuffy. She was orange with a bushy tail, and believe me when I tell you I'm no animal lover but I was crazy about her. Anyhow, one day she just walked across the fire escape into my neighbor's apartment and never came back. I couldn't believe it. I even tried to bribe her by leaving out some caviar some guy I was dating gave me, but she came by that morning, sniffed it, turned her little whiskers up, and walked away, and I cried my eyes out. Can you imagine?" she asked. "Abandoned by a cat?"

The memory made her laugh now, with a giggle that built into a guffaw, and the laughter felt good for a minute, but then she felt guilty about laughing until she saw Nina's back shaking with giggles too and when Nina turned to look at her, the child's eyes were wet, but her mouth was smiling.

"Well, you know *I'm* not going to leave you because *I've* got no place else to go," the little girl said.

"And I'm not going to ever leave you either, honey," Cee Cee said, and just as she did the sun went behind a cloud and the sky dimmed and Cee Cee felt more guilt shoot through her, as if the sun disappearing just then was God's way of saying, You're lying, Bloom. Because the truth was she was already *about* to leave the kid, at some hootsy-snootsy boarding school, and she felt her mouth starting to turn down involuntarily the way it sometimes did just before she cried.

Where the fuck was my mind when I begged Bert to give me this child? she thought. *Shallow me was thinking about going out to buy pink party dresses and patent leather shoes for her as if that was what being a mother was all about. I was already imagining how cute we were gonna look together at the celebrity mother-and-daughter luncheon. But how in the hell can I be a mother to somebody else when I'm bleeding to death myself? Maybe by the time her first school vacation comes along I'll be feeling a little better.*

"We'll go away somewhere together on your first school break. Thanksgiving. I'll take you anywhere you want to go," she said, knowing Nina had to be able to tell how forced this life-is-just-a-bowl-of-cherries voice was that she was using. But if she did, she didn't say anything, in fact she seemed to perk up at the idea of a shared vacation.

"What about Vail?" she asked.

"Huh?"

"On the break?"

"Where?"

"Vail, Colorado. Three years ago my mom took me there."

"Great, we'll do it. I promise. Whatever you want."

"Ever been skiing?" Nina asked, and she took her dark glasses out of her little purse and put them on as the car chugged into the sunny day.

"*Moi?* Are you joking? The thinnest book in the world is called *Jewish Downhill Racers*. May I quote my beloved friend Joan Rivers,

who said, 'I won't participate in any sport that has an ambulance waiting at the bottom of the hill.'"

"Then I guess Vail's out," Nina said quietly.

God, I'm a rat, Cee Cee thought. Like Miss Hannigan in *Annie*, or
Maleficent in *Sleeping Beauty*. One of those villains in children's stories
who treat kids like dirt, but what in the hell else can I do? Santa Cruz.
It'll have to be okay. Just for now. She would explore the school with
Nina, look it over, help her unpack, maybe even have lunch with her,
and by the time she called tonight, the kid would be all settled in,
with roommates and a whole new crew of pals, and that's how it was
supposed to be. Other parents did this. Families with real mothers
and fathers sent kids away to school all the time because they thought
it was good for the kids.

"Ever snorkeled?" Nina asked.

"Is that where they stick a tank on your back and you dive down
and look at a fish?"

"No. That's scuba diving. Snorkeling is easy. You wear a little
mask with a breathing tube, and mostly float on the surface of the
water. It's like watching fish on television."

"If I want to watch fish on television I'll tune into *The Undersea
World of Jacques Cousteau*," Cee Cee joked.

"So much for Hawaii," Nina said quietly.

They were nearly at the turnoff to the school before Nina spoke
again.

"Well, what *are* we going to do?" she asked with real concern in her
voice.

"About what?"

"Thanksgiving break."

"You know, I'll bet you're not going to believe this," Cee Cee said,
"but at that time of year? November? There are very few places that
can compare to Las Vegas."

Nina looked at Cee Cee's face, and when she realized she'd been
teasing, she smiled, and Cee Cee did too, and they held hands over
the console.

"We'll work it out, kiddo," Cee Cee told her. "I swear to God, we'll
work it out."

*   *   *

The school in the foothills of the Santa Cruz Mountains, on its acres of land with its college-like grounds, intimidated Cee Cee. Just the idea of a place where all those kids knew so much more than she did made her uneasy. In her own life, school had always been the place where she was either in trouble with the teachers because she'd been cutting to go into the city to auditions, or where she was thought of as a tap-dancing weirdo by the other kids. That was why she was quiet during the entire tour today, worrying the whole time that the headmistress who led them from building to building might ask her some question she couldn't answer. Nina, as always, was aloof, her little face strained with feigned interest.

"The amphitheater. Our productions of the classics are known for the authenticity of their costume and scene design. Recently we had productions of both Sophocles' and Anouilh's *Antigones*. I'm sure, Miss Bloom, that you, with your theatrical orientation, would have appreciated the detail and care with which they were mounted."

Yeah, sure. Sophocles and Anouilh, Cee Cee thought. I never got past Dick and Jane.

"Are you interested in the theater?" Miss McCullough asked Nina.

"I like movies better."

"We have a film society here. And what film is your favorite?"

"*Jilted*, starring Cee Cee Bloom," Nina said, and Cee Cee wanted to kiss her cute face.

"Private bathrooms," Cee Cee said after the tour. She was sitting on the chair across from the bed in Nina's new dormitory room. She could see the sprawling campus all green and lush through the open window, and the parking lot in the distance, where the Chevy and its contents waited for her.

"Cee Cee, they just showed us a huge science hall, a polo field, a language lab, and a big amphitheater, and all you keep talking about is the fact that the dorm rooms have private bathrooms."

"Hey, I'm impressed. You're looking at someone who didn't have a bathroom to herself till she was twenty-nine."

Nina was slowly and painstakingly making the single bed, lifting each corner of the light mattress in order to tuck in the hospital corners. Bertie had taught her to do that and everything else perfectly. Cee Cee tried to imagine the proper and orderly life Nina would live here just to console herself, but still she felt like a rotten shit.

Earlier in the week Cee Cee had called Hal Lieberman in Los Angeles. He was house-sitting at her place in Brentwood and she told him the news about Bertie's death, knowing he was someone she could trust with her raw feelings. A *mensch*, her mother would have called him.

"Cee, I'm sorry," he said. "Is there anything I can do to make your return here easier?" Hal's own home was a studio apartment containing a bed, a chest of drawers, and the baby grand his grandfather gave him for his bar mitzvah, so he had readily accepted the assignment to stay at Cee Cee's big, roomy rented house.

"Keep the porchlight burning," she told him. "I'm dropping Nina at school and coming home to try and glue my life back together. Am I still in the business?"

"Are you kidding? You *are* the business," he joked, then added gently: "Don't be too tough on yourself. Everything will shake out and be okay." Shake out and be okay. No chance. She was copping out on her promise to an orphan, how could anything make that okay?

"Neen, this place is lovely," she said, sounding like Jayne Meadows describing a float in the Rose Bowl Parade. "The classrooms are fancy, the other kids look great, you'll wear the lovely plaid uniform so you don't have to think about clothes every day. And that lovely woman who gave us the tour, seemed so . . ."

"Cee," Nina said stone-faced, "I'm sorry to interrupt you, but anytime *you* use the word *lovely* three times in one breath . . . I know you're freaked out. But it's okay. I'll settle in here. I'll be with lots of kids, and you can call and tell me all your adventures, and I'll mark off the days on the calendar until our trip to Las Vegas. You'd better pull yourself together or you're going to hurt your career even more."

That little face. Those big-girl words coming out of that little sweet face, that look in her eyes which, now that Nina had removed the sunglasses, Cee Cee could see looked too old for someone so young.

"You're amazing," Cee Cee said. "So amazing you make me feel like a complete jackass. And it must be in your blood, because your mother had a way of doing that to me too. On a regular basis." She walked to Nina and hugged her and gave her a little kiss on the top of the head, and as she did she inhaled the sweet clean smell of the little girl's hair. Then she held her at arm's length and said, "I promise I'll call you every day," then, trying not to make a big deal out of it, she turned and walked out of the room. When she was about halfway down the hall, she thought she heard Nina say, in a voice that sounded like it was pushing to come off as cavalier, "Once a week will probably do it." But she kept walking and when she got outside the building and moved toward her car, she could feel in the back of her neck that Nina was watching her from the window.

For a while she sat behind the wheel, looking back at the school buildings, so torn apart she couldn't even start the car. Finally she did and she drove slowly away, back to Highway 1 and south, this time toward the Monterey Peninsula Airport, with the memory of Nina's little face lodged in the front of her brain and a burr of sadness stuck in her heart.

According to the clock on the dashboard of the Chevy she was early, so she pulled into the parking lot of Del Monte Aviation, where she sat for a while looking out at all of the airplanes, then with a resigned deep breath she made herself get out of the car and walk around to the trunk, which she opened so she could take out the box wrapped in white paper.

"Dying and flying," she said, "my two biggest phobias, and *you*, the woman who called herself my best friend, have managed to make sure I had to deal with both of them at the same time. Well, don't worry, Bert. I fully intend to get back at you for this, as soon as I find out how to reach you from Shirley MacLaine." Then she got back into the car, put the box on the passenger seat, and sat looking out at the rows of private airplanes parked just beyond the fence, and finally too aware of its presence to ignore it, she looked at the box again, leaned over, and tore at the wrapping paper to uncover the package inside. Then, filled with a mixture of horror and curiosity, she pulled up on the lid, and unwound the top of the plastic bag inside the box.

The color. The first thing that struck her was the color. Not black or gray the way she pictured it would look. Not at all like cigarette ashes. But a light color. Like chopped coral, or seashells. Coarse and uneven pieces of what looked like . . . oh God. Bones. She closed her eyes.

"Bert," she said, "I always told you I loved you to pieces, but I didn't mean as small as these." Hearing herself say that made her laugh, a horrified laugh at her own black humor. The kind Bertie loved. And she knew Bertie would have laughed her ass off at that. What would ever be funny again? Hysterical, the way things used to be when she was with Bertie. Even things that didn't seem funny when she was alone, somehow, when they were together, could make them both laugh like idiots. Like that dopey running gag they had for years where Cee Cee would say, "If one of us dies, *I'm* moving to Miami Beach." It had been Nathan and Leona's joke that Cee Cee used to overhear all the time when she was a kid. And after she told it to Bertie, the two of them had adopted it as their own.

One night when she wasn't kidding, but long before she ever got sick, Bertie said, "Cee, you know I was thinking recently, I hope I die before you do." It must have been one of those times Cee Cee was visiting her in Sarasota. Yeah. It was one of those conversations they had until four in the morning. Bertie was real maudlin that night, probably because she was pregnant and her hormones were on the fritz. And after talking the night away they had decided to make some popcorn because it was a low-calorie snack. Of course they'd smothered it in butter and Cee Cee had washed hers down with a little Sara Lee chocolate cake she'd found in the freezer and defrosted in the oven. "Because if you ever died first and I was still on this earth without you, I'd be miserable."

"I'll tell you what, kiddo," Cee Cee had offered, polishing off the last bite of the cake, "just to make sure *that* doesn't happen, if I ever get real sick . . . we'll have *you* killed." Bertie had laughed a lot at that one. So look what happened. She got her wish. She died first and it was Cee Cee who was left to go on without *her.* And now they wouldn't get old together the way they always swore they would, from the time they had noticed two little old ladies together, walking arm and arm down a street, maybe it was in Hawaii.

One of the ladies walked with the help of a cane, and the other one was very rounded forward at the shoulders, so it wasn't exactly clear which of the two was holding the other up, and Bertie had elbowed Cee Cee, making her stop and look at the ladies, and whispered, "That's *us* in fifty years." Now there wouldn't be any Bertie in fifty years to hold her up and walk slowly with her when nobody else wanted to. No Bertie who would remind her to suck in her stomach when she forgot, or to tell her when she had lipstick on her teeth, or food on her chin, or to point out that one of her shoulder pads had slipped back so far she looked like Quasimodo, or that she was acting too desperate with some man, or spending too much money on dumb things. No Bertie who believed in her, and always had from the day they met. She used to sign her letters *YOUR FAN CLUB, B.W.B.* And it wasn't just because she believed in Cee Cee's future as a star the way Leona did. Bertie believed in Cee Cee as a person. Bertie had pressured her to stop snorting cocaine. Shrieked at her in an un-Bertie-like way to stop destroying herself because she had too much to offer the world, and Cee Cee had stopped.

Well, maybe she'd slid back to it after that once or twice, but it was always Bertie's letters to her begging PLEASE, CEE, YOUR TALENT IS SO BIG, DON'T DO SOMETHING THAT WILL EAT AWAY AT IT! that had helped her to feel strong, knowing in order to accomplish what she wanted to do, she had to force herself to be more disciplined. It had changed her life having Bertie out there to remind her, pound into her head the reasons she needed to stay away from cocaine, avoid pig-outs on food, and be sure to keep the list of passionate strangers short, though that one was the easiest to control, since the number of volunteers was so small.

"Do what I do," Bertie said, advising her about men.

"I *do* do what you do, honey, and it's lonelier than hell."

"Find other outlets. For example two nights a week, I'm taking a course on how to repair my car."

"The only way they'll get me under a car is with the mechanic," Cee Cee said. "Look for our feet locked together in love."

Bertie laughed. "You are such a slut."

"Talk is cheap," Cee Cee said, "and so, dear girl, am I." But teasing aside, finally Bertie had proven without a doubt how much she believed in Cee Cee by changing her will and declaring Cee Cee Nina's guardian, instead of the aunt and uncle in Miami Beach. So what if, in a way, Cee Cee had pushed her into making that decision? There was no doubt in the world it was the right one for the kid, and Cee Cee would prove it to anyone who didn't think so.

"Bert," she said to the box of ashes, "I swear you did the right thing by giving me Nina. I promise I won't smother her the way Leona did me. I'll be understanding, but I won't spoil her, I'll be tough, but I won't lean on her too much. In fact I've been reading a lot about what to do with kids because I know somewhere up there you're worried that I won't be able to pull this off. But you're wrong, Bert, because I'm here to tell you that I'll be such a good influence you'll think I'm Mary Fucking Poppins. Hah!" That made her laugh. That and the fact that she was talking animatedly to a box. Dear God, this was bizarre. Now she patted the box warmly.

"Ahh, Bert, if this wasn't so sad it would be truly hilarious. If you were here with me, I mean really here, we'd be killing ourselves laughing the way we always did about this kind of stuff. You always loved those sick jokes I made when you were on the way out of this life, like when I said we should date two ambulance drivers just in case, or that maybe I should do it with a mortician so we could get a discount." That brought a laugh which caught in her throat and turned into a cry she tried to hold inside. Dear God, this was too weird, too fucking over-the-top weird. This was not exactly your run-of-the-mill way to pass the time, sitting in a car talking to a box full of your dead best friend. Finally she wiped away the crying tears and the laughing tears with the sleeve of her sweatshirt, looked at her watch, and saw it was time to go into the charter office.

"I figure if you're graying at the temples, you must have been doing this for a long time," she said to the pilot, noticing how high-pitched and nervous her voice sounded as the two of them walked out through the glass doors to the tarmac. He was a husky man in his fifties who hadn't said a word but "Howdy" when they were introduced, and if he knew or cared who Cee Cee was she couldn't see it in his eyes. Now, as they made the long walk across the airfield, she jabbered unthinkingly in her terror, trying to elicit some assurance from him, but there wasn't a shot this guy was gonna make it easy for her.

"I'm a real white-knuckler," she tried. "I worry about every noise. Once on a flight to New York, I heard this snap and then a hiss and I grabbed my piano player's hand and said, 'Oh my God. What was that sound?' and he said, really calmly, 'It was the sound of the stewardess opening a cola can!' Hah! Of course there probably won't be any stewardesses on *this* flight though, so I guess I don't have to worry."

They were moving in the direction of a herd of small planes

grouped together like a bunch of seagulls on the beach. Their white-ness flashed the sun's glare in Cee Cee's eyes, and when she could make them out clearly she said eeny meeny miney mo, trying to figure out which one of those metal pieces of crap was about to fly her out over the ocean.

"The plane's a Cessna one seventy-two," the pilot said, stopping at a funny-looking little job with the wings high up on the top. The silly little son-of-a-bitch airplane was almost as tiny as a toy. Not exactly the streamlined craft in which she thought she'd be sitting slouched tragically in the co-pilot's seat when she'd pictured herself doing this, and it occurred to her there was still time to back out of it. To hand the pilot the box of ashes and a big wad of dough, say, "Good luck to you," then drive down the coast to Big Sur and watch as he flew over.

"We'll fly out down the coast, somewhere over Big Sur, and that's probably the best place to do what you want to do," he said, unlocking the door on his side first.

"What are *those* things?" Cee Cee asked pointing to two small wheels that extended on either side of the plane.

"That's the landing gear."

"Thank God," Cee Cee said. "I thought they were training wheels." She laughed. The pilot didn't.

"We're taking this particular airplane up," he said, "because the passenger window opens, and in my instructions it says you wanted to disperse the ashes yourself rather than have me or one of my assis-tants do it. So when it's time for the dispersal, I'll slow down the speed of the plane so you can open the window safely, and I'll teach you now how to hold the box below the window level to get the ashes to blow out to sea."

The pilot climbed into his seat, then leaned over and unlocked the passenger door, and Cee Cee stood for a moment, afraid to get in, wondering why she couldn't just go back to L.A., stand on the Santa Monica Pier and open the box lid.

"I can assure you," the pilot told her, seeing her expression, "I've been flying these planes for a long time, and they're perfectly safe. Safer than your being on the freeway."

"You've obviously *heard* about my driving," Cee Cee said. Again he didn't crack a smile, and looked as if he wasn't planning to. Maybe ever. "Let's go for it," Cee Cee told him and climbed into the plane through the open passenger door, placing the box of ashes between her feet.

"Let me show you how you'll open the window once we get over the ocean and I give you the signal," the pilot said. "You see the window's hinged on the top, and you're going to press that small metal lever and then push very hard on the window itself. It will open far enough for you to reach out with the box in your arms, and then you're going to make sure you hold the box low, on a level under the window, because of the wind and the prop wash. Got that?"

"Got it," Cee Cee said.

"Let's practice," the pilot said, and closed her door. Cee Cee pulled on the metal clip, put both hands on the window and pushed. It opened. A cinch. Then she picked the box up from the floor in front of her and leaned out of the open window, moving the unopened box to a level below the window.

"Good job," the pilot said.

Cee Cee nodded an oh-it-was-nothing nod, pulled the box back in, closed the window again, and buckled her seat belt. Not bad.

"Ready to go up?" the pilot asked, closing his door, which sounded to Cee Cee like the lightweight door of an economy car.

Ready to throw up is more like it, she thought, as she nodded. She and the pilot were sitting shoulder to shoulder, as close to one another as if they were in a tiny sports car. And in a second, he had put on his headset and the engine was running and the loud noise blasted in her ears as the Cessna began to taxi slowly toward the runway. The pilot was talking into the microphone on his headset, and Cee Cee wondered if he had a sense of humor in case she got sick all over him, which felt like a distinct possibility, and then the plane began to start down the runway slowly, picked up speed and then more speed, and as Cee Cee took a few shallow nervous breaths, the tiny airplane lifted into the clear blue Monterey sky.

In all the years she'd flown in commercial airplanes, even large private jets, she had never been anywhere near the cockpit. Always it was some magical off-limits place she didn't want to think about, probably to avoid the idea that humans who were capable of making mistakes sat in there working the big mechanical bird. But today the exhilaration she felt at the moment of takeoff thrilled her. Made her feel as if she were part of the sky. Looking right out the big front window and feeling the lift of the aircraft and seeing the ground disappear below, and seconds later having the tops of mountains at eye level, and the view of the Monterey Bay below, made her feel so elated she nearly forgot the reason she was up in the airplane to begin with.

"Now this beats the shit out of TWA!" she said very loud to the pilot, who nodded at her but probably couldn't hear her because of that headset of Mickey Mouse ears he was wearing. "I mean I could seriously get into this. My God. Look down. You can see *everything* from here. I might even decide to get my pilot's license. Wouldn't *that* be a pisser? Amelia Earhart Bloom. Flying myself all over the place in my own plane," she said to the pilot, who was flipping a bunch of little switches and not listening to her. "Like Meshulam Riklis. Ever see his plane? On one side he has painted the words 'Here Comes Pia!' for his wife, Pia Zadora; well, mine could say, 'Boom Boom, here comes Bloom.' Right?"

With relief she leaned back against the seat, proud of herself for actually pulling this off. Doing at least part of what she'd promised Bertie she would do. Going up in a little model airplane that looked like it was made of balsa wood and Duco Cement, to disperse her ashes and to say goodbye. How 'bout *that* for an act of love?

The pilot flew south down the coast, and Cee Cee continued to look out at the mountains and the expanse of ocean below with a comfort that amazed her. For years in her therapy she had talked about the fears she had about so many things and how she hated herself for letting those fears run her, letting them determine what she would and wouldn't do. In fact the only time she was really brave was onstage. Out there when she was performing she would say anything, try anything, wear anything, and not give a rat's ass about the consequences. But in real life, she held back. Crippled and stifled by her fear.

All that stuff she had made jokes about with Nina were real. Perfect examples of her chickenshit life. She wouldn't dream of snorkeling, or be caught dead skiing, and the only time she flew was to get to a job in some faraway city. But worst of all was the way she'd even been afraid of Bertie's persnickety lawyer. Afraid if she didn't do what he said and picked a school for Nina herself, she'd fuck up and scar the kid for life. Afraid to keep the kid with her in Los Angeles, or if she had to go on the road, afraid to educate her with a tutor who came with them, terrified that her crazy unorthodox life would shock an eight-year-old girl. Well, so the fuck what? The kid was hers now, and if something about her life or somebody in her life shocked her, Nina would get over it. After all, wasn't the whole point of Cee Cee's taking the kid to put some color into her little black-and-white world? Now she was pissed off just thinking about the way she'd lamely agreed to that boarding school. Sophocles and Anouilh, my ass, she thought.

The airplane was flying out over the water, and all she could see below them was the slate blue ocean. Jesus, she thought, any minute Mister Charm would be telling her it was time to open the window. If only Leona could see her this minute, in the co-pilot's seat of some flying teakettle, she'd shit a brick. Leona, *that's* who it was who put all those bullshit fears in her head. That's whose fault it was that Cee Cee didn't even learn to ride a bike until she was a teenager because Leona said to her, "What do you need it for? You could break a leg and then you'll never be able to be a Rockette." "I'm too short to be a Rockette, Ma." "So now you want to have *two* strikes against you?"

Leona, who also told her, "Never trust another woman if there's a man around," which was probably why Cee Cee had made only one real friend in her life. And of course it was Leona, that fountain of unwanted information, who had told her on at least a dozen occasions, "Believe you me, sweetheart, when it comes down to it . . . men only want *one thing*." Okay, Cee Cee thought . . . so *some* things the old bat *was* right about.

That thought made her chuckle, and as she did, she could feel the plane starting to slow. The moment had arrived. This was what the pilot told her would happen. He would slow the plane down so it would be okay for her to open the window, and that's what he was doing now. *Oh my God, it's my cue*, she thought, and reached down to the floor and with two hands pulled the box onto her lap. Then she removed the lid again, slowly unwound the plastic, to look long at the ashes one more time.

Okay, Bert, she thought, *here we go. I'm trying to do everything right. I'm up here like I promised, about to strew your remains over the deep blue sea like you asked me to, and I hope this cancels out the time I had that real fancy pin of your grandmother's wrapped in a Kleenex and accidentally flushed it down the toilet, or the time I yelled at you in the lobby of the hotel in Florida, or any other time you were mad at me.* Now she closed her eyes as if that would make Bertie's spirit more able to hear her, and thought about all the last minute things she wanted Bertie to know, feeling as if she needed to cram them in before she parted with the ashes.

Bert, I'm trying to make things the way I think you would have wanted them to be but I know how particular you are about stuff, so sometimes it's hard. Like for example I'm gonna keep buying Nina all those smocked little dresses you like her to wear, and that she likes too, I even took her to Saks in Monterey to buy her some more of them in spite of the fact that I personally think they're so matronly my grandmother would have returned them. But I'm trying not to be too tough on her about it. After she insisted that was what she really liked to wear, I only told her once that she looked like a member of the D.A.R.

"Miss Bloom," the pilot said, and Cee Cee opened her eyes. Obviously he was about to give her the signal. Any second he would tell her to open the window, so she would have to hurry up through the rest of what she wanted Bertie to know. "Yeah, yeah," she said looking over at him, then she held the box close to her chest continuing her silent inner monologue to Bertie. *And that school. Bert, I've got to tell you, I hated to leave her there, because that girl was not happy. I mean she acted real brave and all . . . but see, that lawyer leaned on me and when I thought about it I guess I figured for the time being she'd be better off there than with me, and once I saw how uptown the place was I worried that you'd think so too, so I . . .*

"Miss Bloom, it's time," the pilot said over the noise of the airplane.

"Okay!" Cee Cee said, feeling suddenly foolish and panicky and not sure she remembered the instructions he'd given her. The latch on the window. Turn it and push. She reached over and turned the latch on the window and pushed it open. It was hard to push now. Much harder than it had been in the airport, and the rushing wind rattled loudly through the cabin, blowing through her hair and her clothes. This was it, the last goodbye. Tears blurring her eyes, and her heart and head pounding, she looked at the pilot, who gave her the high sign, and probably because she'd been screwing up the timing talking to Bertie, the guy looked a little pissed, and he wasn't exactly the winner of the Mister Congeniality award to begin with.

"Goodbye, Bert," she said out loud now, the overwhelming force of the wind pounding at her face. "I sure as hell hope you think I'm doing the right thing by Nina." And wincing from the wind, she lifted the box to the window, trying nervously to remember everything the pilot told her, and in one fast move, turned it over to dump the ashes straight down, when she instantly felt the powerful slap of an enormous gust of wind that forced Bertie's ashes back into the window at her, spraying, splattering directly into her stunned, gasping face, covering her eyes, her nostrils, her ears, her hair, her clothes while the rest of the little pellets flew wildly all around the cabin. Hastily she pulled the box back inside and grabbed for the window, which she managed to pull shut and latch.

"Oh, no. Oh, God. Oh, no," she wailed, horrified, weak and devastated by what she'd done because she'd been too rattled to make sure her arms were in the right position.

"Goddammit," shouted the pilot, wild-eyed with rage. "What in the hell were you goddamned doing? Don't you remember how I told you to hold the box?" There were ashes all over *his* face and hair too, and his jacket, all over the front of his jacket. "I don't believe what you did to my plane." This guy is gonna kill me, Cee Cee thought. He's so bummed out he's liable to open the door and push me out, like in some James Bond movie.

"Oh, God," she said. "I'm sorry. I'm sorry." The box was empty. "Oh, Bert," she said. "Oh, Bert, I'm so sorry," and then she couldn't control the bellow of a laugh that came next. The ashes were everywhere. On her, and the seats and the instrument panel, even on the pissed-off pilot who was turning the plane around now, heading back up the coast, while he brushed his hands through his hair and then over the shoulders of his jacket as if he were in a commercial for dandruff shampoo.

"Well, Bert," Cee Cee said, trying not to laugh anymore, which only made her laugh harder as she pulled the empty cardboard box to her chest, smashing the cardboard when she did. "I guess I should probably take that as a no!"

Back at Del Monte Aviation she had to pay an extra cleaning fee for the damage she had caused the interior of the airplane, and after that she spent a long time in the ladies bathroom in the Monterey Peninsula Airport terminal, brushing, washing, and trembling with the courage of her convictions, and soon she got into the Chevy and drove in a fever back to Highway 1 and up to Santa Cruz.

At first it looked to her as if everyone on the playing field had long brown curly hair, but when the girl she had been certain was Nina separated herself from the others to run down the field, Cee Cee realized she'd been mistaken. For a long time she watched the beautiful little girls playing. Each one was prettier than the next, their pink faces flushed with the excitement of the game. Sometimes they would whisper to one another as they huddled together on the bench or braided one another's ponytails while they watched the game, and each time a goal was scored, they all shrieked and leaped and hugged.

This is a mistake, she thought for a panicky moment. I should leave. Not even let Nina know I'm here. This is the way that child's life is supposed to be. Playing soccer at a ritzy school and having friends and wearing a proper little uniform. This was just where Bertie would have put her, not in Hollywood where the cuckoos are. It's exactly what Bertie would have wanted for her, and the ashes flying back at me was just an accident caused by my stupidity. Not a signal from Bertie. I should leave, and I'm going to

"Cee?" When she turned, there was little Nina. Not in a soccer uniform at all, but in the plaid day uniform of the school. And the relief Cee Cee felt when she saw her renewed the certainty that had fired her as she had raced here from the airport.

"Did you forget something?" Nina asked, looking up at her.

"Neen, I came back to see you and I want to talk to you and the people at the school, because I have this really powerful feeling that maybe you shouldn't . . . maybe it would be better for you, since I'm your parent now . . . if we . . . if you didn't . . ."

"Didn't go to boarding school?" Nina finished the sentence herself, then looked into Cee Cee's face hopeful that the end of the sentence she had chosen was correct.

"Didn't go to boarding school," Cee Cee repeated, nodding.

Nina brightened for a second, but then doubt filled her eyes. "But what about the lawyers?" she asked.

"Honey," Cee Cee said, "we're just gonna do to the lawyers what lawyers have been doing to everybody else for years. And you're coming home with me. To be with me and stay with me wherever I go."

"I am? Oh boy!" Nina said, hugging Cee Cee hard around the waist, her eyes closed and the side of her face pushed against Cee Cee's chest.

"Neen," Cee Cee said to the top of her head, "this isn't gonna be like anything you imagine. Especially if I don't get my television show back on the track, because maybe I'll have to go on the road, or maybe I'll have to go on location, or worst of all I could have to go off to Reno or Tahoe with an act, and that can truly be the lowest."

"I think I can handle it," Nina said, her eyes lit from the inside, as she held her head back so she could look up into Cee Cee's face. "You know, a couple of times I heard my mom saying you were too much of a pushover. Is this the kind of thing she meant?"

"Sort of," Cee Cee said, and her eyes were dancing with light too.

Miss McCullough, the headmistress who had given them the tour, responded to the news of Nina's departure in a way that Cee Cee later described as "so cold you could hang meat." The woman stiffly informed Cee Cee that the school would have to keep the non-refundable five-thousand-dollar deposit they had received from the child's trust fund, since Nina had occupied a place which deprived another child from entering this semester, and Cee Cee smiled a big Cee Cee smile and said, "I'm sure you can find somewhere to put the five grand, toots." Then she gave the woman a little wink and hustled Nina out of the office and the administration building and into the Chevy, where Nina's already repacked suitcases had been piled into the trunk and the backseat, and as she did she said out loud to herself, "Maybe I should have phrased that another way."

"I left one of my Cee Cee Bloom albums with my roommate, Heidi," Nina said as she slid into the passenger seat.

"You had one of my albums with you?"

"I had all of them. They were with my things Aunt Neetie sent from Florida."

"And that girl Heidi wanted it?" Cee Cee asked with surprise, starting the car.

Nina turned to look at her and nodded. "After I told her who you were."

"So you gave her yours?"

"I traded it to her. I figured I could always get another one, and she gave me a black turtleneck sweater."

"Well, who do you think got the better deal?" Cee Cee asked, pulling out of the parking lot, so positive now that taking Nina home with her was the right thing to do, her heart seemed to lift in her chest as they sailed along Highway 1.

"Oh *she* did. Because the album was autographed."

"What did I write on it?"

"You didn't write anything. I autographed it *for* you," Nina told her. There was a long silence, then Cee Cee reached over and touched Nina on the top of the head.

"Thanks, kid," she said. "Thanks a lot."

"You're welcome, Cee," Nina said, grinning as the car headed toward home.

Seven hours later when they arrived in Los Angeles, it was dark, but the outside lights at Cee Cee's house were on and Hal waited for them at the front door. When he hugged Cee Cee to welcome her, she wondered if he could smell the heavy odor of death she knew had to be in her hair and her clothes. He didn't mention it. All he said was "Welcome home."

"This is Nina," she told him as Nina followed behind her. Hal waved a little wave at Nina, who nodded shyly in return, and within minutes the tired-eyed little girl was bored with their conversation about telephone messages and mail and took off on her own to explore the house.

"I would have had a room ready for her," Hal said apologetically, "but I thought you were dropping her off at boarding school." He was carrying some of the suitcases upstairs, with Cee Cee behind him carrying the rest.

"Boarding school did not work out," she said as Hal dropped some of the suitcases containing Bertie's things and Cee Cee's small overnight bag in her room, and she looked around at the familiarity of it, thinking how long it had been since the last time she slept in that bed, and about all that had happened to her since then. "It was an idea whose time had not yet arrived, and may I say it fostered hostility and fear and scads of ugly resentment."

"No kidding?" Hal said.

"No kidding. But *I'm* all right now." The two friends smiled. "Nina was great about it, a trooper in fact, but I knew leaving her there would mean cheating her out of what I promised Bert I would do, and also promised myself I would do, so I figured what the hell. I keep thinking about that 'Peanuts' cartoon I have pinned to the wall in the kitchen where Charlie Brown is sitting against a rock saying 'I've developed a new philosophy. I only dread one day at a time!' Well, for the first few years, that'll be me, and then maybe I'll mellow out."

Hal squeezed her hand. "I'm glad you're both okay."

They stood at the top of the stairs and shared a gentle hug, until Cee Cee pulled away to listen to the music she heard floating up from downstairs in the music room. Nina had put one of Cee Cee's albums on the turntable there and was listening to it.

> Nights are long since you went away
> I dream about you all through the day
> My buddy, my buddy
> Nobody quite so true.

Hal, who had played backup piano on the recording session of that album, listened a little mistily to the music, then nodded remembering. "That was the first cut," he reminded Cee Cee.

"Yeah," Cee Cee said, sighing. "And it's always the deepest." Then she put her arm around Hal, and the two of them walked downstairs to be with Nina, listening to the song as it rose.

> Miss your voice, the touch of your hand
> Just long to know that you understand
> My buddy, my buddy
> Your buddy misses you.

ANDREWS, KROLL, SCHULTZ AND STEIN

Dear Cee Cee,

Per our recent telephone conversation, I reiterate how sorry I was to hear of the death of your friend Roberta Barron. Although I never met her, you told me more than once how important her friendship was to you. Regarding your role as guardian of her minor child, I am enclosing the following forms: a petition for your appointment as guardian of the person of Nina Barron and a waiver of notice and consent. Per Mrs. Barron's attorney in Sarasota, I will also forward copies of the waiver to Roberta Barron's aunt Anita Bennet in Miami Beach, Florida, and the child's natural father, Michael Barron in Pittsburgh, Pennsylvania.

The petition will be filed with the State of California and a date for a hearing will be set for sometime within the next six months depending on how much independent investigation the court wishes to make before appointing a guardian. Despite what you told me on the phone about the ominous words from Mrs. Barron's representatives, rest assured that the court will give great weight to Mrs. Barron's nomination.

Because the firm of Barmen and Wolk in Florida has been appointed as guardian to the estate, and the child's natural father has shown no interest in Nina since birth, and the aunt is elderly and I gather relieved to be rescued from the responsibility, I foresee no problems in closing this matter swiftly.

Again, please accept my deepest sympathies for your loss, and if you have any questions regarding these documents please feel free to call.

Sincerely,

Jim Andrews

Dear Cee Cee,

I got the waiver yesterday from the California court, and I signed it because I know that's what my niece said she wanted. Personally I worry about the welfare of a child who is living in that kind of environment where there are so many terrible types. (No offense meant towards you, but you know how most people in your line of work behave. Like that Cher and others I don't have to mention.) I have also put in the envelope a copy of something which I went over to the library to the copy machine to make for you. It's a letter which was sent to me by my niece, a few months before she died. You can tell by what she says in it that it was sent during the time when she still intended to give Nina to me instead of to you. I came across it last night and thought that maybe you should have it because of what it says. The handwriting in it is so poor and childlike that she must have already been very ill when she sent it off, and I'm pretty sure she wasn't really in her right mind at the end. Now and then I get a letter from Nina. If you could make her write to me more often, it would cheer me and my husband quite a bit.

Sincerely,

Anita Bennet

From the Desk of Roberta Barron

Dear Aunt Neet,

I have begun this letter to you again and again over the last few weeks, each time destroying the draft halfway through, probably to deny that eventually I would have to finish and send it, since my intention herein is to outline some of my thoughts about your future with Nina, and that brings home the very painful point that you in fact will be having a future with her, and I will not. Nevertheless, it's becoming increasingly clear that my rapidly declining physical health will soon prohibit my getting a letter of this sort off to you at all, and it's crucial to me that you understand what it is I am about to set down here.

Essentially what I want to write to you, and had the situation been otherwise would have preferred to say in person, has to do with what I will call her care and feeding after I'm gone.

To begin with, let me say that from the very first day of her somewhat unorthodox life Nina has been the dearest and best girl in the world. Yes, she is willful at times and bossy too, but I think that comes mostly as a result of being the fatherless daughter of a living father who, though he admits that she exists by sending money, continues to refuse to see her. That has never been easy for her and I'm sure it never will be. That said, I have to tell you I am terrified that her further rage at my death will tear the goodness from her. And that's why, even though I know you will do everything you can to take splendid physical care of her, educating her per my lawyers, etc., there is so much more that she will need in order to survive.

Oh, Aunt Neet, what I'm trying to say is please, please, please, love her! Try to look beyond her very proper little person facade and you won't be able to resist loving her. See the funny spark in her, appreciate her wonderful mind and indulge her wild imaginings. And as many times as you can find a moment, promise me without a doubt that you will take her in your arms and hug her long and hard. Let her feel grown-up arms around her, reassuring her that even though it seems as though events have conspired against her, she really is loved and special, and maybe that will serve to give her hope that down the line she will be able to find some happiness of her own.

I don't care if her grades in school are not the highest in the class. I don't care if her room is perfectly neat, though I realize I can't dictate the rules for your home. I don't even care if she's sometimes irreverent and more outlandish than I ever was. (Which heaven knows, wouldn't take much, after old Straight Arrow's life. The only unusual thing I ever did was to raise her alone, and I thank God for that decision every day.)

Thank you, Aunt Neetie. My memories of the times I spent with you during my childhood are many and precious to me. You were my mother's dearest sister, and she would approve of my leaving Nina in your care. The truth is, you are my only real family, and I am grateful that you have agreed to shoulder the enormous burden of raising my girl . . . my dear dear girl.

Know that I will be looking on from wherever my spirit lights, smiling with gratitude on both you and Uncle Herb.

Your niece,

Roberta

Dear Aunt Neetie:

I have only known you as Aunt Neetie, so I hope it's okay if I call you that.

I'm sending this to say thank you a lot for the copy of Bertie's letter to you. I knew about the letter but in the middle of all the stuff that's been going on here, I guess I forgot about it. What I'm trying to say is that if you look closely at the original, you'll understand that the reason I already knew about the letter is because the person with the lousy handwriting wasn't Bertie, it was me. She dictated it to me one day when I first started caring for her during her illness, and she was feeling too bad to write it herself.

The one thing I want you to know for sure is that she was not in any way out of her mind when she wrote it, or when she agreed to let me have Nina instead of sending her to you.

I'm knocking myself out to try and carry out Bert's wishes for Nina. And I promise I'll tell the kid to write you more often.

Cee Cee

We have moved

to 29 Malibu Colony Road

Malibu, California   90265

Cee Cee Bloom

Nina Barron

LOS ANGELES, CALIFORNIA
August 1990

T HERE WAS no missing Kevin in a crowd. It wasn't just his rolling walk that always stuck out so dramatically when he moved down the street with the other boys, but the high-spirited whinny of a voice ringing above the others, as he cracked endless jokes, teasing his friends mercilessly, always confident not one of them would dare to retaliate.

Cee Cee caught sight of him the minute he walked out of the front door of the school, and she watched him, surrounded by his usual gang, as they all walked down the front path. She had been sitting outside the school in her car for half an hour, waiting to tell Kevin the news face-to-face, afraid if she didn't get there early she would miss him. Her hands clutched the steering wheel at ten and two o'clock, the way her teacher at the California Driving School had taught her to do so long ago, only now she was parked.

See me, Kevie, Cee Cee thought, staring at his face, which was contorted with animation while he told a story to a few of the guys who responded with a laugh so raucous that even Cee Cee at a distance was sure it had to have been a dirty joke. *See me, Kevie*, she thought again, and then as if in answer, he looked right at her, nodded a special Kevin nod, and then moved away from the others toward her car as she opened the window on the passenger side.

"You cruising high schools now, lady?" he asked leaning in the window. "I mean, I know a good man is hard to find . . . but really, Cee."

Cee Cee got out of the car and walked to where he was standing to give him a hug, startled when she did at the bony frailness under the layered clothes.

"Kevin," she said, "I guess you know what's been going on in our lives."

"I've known for a long time."

"Hey, Myers, you coming with us or what?" a voice yelled from the parking lot.

"Tell him I'm taking you home," Cee Cee said. "Please."

"I've got a ride," Kevin hollered.

"What'd you say?" the kid hollered back.

"He's got a ride," Cee Cee shouted back toward the parking lot.

"Wow, you've got a nice set of lungs. Ever think about being a singer?" Kevin laughed at his own cuteness.

Cee Cee opened the car door for him.

"Get in," she said to him, "before I punch your lights out."

"Oooh, sweet-talk me and you own me," he said, and sank slowly onto the black leather seat of the BMW. Cee Cee walked around to her side, got in, and started the car. She drove back to the Coast Highway and when she reached the parking lot just north of the pier she made a right and pulled the car into a parking spot facing the sea. It was a clear day and there was a line of white sailboats on the horizon. Cee Cee could tell by the way Kevin's right hand held on to the open window that he was bracing himself for the worst. Bad news, otherwise why would she have come to tell him in person?

"Well," she said, "I thought you should hear this from me instead of on an answering machine after a beep."

"Jesus, the suspense is killing me," he said, laughing an uncomfortable laugh, which she interrupted by telling him the news. Then the laughter stopped and she saw him try to act as if he wasn't feeling choked up, but he was.

"So can I count on you?" she asked him.

"I can't think of anything that would keep me away," he promised, and then he reached out a hand and took hers. After a while he let out a little giggle.

"What's funny?" Cee Cee asked.

"Remembering when I met you when you first moved to Malibu. The first time I was ever in your house." Cee Cee grinned as she remembered too, and then they reminisced, looking out at the view for so long that eventually they watched the sun, which had moved slowly down in the sky, drop like a giant orange egg yolk into the sea.

MALIBU, CALIFORNIA
October 1983

CEE CEE sat on the deck of the new house in Malibu wearing a frayed white terry cloth robe she'd had for so long it might have belonged to her ex-husband. She always pulled the now ratty thing out of the closet and wrapped herself in it when she needed to be near something familiar and homey. The breakfast tray she and Nina had shared earlier still sat on the glass and wrought-iron table piled up with their dirty breakfast dishes and the empty milk glasses they had clicked together in a toast to their own cleverness for moving to the beach.

The toast was one Nathan used to say when he drank his rare glass of schnapps on one of the Jewish holidays. "Look out teeth, look out gums, look out kishkes, here it comes." Nina had never heard the word *kishkes* before and the sound of it made her laugh so hard, her milk bubbled up in her mouth and her eyes watered. Cee Cee loved the way the kid was starting to learn to be silly, giddy, childlike. And as odd as it seemed, so was Cee Cee for the first time in her life. Neither of them, in the years before their union, had ever learned much about playing or really letting go. Nina because most of her life had been filled with grown-up problems, and Cee Cee because her own childhood had been so focused on the pursuit of a career.

"I'm getting this mother thing down to a science," she told Hal one day. "For example, I already know that you can't go to the playground in three-inch pumps. The goddamned heels stick in the grass and the next thing you know, *you're* still walking, but the shoes are a half a mile back! After I figured *that* out, all was well until yesterday when my tiny little ass fell right through the humongous hole in the tire swing. In fact it took two very attractive single fathers to pull me out. Did I mention that the park is a veritable treasure trove of parents without partners?"

This morning Nina was down the road at the home of one of her new friends and Cee Cee scrunched down a little lower in the lounge chair wondering how she'd been crazy enough to put herself so deeply in debt by impulsively buying this big expensive house on the beach. At first when her business manager grumbled about it being more than she could afford, she used the excuse that she was buying it because of Nina. That she wanted the child to feel at home after living near water all her life in Sarasota.

Then she said it was because the house was on a street protected by a guard gate and that would keep the paparazzi out. Which it did, for a while, though an army of them seemed somehow to know where she was going at all times and managed to show up everywhere, snapping and flashing away at her and at Nina, immediately selling the pictures to the tabloids, which printed them constantly. But her real reason for buying the house was much more selfish than any of those.

She had come back to Hollywood feeling like an alien. Realizing, though nothing there had changed, that after her months in Carmel she was seeing it all through new eyes. A perspective that had been changed by the lesson of those bleak and endless days and nights of sitting at Bertie's bedside where under fire she had learned about how fragile the line was between life and death. And the time with nothing to do but care for someone else had given her the opportunity to think about the unimportant attitudes and ridiculous posturing that got in the way of most people's living their lives.

So when the painful vigil was over and she came home and looked at the years stretching before her, her first impulse was to goddamn enjoy them in a big way, to live it up. There were no men who interested her and vice versa, she knew from past experience that indulging in too much food would be bad for her career, she already had a great car, so she bought a house, a big gorgeous house on the beach for herself and for Nina.

Every day since they'd left Carmel she had taken an emotional tally of how they were doing together, watching and monitoring the ups and downs. Worried because there had been quite a few little explosions between them. Like the one last week when Nina had given her some of that haughty more-elegant-than-thou shit at which she was an expert and which could always start some sparks flying. There was no getting away from the fact that this kid had been so well trained by Bertie, she could go to lunch with the Queen of England and know what to do, and just like her mother, she didn't hesitate to make a point of telling Cee Cee what *she* was doing wrong.

"Did you send a thank-you note for those flowers?" she asked Cee Cee the other day. That was what started it.

"A what?"

"The world doesn't owe you a living, Cee Cee. Your agent didn't *have* to send those roses just to welcome you back."

"Do you have any idea how much money I made for that agency last year? Believe me, my agent *had* to send the roses. He ought to send *me* a thank-you note for the privilege of sending them."

"I don't agree. My mother taught me that when someone takes the time and effort to send you something —"

"He had his *secretary* send them," Cee Cee had said, her voice rising, astonished at how much the kid's getting on her case like that really bugged her.

"But the thought was *his*," Nina replied in a tone calm enough to make Cee Cee's flaring temper feel stupid.

"I already had a mother," Cee Cee said, steaming.

"Well, she must have forgotten to mention thank-you notes."

Hah! That time Cee Cee had burst out laughing, because the idea of Leona mentioning thank-you notes was pretty funny. "The only person Leona ever thanked was the doctor who told her after I was born that she probably wouldn't have any more babies." Of course the truth was Nina was right about a lot of things. Especially the goddamned thank-you note. It took exactly three minutes for Cee Cee to dash off this really full-of-it thank-you note, and the other day when she stopped by Larry Gold's office, she nearly fainted. The little twirp had framed the goddamned thing and it was hanging on his office wall.

Then there was the constant battle about clothes. Cee Cee remembered how the saleslady at Saks had just about bust a gut overhearing *that* conversation.

"Why?" Cee Cee asked looking at Nina's choices for school clothes, "does an eight-year-old kid want to dress like a forty-year-old woman?"

"And vice versa?" Nina had asked looking Cee Cee right in the eye, and when she did, Cee Cee glanced over her head at herself in the three-way mirror and realized she was wearing an off-the-shoulder sweatshirt, bicycle pants, lace tights, and high-topped basketball shoes.

"Good point," she said, and the subject was closed.

And naturally, since Nina was Bertie's daughter there had to be the whole discussion about language, just like the ones Cee Cee used to have with Bertie all the time. In fact sometimes when Nina opened that mouth of hers, it was so spookily like talking to Bertie, Cee Cee had to look around to make sure it was the kid.

"I'd like to ask you if you'd kindly stop saying F-U-C-K in front of me," Nina said one night at the dinner table, pronouncing the letters of the word as carefully as if she were a finalist in a spelling bee.

"I didn't realize I ever *did* say it in front of you."

"That's because it's a bad habit."

"Huh?"

"You say it automatically at least ten times a day."

"Me? Get the fuck outta here."

"Just like that."

"Ten times a day is impossible."

"Well, if you think it's impossible, what if I fine you for every time you say it, and I get to keep the money?"

"How much?"

"A dollar."

"A nickel."

"A quarter."

"You're on."

Okay, so by the end of the first week she owed Nina six bucks. But last week it was only a buck seventy-five, which was a big improvement. And now they had made it through six weeks. Six weeks of settling in, getting that this was forever. Figuring out what they were going to do next. Six whole weeks since the day the people came and carried Bertie out of the house in Carmel shoved into a body bag, so just the fact that it was still that fresh, and she and the pipsqueak had already survived tons of little battles and the big one of moving out of one house and into another, they were doing all right.

Consider what happens when we are learning any new skill, whether it is playing bridge, playing golf, riding a motorcycle, playing the piano or anything else. We learn by making literally thousands of mistakes. Why should learning the complex skills of raising a child be an exception to the rule? We should take it for granted that we will make mistakes and not berate ourselves or feel guilty about it.

Cee Cee had closed the over-the-counter child psychology book after reading those words and said, "Yeah!" out loud. This was new to her, but eventually she'd get the hang of it and be great. Now she needed to get back into the swing of things in the business. Needed to call people and tell them she was back, needed to get a real good job to pay for this big fucking house. Frigging house. Fancy house. Some days she would call her agent five times in a row with ideas about how to get her career back on track, but other days she would sit incapacitated, numbly staring at the ocean for hours, not knowing or caring what time or even what day it was.

And most important of all she had to find a school for Nina. In the last few days, after talking to everyone she could think of who had a child, she compiled a list of all the recommended private schools within a reasonable distance of the beach house, then she phoned the admitting offices of those schools and set a time to visit. This afternoon the two of them dressed, and as usual looked one another's outfits over with patent disapproval, then headed off to the Buena Vista School, which had been recommended highly by Larry Gold, whose three kids were all registered there. While Nina was escorted on a tour of the place, Cee Cee sat talking with the headmaster. She had a list of questions a mile long, and after he had answered all of them, he took a long deep breath and launched into what, she could tell by the way he delivered it, had to be an often-repeated sales pitch.

"Cee Cee, listen to me, our school caters specifically to the special needs of the children of people like yourself. Let's face it. We all put our kids into schools where *we're* comfortable, right? Of course I mean by that where the policies of the school are the same ones we live by at home. But also where we ourselves fit in with the parent body, if you know what I mean." He waited for Cee Cee to nod and let him know she knew what he meant, then he went on. "Now it's pretty hard for me to believe *you'd* be more comfortable than in a school like ours where you're surrounded by your colleagues." He handed her the school's roster. "Go ahead," he said, "feel free to look through it. We've got more stars than the Milky Way. And the reason for that," he added, "is because we're cognizant of the needs of these families for privacy."

Cee Cee wanted to ask this guy if the school had such a great respect for privacy, why he was letting *her*, an outsider, look at the list of the names of people who were registered there. But instead she just shuffled through it, and had to agree that a lot of well-known people's kids were registered in that school.

"This child has had a few tough breaks," she said, looking into his eyes.

"Oh, I know." The headmaster's name was Jason, and the more Cee Cee looked at him, the more she thought he looked too young to even be a teacher, let alone a headmaster. "I read about it in the paper," he said, nodding, and Cee Cee wondered if he meant the *Enquirer.* "But she'll be in understanding company here, because there are many kids from unusual situations, multiple stepfamilies, cohabiting parents who have never married one another, single parents whose spouses aren't around anymore, or single parents who never had spouses in the first place. In fact in *this* school it's the nuclear families who are unusual." When his smiling eyes met Cee Cee's concerned ones, he shrugged, laughed a little laugh, and said, "That's show biz."

Cee Cee looked around his large office. There were a lot of pictures of this guy on every wall, eight-by-ten framed pictures of him standing among small groups of people. Now Cee Cee looked more closely and saw that one of the groups was Sylvester Stallone and one of his kids, and in another he was with Lesley Ann Warren and her son, then there was another of Jason with Goldie Hawn and her kids.

"Well, we'll give it a lot of thought," Cee Cee said, standing, relieved that at that moment, through the floor-to-ceiling window that faced the school's back lawn with a wide-angle view of the ocean, she could see Nina on her way back toward the administration building. Cee Cee shook the young headmaster's outstretched hand and thanked him.

"So what are you working on now?" he asked, walking out the door of his office with her, and the question felt like a blow to her stomach. Larry Gold was trying to get a meeting for her with the network people she had walked out on when she went to Carmel all those months ago, but so far they were refusing even to listen to her apology. Trouble, she was known in the industry as trouble, her agent told her bluntly, but he was trying to smooth things over.

"I've got a lot of stuff cooking," she said, trying to sound even.

"Well, that's good," the headmaster said, "because I'm a big fan."

Now Nina was standing next to her. When the headmaster put out his hand for the girl to shake, she gave him a look-in-the-eye-firm-grip Cee Cee knew Bertie must have insisted on, said, "Thank you so much for your time," and she and Cee Cee were off down the hall.

"So, what do you think?" Cee Cee asked her when they got into the car.

"I think I should go to the public school in our neighborhood," she answered. "I don't want to go to a school for weird kids from weird families. I want to feel like I'm with real kids. And anyway, all they did on the tour was drop names and ask me what *you* were like."

"Neen, your life is special now and your circumstances are too."

"I'm not special, *you* are."

"Well, the public school in our neighborhood won't work," Cee Cee said.

"And Buena Vista won't either," Nina snapped.

Cee Cee drove silently for a few blocks, their mutual frustration hanging in the air.

More stars than the Milky Way. The kid's right, Cee Cee thought. That's not the place for her. But somehow she had to find a school that offered some degree of safety and privacy to a child whose family profile was so high, one that would give Nina the feeling of normalcy her homelife with Cee Cee would never provide. Someplace where she could see that another lifestyle was possible, and where she would be among lots of families, whole ones, the kind she might want to have herself someday. "Don't worry. We'll find the right place," she said, not sure if she was talking to herself or Nina. It would have to be a good school too, because this kid was one smart little cookie, very intense, with an overanalytical mind that never quit. At bedtime she

and Cee Cee would take turns reading to one another, and Nina
always had a million serious questions about even the most frivolous
storybooks.

"*At Piglet's house the water was coming in through the window. He had
just written a note which read 'HELP, PIGLET, ME.' Piglet put the note in
a bottle which floated out of the window and out of sight. And then Piglet
floated out of the window and out of sight.*" Nina had stopped after reading
that paragraph aloud to Cee Cee and asked, "Do you think Piglet
wrote 'Help Piglet' and then signed the note 'Me'? Or do you think
he wrote 'Help' at the top and 'Me' at the bottom and then only had
room in the middle to sign it 'Piglet'? Or do you think he wrote 'Help
Piglet' and then thought he should explain that the note was written
about himself so he wrote 'Me' in the middle of the page?" Cee Cee
couldn't believe the worried expression on the little girl's face while
she waited for the answer to those questions. And that was the way
her compulsive little mind worked all the time.

"Honey, I think," Cee Cee had said, putting an arm around her,
"that when the water's too deep, we just blurt out the message and
don't stop to think how it comes out." That seemed to satisfy Nina
for the moment, and as they read on, Cee Cee thought about her own
life. Like Piglet *she* was in too deep. When Larry Gold called and said
Peter Flaherty at the network had finally agreed to "take a meeting"
with her, she knew she was supposed to be happy, but instead she felt
afraid, because she was so desperate for it to work out.

"Tell them I have a child now, Larry. Tell them I'm the new
Nixon. Say I need to work more than ever. One of those people must
have kids, somebody there should understand that." She couldn't
believe his response.

"Trust me, you're gonna have to kiss a few asses to pull this one
off. Cee Cee, you *know* what the numbers were. You cost them a
million five by walking out and going to be with your sick friend.
And don't get me wrong, because I understand that kind of stuff, I
cry at the drop of a hat, but you're nuts if you think Peter Flaherty
gives a shit. Remember the joke about the guy who needed the heart
transplant, and he couldn't find a donor? And finally they brought in
Denton Cooley, the specialist, who looked the patient over and said,
'I recommend giving him Peter Flaherty's heart. After all, *he* never

uses it.' I promise you, Cee, the network only cares about people who are dying if there's a Movie of the Week in it."

The next morning on the way over to the meeting in Larry's Jaguar XJS convertible with the top down, the wheel of which he was barely tall enough to see over, he said, "It's pretty amazing that even after the article on the front page of the Calendar section, Flaherty is still in that job. I mean, you know every word of it was true."

Cee Cee wondered as she looked at Larry Gold's tiny hands clutching the wheel of the Jaguar, then at his serious little face, if when he drove the car and there was no one in the passenger seat, whether people who were driving behind him thought his car was a runaway vehicle. The idea of that made her smile.

"Yeah, pretty funny, wasn't it?" Larry said, taking her smile as a response to his question.

"Wasn't what?" She hadn't heard a word.

"That article in the *Times*. Oh maybe you were in Carmel when it came out. About Flaherty and the psychic?"

Cee Cee had no idea what he was talking about, and she could see that Larry Gold warmed to the telling of the gossip the way the old women on her front stoop in the Bronx always did, just after some neighbor passed by whom they were eager to trash.

"Flaherty actually had some girl on the network payroll, with a three-year contract, and the girl was a psychic who told him which shows to pick up and which to cancel and where to slot them in the lineup."

"Didn't seem to do him any good," Cee Cee said, pulling down the visor in front of her and looking at herself in the mirror. "His network is still number four out of a possible three."

"Which is why after two years of bad predictions, Flaherty dumped the girl, who was not too happy about it."

"If she was any kind of a psychic, she'd have seen it coming," Cee Cee said, and she and Larry both laughed.

"So instead of just saying, 'I had a nice ride for a couple of years on the network's dough,' the psychic . . .'"

"Calls the *L.A. Times* and tells them the story," Cee Cee interrupted.

"Yeah. How did *you* know?" Larry asked driving up Highland Avenue toward the freeway.

"I'm psychic," Cee Cee said.

"Everyone went crazy while it was in the papers. Even Johnny Carson was doing jokes about it, but I guess it passed."

Cee Cee's hair blew wildly around her face as they sailed along the Hollywood Freeway. She hadn't had a haircut or hair color in more than three months, hadn't done anything for herself the entire time she was in Carmel, and then this morning in anticipation of the network meeting she'd spent hours trying to get her hair not to look like a bad imitation of Harpo Marx. But after this ride there was no hope. She hated that she felt nervous, and that she couldn't even seem to calm herself with the news that she was on her way to meet with a man who was so insecure himself he had to hire a psychic to tell him what to do.

"Hey, these people were ready to sue you," Larry told her as he pulled into the parking lot at the network, gave a friendly wave to the guard, and found a spot next to what Cee Cee recognized as Peter Flaherty's Ferrari, "but I parlez-voused a little, and I think now they get the idea that when you walked out on the show, you had no choice. I mean, that's what I told them. I said to them . . . 'People, this girl is not difficult, this girl is not Judy Garland. She doesn't even touch drugs anymore.'"

"Did you *say* that?"

"No! Are you crazy?" Larry Gold laughed. "I'm kidding you. It's like that joke. 'When did you stop beating your wife?' No, what I said to Flaherty and that girl who works for him, Michelle, I said, 'Do yourself a favor, let Cee Cee come in, we'll sit, she'll explain it, you'll hear her side of the story and we'll get the whole thing back together in no time.'"

Peter Flaherty's office was furnished with white sofas, white chairs, and glass tables on chrome bases so that the sun pouring in through the floor-to-ceiling windows bounced off the reflecting surfaces, making Cee Cee want to put on her dark glasses, but she didn't because she was afraid that would make her look too Hollywood, and for this meeting she had to look down-to-earth and sincere.

Flaherty was wearing a tailor-made shirt and an expensive tie and gray suit pants. The jacket was hung neatly on the back of his desk chair. He had a slim, boyish body, a fair complexion with freckles, and perfectly coiffed strawberry blond hair. There was no doubt the guy was great looking. Cee Cee knew that in television circles he was known as a cocksman and was sometimes referred to as "The Red Fox." Probably, Cee Cee thought, he had given that name to himself, then hired a press agent to pass it around. As she watched him chatting with Larry Gold, she remembered one night at a party at Jerry Weintraub's house when Flaherty had pulled her into the powder room and made a pass at her. He was the president of the network.

The girl, as Larry Gold had called her, was Michelle Kleier, the executive vice-president of programming. She was bouncy and cute with short blond hair and big brown eyes, and she was very obviously pregnant. Her greeting to Cee Cee was a little warmer than Flaherty's, but there was a strain in her smile that made Cee Cee know this wasn't going to be a welcome home party.

The third henchman was Tim Weiss, vice-president of specials. He was young and handsome, with dark wavy hair and horn-rimmed glasses, and he looked as if he had just walked straight out of some magazine ad for men's cologne. Cee Cee remembered him from last summer, when he was the executive assigned to her special, as being wide-eyed and idealistic. This morning he looked at her with the helpless look people give to the mourners at funerals.

When everyone had greeted one another, Peter Flaherty announced to his secretary that he would stop taking phone calls, the door to the outer office was closed and everyone was seated, and then there was a long cold silence during which everyone looked at Cee Cee, making it obvious that she was the one who was supposed to talk first. She had made a big expensive mistake, and now they were waiting for her to explain why and to apologize humbly. All of their faces blurred in front of her, and she was sure she would never remember what it was she had rehearsed and then promised Larry she would say, but she started talking anyway, hoping it would come to her, and it did.

"Larry and I both thought it would be a good idea if I came in and told you why I walked out on the show. I'm sorry if it seemed irresponsible to you, and I understand why you'd be angry, but something very emotional happened to me and at the time I felt as if I had no choice but to do what I did." Dumb, she thought to herself as she said it. I sound like a fourth-grader, apologizing for cutting school.

"Yes," Peter Flaherty said, "we heard there was a death in your family, and that kind of threw you for a while."

"It was my best friend. She called me one day when I was in rehearsal for the show and said she needed to see me right away. So I rushed out and went up to Carmel, thinking I'd just stay the night and be back at rehearsal in the morning. But when I got there she told me she'd invited me because she wanted to let me know that she was dying and to say goodbye, and she wanted to do that in person in order to let me know she was okay about it.

"And she *was* okay. Brave and tough, with all her papers in order and ready to hit the road. Only the thing was that *I* wasn't okay about it because she was the first real friend I ever had in my life, and also the only really close one I ever had, and I wasn't ready to let her go. So I never stopped to figure out what it was going to cost anybody down here if I stayed with her until she died, because all of a sudden, all I could think about was that I couldn't let her be escorted out of this life by people who might do a good job of keeping her sickroom clean and getting her fed, but who had already written her off as dead when there was still enough life left in her that she could be enjoying.

"So I stayed. I didn't take the time to come down here and work out how and when to reschedule everything, because there wasn't any time to take, and I guess I knew if I called to discuss it with Larry or my business manager, Wayne, they'd try to convince me to come back, and I *couldn't* come back. Because, my plan was to escort her out laughing, since that was how she and I always handled everything bad in our lives. We laughed about them and made them okay. So when she was feeling low because she probably wouldn't make it till Christmas, I got a tree and we had Christmas in July, and I sent for her daughter and got her to come out from Florida and be with us, and we all sat out on the beach and laughed and argued and did dumb jokes about dying. We really enjoyed the time until finally my friend had nothing left . . . and I had to let her go."

That was the end of what she had to say, and the minute she spoke those last words, she knew there was something irreverent and wrong about making the speech in the first place. Because now she understood that what Larry Gold told her was true. These people would never understand in a lifetime how much it had meant to her to be able to spend those months with Bertie.

"Look, I apologize for screwing up the show by walking out, because when I finally took time to think about it I realized *that* part was wrong, very wrong, but I also know that staying with my friend in Carmel was right. The rightest thing I've ever done."

The two men didn't react at all, and the woman lowered her eyes and looked down at the floor.

"And now I'm okay," Cee Cee said, knowing it was a dirty lie, because she wasn't anywhere close to okay. She still woke up in the middle of the night feeling around for Bertie's medication, sometimes jumping up out of bed to go to her, and some nights getting as far as her own bedroom door before she realized where she was and that Bertie was dead. But she needed these people to think she was okay so they'd give her back her show, and then she *would* be. She'd take off the extra weight she'd put on while she was in Carmel, work any hours she had to. Do whatever it would take to get the old show happening again.

"I'm ready to go back to work. In fact I need to work. To do something that'll keep me busier than hell," and while she was talking, hearing her own voice ring through the room, she could tell that though they might be listening they weren't really hearing her. She was looking now at Michelle and Tim, and out of the corner of her eye she saw Peter Flaherty push the edge of his cuff up surreptitiously to take a peek at his watch, and she wondered how much time he had allotted in his day for this meeting. How did somebody figure those things out? Amount of time it takes for out-of-line former big star to beg forgiveness. Two minutes? Five? Ten?

She was losing them. In fact they all looked so uncomfortable they probably couldn't wait for her to get out of there. This was a lot worse than the flop sweat she felt onstage when her jokes weren't working, because at least in those cases she knew she could rewrite the jokes and try them again the next night. But if these network people wouldn't put her on the air because she'd been trouble, they would tell everybody in the industry the reason why — that Cee Cee Bloom was a flake, difficult, unpredictable — and then she wouldn't be able to get work anywhere.

"Well, you're great to come in, Cee Cee," Peter Flaherty said.

"You're great," Michelle Kleier echoed.

"Great." The word made Cee Cee cringe. It always reminded her of that character Warren Beatty played in *Shampoo*, the hairdresser who went from woman to woman telling each one of them, "You're great, baby. Great."

"Thank you," Cee Cee said. She had to keep talking. Had to get Flaherty to say he would give her another chance.

"Please, take a shot with me," she said, trying to catch his eye, because it always seemed as if he was looking just a little bit past her, as if that was a way he had learned to look at people to throw them off balance, and she was off balance all right, but still in there pitching. "You know if you put this show on, I'm gonna bring in a big audience share. This is the first time I've done television in years. People will be tuning in left and right to see me. You'll make your money back. I'll even do the show for free." That sounded like a valiant thing to say, and she meant it, but she heard an intake of air from Larry Gold as he moved forward in his chair, and she suspected if she looked at him he would make some gesture for her to shut up.

"It would be nice if we could resurrect something, Cee Cee," Peter Flaherty said, his brow furrowed, "because you know we've always believed in your talent, but frankly I'd have a hard time recommending it. Even with your promise, how could I ever be sure some other whim might not just take you off the set again, and that for some other reason which felt urgent to you at the moment you might not do the same thing again?"

Cee Cee sat back in her chair with an acidy ache in her stomach. A whim. Peter Fucking Flaherty didn't give a shit about what she'd lived through. Wouldn't give a shit if the story she had just told him had been about his own mother, and that made an anger rise in her like hot lava, so that she had to hold on to the arm of the chair to keep from getting up and walking out.

Okay, he was right she'd been irresponsible to leave the show the way she had, but to characterize it as a whim was cold and wrong. She thought about what Hal always said to her when they were on the road if she got upset by a bad audience or a rotten review, "It's just a show. It ain't life and death." Well, spending those months with Bertie *had* been life and death, not just another television show people forgot the day after it aired.

Flaherty's eyebrows were raised, and his lips were pursed together as if he was expecting an answer from her. "I mean how would I know?" he repeated the question, like a teacher waiting for a student to respond.

Cee Cee's blood boiled, her face was hot, and she knew with a kind of drunken headiness that she was about to lose it and say what was on her mind. Later she would replay this scene in her mind and wonder how she'd let that rage take her over so completely at that moment to make her mouth shoot off at the president of the network.

"Maybe," she answered, "you could ask your psychic."

Flaherty went pale. There was a split second when he seemed to be thinking about how to react, when it could have gone either way, maybe he would even take it as a joke, but then Cee Cee saw in his eyes the decision that there was no way he was going to accept this kind of abuse from some former superstar prima donna who should be sucking up to him and begging for her show back. Who in the hell did she think she was? Now he stood, signaling that the meeting was over.

"Thanks for stopping by," he said, his jaw clenched, his eyes completely drained of expression. Then he walked to the door and opened it. His lieutenants stood too. Cee Cee couldn't look at Larry Gold, because she knew he was probably on the verge of a full-out stroke, that he would go apeshit over this, tell her what he always did, what Bertie always used to, that you didn't always have to say the first smart-ass thing that comes into your head . . . but she didn't care. These unfeeling schmucks would never know, never understand why she did what she did, and if that meant she was drummed out of the business, that would have to be the way it was. When she got to the doorway where Flaherty stood, she looked up at him, and said to his indifferent face, "It's a good thing you've got *crystal* balls, honey, 'cause you sure don't have the other kind." And she stormed out, with Larry Gold rushing down the hall of the network building after her.

All the way back out to her house in Malibu, neither of them said a word, and Cee Cee feared with a sick feeling that probably she had made a big mistake taking Nina out of that boarding school so fast. Up until now there had been a shred of hope that things could fall into some state of normalcy, but for certain now her life would be a rat's nest. She'd be traveling around, doing concerts, hoping for a good script with a breakout part to come along in a movie that could shoot God knows where.

She shuddered when she thought back to what the concert tours had always been like, and some of the animals she had had to deal with. Not to mention the scrungy hotels and horrible hours. That was a lifestyle she wouldn't wish on her worst enemy. Finally, when Larry Gold pulled up outside her house, he stopped the car and turned his small body in the seat so he could face her.

"You were wrong, Cee Cee. You should have been humble. What'd you *get* out of it? One second of making Flaherty uncomfortable versus getting your show back on the air."

"They knew they weren't gonna do another show with me before we walked in there, Larry, believe me," she said, getting out of the car. But the truth was he was right, and she knew it.

"What do you want me to do?" he called after her. She turned around and looked at his helpless expression. She had behaved like a dumb headstrong jackass who didn't know better, and if there had ever been a prayer to get the show back, she had blown it.

"Get me a job," she answered, then turned and put her key in the front door, realizing how glad she was to be able to come home to Nina.

Hal's high-pitched singing voice was the first sound she heard as she pushed the door open. He was belting out some old silly song he had written about a frog prince, and Nina was singing along, laughing at all of the funny lyrics.

"Well, what'd they say?" Hal asked, stopping the music as Cee Cee walked in.

"Wait. I've gotta clean the rug burns off my knees from where I was down on them begging their forgiveness."

"And?"

"And after that I succeeded in big-mouthing my way right out of the business."

"How'd you do that?"

"Never mind how. I'm ruined, I'm cold potatoes, dead meat. They don't care why I left the show, and they'll probably see that I'll never work again. I'll be back playing the High Sign Café in North Hollywood. Remember that place, Harold? With the mice? And I can promise you they were not the ones from the cast of *Cinderella*. They didn't make me *one* dress. In fact, you may recall I stood on a chair most nights when I sang just to avoid coming face to face with the little rodents." She turned to head for the kitchen. "I'd better go call the real estate broker and put the house on the market."

"Hey, Cee," Hal said.

"Yeah?" She turned back.

"If I were you, I'd get off the cross. You'll probably need the wood for fuel."

Cee Cee couldn't help but laugh. And when she did, Nina did too.

"Flaherty is one network. There are two others. There's cable, there's theater, there're other studios who would kill for you. You'll have a gig in no time," Hal said.

"You think so?" Cee Cee's eyes tested his for the possibility of a lie.

"I do," Hal said. "And I don't say 'I do' to just any girl."

But no one was calling for her, the phone in the Malibu house was stubbornly quiet when they were at home, and the answering machine light didn't blink with waiting messages when she and Nina came home from their visits to the various schools. For weeks they'd tried to find just the right one, but they were getting more and more discouraged.

"Today we saw 'the free to be me school,' where they wore Spandex pants, streaks of green hair, and everything visible that was piercible contained a cubic zirconia."

"They let the kids walk around looking like that?" Hal asked her.

"I haven't gotten to describing the kids yet. Those were the teachers. And did I mention the hoity-toity one where they asked if I'd like to build a gymnasium in memory of Nina's mother? Or the very regimented one where the headmaster asked if I believed corporal punishment was ever warranted, and when my answer was 'Only during foreplay,' he had me removed from his office. It's getting exhausting, Harold."

The next school they looked at was Elmhurst. On the way, Nina asked again, "Why can't I go to our neighborhood public school? My friend Kevin goes there and he —"

"Neen, listen carefully. Those other kids, the ones you're meeting on our road. Their homes aren't listed on 'Maps to the Stars' Homes' that any kidnapper can buy on the corner of Sunset and Doheny for five bucks."

"What does *that* have to do with school?"

"Your needs are special now, kiddo. Because as Cher once said to Sonny, 'You've got me, babe.'"

"That was way before my time," Nina said. "But I think what she really said was, 'I've got you, babe.'"

"Yeah? Well, what she meant was stuck is stuck."

The physical plant of Elmhurst was shoddy, a group of ramshackle buildings sitting on a lot in Topanga Canyon that could hardly be called a campus, but the cheery mural of a playground painted by the children, which covered the side of one of the buildings, brightened up the look of the place. This morning Sandy Lowe, the director of the school, a tall heavy woman with long straight gray hair that she wore pushed back from her face with a plastic pink headband showed Cee Cee and Nina around the tiny campus, and she talked to both of them in the tone and cadence of somebody who spent most of her time with young children.

"Those are our little buddies, the mice and snakes and hamsters and rabbits, and Fred and Wilma over there are our baby rats. They're very tame and the children get to take them out of the cages to feed them and hold them," she said as they stood in the makeshift science lab where Nina wandered over to the animal cages.

"No!" Cee Cee said, surprised. "I spent years tryin' to get out of my old neighborhood so I wouldn't have to get anywhere *near* a rat. Now I've got to pay ten grand so my kid can hold one? You gotta be kidding."

The director smiled, a very slight smile. Nina walked over by the far wall where there was a display of the children's work.

"The school is a family corporation. Many of our activities are completely parent run. The parents care for the school building, as well as sit on the board that governs the corporation. And the parents work regularly with their children on the various projects. For example, what Nina is looking at right now is a parent-student science project about weather. Precipitation. Why it snows. How to make it rain."

"I know the answer to that!" Cee Cee said in a loud voice. "I just go and get my car washed." No reaction.

Dumb joke, Cee Cee thought. Dumb friggin' joke, just like when

I was a kid. Make a joke to cover how stupid I really am. I was afraid the director was gonna ask me to tell her how rain actually does get made, and Nina would see how dumb I am because I don't know.

"Calm down, Cee Cee," Nina said softly to her when they were a distance away from the director, following her back to the office. "It's me who's trying to get into the school. Not you. This is the best one so far, so don't mess it up."

"Why doesn't Nina stay with me for a little while so we can talk some more?" Sandy Lowe said, coming over and patting Cee Cee on the arm. "And you can go over to the development office and talk with Barbara Gilbert. She's the head of the parent organization and she'll be able to tell you better than I can about what, if Nina is accepted at Elmhurst, they'll expect from you."

"Great," Cee Cee said. Nina walked away with Sandy Lowe, looking particularly tiny next to the tall wide woman, and Cee Cee thought before she turned away that the little girl had had a look on her face that said she was relieved to get away from her. She liked this place. So did Cee Cee. Settled. This was it. The school for her. Cee Cee's step felt lighter now.

The development office had two desks, both of which were piled high with papers. A small brown-haired woman with a blunt-cut bob that accentuated her large nose sat behind one of the desks, talking on the phone. She was holding a Diet Coke in her free hand, and when Cee Cee stood in the doorway, the woman tucked the phone under her chin and waved Cee Cee in with her now free hand.

Cee Cee took a seat in a chair on the other side of the desk, and after a while when the woman continued to talk on the phone, she felt awkward sitting there listening, so she opened her purse and rifled through it, just to have something to do. I'm so relieved we found the school for us, she thought. After she had yanked Nina out of that school in Santa Cruz, and would really get shit from Bertie's lawyers once they discovered she had, she'd better get the kid's education on the ball already. This school seemed to be the best choice so far.

Barbara Gilbert laughed a nervous laugh in response to the person on the phone then said, "I have to hop, Katie. I have a parent interview. Talk to you later."

A parent interview. Cee Cee sat up straighter. She thought she was stopping by to get some information and say hello but clearly this was an audition.

"I'm Barbara Gilbert."

"I'm Cee Cee Bl—"

"Oh, believe me, I know who you are."

"Well, Nina and I really like the school," Cee Cee said.

"Isn't that nice?" Barbara Gilbert said. "And you met Sandy Lowe? She's a love." Cee Cee forced a smile. "We couldn't survive without her. The kids love her, and she's so guileless and unthreatening and childlike herself."

Oh brother, Cee Cee thought. I may not know how you make rain, but I've been around long enough to already know by the way she said that, that this broad has it in for the director and isn't too sure about me in the bargain.

"Cee Cee. How can I put this in a way that won't insult you?"

What did I tell you? Cee Cee said to herself. "Gee," she said out loud, "when you start like that, I can hardly wait to hear the rest. Insult away." Barbara Gilbert laughed a shrill laugh. She was edgy and tense, as if she'd just had a lot of caffeine. More than you get in just one Diet Coke.

"I personally feel that you're not the kind of mother who will be happy in our parent program."

Cee Cee felt weak. This didn't sound so hot. It was definitely a rejection. Not now, after all the schools they'd looked at, and finally they'd found this one, the one she thought felt right and Nina seemed to like too, this woman was saying no.

"How can you possibly know what kind of mother I am? I just walked in here. Not to mention the fact that I've only been a mother for less than a month to begin with, so *I* don't even know what kind of mother I am," Cee Cee said, her anger all over her face.

"I mean you work, Cee Cee, and even though many of our mothers do, they work in jobs which give them the freedom to come here regularly and get deeply involved in our program, because that's what we require."

"Well, at the moment I'm out of work," Cee Cee said, in a voice she hoped didn't sound like it was begging. "So I have tons of time,

and besides I *want* to be involved. I'm interested in this school because
I've looked at others and I knew that if Nina went to school here I'd
have to take a few hours out of my week to be around as if I was . . ."
She stopped herself from saying the words *a real mother.*

Barbara Gilbert had a little smile on her face, which looked more
like a smirk. "Let's be realistic," she said. "You're a famous star with a
schedule I'm sure isn't going to leave you the kind of time Elmhurst
demands from its families." No, she was telling Cee Cee no. Because
Cee Cee wasn't the right type, they were going to reject Nina.

"Have you looked at Buena Vista?" she asked.

"We have," Cee Cee said, and the sinking feeling in her stomach
felt familiar. She was amazed that her hands were as clammy now as
they had been in the network meeting the other day. "And we didn't
think it was right for us. It would be so good for Nina to come here,"
she said, trying to keep her voice sounding even. "I want to do this
for her, because she needs to be in a place where there are a lot of
family things going on. So she can see how real families operate and
support one another. She never had a father, and her mother . . ."

"I *know* the story," Barbara Gilbert said, cutting her off. "I read it
on your admissions application, not to mention in all the newspapers.
But frankly, I don't think you have any idea what it is you'd be getting
into. The families in our school run the school. And that means work.
We have a mothers' committee that comes in twice a week and makes
hot lunches. Certain mothers come in and straighten up every day.
Every other Friday morning all the mothers and some of the fathers
come in and we clean the building ourselves, we repair things that go
wrong on our own, we do all the dirty work, if you will, and we do
it ourselves." Her face was tense with self-righteousness. "We've had
some families with working mothers who have asked if they could
send their housekeepers in to do the work for them, but that is not
allowed. It's missing the point of why we exist at all."

"Yeah? So?" Cee Cee said, "I understand, and Friday mornings are
good for me. Hey, believe me, I can clean as good as anybody else. I
wasn't born a star, you know. I grew up in the South Bronx in a sixth-
floor walk-up. When my father's dry cleaning store was in trouble, I
had to teach tap dancing to little kids so I could get my own lessons
free. And after I practiced my tap on the linoleum kitchen floor, my

mother used to make me scrub it with a toothbrush. Don't be prejudiced against me 'cause I'm famous. I swear I'll work ten times as hard as anybody."

Barbara Gilbert looked down with a sigh. This was not what she wanted to hear. Clearly, she had hoped to scare Cee Cee off. Was sure that by now she'd be seeing her to the door, sorry she'd ever thought of putting the little girl in a co-op. When she looked Cee Cee in the eye now, it was with an expression which meant, Now I'm going to drive my point all the way home.

"Besides our group responsibilities, each family has to have a job. Cleaning the animal cages, scrubbing the floors, buying supplies in bulk, delivering them to the school and putting them away, fund-raising, organizing and refurbishing the library." She rattled off the list with raised eyebrows then asked, "Which job in those I listed do you think you would want to do?" as if it was a trick question.

Cee Cee's mind raced. She was afraid if she gave the wrong answer Barbara Gilbert would suddenly pull a lever that would release the floor beneath her feet and she'd find herself standing outside in the parking lot. "How about fund-raising?" she tried. "I've got lots of good ideas for that. I could maybe get donations from the studios, or how about after I do my next picture we could have a special premiere of it and charge a high ticket price and every cent could go to the school. I could probably help the school make some dough. So much, that maybe you could afford to hire a janitor!"

Barbara Gilbert looked up sharply.

"A joke," Cee Cee said apologetically. Very apologetically. "That was just a joke."

Barbara Gilbert thought about it for a while, then Cee Cee saw the moment when it turned, saw in her face that she realized maybe the idea of having Cee Cee Bloom at the school might not be as terrible as she'd imagined. There was something to be said for the ability of someone like Cee Cee to help bring in some badly needed money.

"Look, I'll be frank with you," she said, "there are many schools in Los Angeles which cater to children of people in show business, allowing the students to go off on locations with their parents at any time and that sort of thing. We're not one of them. Also there's no doubt in my mind that you are not co-op material. But since you're so insistent and I feel very sorry about the child's situation, let me speak to the others and get back to you."

Relief. Cee Cee wanted to pinch Barbara Gilbert's little birdlike face. She was right in a way. The old Cee Cee wouldn't have been co-op material. She was obsessed with her work, fixated on her career, had let too many important things fall by the wayside because of her work. But that was not who she was now, or at least who she wanted to be. She wanted to have her priorities in order, and Nina was at the top of her list. Now Barbara Gilbert pursed her lips and Cee Cee thought of Margaret Hamilton in *The Wizard of Oz* saying, "I'll get you, dearie, and your little dog, too," only instead she was saying, "I'll let you know."

"Maybe I won't send her to school," Cee Cee said to Hal that night. "Maybe I'll just keep her home and teach her everything I know."

"That sounds great," he said, "but what's she going to do the *next* day?"

"Funny," she said, poking him in the side as she sat down next to him on the piano bench.

"Why don't you just put her into the neighborhood public school?" he asked.

"Now you sound like her," Cee Cee said. "Because her life situation is special and she needs a special place. And I picked a co-op so I could be around her a lot and we could bond."

"Yeah, right. I know that's the big word in child-raising these days. Bond. When I was growing up it's what everyone gave you as a gift for your bar mitzvah. When did *your* mother ever come to school?"

That was a funny thought. Cee Cee knew Leona only cared about her show business career, and didn't ever give a damn about what was going on with her in school. Once when she was a teenager, she and some other kids had cut school and gone into town to see a Vincent Price movie, and when she got home at dinnertime to eat with Leona because as usual Nathan was working late, Leona asked her, "So what did you learn today?" Cee Cee, who knew her mother wasn't listening anyway, had answered, "I learned that if you're gonna have your molecules teleported, you better make sure there's not a fly in the other booth, 'cause if there *is*, you're gonna come out looking very weird and so is the fly." And without skipping a beat, Leona had said back, "Well, isn't that interesting?" Then pushed a bowl filled with a mountain of buttered mashed potatoes in front of Cee Cee, spooned half the mountain on Cee Cee's plate, and it wasn't the first time she got the message that her mother never listened to a word she said. No, she would never be that kind of parent. The co-op would be the perfect place for Nina and for her.

But days went by and Barbara Gilbert didn't return any of Cee Cee's many calls to her, and neither for that matter did Larry Gold, and every time Cee Cee called his office the secretary told her he was in a meeting or on the other line or in New York or still at lunch, and he wasn't rushing to call her back either. One day she got past his secretary and as far as his agent-in-training, Mel.

"Oh yeah. Hiya, Cee Cee. Listen, it's a zoo here, and Larry's been really snowed under, so is there something *I* can handle for you?"

You've got to be kidding, she thought. I'm not only getting the cold shoulder from this asshole, but now he's passing me down to the kindergarten? "Yeah, there's something you can do. Tell my agent I want to know what's going on in my career." I should hang up. I'm talking to a twelve-year-old here, she thought.

"Oh, hey. Not to worry. Because I know he's got a whole long list on you right here. And you're up for tons of stuff."

"Like what?" The lying little cuff-snapping sack of shit.

"Let's see, let me look. Ummm . . ."

She felt belittled and stupid. Here she was, waiting like a hungry dog for some kid, fresh from the mail room, to throw her a bone.

"There's an offer out for you to do 'Zone.'"

Zone. A movie. An offer to do a movie. Real interesting. The title sounded as if it was science fiction.

"What's that?" she asked.

"A feminine hygiene product," Mel said, and Cee Cee laughed out loud, but while she was laughing she realized he wasn't kidding. "But I think Larry told them you don't do commercials. And then there's a possible *Love Boat*, and they want you to be a presenter at the Daytime Emmys, and there's a possible running part on *Dallas* . . . but I think they may be going a little younger."

Without saying another word she hung up. At eight o'clock that night Larry Gold called her.

"Cee Cee . . . don't get crazy. The kid made a mistake," he said after she had shouted at him so angrily it threw her into a coughing fit. "He got mixed up. He's a young kid. He's Garry Marshall's nephew, so I gave him a break. He must have gotten you confused with Juliet Prowse and read you *her* list. Big deal. Believe me. You're not up for any commercials."

"What *do* you have for me?" she asked.

"I'm working on it," he told her. "I'm working on it," which in agent language means I hope you have some dough stashed away, because there isn't a job in sight. And she'd better go back to her list of schools because the bitch from Elmhurst wasn't exactly busting her ass to call her back either.

Ironically, for someone who couldn't get a job, she was still in the tabloids all the time — "Who's the father of Cee Cee's love child?" "Cee Cee begs judge, 'Don't take my kid away'" — and the paparazzi continued to lurk everywhere she and Nina went. The nosy snooping sons-of-bitches snapped their cameras in her face and Nina's while they called out to Nina by name to try to get her to look at them. But within weeks Nina had learned how to affect the glazed-over look-right-through-them expression Cee Cee always assumed when she spotted them. Sometimes they would even be so brazen as to camp outside the gates to the Malibu Colony waiting for Cee Cee's car to emerge. And they always seemed to be waiting at the front door of a restaurant when Cee Cee, Nina, and sometimes Hal with them, made their exit. Finally one evening Cee Cee decided they should just stay in, and she ordered out for a pizza.

She didn't count on the photographer who stopped the pizza delivery boy before he turned the corner at Webb Way heading toward the Malibu Colony gates, and offered him fifty bucks to reveal where he was going and another hundred bucks to let the photographer stand in and deliver the pizza. And when the photographer with the pizza got into the house, acting deferential and delivery-boyish in a way he couldn't wait to describe to his colleagues, while the unknowing Cee Cee and Nina searched for cash to pay for the pizza in their purses on the hall table, he quietly took the opportunity to snap a few pictures of them in their pajamas with a tiny camera they didn't notice. Within a few days those pictures were all over the tabloids. The sleazoids.

The day Cee Cee stopped at the Colony Market to pick up a few groceries and spotted the issue of the *Enquirer*, she felt as if she'd been slapped, wanted to call an attorney and sue those lousy sneaky low-lifes, in fact she was about to pick up the phone and call her lawyer to see if there was anything they could do to avoid that kind of invasion of privacy when the phone rang. It was Barbara Gilbert.

"Cee Cee," she said, "I apologize for taking so long to get back to you but I had to present the idea of you and Nina to our board, and I'm so sorry to say, they don't feel your family will work in our school community. But thanks for thinking of us, and I wish you luck."

Cee Cee put the phone down and went back to get her list of private schools. Nina was in the kitchen reading *Weekly Variety*.

"Boy, if this is the schedule of shows that are coming on," she said without looking up, "I'd think they'd be begging you to come back and do yours." Cee Cee had to hold in a snort of surprise at the attitude of expertise that accompanied the comment.

"Thanks," she said moving nearer as Nina closed the paper because an item on the front page caught her eye. FLAHERTY EXITS WEB FOR INDIE PROD. Her eyes skimmed the column which was written to make it sound as if Peter Flaherty had chosen to resign from the network to become an independent producer, but probably, Cee Cee thought, the psychic scandal had finally caught up with him.

"Neen, they won't take us at Elmhurst . . . but I want you to know it's because of me . . . not because of you . . . so I think we should . . ."

"I don't care," Nina said. "I'm glad. I want to go to the public school."

Cee Cee sighed and looked down at her list. She was not going to let an eight-year-old girl decide what was best for herself. She would continue the search until they found the right school and that was that. "I'll call Crossroads tomorrow," she said. Crossroads was another private school in Santa Monica.

"Oh, while you were at the market, Larry Gold called," Nina remembered. "It's important too. You're doing *The Tonight Show*."

Cee Cee had a simultaneous surge of elation and terror.

"When?"

"This afternoon. He said somebody dropped out at the last minute and the talent coordinator wants to see you as soon as you can get there. Can I come and watch?"

"Of course," Cee Cee said.

"Larry Gold's office."

"It's Cee Cee Bloom for Larry."

"Hold on."

Larry Gold clicked on. Cee Cee heard the triumphant note in his voice. "So, you told me to get you a job. I'm still working on it. In the meantime I got you an appearance on *The Tonight Show.* They're excited to have you."

"Larry, how can I do *The Tonight Show* with no notice? I'm a wreck here. I haven't sung in months, I look like something the cat dragged in, I have nothing planned to talk about. I'll bomb out there. You know if you don't get big laughs, Johnny gets that bored look on his face and never wants you to come back. I can't even find a writer with this kind of notice."

"Cee Cee, calm down. There's a hairdresser over there, a good makeup man. I'll drive you over, you'll pitch some ideas with the talent coordinator about what you want to talk about with Johnny. I just put down the phone with Hal, he's going to meet us there with a half a dozen or so songs you've sung a million times. You bring any music you like, and Doc is going to be there to rehearse the music with you. You're not going to bomb."

"How do you know?"

"I know," he answered. "And if you do? You're no worse off than you were a few weeks ago."

"You mean it isn't too late to say yes to the feminine hygiene commercial?" she asked, but Larry had clicked off.

There was an eerie, dreamlike state that went along with being on *The Tonight Show.* Maybe, Cee Cee thought, it was because the scene of Johnny Carson at his desk and the famous sofa with the hot seat next to him was so familiar after seeing them on TV year after year, that suddenly when they were there, real and three-dimensional and it was *you* sitting next to Johnny in the seat usually occupied by Burt Reynolds or David Steinberg, it was like stepping into a familiar book and becoming part of the story. And it was the *real* you Johnny was talking to, whoever the hell *that* was. Not a character you were playing in a movie.

Or maybe the whole thing was so strange because it was loaded with pressure, since everybody knew that a shot on *The Tonight Show* was always seen by so many people, which meant that scoring could make a nobody into a star or revive a flagging career. So the urgency of having every second count must be just like it was for a batter who stepped up to the plate during the World Series. Cee Cee remembered reading articles about ballplayers who described the moment when the ball was hurtling toward them, as seeming to be slowed in time, when the ball looked huge to them as their expanded consciousness readied them to slam the home run. And it was with her adrenaline pumping and that same kind of altered perception of time during which she heard Johnny set her up for what she planned to say, loud and in quotation marks.

"We haven't seen you around for a long time. How've you been?" he asked, eyes twinkling, after the applause which followed her entrance.

"How have *I* been?" she asked, then held up two tabloid covers she had brought with her from home. Each of them had a full-page color picture of Cee Cee and Nina at home, candid photos of them in their pajamas. "You'd have to live on Mars not to know how *I* am."

There was a close-up shot of the pictures. "That's you at home with your little girl," Johnny said. "How do they get pictures like that?" he asked, with his perfect timing.

"Well, in this case, I ordered a pizza and the deliveryman came and asked us, 'What did you want on your pizza?' So we said, 'Cheese' . . . and he took our picture."

The audience laughed, and the glorious sound of the laughter sent a flush of triumph through Cee Cee.

"No!" Johnny said, in feigned disbelief, tapping his pencil. Cee Cee nodded.

"Some people get pepperoni with their pizza?" she told him. Beat. Beat. Beat. "I get paparazzi."

Another big laugh. Johnny laughed.

"Well, you *too*. Right?" Cee Cee asked him. "I heard the photographers were hiding on the beach right outside your house in Malibu. In fact, if I'm not mistaken, all America drooled over the picture of the gorgeous creature sitting on the deck in a brief little bathing suit." Johnny nodded, as Cee Cee added, "And your *date* wasn't bad either." Big laugh and then she turned to the audience and just as the laughter was beginning to ebb she asked, "The old boy still looks pretty good, doesn't he?"

The audience applauded, Johnny pretended to blush, and the rest of the interview sailed along with laughs and approving nods from Johnny and it seemed as if only seconds had gone by and then he asked her to get up and sing. Singing would be the easy part. She'd been vocalizing all afternoon.

"This song is for Nina," she told Johnny. "She's in the audience." Then she turned to the camera and said, "For those of you who *don't* read the tabloids, her mother was my best friend and she died, and now I'm her guardian, and I'm sorry I lost my friend but I'm glad I have Nina." The camera got a shot of Nina, dressed up for the occasion, grinning, while Cee Cee walked over to the piano where Hal sat waiting, and as Cee Cee perched on a stool he played the intro and she sang,

> You and me against the world
> Sometimes it feels like you and me against the world
> When all others turn their back and walk away
> You can count on me to stay . . .

It was a Paul Williams song Cee Cee had always loved, and the way things had been going it felt right to sing it to Nina.

> And for all the times we've cried
> I've always felt that God was on our side . . .

When the song was finished, the studio audience, especially Nina, applauded, and even Johnny wiped away what might have been a tear before he pointed the eraser end of his pencil at the camera and said, "We'll be right back."

That night when the show aired Cee Cee couldn't bring herself to watch it, and when no one called after it was over she told herself it was because it was too late at night. As she tried to fall asleep, the beats of everything she'd said earlier at the taping of the show played themselves over and over in her head. "And your *date* wasn't bad either." In the morning she woke up so early it was barely light and she slipped on a kimono and sat for a long quiet time in the window-seat of her room looking out at the people already on the beach. A man with white hair walked south along the water's edge with a big black dog splashing happily through the surf next to him, and jogging along in the other direction a hot-looking young hunk of a guy, his big chest wet with the effort of the run, his blue-and-white-striped shorts clinging to him. Cee Cee watched him all the way up the beach, thinking she couldn't even remember the last time she'd had a good hard man next to her, on top of her, wanting her.

Of course being at the beach seemed to magnify her lack of a lover because it was such a sexy, oily, half-naked, lusty place, and when the sun set, the balmy evenings seemed to scream for someone to love, hold, be with, and failing that, she laughed to herself, a nice hot little roll around in the sack. But there was no one. This morning she padded downstairs and made herself a pot of coffee in the kitchen which was silent, except for the crashing of the waves outside, then she sat down at the round oak breakfast table to look again at the list of remaining private schools.

What was she doing to this kid? If she didn't get her into a school soon, some truant officer or welfare person was going to come and put Cee Cee in bad-parent prison. No joke, she thought, since there would, in fact, be a hearing coming up about her guardianship and surely they would want to know not only all about Nina's education so far, but whether or not Cee Cee had a job.

Ass in gear, she thought. I've gotta get my ass in gear and find a school today. At eight o'clock she was on the phone to all the private schools left on her list. Some of them had no room in Nina's grade, some said they would be glad to interview the child and put her on a waiting list for next year. By ten o'clock she had found a few private schools on her list with available spots for Nina, so she made two appointments a day for the next three days at those, and then stood to go and tell Nina. She could hear by the laughter in her room that she was in there playing with one of her friends. God, she thought, aren't kids lucky, the way they can just meet another kid and say,

"Wanna play?" and two minutes later they were in business. Too bad that wasn't the way it worked with grown-ups.

"Hi, kids," Cee Cee said, trying not to trip on all the toys on the floor of Nina's room.

"This is Kevin," Nina said.

"Yeah, hiya, Kevin," Cee Cee said, nodding in the boy's direction, then looked down at her list and proceeded to read off the names of the schools they were going to visit and the times of the visits.

"Cee Cee . . ." Nina said when she'd finished. "I don't want to go to a private school."

"I know you don't," Cee Cee said, hoping they weren't going to end up in an argument in front of some kid who had come to play. "But there's no choice so let's not go through it," she said, trying to keep her voice even.

"I want to be a real person," Nina said, her voice sounding suddenly adult. "Kevin doesn't go to a special school for the same reason. We don't want to be weirdos," Nina said, standing, and Kevin stood too, and now Cee Cee looked at him for what was really the first time.

His hands were knotted fists, and his arms were raised in a V, upward from his elbows. His head was tossed loosely back as if he needed to look at her from his lower eyes, since heavy and unmoving eyelids covered his upper eyes.

"Don't worry," he said. "You didn't have too much to drink. I *always* look like this. I have cerebral palsy." And then he laughed, a kind of cackle of a laugh, and Nina smiled a big smile.

"He lives on the Old Road just down from here, and he told me his mother *fought* to be able to get him into the public school. She went into the office and hollered at people to let him stay there."

Kevin wasn't easy to look at. He was only nine or ten, but the struggle he must have already lived was apparent in his wise gaze, and Cee Cee leaned against the bedpost of Nina's canopied bed for support. Dear God, she thought as she got the point loud and clear. If you're unusual, you long for sameness. To be part of the mainstream. The same way she had longed just to go to school and out for a cheeseburger with the other kids instead of going to dancing school to become a funny-faced tap-dancing outcast, the way this kid Kevin must long to be treated every day of his life and Nina too. Maybe, she thought, I have to let this one go.

"Let me think about it," she said folding the paper with the private school names on it, and folding it again and again and one more time, then slipped it into the pocket of her kimono. Later that day she called Webster Elementary School, the public school in her neighborhood, to tell them that tomorrow she would bring Nina by to register.

"There's a to-die-for part in a picture at Universal," Larry Gold told her a few days later.

"Thank God," she said.

"But they want you to test for it."

"Test for it? Come on."

"Big people are testing. Not just you."

"You mean a lot of people are being considered for the part besides me?"

"I mean you're on a list, Cee. I'm not gonna lie to you."

"I'm doing a screen test? Like an unknown?"

"Teri Garr is testing. Madeline Kahn is testing."

"So it's a second banana part."

"Well it's the part of —"

"The friend. The star's zany but loyal friend. That's who those people play."

"Yeah . . . but it's a major —"

"I'm not testing. I'm not testing against those people. I don't do good on tests. Every time the guy got into my car at the Department of Motor Vehicles, I forgot which was the gas and which was the brake, and I failed, even though before the guy opened the car door. I was Andy Granatelli. No tests."

"Then how am I gonna get you a job?"

"Larry, that's why God made William Morris, so you guys could figure it out."

"Cee?" It was her business manager, Wayne. "Can you come in here next week so we can talk? I'd like to do a tax projection and I need to know what you have coming up so we can figure this out together."

"I don't *know* what's coming up," she said. "It's a little slow for me right now."

There was a silence and then he asked, "Well, what are you going to do for money?"

"Don't I have any?" she asked.

"Not a whole hell of a lot," he told her. "With a monthly nut like you've got, I think you ought to be trying to get some steady work if you can, and failing that, start doing some guest shots, commercials. That kind of stuff ever occur to you?"

"Yeah, sure. It has, but —"

"It would probably make sense for you to take some work like that just to pull in some bucks until something big happens. You know what I'm saying?"

"Sure. Sure. I know."

"Look, why don't we schedule a meeting for tomorrow or the next day and in the meantime you can sleep on it."

Sleep on it. Whoever invented that catchy little phrase sure as hell didn't have her in mind. Every night for the last few weeks when she put her head on the pillow her brain moved from one fear to the next the way her car radio once moved from station to station because the SEEK button was broken. No money, no show, no man, too flaky, a kid to raise but how to do it, too fat, *The Love Boat*, too old, a commercial for feminine hygiene, sell the house, Juliet Prowse, and on *Dallas* they're going younger.

Nina had started school at Webster Elementary, and she loved it. Some nights Cee Cee would get out of bed and walk around the house, stopping outside of her room and looking in the open door at the peacefully sleeping child, and when she did she'd think, *I'll do a shot on the goddamned* Love Boat. *That's not too small for me. On any show, whatever it is. And when I get through they'll give me an Emmy for it, because I'll chew a hole right through the scenery.* But when she tried to reach Larry Gold to tell him that, Mel said he was in London for the next few weeks.

One night Hal and Nina were conspiring to cook dinner for Cee Cee, who had just come from a meeting with a producer who wanted her to be in his off-Broadway musical, but wanted her to invest money in it too, when the phone rang and Hal answered it.

"Cee," he called. "It's for you. Tim Weiss."

Tim Weiss. It took Cee Cee a minute or two to figure out who that was. The guy at the network. The one who had worked for Peter Flaherty. Cute young guy.

"Cee Cee," he said in a very warm voice, "how are you?"

She felt suspicious. Why the call? "I'm grand," she said, no emotion in her own voice. "And yourself?"

"Well, I'm great because — I don't know if you've heard — Flaherty's gone."

"I've heard," Cee Cee said.

"And I've been promoted."

"Congratulations."

"I'd like to get together with you, Cee Cee, and talk as soon as possible. Would you be willing to?"

To talk. Flaherty was gone. Maybe things could be turned around.

"Sure."

"When?"

"What time is it?" she asked him.

"Five o'clock."

"How's five thirty?"

She could hear Nina and Hal in the kitchen making Hal's mother's roast chicken recipe for dinner, while she sat on her chintz-flowered sofa across from Tim Weiss. He was very attractive looking and smelled of some lime aftershave she recognized as the same scent one of her long-ago lovers had worn but she wasn't sure which one, and his attitude was apologetic and kind.

"Cee Cee, I came here for two reasons. The first is to say that I understand from a very emotional and personal point of view about your leaving the show to be with your dying friend. A few years ago, my own friend was dying too, in Europe, but by the time I had the guts to tell Flaherty that I needed to take some time off so I could get to him, I had missed him, by an hour. I only wish I had had the last few months of his life to do what you did for and with your best friend."

Cee Cee was stonefaced as Tim went on. "I also want you to know that I wish I'd been able to say what I just did in front of Flaherty at our meeting in his office, but frankly, I was afraid. He was volatile and irrational and I would have been fired on the spot. Now he's gone. I don't have his job, Michelle Kleier does, but she and I are very close, and I know she feels as I do that we want to give you a show."

Cee Cee felt weak with relief and buzzing with joy. Every meeting she'd had with producers had come up dry, and even though there were a few products for which she agreed to do commercials, finally none of the clients wanted her.

"Not just a special, but a series if you'd do it. We'll work out the guarantees with Larry Gold, and your company can produce it. Both Michelle and I saw you a few weeks ago on *The Tonight Show*, and Michelle called me afterwards and said, 'There's no one like her.' And it's true. But you're so unorthodox it took us a while to sell the concept of a series to the powers that be. Now we've done it and we think we can pull it all together, and that's why I'm here." He bit the inside of his lower lip now that his speech was over, and sat waiting for a reply.

"I'd want my accompanist Hal Lieberman to be my musical director," she said quietly, not certain she had better put any belief in this turn of events.

"I know Hal and he's very gifted. I'm sure we can work that out."

"And I have to have a schedule that's not so killing that I can't spend time with my kid."

"I understand," Tim said.

"I'll talk to Larry Gold tonight and we'll call you in the morning," Cee Cee found the voice to say.

Tim nodded and she walked with him to the front door where she shook his hand. "I'm sorry about your friend," she said.

"And I'm sorry about yours," he said, and when he left, she watched him through the sidelight windows of the front door as he got into his two-seater Mercedes convertible and drove away, then she walked into the kitchen. It was a mess. Garlic and onion and fresh spices and dirty pans and chopped breadcrumbs were everywhere. And then there were the sweet expectant faces of the apron-clad Hal and Nina looking at her.

"I've got good news," she said. "I got a job so we won't have to eat the dog."

"We don't have a dog," Nina said.

"Well, then, that means it's better news than I thought," Cee Cee said.

"What kind of job?" Hal asked.

"Nothing much," she told him, pulling an apron from a hook and tying it around her waist. "Just my own show. It was a brief but satisfying retirement, but La Bloom is definitely back in la show business," she said doing a little dance step of joy, carrying the dirty pans to the sink and turning on the hot water.

"Oh, and Harold," she said as the steam rose around her. "I forgot to mention that if you want one, you've got a new job too, as my musical director."

"Ooh, I think I could put up with that," Hal said. Then he walked over and opened the oven door to look proudly at the crisp, bubbly chicken, whose aroma filled the entire room.

"Now *that*," he said, "is what *I* call entertainment."

VANITY FAIR

March 1984

"Why doesn't somebody bring back the old-fashioned variety show?" That's been the question since we bid a fond adieu to our favorite ones like *Carol Burnett* and *The Smothers Brothers* and *Sonny and Cher*. But it seemed as if the versatile talent who could pull off the jokes, the songs, and the hosting of guests with the sophistication of the eighties didn't seem to be around. In her many years in the business, Cee Cee Bloom has starred on Broadway and in films, recorded hit singles and albums, has survived as many ups and downs as Wylie Coyote. So this year, when to the supreme delight of her fans, she picked up the variety show gauntlet, by not only starring in one of her very own but by producing it as well, all of us crossed our fingers and hoped for the best. Well, good news. Variety is once again the spice of life!

Cee Cee's talented, she's funny, you can't stop looking at her, and somehow, even though we've known her for so long, she's in a package which works for the eighties! In her first season she's done every funny turn imaginable, from Camille to Clarabel the Clown, and as if that wasn't enough, with her newly worked-out and very voluptuous body poured into a sequined dress, she sings so soulfully it can make you cry. In addition to which she has a roster of guests (Michael Jackson, Paul McCartney, Mister T) that would make any rival counterprogrammer shudder.

And as smashing and surprise-filled as the first several shows were, up-and-coming entries promise to be even more exciting (Bruce Springsteen's already on tape). Isn't it good to know Cee Cee Bloom, who seems to have more lives than any cat we've ever heard of, is back on top again. And so, thank heaven, is variety!

VARIETY

1985

The *William Morris Agency*
congratulates their client
CEE CEE BLOOM
on her Emmy nominations

Variety, Music, or Comedy Series —
THE CEE CEE BLOOM SHOW

Variety, Music, or Comedy Special —
THE BEST OF THE CEE CEE BLOOM SHOW

Individual Performance — Variety or Musical Program —
CEE CEE BLOOM: *THE CEE CEE BLOOM SHOW*

Dear Aunt Neetie,

Cee Cee and I are living in Malibu in a house she told me she is busting her ass to keep. I go out on the beach on the weekends and play with Larry Hagman who is J.R. on Dallas. Remember when he got shot? Also I go to school. The first school I went to was in Santa Cruz but I heard Cee Cee tell the headmistress where she could put the five thousand dollars, and we came back here. The co-op school wouldn't take us because of Cee Cee being unacceptibel and now I'm in the school I wanted which is where my best friend goes who is crippled.

I have met lots of people who are famis, like Michael Jackson and also Richard Pryor who set himself on fire once while he was taking drugs, but he's okay now. It's pretty good to live with someone who has her own television show which I guess you know Cee Cee does now, because we get to go everyplace in limosines and the fan magazine guys can't see into the black windows and that's important because last year one of them got into our house and took pictures of us in our pajamas.

It's really lies what they print in those papers. Don Johnson and Cee Cee are not lovers and she did not go with Bruce Willis to Spago. Cee Cee told me those pictures are called paste-ups, a picture of her and one of Don Johnson, and the newspaper puts them together and makes it look like they are what she calls an item, only it's a lot of bull you-know-what. So far it's pretty much okay here, except for how much I miss my mom which is so much that some nights I dream she is alive and wake up crying because she's not.

Love, Nina

Michael Barron
c/o Barron, Malamud and Stern
1600 Golden Triangle Way
Pittsburgh, Pennsylvania 15213

Dear Michael,

    This is a very informal request from me to you
just to ask if there might be a chance for you to spend
even one hour with your daughter Nina. I will fly her
to you anywhere in the world if you'll just say you'll
meet her and say hello.

Thank you,

Cee Cee

LOS ANGELES, CALIFORNIA
August 1990

FROM THE BACK of a limousine parked at the airport curb, Cee Cee sat looking out of the black-tinted windows watching the people hurry in and out of the automatic doors. The couples, the families, the business types, some of them squinting hard when they looked at her car windows curiously, as if squinting would help them penetrate the one-way glass to see who was inside. When she saw Richie Charles emerge through the doors surrounded by his usual entourage of bodyguards, moving with that famous swagger of his toward his waiting limo, which was parked in front of hers, she threw her door open and called out to him.

"Richieee." She hoped he would hear her over the bus that was pulling away with a smelly gray puff of exhaust. When Richie turned in her direction, he was wearing a patronizing look she'd seen him give to fans. His new late-night talk show was such a hit, the press was calling him "the black Johnny Carson." Now when he realized the person who had called out to him was Cee Cee, the stiff smile changed to his real one, and he moved toward her, his arms out to embrace her.

"Gimme one of them big titty hugs," he said and pulled her close. He was lean and muscular and smelled of some exotic men's cologne. When she backed up to take a better look, she had to smile at the Armani suit and the sockless Italian loafers he now wore as a testament to his success.

"I wasn't sure if you'd make it," she said.

"Get outta here. And miss this? Who are you talking to? I've got to stop at my office and then I'll see you on over there."

"Thank you, Richie. Thank you from the bottom of my heart," Cee Cee said. Richie held her close again and she knew the facade had slipped and he was straining to hold back emotions he liked to pretend he didn't have. Dozens of airport passersby hurried along the sidewalk, and every now and then one of them, noticing suddenly who they were seeing there, stopped for a moment to gawk.

"Cee Cee," Richie whispered into her hair after they'd been clinging on to one another for a long time, "I just realized I'd better get out of here fast."

"Why is that?" she asked, looking concerned.

"Because darlin' . . . you and I are standing in the White Zone."

Cee Cee chuckled as Richie squeezed her hand and gave her his reassurance that he'd see her in a matter of hours, then fell easily into his waiting limousine, which pulled away from the curb and moved slowly into the Los Angeles day.

ATLANTIC CITY, NEW JERSEY

1985

"ON THE BOARDWALK in Atlantic City, we will walk in a dream. On the boardwalk in Atlantic City, life will be peaches and cream." Leona used to start singing that song the minute the bus pulled out of the Port Authority, and keep singing it all the way onto the Garden State Parkway until Cee Cee, who always felt sick on buses anyway, wanted to scream at her to stop. And if Leona's singing and the stinky odor of the bus fuel weren't bad enough, those Hebrew National salami sandwiches Leona always packed for the trip and unwrapped and devoured, and occasionally pushed into her daughter's face to offer her a bite, would eventually make Cee Cee green with nausea.

This time she was in Atlantic City to play Caesars Palace. Not exactly Carnegie Hall, but the money was great and after her business manager heard how high the offer was, he told her to grab it.

"You want me to take a nightclub act to Atlantic City? Now? When my show's a big hit? Wayne, it's my time off and I'm going to go sit on a beach somewhere."

"Atlantic City *is* a beach somewhere. During the day when you're not onstage, you'll sit on it. Take the kid, she'll love it there."

"No shot."

"Cee Cee, you people in your business," he began, and she knew he was about to launch into his voice-of-doom speech, "you make a mistake when you live your lives and plan the rest of your lives based on how much you make in your best year. And the truth is, if you live like that even with a hit show, you'll run out of money."

No matter how much money Cee Cee had, and she was never sure exactly how much that was, she always worried about it. She had never been able to forget the scenes from her childhood of Leona sitting over a dining-room table covered with bills every month, frantically trying to decide which ones she could get away with not paying for a little while longer, all the while muttering, "The poorhouse. Pretty soon they'll be sending my mail to the poorhouse."

And all those times in Wayne's office when Cee Cee sat across the desk from the furrowed-browed "accountant who got lucky" as Hal called him and Wayne tried to explain why she had to incorporate and become a production company, or whatever the hell else he told her, like what he was going to do about her tax problems, she didn't understand a word of it. Sometimes he sounded as if he was talking to a two-year-old, and finally, still in the dark but wanting to end the dizzying confrontation with the sheets of numbers, she would say, "Look, here's our deal, I'll *make* the money, you take care of it."

Bertie used to tell her she was being infantile by evading the issue of her own finances and that an artist had to be a businesswoman too, and Cee Cee knew that was probably true. Because when you put your money into somebody else's hands, you ran a risk they could lose it or steal it or, as the song went, "run Venezuela," but she decided she'd take that chance instead of clogging up her brain with the problems.

"Cee Cee," Wayne urged, and when he urged he always made it sound as if it was for her good and never his commission, "do yourself a favor. For a lousy two weeks in New Jersey, you'll make a shitload of dough, and then if your television show gets canned, you'll have a cushion." Mister Tact.

"My show is number three in the country. Why would it get canceled?" she asked, hearing the panic in her voice because she immediately suspected he knew something she didn't.

"Hey, no reason. I'm just saying that plenty of people in your position who started out as big stars died without a pot to piss in."

"*There's* a happy thought."

That night she had walked from room to room trying to decide how much of a comedown it would be when people in the business found out she was playing Atlantic City, the armpit by the sea. Why would she *do* that to herself? She didn't even like playing the place when she was a kid and she had no other choice. At the moment she was a big television star, and eventually she'd make movies again. Or maybe not. Maybe she'd die without a pot to piss in.

Probably it was hearing that her two allies at the network, Tim Weiss and Michelle Kleier, were both leaving their jobs that finally made her call Larry Gold and tell him she was willing to do the gig in Atlantic City. Michelle was leaving the network job because she was pregnant again and this time she didn't want to have to leave a baby and rush back to work, and Cee Cee hadn't heard anything about where Tim was planning to go, but he was definitely out of there, and he had been her strongest champion.

She could remember so many of the people at the networks and the studios whose names had reverberated through the show-business community at one point or another because of their power positions, and who were now nowhere to be seen or heard from again. The turnover was almost comical. And of course, the new people liked to come up with new projects of their own and not inherit shows from somebody else's regime. Cee Cee had known from the start how both Tim and Michelle fought to get her show on the air, then defensively changed the format, the time slot, the promotion techniques to keep it on top. And each time the show would do great and their belief in her would be lauded. But if neither of them were there, she wasn't sure what would happen.

The day after she talked with Larry she sat down at the kitchen table and on the long thin pad the housekeeper used to make shopping lists, she made a list of the best writers of special material and jokes, choreographers and boy dancers, lighting and costume designers, and then started worrying again so she called Hal in New York. After two seasons as the musical director of her show, he had taken his original musical to a small theater off-Broadway. Now a move to Broadway was in the works, and he was up to his ears trying to make the show bigger to fit the bigger venue.

"I have to put an act together to take to Caesars Palace in Atlantic City," she told him.

"Why? Who'd you murder?"

"Funny. But Wayne says the offer's too big to turn down. And there's always the threat my series may get canceled, so I may as well have an act ready to take on the road."

Hal sighed. "The timing couldn't be worse for me. I'm overwhelmed with work," he told her in an apologetic voice, and she knew he didn't have a minute to spare to help her with some nightclub act.

"I understand," she said.

"But I'll send you some ideas, and I'll call some people I think you can use, and come to think of it, I do have an idea or two in my trunk you may like."

"Thank you, Harold," she said gratefully. She was about to go on and tell him who she'd put on her own list to call when he said, "Cee Cee?"

"Yeah?"

"I'll fly in for a couple of days and help get you started."

Within ten days of Hal's arrival in Los Angeles, the act was complete. Between his contacts in the creative community and Cee Cee's, they put together a team of unbeatable talent, and rehearsals began. There were ballads and blues and soft shoe numbers and funky getdown rock numbers, and Cee Cee's tribute to the saucy sexy ladies, Belle Barth, Mae West, Totie Fields, was funny and original. The act was drop-dead great and showed a versatile Cee Cee no small screen production overseen by a Standards and Practices censor could ever possibly produce.

But even after the long flight from L.A. to Kennedy Airport and the limo ride from New York, she couldn't sleep at all. At first she thought it was because she was nervous about the opening tomorrow night. But that was impossible. She knew the act backward and inside out, to the point where every gag sounded like an ad-lib and every haughty toss of the head was a guaranteed laugh. No, the fact that the opening was hours away wasn't what had kept her awake. It was knowing that for the first time in almost thirty-five years, she was back in Atlantic City, New Jersey, and she was feeling an unexpected tug of sentimentality about the old days she'd spent here.

This was the place where all of it had started for her. Onstage at the Steel Pier in the Jerry Grey Kiddie Show, a show in which she had first appeared when she was five years old, and from which she had retired at age ten. And it was in those shows where suddenly she had felt her power as a performer and had known that if nothing else in the world ever worked for her, when she stood on a stage and sang a song, even in the light of a bare lightbulb, for that moment people loved her, or thought they did anyway, and for years that brand of love had almost made up for the fact that she wasn't pretty, and her mother was fat, and boys didn't exactly fall all over her. Atlantic City was where she had first met Bertie. Bertie who was already gone for two whole years. How could it be?

And just forty miles north of Atlantic City on Long Beach Island was the place where she had met and married the only husband she would probably ever have. John Perry. She had been nineteen and he was thirty-one, the owner of the theater where she was working. The one who had predicted the eventuality of the success she was having now. And one night, aching with a girlish crush on him, she'd gone to his house on the beach, wanting him, begging him to make love to her, and instead he told her she was fabulous and brilliant and how famous she would be some day, then patted her on the ass and sent her on her way.

Of course later that summer, almost as a vote of confidence in her future fame, he had asked her to marry him, swept her off her feet, managed her career until she started actually to approach the fame he'd predicted, and then he left her. Not because he didn't love her, but because he said he couldn't handle what he knew would become her superstardom. Told her one heartbreaking night, the memory of which still hurt, that he wanted a woman, needed a woman who would bask in *his* glory.

Now it was six-fifteen in the morning of her opening night at Caesars, and she knew she ought to turn over and try to catch at least a few hours of sleep or tonight on stage she'd be a dishrag, but she was too wide awake, thinking about the old days, and soon she was on her feet, padding around trying to find some sweat clothes to throw on so she could go out for a little walk on the boardwalk. Last night, by the time she and Nina had arrived it was late and they were both too tired from the trip to feel like going out to explore. They had ordered dinner to be sent up to the suite, and when Richie Charles called to say he had arrived that afternoon, they invited him to join them. Richie was in Atlantic City to be Cee Cee's opening act, and Nina had taken an immediate liking to the funny black man, who after dinner taught the kid three new card games before Cee Cee told them to break it up, and sent Nina to bed.

For a minute Cee Cee thought it might be a bad idea to let Nina and Richie become friends, because the comic's outrageous, X-rated, foulmouthed behavior was well known, but then she decided it was mostly the character he played onstage who was whacky and not so much the quiet, lonely, brilliant comic she had known for years as they both had worked their way up. Onstage Richie did a lot of jokes about using drugs and getting laid. He had even been reputed to drop his pants and "moon" the audience, or unzip his fly, as the women in the audience shrieked and he did some material about "the truth about black men." But the offstage Richie was gentle and thoughtful and as childlike as Nina herself.

This morning as Cee Cee opened the door from her bedroom and stepped into the living room of the garish suite, she remembered that she didn't have to tiptoe out, because last night Nina and Richie had made a plan to wake up early, rent bikes, and go for a long ride on the boardwalk at sunrise, and Nina had probably met Richie in the lobby before six so that by now the two of them were well on their way.

The jangling sounds of the casino jarred the early-morning hum in Cee Cee's brain, and she passed through quickly, amazed as she'd always been in Las Vegas that even at this hour there were rows of white-haired ladies holding plastic cups filled with coins, and pulling at the slot machine handles. Some of them even sat on folding lawn chairs they'd brought from home and parked in front of a favorite slot machine. Now she was out the door onto the boardwalk, where she stopped for a long nostalgic time to breathe in the salty fishy smell and watch the sun coming up over the ocean and the waves rolling in to an empty beach.

For an instant she closed her eyes to take herself back, to pretend that no time had passed at all since the days she'd spent there as a kid, sure that she could still smell the unchanging carnival smell that must be wafting from Fralinger's Salt Water Taffy, down a few blocks, which someone in New York had promised her was one of the institutions still standing.

I can't believe I'm actually getting a thrill out of being in Atlantic City, New Jersey, she thought, and turned left because some vague memory told her it was in that direction where everything would be that she wanted to see. A group of bike riders moved breezily past her and set a flock of pigeons fluttering, and she was excited to be on the boardwalk, passing chintzy little souvenir shops crowded with schlocky merchandise, where she used to rush every summer just before she went back to the Bronx so that she could buy her father a tin ashtray. She remembered how painstaking the decision was over which ashtray it should be, and how she would carefully count out the change Leona had given her with the warning not to spend it on "*chazerai*," nothing junky or worthless, which was why she bought ashtrays, because they were useful.

The city's new look was disorienting to her. The marquees of the casinos jarred her, and in the store windows she noticed the featured T-shirts, which used to say on them FUTURE MISS AMERICA, now said I LOST MY ASS IN ATLANTIC CITY. There had always been a kind of low, carnival atmosphere about the place which she'd recognized even as a kid, but in those days it was a high camp, ricky-ticky kind of cheapness, now it felt tawdry and overdone. She started walking faster, knowing now exactly where she was going, and when she finally saw what used to be the Steel Pier in the distance jutting out into the water, she felt as if someone had kicked her.

Even from that distance she could see what was now a closed-up and deserted building surrounded by a wooden construction fence. The pilings were still up and a geodesic dome that must have once housed a theater or ballroom after Cee Cee's time stuck out over the water, but there was nothing left of the life of the place Cee Cee had once believed was the epitome of the entertainment world. With the star-filled stage shows. And elegant movie theaters, and the famous diving horses and the Auto Show, with all of the tall gorgeous show-room models standing on the revolving platforms next to blindingly shiny cars that looked as if they had just landed from outer space.

She continued to walk toward the remains of the pier, passing pizza parlors and submarine sandwich shops and frozen custard stands, but now she moved more slowly because the closer she came to it the more obvious it was how desolate the spot was where the dazzling show-business center had once stood. And probably, she decided, the closer she got the more painful it would be, so she stopped and for a while, with the squacking of sea gulls over her head, she stood and looked over the railing above some steps leading to the beach.

It wasn't until she was about to turn and go back to the hotel that she looked down and realized with a warm feeling and misty eyes that she knew those steps as if she'd just walked down them yesterday, because it was beneath this very spot under the boardwalk where she'd been asleep in 1951 and a little girl's crying had awakened her. The little girl was Bertie, and that was when the two of them had their first conversation.

The memories of that morning bubbled up around her and she stayed holding on to the railing remembering it so vividly she could even see the bathing suit Bertie wore, and how she'd felt when she'd snuck away from the snoring Leona that morning to come down to the beach, where real kids went. Kids whose lives weren't devoted to show business, who didn't feel more worn out than a kid ever should from the late show she'd appeared in the night before. It was the way she always remembered feeling, because from the time she was five she was already living some grown-up show-business life. And that was why she'd been so wiped out that when she finally did get to the beach, she'd fallen asleep under the boardwalk, until Bertie's sobs woke her.

Of course the beach had been different then. Not littered with soda cans and newspapers and cigarette butts the way it was today. Now remembering how it was, superimposing a mental picture of those days on the empty beach, filled her with a glowing nostalgia as she walked slowly down, and stopped holding the bannister halfway to the bottom. In the distance near the shoreline she could see an old woman wearing a big straw hat and carrying something that looked like a Geiger counter, sweeping it across the beach, probably searching for lost coins. A cool morning breeze moved over her and she felt a chill she wasn't sure if she should attribute to that or to the fact that she was reliving a moment which, in retrospect, had changed her life.

Never in the five summers she had spent here working the kiddie shows, with all of the late-night performances, had she been awake early enough to see the beach as empty as it was now. In those days, by the time she had a chance to be outside, the sand was always covered with families playing ball and playing cards and buying ice cream from the wandering ice cream men who walked up and down shouting, "Hey, ice cream! Getcher ice cream." Cee Cee's favorite ice cream had always been Dixie Cups, which she dug at and ate with a little flat wooden spoon. Now she looked up at the white clouds looking like bubble bath against the blue sky and hoped Nina would like it here.

That little girl was getting better every day, Cee Cee thought to herself. Loosening up the way Cee Cee had hoped and prayed she would. She was ten now and filled with imagination and ideas. At school last semester she'd been the director of her class play, which was *Peter Pan*. She had long ago grown tired of Barbie dolls and was passionate about her dance classes, and told Cee Cee that someday she was going to marry Baryshnikov, and kept the autographed picture of him, which Cee Cee had been able to get her, framed over her bed.

They were close, and for Cee Cee who hadn't had a real relationship with a man in years, and whose only real friend was gone forever, it was probably the closest relationship she was destined to have. Sometimes that thought made her feel depressed and empty, but most of the time she figured what the hell, having Nina and having her career was so much more than almost anyone else she knew had, she was infinitely blessed.

When she got to the bottom step and was about to duck under the boardwalk to her spot, she stopped short and her heart pounded, because there where she'd first laid eyes on Bertie, as cracks of the morning sun came through making stripes of light all around, slept a bearded scruffy man probably in his sixties. He was wearing an old, dirty plaid flannel shirt, and worn shoes, and lay on top of a sleeping bag, with a tattered backpack hooked onto his back.

Her first instinct was to turn and run up the steps, before the man woke up and pulled a gun from his bag and tried to rob her, or maybe unzipped his pants and tried to flash her. But the poor guy looked a little too old and weary to be dangerous, and maybe that was why she wasn't running, even moved a step closer for a second wanting to wake him and tell him this was her spot and that he was ruining what was supposed to be a sentimental moment. But she didn't wake him. Instead she pulled her wallet out of the pocket of her sweat pants, removed five one-hundred-dollar bills from her wad of spending money, walked over to the man and slid the bills into the pocket of his shirt, and walked back to the hotel to do a sound check for her opening night.

"Atlantic City, what a place! Every year a bevy of hopeful young beauties come here and parade in bathing suits and evening gowns displaying their looks and their talents, vying against one another to be the one chosen to serve. And *those* are just the hookers." Gotta work on some better Miss America stuff.

Before Cee Cee's show every night Nina would have room service deliver her dinner to the suite at Caesars Palace. After the waiter left, she would take her plate of food out from underneath the silver cover, and her glass of milk out of the ice-filled holder, put them on the floor next to the sunken Jacuzzi, turn on the power, and modestly slip out of her robe at the same time she slid into the steaming water. Then she would eat her dinner with the water bubbling wildly around her.

"Now *that's* got to be bad for the digestion," Cee Cee would always say, walking through the suite pushing the buttons to close all of the floor-to-ceiling drapes as she vocalized to get ready for her show.

During the day Nina would sit out by the pool ordering ginger ales, which she charged to Cee Cee's tab and sipped while she sat in the sun playing gin rummy for money with a former show girl named Donna who was now a change girl at Caesars.

In the late afternoon while Cee Cee had a massage or rehearsed or shopped, Nina would go with Richie Charles to Tivoli Pier, or to Margate City to see Lucy the Elephant, or take a ride in a rolling chair, or just sit on the beach with him and build sand castles. Some afternoons she lolled around in the air-conditioned suite on the big round bed, reading or talking long distance to Kevin back in Los Angeles. Kevin loved to be filled in on which shows Nina had seen, which stars she'd met when they stopped backstage to congratulate Cee Cee, and which dirty jokes she remembered from the various comics, jokes she wrote down and then read to him over the phone so he could explain them to her.

"A guy is sitting in a bar and a beautiful woman at the other end of the bar says to him . . . wait a second, I think I heard Cee Cee walk in . . . hold on, Kev," she said, then put the phone down and ran to the bedroom door to peek into the living room and check.

"Nope, she's still at rehearsal. Where was I?"

"A beautiful woman at the other end of the bar says . . ." Kevin reminded her in his halting voice.

"Right . . . the beautiful woman at the bar says to the guy, 'I will do anything you want, fulfill your wildest dreams, and all *you* have to do is be able to ask me for whatever it is you want in three words.'"

Kevin giggled, a silly giggle on the other end of the phone. "Yeah?" he said.

"So the guy looks at the woman and says, 'Paint my house.'" Nina paused, waiting for an explanation of why in the world that was funny.

"Tell you in two years why that's funny."

"Hey, you're only twelve."

"That's two years older than you."

Kevin laughed for a long time, and when he finally stopped, she asked him, "Well? Why is it funny?"

Kevin was still giggling. "Because the woman thought the man was going to ask her to do something sexy."

"Yes? *And?*"

"And he didn't."

"So?"

"Neen, let's talk about this in a few years."

"Paint my house. Paint my house. I don't get it. And I'm never telling you any more jokes."

"Are you still hanging around with Richie Charles? I saw him on his comedy show on HBO. My God, he's raunchy."

"He's my best friend here," Nina said in a voice serious enough to let Kevin know that to say anything negative about Richie would be a violation. "Of course, Cee Cee won't let me watch his act. He opens for her and she doesn't let me leave the dressing room until she walks out to go on. She turns down the volume on the speaker so it doesn't pump into her dressing room, and I can't hear it. After *she* does *her* version of Mae West, how much worse could he be?"

"Worse."

Every night she sat in Cee Cee's lavish dressing room, perched on a tall director's chair near the makeup table, telling Cee Cee all the events of her Atlantic City day. And when Richie came offstage and the stage manager knocked, Nina would hold Cee Cee's hand, feeling the sweatiness of her palms which never went away no matter how many times she did the show, and walk out to the wings with her. Then she would give Cee Cee a good-luck hug, smelling the thick pancake makeup and feeling Cee Cee trembling slightly with her pre-entrance jitters.

"Ladies and gentlemen, Cee Cee Bloooooooom!!!!!" And off Cee

Cee went, doing her little strut of a walk as the crowd went wild, and Nina, who had seen the act so many times she knew it by heart, went back to sit in the dressing room with Richie, who was teaching her everything he knew about cards, which was considerable.

"Okay, now you got it? Never hit fifteen, seldom hit fourteen, think about hitting thirteen, and take a look at what the other players have before hitting twelve. If there are a lot of face cards, then *maybe* you hit twelve because then you think there's a good shot another face card isn't coming up."

"Got it," she said as he dealt.

"You sure?"

"Yes. It's about quick adding and figuring out all the possibilities fast," she told him matter-of-factly.

"Are you a kid?" Richie asked squinting at her. "Or are you actually a dwarf pretending to be a kid?" Now Nina had two cards and so did he.

"Hit me," was her reply.

"I like Atlantic City. Some people say it's low class. But I don't notice that. Probably because I live in Los Angeles where *their* idea of culture is frozen yoghurt."

The jokes. Cee Cee decided she'd better call Bernie Adelman in Los Angeles and ask him to do a little work on the jokes. Like the frozen yoghurt joke. That wasn't working so great because this audience didn't know what culture had to do with yoghurt. Or maybe even what yoghurt was. And maybe she ought to change the order of some of the songs. For the first few minutes after she made her last exit, Cee Cee's head would always spin while she tried to come down from the pounding adrenaline-high she had to produce every night in order to do her demanding act.

Covering every inch of that huge stage and never dropping her vivacious, outrageous character for sixty-three minutes was a killer, with only two brief breaks when she rushed into the wings to change costumes while the boy dancers did their interlude. Probably, she thought, this was what it was like to be an Olympic athlete.

Her body had to be stretched out and limber for the dancing, her voice had to be warmed up and loose for the singing, and the energy behind every move and every sound had to be bigger than anything she put out for films and television. Grand enough to fill the Circus Maximus so that each person who paid their money to see Cee Cee Bloom that night felt that she had been there just for them.

Once, years ago in New York, she had gone to see a matinee of *Mame*, and during the curtain call, Angela Lansbury had looked down into the front section where Cee Cee sat looking up at her with awe, and Angela Lansbury winked. In spite of all the sophistication Cee Cee had about the theater, she still remembered believing on her way home that day that Angela Lansbury had winked specifically at her, Cee Cee Bloom, and it was that kind of intimacy she now wanted to make every person in her audience remember when they went home from her show.

Wanted them to remember all of the jokes and songs, her "Saucy Sassy Ladies" segment where she brought the house down in a clingy dress, singing as Mae West,

> A guy what takes his time
> I'll go for any time
> I'm a fast movin' gal that likes 'em slow.
> Got no use for fancy drivin'
> Want to see a guy arrivin' in low.
> I'd be satisfied
> Electrified
> You know
> With a guy what takes his time.

And every night she fine-tuned the moments, never happy unless it all worked perfectly. Sure it was only Atlantic City, but if you were going to do it, you might as well goddamn do it right. Some performers came offstage and didn't want even to think about their work until it was time to go on again, but Cee Cee was already making mental notes during the encore and the curtain call, pushing herself to make her show its best.

The few minutes immediately after her final bow was usually the best time to do the postmortem, because everything was still fresh in her head. She stood sweating in the wings, wiping her face with a cool towel handed to her by her dresser, who placed another larger towel around her shoulders, and a big plastic Evian bottle in her hand,

and Cee Cee caught her breath and drank the water, rerunning her performance in her head.

"Great show," she told the dancers as they passed her with a sweaty grab of the hand or a pat while she waited for the band to finish their final notes, and for Artie Butler, her musical director and conductor, to come offstage, so they could rehash the show together. Where did it feel rushed? Slow? When did the audience seem restless? What needed to be cut? Added? Revamped?

So much had changed since Cee Cee's days of performing live. Now light cues were all computerized so there could be no making changes at the last second when it would be too late for the lighting designer to reprogram the timing. Cee Cee remembered wistfully those days of playing small clubs with Hal, and how she used to be able to stand offstage about to do her encore, and peek through the curtain, trying to psych out the mood of the audience by their faces, and to figure out if they'd prefer "Knock Me a Kiss" or "Guess Who I Saw Today." A nod to Hal was all he used to need, and a nod from him was the cue to the lighting man who stood in the back.

"I notice that Atlantic City seems to draw a much older crowd than Vegas. I just saw a waitress ask a man who finished dinner at that table if she could take his plates, and the man handed her his teeth."

Dumb. Dumb. It gets a laugh, but that joke always sounded to her like one that Milton Berle stole from Henny Youngman who borrowed it from Fat Jack Leonard. Tonight, as she and Artie talked, they walked toward several well-wishers who had found their way backstage to congratulate her. Every night of the run there was a group of people who had either come to the show from New York, or were working on the boardwalk themselves and were about to open in a few days. Tonight she gave a hug to Merv Griffin, remembering her first shots on his television talk show years before, and how kind he'd been to her when she was nervous, assuring her every time his show broke for a commercial, "You're doing great."

Behind Merv there were several other people Cee Cee didn't know, who had somehow managed to get backstage to meet her, and she shook their hands and said her thank-yous to their compliments and then was glad to see Steve Lawrence and Eydie Gorme waiting to say hello too. Steve and Eydie were opening next week. They were raving about Cee Cee's show, and when Cee Cee happened to look at the man who was waiting to talk to her standing behind Steve and Eydie, her heart stopped and she didn't hear another word Steve or Eydie said, because the man behind them was John Perry, her ex-husband, who was smiling now, knowing she had seen him.

Steve and Eydie's lips were moving and Cee Cee was nodding to them and saying an automatic "thank you" every now and then, hoping they thought she was listening, because she couldn't be rude but, dear God, she prayed, let them hurry up and finish what they're saying and go. And finally they squeezed her hands and said goodbye and congratulations a few more times, and when they were gone she was standing in the cool darkness of backstage, face-to-face with the only real love she'd ever had in her life.

Neither of them spoke, and after a minute of sizing him up, still slim, no paunch, gray temples, hardly a wrinkle, eyes still as big and blue as ever, Cee Cee counted on her fingers behind her back, trying to figure out how old he had to be by now. Let's see. They were married in 1960, broke up in '70. Now it was what? 1985. So she hadn't even seen him in fifteen years, which meant that he was . . . had to be . . . holy shit, the man was fifty-six years old, and goddammit, did he look great.

"I know you," she said to his smiling face.

"And I know you."

"Boy, do you look good!" she said. His skin, the springy rosy way it looked, his big chest and muscular arms, and his wonderful brown curly hair, which now except for a little bit of gray in it was the same as she remembered. The son-of-a-bitch still had looks that could break your heart. And best of all was that expression on his face she knew so well, the one of abject appreciation when he took her in, his eyes seeming so grateful to look at her, as if no one else in the world existed and nothing else could distract him, as if a bomb could go off right next to him and he wouldn't notice because he was so rapt looking at her. How she had missed feeling the warmth of that look.

"And you, Cecilia, not only look great, but apparently are still tearing the world apart with your extraordinary talent." There was a long silence as their eyes searched one another's, but Cee Cee broke it.

"So let's fuck," she said. Then she howled with laughter at her own joke and he did too, and they fell into one another's arms, alternately holding one another tight for long warm hard hugs, then at arm's length to look at one another and rejoice, and then hug again.

"Where in the hell have you been? In Ohio, for Christ's sake? Who stays in Ohio all these years and doesn't surface once in a while and call a person?"

"Well, *I* was lucky," he said. "I had the distinct advantage of being able to see you whenever I felt the need. All I had to do was turn on the television or pick up a newspaper or a magazine or drive by a billboard."

"Yeah. I do have a tendency to be rather high-profile, don't I?"

"You *are*, shall we say, visible."

"J.P., I can't believe I'm actually looking at your face. I was always kind of figuring I'd just never see you again. I knew you got married. You wrote me that years ago. But I didn't know if you . . ."

He nodded. "I've got three kids. Two boys and a girl. All in various stages of trying to be in show business. And they'll be envious as hell when I tell them I stopped in to see you. After me, they're your biggest fans."

"Where *are* they?"

"In Ohio with Katie. Their mother. I'm here, believe it or not, on business."

"What kind of business?"

Now he flushed, and for the first time she noticed a little sweat on his brow, even though there was a draft of air so cool in the wings where they were standing that it made Cee Cee need to pull the towel she wore tighter around her shoulders.

"It's nothing. It's silly. Look why don't you go and do whatever you're doing and I'll call you tomorrow if that's all right. Maybe we can get together and just talk?"

Tomorrow. How could she wait to talk to him until tomorrow? She wanted to take his hand and drag him into her dressing room and have him fill her in on what he'd done every second since they'd been apart. And okay, maybe she did feel an urge to hold him close and see how it felt to kiss him again, touch him again, find out if he still had any feelings for her besides admiration for her stardom. Liar, she thought, you could drag him into bed this minute with the rush of feeling you're having. Crazy and wrong as she knew that was, she was afraid that was what she would do if it wasn't for . . . Nina. My God.

Wait until John saw Nina. He would know the instant he saw her that she was Bertie's daughter. The first time he ever met Bertie she was sixteen. Not so many years older than Nina was now. Cee Cee remembered telling Nina about those days only recently.

"You never knew John Perry," she had said, feeling melted the way she usually did when she thought about him. "We split up long before you were born. I met him when I worked in his funny little theater in Beach Haven. He was someone out of this world. Your mother thought so too. She was an apprentice at the theater and I was a singer."

"For a while my mother was in love with him too," Nina had said, and hearing that truth come from her surprised Cee Cee.

"Did *she* tell you that?"

"My mother wasn't like you, Cee Cee. She never told me anything. But I didn't have to hear the words. It was just the way she always talked about meeting him when you two were young, and how handsome he was, and then she would say, 'And all the girls were crazy for him,' with this look in her eyes, and then she'd say, 'But he married Cee Cee.'"

"Funny," Cee Cee had said, liking the story because it made her sound so triumphant over every other woman in the world, until Nina added, "I think she was trying to tell me that you don't have to be pretty for someone good to fall in love with you. To say that it's what's inside that counts. You know?"

"I *do* know," Cee Cee had said, hurt with the kind of a wound she now understood a daughter could give to a mother under the guise of being matter-of-fact.

"How *is* Bertie?" John asked. He beamed as he waited for the answer.

"She's gone," Cee Cee said, then saw right away that he hadn't understood what she meant by gone, because the smile was still on his face. "I have her daughter because Bertie died. Two years ago."

Cee Cee tried to identify what came into his eyes next. From the minute she had seen him watch Bertie walk across a room that summer in Beach Haven in 1960, before she'd admitted to Bertie or even to herself that she loved John Perry, Cee Cee had been afraid that it would be John and Bertie who would get together. Both of them were so beautiful, so confident, and part of some cool Christian world a

person like her would never understand or be able to enter. And somewhere in a sick, niggling little place in her chest she'd always held the
fear that it was only a matter of time before the two of them fell in
love. She could still recall every detail of that night in 1960 at the
Sunshine, the theater John once owned.

It was after the cast party for *Damn Yankees*, in which Cee Cee had
starred as Lola. She and Bertie had taken a walk on the beach. There
were tiki torches blazing everywhere, making the night seem roman-
tic, and Cee Cee had felt confident and important and strong about
her future as a performer. And as the two friends walked Cee Cee had
searched her mind for a way to talk to Bertie about how much she
loved John. To tell the only person in whom she had ever confided
how much she wanted to make love to this man, and how she was
living on the secret fantasy that someday he would be hers, and before
she could get the words out, to her horror, Bertie confessed to her
instead that only the night before John had taken her virginity.

After that, even when Bertie was far away and Cee Cee and John
were married and Bertie was safely married to Michael, Cee Cee hated
herself for wondering if every time Bertie asked about John in a letter,
or John casually asked, "When did you hear from Bert last?" if the
two of them weren't secretly longing to be with one another.

"My God. I remember now reading that you'd become the guardian of a friend's child, but I had no idea it was Bertie's. What happened?" John asked. The look on his face was pure sorrow.

"She had ovarian cancer. She moved away from Florida where she
had been raising Nina because she wanted to die alone in peace and
quiet."

"And?"

"And she made the mistake of calling me to say goodbye. So I flew
up there and took over her care."

"And God knows, that was certainly the end of the peace and
quiet."

They both grinned.

"You *do* know me, don't you?" she asked.

"Is the child okay?"

Cee Cee nodded. "Considering the circumstances. And that she's
stuck with me."

"What's she like?"

"You'll meet her. She's like her mother, as raised by me."

"Now *that's* a combination to be reckoned with."

"You bet it is," she said, putting her hand out and reaching for his.

"So come along and start reckoning."

"You want me to meet her now?"

"Unless you can't. Unless there's someone waiting for you?" Please let there be nobody waiting for him, she thought and almost let out a whoop of joy when he gave her his hand. And the instant she felt its familiarity, she was flooded with a series of flashbacks of their years together. Years of deep love and great fun and very hot sex. The bad part had been the way he had taken over her life where Leona had left off. Pushing her to achieve and then standing back and taking the credit when she did. Living through her success, and on the one hand loving it because it took them to a height and a lifestyle he might never have had without Cee Cee, and on the other hand resenting it mightily because he was completely dependent on her for that high.

For Leona it had been okay, because she had no talent of her own and had always known it would take Cee Cee to get her anywhere. But John had aspirations for himself and a male ego she had tiptoed around for years, stopping herself a million times from telling him his ideas for her were too small, clichéd, wrong. Instead she had tried desperately to please him, to make his ideas work for her, terrified if he ever knew how little she really needed him professionally, he would lose interest in her personally, sexually, completely. And finally, after ten years of his being told, "Hey, buddy, would you get outta the way," when he stood in the wings, and after signing endless bar tabs and credit-card slips and hotel charges "John Perry for Cee Cee Bloom," he sat depressed and hurt in a dark Miami Beach hotel room one night smoking a cigarette, and told her what she knew he would have to say to her sooner or later which was, "I want a woman who will bask in *my* glory."

"You breathe all the air in the room," Bertie used to tell her. "And there's no more left for anybody else." It was funny when Bertie had said it. And it had always been all right with Bertie for Cee Cee to be the one with the big hungry ego. Bertie was content to play the part of the fan. But J.P.'s frail ego had doomed the continued success of their marriage.

When they walked into the dressing room, Nina and Richie were each staring at their respective hands of cards. Nina picked one up from the pile on the table then shrieked a winner's shriek.

"I cleaned you out," she said giddily, then jumped to her feet and did a little dance.

"The kid's a mechanic," Richie said, "I never saw anybody that lucky in my life. I'm taking you out to the casino and getting you a job as a dealer."

The two of them were oblivious to Cee Cee and John in the doorway.

"Hahhh!" Nina hollered. "Pay up, pay up." Then she looked over and said a casual "hi" to Cee Cee, who introduced John Perry, but there was no recognition from Nina at the name, she just nodded an uninterested hello, then gathered up the cards and shuffled as John watched appreciatively, smiling at the characteristics he immediately recognized in her.

"Looks just like the Bert I remember," he said.

Hearing that made Nina look up at Cee Cee. "You mean this is John Perry, your ex-husband?" she asked surprised.

"One and the same."

Richie looked at John now for the first time too.

"Wow, this is an honor," John said, reaching to shake Richie's hand.

"John Perry, this is Richie Charles . . ."

But before Cee Cee finished John was already going on about the HBO special of Richie's he had seen a few weeks earlier, remembering some of Richie's jokes and talking about them with a fan's wide-eyed admiration while Richie smiled a half smile, which looked more to Cee Cee as if he was baring his teeth. It was an expression she knew Richie gave to strangers he didn't trust. Silly, she thought. It's just harmless old J.P. And starry-eyed at that over meeting Richie. How the worm turns, she thought, remembering the way she had idolized John the year they met, trying to act as if she had it all under control when all along she could barely sleep at nights for fantasizing about him. And now here he was, looking kind of down at the heels and acting like some fan who just fell off the turnip truck. She could even see an expression on Nina's face as she looked at him as if she was wondering what the big deal had been about this guy.

"I owe you two bucks," Richie said to Nina. "I taught you too good."

"Well now, how's this for an idea? What if I get room service to bring some food up to the suite and we have a little party?" Cee Cee asked.

"Not for me." Richie stood. "I'm gonna turn in and lick my wounds after the beating I just took from the hustler over there. Nice to meet you," he tossed over his shoulder to John as he left.

"I'm tired too," Nina said, following Richie, "and I already ate. Goodnight," she said and was out the door.

"She's gorgeous," John said, looking after her, and Cee Cee was glad when she felt a surge of pride instead of jealousy.

"I'll change," she said, and after she took her clothes down from a hanger in the big mirrored walk-in closet, she stayed in there to change out of the dress she'd worn onstage, thinking it was oddly modest of her since this was someone who had seen her naked every day for more than ten years. But this was a different naked body, she thought, looking down at herself. The aging version, and she didn't want him to look at it and compare it to the way he remembered her. Stop, she thought. Don't get all hot and bothered about this visit. He's married. He's here on business. She emerged wearing a black sweater and black pants, holding her stomach in, trying to decide if she should remove the elaborate stage makeup and risk him seeing the comparison to her own pale skin.

"You've never looked better to me," he said, and there was that look on his face again. Maybe she'd leave the makeup on.

"It's the first time in my life I can eat anything I want, because I probably sweat off five pounds a night out there," she said, wondering if she should take him upstairs to the suite and order some champagne. No, that would be seductive and she didn't want to do that. Somewhere in Ohio this man had a family waiting for him to come home. Too bad, she thought, then wondered to herself if maybe fucking your ex-husband shouldn't count as cheating. After all, she'd already done it with him so many times in this lifetime, how could a few more hurt?

"Your act is wonderful," he said. "You're better than you've ever been."

"For an old broad," she joked.

"Not old to me," he said.

"True. But then, you *are* a senior citizen."

"Don't knock it. We're an interesting group. We've lived. We've loved. What's the song from *The Boy Friend* about artists?"

Cee Cee thought, then laughed when she remembered the song and sang, "'The modern painters of today may paint their pictures faster. But when it comes to making love, you can't beat an old master.'"

"Precisely," he said.

A seduction. Was this a seduction? Boy, it felt good. Stop, stop. He's married, she thought, but she couldn't stop the fantasies that danced in her head, and the rush of physical memories her body had of his. He had been one hell of a lover. Of course, at that time in her life she knew no comparison.

"How's your father?" he asked.

"He's okay, just okay. Sick enough lately to have to go back to a nursing home where he sits and grumbles about everything." Again they looked long at one another.

"I've never stopped loving you," he said all of a sudden, and those were exactly the words she'd been thinking about him just before he said them, but she was afraid to say them back to him, couldn't say them back to him. He was married. Married.

"My marriage to Kate is over," he said, as if he'd just been reading her mind.

She tried to see if there was any flicker on his face that might let her know whether or not that was a lie.

"Who asked you?" she said afraid now and turned away to busy herself, packing up a little cosmetics case she carried between the dressing room and her suite upstairs every evening, John's last statement resonating inside her, making her heart beat faster and her face feel hot. What if what he had just said was true and the reason he had come here was not business but to test his feelings for her. To see if now that they both had changed and grown he would finally be capable of handling her success.

"Nobody asked me," he said gently, "I was just confiding in an old friend. Maybe just looking for a shoulder to cry on."

"I'm sorry to hear it's not working out," she said, but it was a lie. She continued to pack her makeup, but she was rattled now and dropped two of her makeup brushes to the floor, stooped to pick them up. One of them rolled away and after she grabbed to retrieve it, she was about to stand when she felt him close behind her, and as she stood slowly he moved tight against her, and she could feel his hardness pushing against her back and his arms go around her.

"I knew the minute I saw you how much I still love you, Cee Cee," he said.

When she looked straight ahead she could see the two of them in her giant makeup mirror, and it was an odd picture. Her stage made-up face, grotesque with huge eyes and the thick false lashes it was necessary for her to wear in order for her eyes to be seen from the back of the massive showroom. And in those eyes the confusion she felt having him there behind her, wanting her, saying the things he was saying.

Now he was nuzzling her neck, her ears, her shoulders, calling up sensations she never thought she'd have again.

"J.P." She turned to face him, and he took her face in his hands, but before he could kiss her she pulled away.

"John, listen to me. I'm not just me now. I'm a family. With that little girl, and believe me when I tell you that both of us have been through the ringer."

"Cee Cee . . ."

"Wait. I'm just telling you, I'm standing here looking at you, and what I see is not just some guy who happens to look good, although you sure as hell do look divine. But I see my husband, okay? Yeah, my ex-husband, but it doesn't feel that way. It feels to me like 'Oh, here's John who went on a little vacation and now he's back.'"

"Well, maybe you're right about that."

"No, I'm not right about that. You married someone else. You must have loved her. You created children with her, children you raised and loved and who would be sick if they thought their father was in Atlantic City right now making a grab for his ex-wife, even if they are my fans. Believe me, J.P., my body remembers everything about yours. I mean, I look at you and I can hardly stand up for wanting to climb all over you and fuck your socks off." He laughed a little burst of a laugh, but Cee Cee's face was serious. "Trust me, in the last two minutes I've already gone so far as to figure out if it would be hotter to do it on the sofa or on the cold tile floor. But as sure as I'm standing here, I know if you come back to me now or next year or when we're too old to remember how to do it, it's got to be after you straighten out your other life first. Go home. Work it out with Kate. Sit down and talk to your kids. And if you're going to get out of Ohio, get out for reasons that are about you, not about me. Because if you don't, after all the shit I've already put that kid through, you can bet I won't let you touch me with a ten-foot pole."

There was no sound in the chilly dressing room until he joked, with a half smile, "So you *do* remember everything about my body." That made her laugh.

"Tell me about the business you have in New Jersey," she said.

"It's silly," he told her. "I mean maybe it's really silly. Though part of me loves the idea. The Sunshine Theater is for sale again. It's been through several owners since I gave it up, and the current owner tracked me down to see if I was interested in owning it again. I still know enough people on Long Beach Island who might back me, and I've got some dough of my own I could put in from the sale of the theater I owned in Steubenville. I've been teaching since then, and directing Shakespeare in Chagrin Park in the summers. So I'd just do my summers in Beach Haven instead, the way I did years ago."

"You were so good at it," Cee Cee said, feeling herself falling into the familiar old position of massaging his ego.

"Want to be my backer?" he asked, but she was sure he was joking. "I'll change the name and call it the Cee Cee Bloom Playhouse. Kind of like the Helen Hayes Theater."

"Thanks anyway," she said.

"Cee Cee, you're right about me straightening out my life first. You should know though that Kate had a four-year love affair with, of all people, our pediatrician, and we almost broke up over that but —"

"No, I shouldn't know that," Cee Cee said, shaking her head. But it was information which made her feel a little less guilty for wanting to drag this married man inside the mirrored closet and watch on every side while she peeled away all of his clothing and then worked on him until he exploded. Drive him crazy the way she had during all the years they were together.

"Go home," she said, "and let me know how it all works out."

After a minute he gave her a pained smile and hugged her. This time it was just a friendly hug, and then he left, and she wondered as she listened to the sound of him walking to the stage door, opening it, and leaving, if she'd ever hear from him again.

The first weeks after their return from Atlantic City were the calmest Nina could ever remember since she'd come to live in Cee Cee's world. At first she thought it was just the comparison of their peaceful Malibu house to the chaos in the hotel in Atlantic City, which had been filled with the constant undercurrent of room service, maid service, laundry service, and the casual way the people from Cee Cee's show felt free after a light knock on the door to wander in and out. Or maybe the calm was the result of Cee Cee's seeming more sure of herself. As if being able to put together an act, and then get the offer of a mammoth five-year contract from Caesars Palace, had given her confidence in her continuing ability to survive no matter what happened to her television show.

But more probably the calm could be attributed to the fact that John was calling every day from Ohio, keeping her up on the progress he was making in straightening out the end of his marriage, making plans with his children, and peace with the wife he was leaving in order to move to Los Angeles. He had already managed, he told Cee Cee and she lightly mentioned to Nina, to find himself a job in L.A., through an old summer stock friend who had become a movie producer. John would be the producer's development executive, which meant he would read scripts that had been submitted to the producer, and then advise the producer as to which of the scripts could be turned into a film that would make a lot of money.

John admitted to Cee Cee that he didn't have a clue what it was that made one film more commercial than another, but he had read William Goldman's book *Adventures in the Screen Trade*, which said that the thing to remember about the movie business was that "nobody knows anything," so he figured it might as well be him making money from not knowing anything as anybody else.

"Are you having R.J. Wagner–Natalie Wood fantasies about your ex?" Hal asked Cee Cee. He stopped by to watch her show shooting one afternoon while he was in Los Angeles for negotiations with Universal Studios because they were trying to buy the film rights to *Penny Candy,* his second Broadway musical.

"You mean do I think I'll marry him again?"

"Forget I asked. There's a funny little look in your eyes that tells me you've entertained the thought more than six or seven hundred times."

"Harold, I don't know what the fuck's going on," she said, while a makeup lady with a sponge was dabbing more concealer under her eyes. "Look up, Cee Cee," the makeup lady said, and Cee Cee tipped her head up a little and kept talking. "He's available. Lonely even, thinks he wants to be with me, seems to have changed, and now he's coming out here to see if he can find happiness in Tinsel Town. So how do I know what'll happen? I'm a shell-shocked, gun-shy, beaten-up broad who's so short on trust that even when the talking scale in my bathroom tells me how much I weigh every morning, I say, 'Bullshit.' So who am *I* to tell you how I feel?"

Within weeks John arrived and was living at the Sunset Marquis Hotel. He looked more professorial than Hollywood, Nina thought, wearing corduroy pants no matter how hot the day and a sweater vest over a shirt, and a brown tweed blazer, that same brown tweed blazer he wore so often Nina joked to Cee Cee that pretty soon it might crawl off him and walk on its own to the cleaners. He would show up a few nights a week for dinner, and sit at the kitchen table with them, telling them funny stories about his adventures in show business.

Cee Cee acted relaxed with him, wearing no makeup and her hair in that funny way it looked after she took off the wigs she wore on her show, or pulled out the hairpins and just let it fly everywhere, and the three of them would eat and talk and most of all laugh at the stories, which came with John's fresh point of view about the Holly-wood whackos and their habits. About the crazy producer who invited him to the racetrack, where John watched the guy lose fifty thousand dollars on one race. The friend of the producer John worked for who had a portable bathroom in the back of his Mercedes limousine. "Hello? Yes this is his car phone, but he can't talk to you now. He's in his car men's room," John said. Nina was starting to like him, even starting to understand what it was about him that made both Cee Cee and her mother think he was attractive. And she also liked that he called his children in Ohio every day. Sometimes she overheard him say things like, "I love you too, and can't wait to have you come here to be with me."

When you do find a man with whom you develop a deep relationship that is leading toward marriage, you will discover that your children will have mixed feelings toward your husband-to-be. Your children will want a father surrogate in their lives, but on the other hand, they have had you to themselves and will be hesitant to give that up.

After Cee Cee read that in one of her books, she tried to include Nina as much as she possibly could so the kid wouldn't feel left out.

One night she brought out a pile of very old photographs she had found. One was taken on the day she and John were married. Cee Cee was wearing the weirdest white dress, and looking really goo-goo-eyed. And while they looked at it they argued for ten minutes about who had taken the picture, the judge or one of those bizarre witnesses they had dragged in off the street because having the wedding had been such a last-minute decision they hadn't invited anyone. One of the pictures was inside a little red plastic viewer that Nina put against her eye and held up to the light to see. It was taken at the pool of some hotel in Miami Beach, and in it both Cee Cee and John wore annoyed expressions as if they weren't too happy that the picture was being taken at all. "That was the week we broke up," Cee Cee remembered to John, and then told Nina. "And the week your mother and I made up after a long fight we had."

"About what?" Nina asked her.

Cee Cee took another turn looking at the picture in the viewer. "I don't remember," she said.

Nina's favorite picture was one she'd seen before, which John looked at now. It was of Cee Cee and John and Bertie in Hawaii. Cee Cee was so skinny it was amazing, and they all looked so happy and young. John shook his head the way people do when they're about to say, "Where does the time go?" But he didn't say that, he just looked at Cee Cee and said, "You haven't changed a bit." And she said, "Neither have you. You're still as full of shit as you always were," and gave him a little punch on the arm.

It felt good to be so comfortable with a man, and the odd part was that she wasn't sleeping with him. Particularly odd since everything below her waist fluttered every time he walked into the room. But for once in her life, instead of being led by the underpants she was trying to behave like a grown woman, to reserve judgment, to see what happened.

The first thing that happened was that John's producer friend was offered a power job at an agency, which he took, so he no longer needed John, which meant that John was out looking for a job every day. Cee Cee called some of her friends at the studios, who said they would look out for something for him, and she asked Larry Gold to try to get some producers he knew to try to find something for John, but after some time passed and he couldn't find any job at all and didn't even have a job interview in sight, he started hanging around at the studio on Fridays when Cee Cee's show was taping.

Nobody seemed to mind him being at the tapings, everyone was friendly to him. He chatted with all of the people on the staff of the show. Sometimes after they'd repeated the same sketch again and again, and he was tired of watching it, he would walk down and sit in the commissary to have a cup of coffee and read the trade papers, and soon people who ate there regularly knew him by name and knew that he had something to do with Cee Cee, probably he was her boy friend. Seemed like a decent guy.

Then he started coming to the rehearsals during the week too, sitting in the back on a folding chair with a little spiral notebook in which every now and then he'd scratch some notes. Later, when Cee Cee was taking a break, he'd come into the dressing room and when everyone was gone but the two of them, he would take out the spiral notebook and say things to her like, "You know that spot in the hospital sketch where you're the doctor giving the patient the reflex test? Well whoever that day player is, he's mugging so much it upstages everything you're doing."

"He's not a day player. He's part of the company of people who do the sketches with me."

"Well, the director is doing you a major disservice if he keeps letting him get away with that behind you."

"I'll look into it," she said. There were more notes like that. They were good notes. Good for Cee Cee, from someone who seemed to care more about her than about the general welfare of the show. It was much more personal care than she'd ever had from Larry Gold. And it felt familiar, because it was the way John had advised her when she was a young struggling singer, and the way Leona had focused on her, from the phrasing of each line she sang to the color of the mascara she wore. But she liked it for another reason too. Because John was telling it to her like it really was and, with very few exceptions, she was already up to her ears in yes-men. People who always said, "You were brilliant, Cee Cee," even when she knew she wasn't.

"That sketch is completely tasteless," John would tell her after watching the rehearsal. "Beneath you and the show. Don't do it."

"Are you sure?"

"Think about what it says. Is that the kind of statement you want to make?"

This man directs Shakespeare, she would think. He must have class. I do hooker jokes. What do *I* know? "I'll have them cut it," she would say after reading it again through newly educated eyes, and go out to face the producer and the head writer to tell them to cut the sketch, knowing they would exchange looks and tell her she was being difficult, but she didn't care what they did. John was right, and she was starting to feel very tied to him again. The man she had been the most intimate with in her life.

How odd that she had been continuing to fend off their sexual intimacy. Hadn't let him lay a finger on her all this time, though they joked about it and it was always in the air between them. But she had to admit she was starting to feel so hooked into him that she didn't want to think of what adding sex to what they had now could mean to them emotionally.

It didn't take people long to start thinking of John as a good way to get to Cee Cee. If the network wanted her to do some promotions or get her to come and perform at the affiliates convention, something she hated, they would start the conversations with John to feel out how he liked their ideas, or to have him help them determine what was the best way to approach her. One afternoon at the commissary a successful television producer named Jay Green put his coffee cup on the table across from where John was sitting, and when John looked up, Jay Green smiled and introduced himself. After they'd talked for a while, he told John he'd like to give him a script to read that was a potential miniseries with a part in it that was perfect for Cee Cee.

"She won't do a miniseries. We think she should only do features," John told him.

The television producer's eyes smiled at that statement, but the rest of his face was serious as he said something about how he was sure John would change his mind when he read the script he had in mind and also, he dropped, it might be something John would be interested in co-producing with him. So John took the script and read it several times, making notes about things in the story he thought should be changed and parts of what the lead character did that wouldn't be suitable for Cee Cee, and over the next two weeks he took several meetings with Jay Green before even mentioning the project to Cee Cee.

The night he did mention it to her, her mind was in a million different places, and later when she thought back to it, all she remembered was John saying he had a chance to produce some television show, and she had thought, Thank God, he's going to have a job, and she said "Great." So when Larry Gold called her at home and said he needed to talk to her without anybody else around, she couldn't imagine what was such a big deal and a secret, but she took the call in her bedroom and closed the door.

"Look, forgive me," he started out. "But you and I have been together for a lot of years. Okay? And I'm hoping we'll continue to be for a lot more years, so I'll be straight with you. Are you shtupping that guy Perry? I mean is that why he thinks he can take meetings on projects and make promises to people that you're gonna do the projects without even checking in with me?"

"What?"

"Jay Green thinks that I should be opening negotiations on your behalf for some piece of dreck miniseries I don't think you would spit on. And he says he knows you're available to do it because Perry's his partner, and that's what *Perry's* saying. Cee Cee, what's the haps here? I thought we decided no miniseries and no Movies of the Week."

Cee Cee searched her mind trying to think if she had said yes to something and forgotten about it, or led John to believe she wanted to do a miniseries. To begin with she hadn't even read whatever script Larry was talking about. But she didn't want to tell that to Larry. It would make John look ridiculous, so instead she said, "Well, we did discuss the fact that it was a terrific part."

"You've got to be kidding!" Larry said. "With a page-one rewrite by Alvin Sargent, maybe it's a good part. But other than that, this thing belongs in the trash masher. Cee Cee, I'm always the first one to tell you how brilliant you are. But, in this case . . . reconsider."

Reconsider. Reconsider what? John had committed her to something and she wasn't even certain what the something was.

"Not really committed. How could I commit you without you seeing it? Don't be crazy," he told her that night. Antonia, the housekeeper, was off, Nina was at Kevin's, and John had brought take-out Chinese from the Mandarin for dinner for the two of them. "Look, I have to admit the script is not one hundred percent. But Jay says once we get the network to say yes, we can afford to bring in a new writer and I'll supervise the writing. That way we'll know from day to day exactly what we're getting. I'll tell you what. On Saturday morning, let's drive up to Santa Barbara. You can read the script in a bungalow at the Biltmore, and we can get away from all the tensions here. I know you're going to see the potential in this, and drop your prejudices about miniseries."

Cee Cee watched him while he said all that, opening all of the little white cartons of Chinese food, as the steam rose from each one, not looking at her while he talked. For a long time she'd recognized that to be in her position was to be a target for every person who thought she could help to get them something they needed or somewhere they wanted to go, and though that had probably been true for years and years, this was the time when she prayed it wasn't the case. Figured that John, since he had loved her when she had been nowhere and nobody, would be exempt from needing her that way. And on Saturday night in the bungalow at the Santa Barbara Biltmore she let him make love to her for the first time in fifteen years, hoping the act of sex would not only ease her worries but rekindle some deeply rooted passions from years before.

Every man she'd been with since him, no matter how hot and sexy, took a while to psych her out, and of course the reverse was true, too. To know exactly where and when to touch one another, how hard to press here, how gently to rub there, which moans meant go on and which meant stop. But within seconds the two of them had one another going the way they always had during their ten-year marriage. He was holding her face in his two hands, telling her how he'd never stopped loving her, knowing how she always needed to hear the words, how protestations of love were more erotic to her than any touch. She was holding his great ass and pulling his pelvis toward her, while he promised her they were going to be together forever, telling her how much he wanted her, how he'd lived his life just waiting to come back to her this way, then pulling her to him hungrily and kissing her with a long searching kiss, during which he moved his hands under her sweater, easily in one move unfastening the front clasp on her bra, then finding her nipples and taking them between his thumb and forefinger the way he remembered she loved it and playing with them first softly, then squeezing until she moaned, and then if only from the long absence of sex in her life she was filled with heat, the aching needy place inside her that had to have him there to fill it, and she felt her knees getting weak.

Again with the agility he'd always had, which she used to think was almost sleight of hand and be jealous of every woman he had been with, since it was obviously a result of years and years of practice, he unbuttoned the top button on her slacks, then unzipped them and gentled them down to the floor by rubbing his own body against hers until the pants moved to her thighs, then to her knees, and when they were piled around her ankles, before she could step out of them he slid his fingers under the lace on the thigh of her panties and pressed them into the swollen throbbing folds longing to be caressed.

Oh, yes, she wanted it, and she pressed her pelvis hard against his fingers so he could feel the urgency in her, and he lifted her and carried her to the bed, quickly removing his own clothes, then the rest of hers, while she somehow managed to find an instant of presence of mind to grab for her purse on the floor and fish around inside it for one of the condoms she'd shoved in there just before she left her house.

But by the time she found it, he was moving astride her, and she helped him on with the balloonlike piece of rubber, afraid one of her nails might tear it, then looked at his very familiar body and his very familiar cock, and his face contorted with a passion she remembered so long ago could make her wild with desire for him, and realized with a sudden discomforting wave of sobriety she never had during sex, as he entered her with a first thrust, that it was only the lubrication of the condom that made his slide inside of her anything but unyielding, because she felt nothing. Then he thrust harder and this time she was wetter as her body responded to the sex, any sex because it had been so long, but she knew as she began to relax into the physical feelings, that this moment she had hoped for was nothing more than what she'd heard people call a mercy fuck. Because all she felt for him now was sorry.

Sorry he was pushing sixty and still trying to find himself, sorry he had left his family instead of hanging in and working on his relationships with them because he had some fantasy that being with Cee Cee could fix his life, and that she had been a party to the fantasy because she'd needed it so badly herself. And now she knew that the security she had begun to feel about leaning on him had been a result of her bottomless need, and also a result of the front he'd developed to get her to depend on him so that he could manipulate her, and the truth was that she couldn't go back again and find solace in him and security and a mind she respected the way she had when they were just starting out their life together. She had come too far to ever go back.

John was lost now in that other world of sexual heat, eyes closed, moving inside her against her to his own rhythm, and Cee Cee beneath him felt as detached as if she was watching from the back row of a movie theater. "Baby, we're so close, we're one person, how did I ever leave you, baby? Oh God, you feel so good to me, you're mine, you're still mine, aren't you, baby? Oh, Cee Cee, oh yes." It *did* feel good having a naked man against her own nakedness, it had been much too long and even in her removed watching-from-a-distance place she had to admit that. But each time she opened her eyes and saw John there on top of her, so filled with the passion she was lacking for him, she knew that though it might be sad to feel anger or hatred about someone you once loved so much, what was much more heartbreaking was to feel pity.

After that night in Santa Barbara things started to slide badly. Cee Cee turned down the miniseries, John went out for a brief spurt of job hunting, and the tension between the two of them became palpable. Once Cee Cee snapped at him and overheard somebody on the crew joke, "Uh oh, trouble in paradise." One Friday night Nina had stayed up late, but shortly after she'd fallen asleep she was awakened by the sound of Cee Cee and John having a fight downstairs. They were probably sitting at the dining-room table, which was directly under her room, so she could hear every word rising from their heated quarrel.

"Hey, nothing personal, but you and I both know television is simply a lot of mindless bullshit for morons, which is why your show has been so successful for so long. Because it has no substance."

"Is that right?" Cee Cee said. She had never thought her show was fodder for PBS, but bullshit for morons was a little low. "If television is such shit, then I'd like to know why you've been kissing up to so many people trying to worm your way into it."

"Oh, now that's funny. Who in the hell have I been kissing up to?"

"Everyone I introduce you to. Everyone I *don't* introduce you to. Everyone in the business."

"You couldn't be more wrong. Of course with your upbringing you wouldn't know the difference between someone with charm and someone who is, to use your classy phrase, 'kissing up.'"

"Oh, honey, let me tell you something," Cee Cee said in a tone Nina recognized as her haul-off-and-let-one-go voice. "You have been *so* charming to *so* many people out here, rumor has it that *your* nose is browner than George Hamilton's."

Nina wasn't sure what *that* line meant, but the giddy triumph she heard in Cee Cee's delivery meant she'd probably been rehearsing it for a while. Then it was quiet and Nina figured maybe they were both sorry for being so mean to one another and had probably made up and were kissing or something, but then she heard John say, "Cee Cee, I've been talking to my wife on the phone every night, and the truth is I really miss her. I love her, and I never should have left her for some unrealistic fantasy I had about what you could be for me, or what we could have together, because you were never right for me and you still aren't."

Nina felt sick when she heard that, because so many times over the last few months she had seen a girlish look on Cee Cee's face when she referred to John as a joke, as her "once and future husband," that made Nina know she wasn't joking, and now she wished she could rush downstairs and put her arms around Cee Cee, who had to feel after that news as if John had punched her in the stomach.

"When did you start talking to her every night?" Cee Cee asked

with the same hurt Nina had heard from her on the first Mother's Day
they had spent together, when Nina had flared at her, "Don't keep
hinting around that it's Mother's Day. You're not my mother and I'm
not getting you any gift." "Oh, I understand," Cee Cee had said in
that voice which had hit a chord so deep in Nina she'd walked immediately over to the Malibu pharmacy and spent ten dollars on a silver
compact and another dollar fifty on a card that said MOTHER'S DAY
GREETINGS TO SOMEONE SPECIAL. But apparently that voice didn't
have the same effect on John, because now he went on to say, "I'm
going home. It's almost the holidays and I want my family back. My
flight leaves tomorrow morning."

There was no response, and Nina leaned over the edge of her bed
to get her face closer to the floor so she could hear the next.

"You talked to her every night? Even when we were in Santa
Barbara?"

"Even when we were in Santa Barbara."

"When? You were with me every minute."

"When you were in the shower."

"You filthy rotten lowlife."

"Likewise I'm sure," he said, and then Nina heard nothing until
the sound of the front door slamming shook the house, and it took
Nina a long time after that to fall asleep.

In the morning when she went downstairs she could smell coffee,
and when she walked into the kitchen, Cee Cee was there, red-eyed
and edgy and fighting to be cheerful. "I think you, me, and Kevin
ought to go to the movies tonight," she said. "Let's find out what's
playing at the Malibu Cinema." She was wearing a silk kimono and
her face looked as if she hadn't taken off her makeup properly the
night before, still smudged around the eyes, and there was a little red
spot on her cheek.

"John went back to Ohio?" Nina asked her as Cee Cee absently bit
into a piece of toast that was black around the edges.

"Yeah," Cee Cee said. "How do you know? Did you hear us fighting last night?"

"Uh-huh. He was really mean to you."

"Yeah, that was pretty bad. And as if he hadn't hurt me enough,
I, like a schmuck, followed him out to the car and stood there crying
while he was putting his things in the trunk. It was like I was saying,

I didn't have enough. Give me more shit. Can you believe it? So he did. He told me I had a star complex, that I take myself too seriously, and that I've lost my sense of humor. I was so hurt by that, I forgot to mention that only six months ago the *New York Times* called me the comedy star of the decade." She giggled a ripple of a giggle at that, then looked at Nina with a pained grin that had toast crumbs all around it.

"Well, why didn't you?"

"Well, I would have but at that moment, I didn't remember."

"What do you mean?"

Cee Cee put her elbows on the table now and rested her face in her two hands. "I mean I lost it. He was rejecting me so I totally lost it, forgot that every day for the last two weeks I woke up with a speech in my head I was planning to make to him, about how you can't go backward in life, and how even though it felt good to see him and be with him, and how I'd be willing, even glad to help his career in any way I could if he wanted my help, I couldn't keep allowing him to take over my life the way he was trying to, and the way he did when I was a kid."

"Good speech," Nina said, putting a piece of bread in the toaster for herself.

"Isn't it?" Cee Cee said. "Too bad it's on the cutting room floor. I was even gonna say that he ought to start to meet some other women and date them because I didn't want to go back to a romance with him, and certainly not a marriage. And all of a sudden when I heard him saying he was on his way back to Ohio, all my plans to be rational went right out the French doors. I mean, I panicked because all I could think was 'He's leaving me. How can he leave me?' And I looked at the same man I couldn't wait to get rid of two weeks before and thought, 'How am I going to live without him?'

"So I said, and this is the part I hate myself for, in this real dramatic voice I said, 'John . . . don't go to her. Stay here and we'll try to work it out.' I still can't believe I was so crazed I was asking him to stay and I didn't even want him to. And then, as if it wasn't bad enough, he said something that really got me. He said that after all this time, he'd better confess the truth, which was that when he showed up in Atlantic City, he was really coming to ask me to be an investor in the Sunshine . . . you know, that theater he used to own?

Not to renew anything, not because he cared about me, but then when he saw me onstage that night he got tangled up in the web of his feelings for me. Do you love that phony bullshit? The web of his feelings? Like I was the spider and he was the fly, and that it took him till now to realize it was all just him reacting to the bad way his wife had treated him a few years back and trying to get back at her was childish and that he wanted to go home. 'Of course, you do,' I told him. 'Maybe *she* can bask in your glory. But as far as I can see, you don't even need any sunscreen to bask in *that* goddamned glory.'"

Cee Cee wiped her mouth with a napkin. Her eyes were full and her face was red, and she stood and walked away toward the sink for no apparent reason except to hide that fact from Nina. For a while she stared out the window at the ocean, then finally she asked Nina, "Can I fix you anything?"

"No thanks," Nina told her, "I'll just have my toast." Then she walked over to the sink and put an arm around Cee Cee as the day filled with sunshine and a couple wearing matching white sweat suits jogged north along the beach outside the window.

Dear Cecilia,

First I'll start by saying don't get excited, it's not a big deal because if it was I would call you up instead of writing it in this letter, but I'm not so hot in the ticker department if you know what I mean. Believe me, you have got enough on your mind with a television show and somebody else's daughter to worry about without having to think about me. So all I'm doing is writing to say "hello" and thanks for all the money you send me from some guy named Wayne Gordon's office whoever he may be.

Time goes by so fast, it's hard to believe your mother, may she rest in peace, is already gone so many years. If she was alive she would be calling you every day saying why don't you come and visit once in a while, but I don't believe in telling children what to do.

You know that old expression "all I know is what I read in the paper"? That's what I should say, since down the street at the newsstand I see your picture in the paper all the time.

Everyone here thinks you're some big deal, and when I tell them you're my daughter, they think I am too.

Your father,

Nathan Bloom

MIAMI BEACH, FLORIDA

1986

IN MIAMI BEACH the light of the day is so soft and flattering, Cee Cee decided, as her taxi drove down Collins Avenue, the reason why so many old people moved there had to be because the light made them look younger. Her father had lived in an apartment in Miami Beach off and on for years in which it had cost her a fortune to keep him, and now he was dying there in a Jewish convalescent home where it was costing her even more. She had been summoned by his doctor two days ago, who told her Nathan was having chest pains and trouble breathing but that he refused to go into a hospital, and maybe her input would change his mind.

The call made Cee Cee want to pick up the phone, call Nathan, and shout, "Daddy, get your ass into the hospital," but a lifetime of guilt for ignoring him prompted her to call off a few days of production meetings for her show and ask her travel agent to book her to Miami (God's waiting room) Beach.

"Can I come too?" Nina asked. She was a skinny beanpole now, with long curly fly-away hair that was always in her eyes and a close-lipped smile she used, to try to cover the mouthful of braces on her teeth.

"Of course you can, but why would you want to?" Cee Cee asked.

"While you're seeing your dad, I could visit my aunt."

Bertie's Aunt Neetie. Cee Cee's first impulse was to say, "No way, José," and close the issue because she couldn't bear the thought of Nina spending even one minute with the Miami Bitch, which was how she thought of Neetie. Aside from Michael Barron, Neetie was Nina's only living blood relative, and she was always hovering out there with something shitty to say about Cee Cee in her letters or phone calls to Nina, or something snide to say about everyone in show business in general as if she knew them all personally, and she was an expert at constantly making the point to Nina that Bertie, if she was alive, would have done everything pertaining to Nina so much better than Cee Cee did. So that when Nina openly and candidly read the poison missives out loud to Cee Cee, it was all Cee Cee could do not to call the old witch in Florida and tell her to fuck off, but she didn't. Instead she took a deep breath and tried to explain away the things Neetie had written, and though there was no doubt in her mind that Nina's spending a few days with Neetie would cost a lot of deep breaths and a lot of explaining, she still answered, "Sure, honey. I'll help you pack."

Things had been a little rough with her and Nina recently, and late at night when Nina was long asleep, Cee Cee turned to the now dog-eared child-raising books looking for answers. This time to read about what they called pre-adolescence. A time when confusion reigned because at eleven they were no longer children and not quite adolescents.

This stage usually hits parents with a wallop. Your stable, reasonable and well-behaved child seems suddenly to have taken an overdose of obnoxious pills.

Nina seemed to fade in and out of surliness. She was a classic case of being neither here nor there, still sleeping with teddy bears but blushing and flirting when one of the crew members on Cee Cee's show kidded with her. And when Cee Cee saw that, she wished like hell there had been a healthy relationship Nina could have witnessed somewhere along the line, a man she could have had some time with, since she had lived her whole life without a father. A man.

Men. Now there was a joke. Each time a new one came into Cee Cee's life, she was amazed to see that no matter how bad the departure of the last one had been, the kid was still ready and willing to pin her hopes on the new one. Once Cee Cee read a quote somewhere that said a woman without a man couldn't meet a man of any age without thinking, even for a second, maybe this is *the* man. And she could see by the way Nina closely observed each man who showed any interest in Cee Cee, the way she asked him telling questions about himself, that she too was trying to test the potential each one had to be the man in their household.

But none had worked out. Some of the men who found their way to their door were too interested in Cee Cee's stardom, wanted to use her power for their own purposes or to be able to say they were involved with a star. Others were intimidated by her lifestyle, and she had to admit it wasn't exactly easy. After all, there was no dating her in a conventional way. Everywhere she went she was swamped with autograph seekers, besieged by photographers, and stared at by everyone else. So the men who stepped forward, as she described it, "bearing bouquets of flowers and cocks that didn't fall to half-mast as they approached my famous and exquisite bod," were rare and unusual.

And even when they did, eventually some interior buzzer of hers buzzed, like the rasping end-bell on a game show telling the contestant the answer was wrong, and Cee Cee would know it was over with this one too, so she would try to explain nicely, then turn down his requests to come over, and eventually stop taking his calls at all, and soon another would be phased out.

"No more Dan?" Nina would ask (or Chad or Mark or Roger).

"Not for me," Cee Cee would answer, knowing she would have to face the disappointment in Nina's eyes again.

Perhaps there is an in-law or a relative, a grandfather or an uncle who can play an active male role with your children. In rare cases a male friend can do this. This person can be invited over to dinner or picnics. He can take the children to movies, take them fishing or camping, take them to sports events, go swimming or sailing with them.

Yeah, sure. There was no one in their lives to fit that bill, except for Hal, but he lived and worked in New York, and these days only came in on occasional visits. Cee Cee's father, who had never been a force in her life, was another story. As soon as she'd started making money she had helped him to move out of an old folks home in New York to an apartment in Miami Beach. Bought him stock, MCA, Warners, enough to give him a reason to get up in the morning, to call his broker and check on his money.

Over the years she had extended vague invitations to him to come to Los Angeles to visit, never sure what she would do with him if he said yes and showed up, but Nathan Bloom had always declined.

Now he was ailing and not long for this world, and the illness had dictated that he move back into a convalescent home, the one toward which her taxi now moved through the bright, sunny Miami Beach day.

"Why don't I take this cab to Neetie's and you take that one to see your dad? You don't need to come with me to see Neetie," Nina had said to her at the Miami airport.

"You mean because she loathes and despises me and that makes you uncomfortable?"

"Yes," Nina answered.

"You got it." Cee Cee felt remiss agreeing to take separate taxis, but she couldn't bring herself to have to see Neetie and her pinched, judgmental face waiting for Nina's cab to drive up outside her building, so she agreed to let Nina get there alone. At the cabstand she gave her enough money to last for several days, exchanged phone numbers with her, and hugged her goodbye, regretting her decision the second the cab pulled away, and she tried hard to fight back the fear that Nina would see Neetie after so many years and love her so much she would beg her aunt and uncle to keep her in Miami Beach.

Even at its worst the L.A. heat didn't have the kind of dense humidity Miami Beach did. By the time Cee Cee had paid her cabdriver and carried her overnight bag to the door of the Beth Shalom Convalescent Home, she was soaked with sweat, and her black silk sweater stuck to her in several wet places. As she pushed the glass doors to the lobby open, she tried to steel herself for what it would be like seeing Nathan after so long. Nathan, who had been a silent figure behind a newspaper for most of her childhood. Cowering from that cow Leona. "Let the kid sleep late, for chrissake, Leona," he would offer now and then on a Saturday morning as Leona hollered for a tired Cee Cee to "Getyertapshuzon." And when he did, Leona would turn on him and yell, "And you mindyerowngoddamnbizness," and he always did. Occasionally there would be a burst of humor from him, a moment when he could ease the overbearing Leona into an uncharacteristic grin or a sudden girlish giggle. Like when the two of them sang together.

"I'm the sheik of Araby," Leona would sing, and Nathan with a sexy little twinkle in his eye would follow every line with the words, "Without a pair of pants."

"And your love belongs to me."

"Without a pair of pants."

"At night when you're asleep."

"Without a pair of pants."

"Into your tent I'll creep."

"Without a pair of pants."

"This is where you got your talent, Cecilia," Nathan would tell her pointing to himself.

"Oh yeah?" Leona would say. "I guarantee ya, Eddie Cantor ain't losing any sleep over you, Bloom." Sometimes by the end of the song he would be wearing a kitchen towel around his little bald head as his costume for the sheik of Araby. Remembering him that way now as she walked up to the desk at the convalescent home made Cee Cee regret all the years she had stayed away from him, and wish she could have them back.

When she asked the nurse at the front desk where 4C was, she answered, "Ahhh, you're Nate's daughter. He's a prince of a man," then gave her directions to her father's room. As she moved down the carpeted hall, Cee Cee looked at the old people who sat slumped and staring in wheelchairs posted outside the doors to their rooms, probably because they didn't want to stay inside the rooms all day but only had the physical wherewithal to get as far as the door jamb.

Now and then the eyes of one of them would meet hers and she would see a glimmer that probably meant, "Look! A young person!" But that was all the contact most of them seemed able to make. On the cardboard plaque outside of room 4C there was a sign which indicated that inside the room there were two occupants. MARTY ELMAN AND NATHAN BLOOM it said, and there was a photograph of each man's face next to his name. Cee Cee looked long at the picture of her father. It was an old one from long ago, in fact it was half of one in which the other half had been her mother standing next to him. Cee Cee knew because somewhere in a box of pictures at home she had the original, and now she wondered if Nathan had used that particular picture because since then no one else had taken another one of him. That thought made her so sad she reached up and put her fingers on the picture.

"They all have them now," someone said, and Cee Cee turned to see a small round blond nurse holding a pile of what looked like sheets. "Originally we started putting pictures up so our Alzheimer's patients could find their way back to their rooms. Then everybody wanted them."

Cee Cee nodded a numb nod in reply.

"I'm your father's nurse, Cee Cee. I would know you even if I never saw you in the movies or on TV, which I did, because he has a million pictures of you in his drawer."

"He does?" Cee Cee wasn't sure why that surprised her.

"He's asleep now, I just checked him," the nurse told her, shaking her head sadly. "Not good. On the first floor alone we lost three this week. They wear out. The human body unfortunately was only designed to last sixty-some years. You take perfect care, you last more. Not such good care, you last less. Your father, he's in his eighties, so it's his time."

"I'll go see him."

"Don't mind the roommate, Elman. He's a pain in the *tochas*. You know what a *tochas* is?"

Cee Cee nodded.

"Anyways, how's that little girl of yours?"

"She's fine," Cee Cee said. "Thanks for asking."

The room was divided by a panel of curtains, and Cee Cee wondered why, with all the money she was paying, Nathan only had a semiprivate room instead of a private one. She made a mental note to ask somebody in charge after she spent some time with her father, whose head was thrown back and his mouth was open in a snore, as he twitched in the throes of a dream.

Overlaid on the disinfectant odor in the room, she breathed in a familiar Nathan scent from her childhood she recognized as Old Spice cologne, and the smell of it brought back the old apartment of her childhood, and the memory of Nathan standing with only a towel wrapped around his waist, his hairless pink chest and fat little arms, leaning over a sink of hot water trying to shave, while Leona hollered at him so much it was a miracle he didn't cut his face to ribbons.

"Hiya, Sheik," Cee Cee said softly now to the soundly sleeping old man. "Long time, no see."

Aunt Neetie looked as if there might be tears in her eyes when she walked out of the lobby of her building to greet Nina's taxi. She was a slim woman with hair dyed too black, and skin that was a kind of muddy brown and very wrinkled from the sun.

"Well, aren't *you* a big girl!" she said. Nina thought by the way she walked toward the taxi with her hand in her pocket that maybe she was about to pull out money and pay the cabdriver, but when she made no move to, Nina opened her pink plastic "Hello Kitty" wallet, took out some of the money Cee Cee had given her, and remembered to add a tip before she handed it to the driver.

As the cab pulled away Neetie explained away her watery eyes. "I'm allergic to hibiscus," she said. "And it's all around now." Nina's suitcase sat on the front step of the building where the cabdriver had dropped it. "Can you manage that bag all by yourself or shall I get Uncle Herb to come down? The Cuban doorman is off today. He says one of his kids is in the hospital. The little spic has so damn many kids there's always an excuse," she said, and then laughed a forced throaty laugh.

Nina picked up the heavy suitcase and dragged it toward the front door of the building.

"You're the picture of your mother," Neetie said, opening one of the glass doors into the foyer of the building to let her in and holding it open. The air-conditioning brought goose bumps to Nina's little arms.

"Thank you," Nina said, pulling the suitcase over the threshold and across the marble-floored lobby toward the elevator. The building smelled of onions cooking and the odor made Nina, who hadn't eaten anything on the flight from Los Angeles, feel hungry and queasy at the same time. The elevator was so small, Neetie and Nina and the suitcase just fit inside. There was a notice taped to the elevator wall, listing a schedule of events which Nina read to herself as she and Neetie took the ride up.

MONDAY NIGHT — SEVEN P.M. BINGO
   (REC ROOM SEVEN O'CLOCK)
   REFRESHMENTS WILL BE SERVED.
WEDNESDAY NIGHT — BOOK DISCUSSION — THIS MONTH <u>AIRPORT</u>.

The elevator doors opened and Nina pushed her body against the suitcase and shoved it into the hall. "It's the third door on the right," Neetie said, walking ahead of her with a kind of stoop-shouldered walk. "Your Uncle Herb is watching television as usual. Herbieee," she yelled out, opening the door to her apartment, "Roberta's daughter is here."

Nina stood in the doorway of the apartment. Neetie, who had obviously been unable to part with the furniture from her larger home, had managed to cram it into the small apartment rooms. After a minute a skinny little man with white hair, wearing trousers and a white sleeveless undershirt that revealed his white armpit hair, opened a door to a back room through which Nina could hear a television show blasting. The man nodded and made a few noises that sounded oddly like burps, and then instead of a voice, out came croaking noises that sounded as if they might have been, "Nice to see you." Nina took a step back. Something was wrong.

"A couple of years ago he had a laryngectomy. Cancer of the voice box. Had to have it removed," Neetie said as if she was talking about a lamp or a chair instead of Uncle Herbie, who nodded in Nina's direction during the narration, watching her reaction carefully. "Now he speaks through a hole in his throat," Neetie said. "I never mentioned it in my letters because I didn't want to worry you." Then she asked with amusement in her voice, "What's the matter, did he scare you?"

Nina looked at her uncle's neck where she saw the hole and then into his eyes where she could see that her answer was important to him, so she lied. "Oh, no," she said, then thought, *I'm going to vomit.*

"Isn't she big, Herbie?"

"Burp, burp, she sure is," is what it sounded like he said.

Nina's sick feeling must have filled her face, because Neetie said, "Don't worry, you can't catch it. It's from smoking too many cigarettes. You don't smoke, do you?" She was making what Nina could tell by the strange little smile on her face was her idea of a joke.

"Burp, burp. Leave the kid alone, Anita. Here, I'll take you to your room," Uncle Herbie said, walking over and picking up Nina's suitcase, and with a wag of his head to the side invited her to follow. Now she had to be alone with him. Obligingly she followed him down a narrow hallway and into the guest bedroom, the door to which, when he opened it, bumped into one of two beds with headboards that matched a large dresser with mirrors over it, two night tables, and a chair. On one of the tables there was a small framed photograph of two women and a little girl of about seven or eight years old. Uncle Herbie saw Nina looking at it.

"Burp, burp, it's your mother and your grandmother and my wife. On the beach in Atlantic City," she thought he said.

Nina wondered if the picture was taken the year her mother first met Cee Cee there. Uncle Herb put her suitcase on one of the beds. "Burp, burp, bathroom's just down the hall," he said. Now she would unpack, and then they would eat dinner. She wondered if when Uncle Herbie ate, some of the food fell out of the little hole, and that thought made her feel really sick. Uncle Herb burped some more and said some more words as he pointed out the closet, the chest of drawers, the clock radio, and Nina tried to be polite and not look at the hole, and nod, and hope he'd leave the room. When he finally did and closed the door behind him, she lay face-down on the bed trying to pull herself together, but the pain of disappointment rushed to her eyes. This was certainly not the Aunt Neetie and Uncle Herb she had conjured up in those moments when she thought about escaping from Cee Cee, times when Cee Cee embarrassed her so horribly, like when she was dating some really awful guy who was too young for her with hair down to his shoulders, or that one who wore the gold jewelry and smoked eight cigars a day. Or those times she came for parent-teacher meetings to school wearing those Halloweeny thrift shop outfits that made her look like a cartoon character.

Nina would pacify herself on those days by writing and mailing letters to the couple she liked to think of as her "real family." An elegant older couple, living in a building she knew from their return address was called the Versailles, which she had always pictured to be like the Plaza Hotel, where she and Cee Cee had stayed last year when Cee Cee had to go to New York for meetings. Surely there would be a dining room with chandeliers and a violinist who played during tea in the lobby. And the aunt and uncle would take her in, clucking their tongues with understanding at what an ordeal it must have been these last few years for her to put up with all the craziness in Cee Cee's life.

Of course after she mailed the feverishly written letters and sent them off to the Versailles, the tide at home would turn because Cee Cee would eventually either dump or get dumped by the guy, or do something marvelous just for Nina like having the Muppets as guests on her show and inviting Nina's entire class to be her guests at the taping, and things would be all right between them again for a while, but soon they'd fall apart again and when they did, Nina would get through it by picturing what her life would eventually be like when she came to live with her real family at the Versailles.

There was a tap at the door, and Aunt Neetie came in smiling. "Well, you must be worn out from all that traveling," she said to Nina as she walked over to the suitcase, opened it, and removed the clothing piece by piece, moving back and forth to the chest of drawers to put them away. "I guess Miss Cee Cee didn't want to come over here *with* you because she couldn't stand to look me in the eye because of what she did to me, and I'm sure you know the story."

Nina knew which story Neetie meant, since over the years Neetie had told her various versions of it in her letters. All this time had gone by since Bertie's death, and still she wouldn't let "the story" go. Somehow she always managed to get some dig in about how Cee Cee had tricked Bertie into giving the care of Nina to her and taking it away from Neetie.

"My ass," Cee Cee had flared furiously when Nina had mentioned it the first time. "Nobody tricked anyone. Your mother knew I was the right one and that's why she let me have you."

"You know, of course you're getting to be the age where you can decide you don't want to be with her anymore. And when you do, you can march right into that courtroom and say, 'Judge, get me the hell out of that nuthouse.' And frankly, honey, I hope you do. And that me and your Uncle Herb will still be around to take you. Maybe move up to the fifth floor to a three-bedroom."

Nina just nodded.

"And I suppose she's raising you as a Jew?" Neetie asked now. Nina looked at her curiously, wondering why there was a sneer on her lips, and Neetie took her look to mean yes.

"I thought so. Well, don't worry, I'm used to Jews. You live in Miami Beach all your life the way I have, all you see are wall-to-wall kikes. And the joke is they think *I'm* one of them because I have black hair. Sometimes they do jokes to me in Yiddish, can you imagine? Well, I'm not here for the company, honey, I'm here for the climate." Now she was putting Nina's pink sundress on a hanger. "I never knew what the hell your gorgeous classy mother ever saw in Cee Cee

Bloom. I tell you, every time I saw your picture in one of those scandal papers — not that I buy them, but they're all over the beauty parlor I go to — I wanted to cry. Anyway, let's talk about happier things. You and I and Herbie are going to have a grand old time. Right?"

Nina didn't say anything, but when Neetie left the room to check on dinner she opened her little purse, took out the wallet inside and looked at the telephone number Cee Cee had left with her, and considered calling it and begging Cee Cee to come and get her.

"Cecilia," Nathan said, opening his eyes. "Is it really you?"

"It's me, Daddy," she said, looking at the old man in the bed who only bore the slightest resemblance to her memory of her father. And Cecilia, the name he called her. Who was that? The little girl inside of her only he remembered who wasn't Cee Cee Bloom the star. The ordinary person who had long ago created the character of Cee Cee Bloom. Made up her walk, made up her flashiness, made the choice that she would be tart-tongued and bawdy, outrageous and sexy, while Cecilia, Nathan Bloom's daughter, watched all of that from the inside, like the puppeteer watches the puppet.

Nathan's eyes flickered with joy and she took his hand gently. "I'm dying?" he asked her. "That's why you came because I'm dying?"

How should she answer a question like that?

"I just came to see you."

"You're doing a show in town here?" he asked her, and she realized he was saying he knew it could only be his imminent death that would bring her to his side, or business, and she hated that he was right.

"I needed to come and talk to you," she said.

"No kidding?" he said, and then winced with pain as he moved himself a little higher on the bed. "I'm not so good, kiddo. I had some prostate trouble a little hip trouble, now I got chest pains."

"I know. The doctor wants you to go into the hospital."

"Forgetaboutit."

"Daddy, it could save your life. Give you years and years."

"Who wants more years?" he asked, making a face that was so familiar because she made it all the time, too. "I had enough years. Your mother, God rest her soul, got a flucky. You know that story?" Cee Cee couldn't believe it. He was going to tell her a joke. "A guy goes to a whoor. Everybody else goes to the whoor gets VD. The doctor tells this guy he didn't get VD, instead he got a flucky. The guy is scared, because he never heard of such a thing. Then he realizes the doctor meant he 'got off lucky.' Your mother got a flucky because she never had to get old. Come to mention it, maybe that's why I'm still here. Leona would have noodged me into an early grave," he said.

"Daddy, they think you might have a leaky heart valve. If that's true, they can replace it and you'll feel good."

"Leaky, sure. Why *wouldn't* it be leaky at my age? You're old, you're sick, you die, that's life." Cee Cee shook her head and there was silence.

"So since I saw you last you're a mother?" he said and asked at the same time.

"That's right. My best friend left her daughter in my care and I'm raising her."

"Why you?"

"I was the best choice."

"Oy vay," he said and smiled.

"What does *that* mean?" Cee Cee asked, annoyed that he had been awake less than three minutes and was already aggravating her.

"I beg your pardon. I was the one who retrieved your turtle from the toilet and sat shivah for all your goldfish. In my mind you're not a mother."

Cee Cee flared. "So who *was* a mother? Leona who drove both of us crazy from morning until night? Grandma who made you walk her from room to room in her house so she could say goodbye to the furniture, and then had the nerve to live so you'd have to do it again the next day and the next for years?"

"Don't get excited. I'm entitled to an opinion."

"Hey, you know what?" Cee Cee said.

"Yeah?"

"Why don't you come out to Los Angeles and see for yourself what kind of a mother I am."

"I'll read about it in the paper," he said.

The nurse Cee Cee had met in the hall came into the room carrying a small metal tray.

"So, Nate. Your famous daughter schlepped here a long way. You think maybe you'll go for a little walk down the hall with her today?"

"No walking noplace. I walked farther in my lifetime than both of you put together ever will, so that's enough walking."

"Nate, it improves the efficiency of your circulation," the nurse told him, and when she put the thermometer in his mouth and held his wrist, while she looked at her watch to get a pulse rate, with the hand she wasn't holding he gave her the finger. Cee Cee had to bite her lip to keep from laughing out loud.

For someone who didn't like Cee Cee, Aunt Neetie sure made a big thing out of the fact that she not only knew her but that her great-niece Nina lived with her in Hollywood. It was something she had obviously talked about to her neighbors who sat by the pool at the Versailles.

"Is that her?" everyone asked, looking hard at Nina. Older people, mostly ladies wearing beach hats and bathing suits and jewelry, were lying on lounge chairs or sitting around tables playing cards.

"That's the little doll," Neetie said, spreading orange-and-blue-striped beach towels across two lounge chairs. Then she made the introductions.

"Say hi to my beloved Mrs. Altschuler and Mrs. Haber."

"This is the one who lives with Cee Cee Bloom?"

"This is the one," Neetie said, gesturing toward Nina as if she were selling her.

"Oh, that Cee Cee! I'm her biggest fan," said one of the ladies, whose giant saggy breasts were falling like too much pleated fabric over the top of her bathing suit as she leaned forward to Nina to make her point. "You tell her Mrs. Altschuler, formerly from Cleveland, never missed any of her shows or any of her movies."

"That goes for me too," an unintroduced woman who was clearly not one of Neetie's beloveds announced. She was tiny, with short gray hair and a smear of pink ointment covering her nose and cheeks.

"I'll mention it," Nina said.

"Is she in town here?" the woman with the falling breasts asked.

"She is," Neetie answered. "She's visiting her sick father in a home on Bay Road. But she'll probably stop by here," and she smiled a knowing smile as if to say that she knew a lot about Cee Cee's schedule.

The women squealed at the idea. "No! Come here? Anita, you have to call us. My daughter would kill me if Cee Cee Bloom was here and I didn't talk to her."

"Well, you know," Neetie said, "people like Cee Cee are funny about their privacy . . . but of course I'll call you."

When the women had drifted away and Neetie and Nina were alone, Neetie said to her, "Those two are widows, rolling in dough. Altschuler's husband was a lawyer and the other one's husband was in louvered doors. When they get dolled up at night you could go blind from the glare of the jewelry." Neetie reached into the straw basket purse where she kept the suntan lotion and pulled out a pack of cigarettes. When she saw Nina's surprise as she held her hand up to shield the match she was lighting from the wind, she said, "Don't tell Herbie or he'll kill me," then she inhaled and blew out a big puff of smoke. "Believe me, I don't envy them. I mean what in the hell is jewelry if you don't have a man, kiddo. Right? Jewelry can't keep you warm at night." Nina tried not to picture Uncle Herbie keeping Aunt Neetie, who was puffing away on the cigarette and unbuttoning her white gauze coverup, warm at night. Underneath she wore a black bathing suit and had a very skinny, sagging brown body.

"My husband left me a couple of times. He was even in the pokey more than once, before you were born, when your mother was a kid. For illegal gambling activities. But you want to know what? I got him back every time. And I stashed away plenty of cash during the good years, and had a beautiful house where your grandmother, my sister Rosie, could come and visit, and now this condominium. I got the world on a string, honey." She puffed away a series of puffs on the cigarette until there was smoke all around her face.

"What was my grandmother like?"

"A doll. A beauty, just like your mother. A widow at a young age, but she never wanted to remarry." Neetie shook her head when she told Nina that. "Personally I think that's what killed her, killed your mother too. The doctors can call it cancer or stroke or whatever you like. I say a woman without a man dries up and dies." She took a long puff on the cigarette, creating dozens of tiny lines around her mouth as she puckered, then blew out the smoke, and asked, "So what about Cee Cee Bloom? Who's *her* latest boyfriend?"

"She doesn't have one at the moment."

"With that face it's no wonder," Neetie said and laughed. "Of course men don't care so much about the face, do they? Just the neck down." She laughed at that, then lay back, the cigarette now burning between her two fingers as she drank in the sun's rays. "Tonight we'll go to dinner to a cafeteria. Won't that be fun?"

Nathan held Cee Cee's arm as he moved haltingly down the hall. He was wearing a paisley bathrobe Cee Cee was sure he'd had when she was a little girl. Earlier she had tried to get him to eat a meal.

"Don't give me any more of those lousy potatoes without salt."

"You're not *allowed* to have salt, Daddy."

"I'm gonna be dead in a little while, who's gonna know if I had salt?"

"Pretend there's salt on them."

"You pretend I'm eating them."

"You need your energy."

"Why? I'm not going disco dancing. I'm lying here waiting to die. For that I don't need energy."

After that the nurse came in to bathe him, and Cee Cee stood in the hall outside talking to the doctor, who looked just the way Cee Cee pictured him when she spoke to him on the phone from Los Angeles. Small and slim with horn-rimmed glasses and wispy gray hair. "As I told you the other day, he has a negative attitude about intervention of any kind, says he's too old. The symptoms he has indicate that he has the mechanical problem of a leaking heart valve, and if it's replaced he could do well for quite a while."

"Then why is there a doubt?"

"He says he's lived enough."

That night, after Nathan fell asleep, Cee Cee checked into the Doral Beach Hotel to a suite that felt as large as an entire floor of the convalescent home, where she took a long bath, got into the big double bed and turned out the light, and couldn't sleep. For hours she paced the floor of the too-lavish room, wanting to blame her sleeplessness on the fact that she could hear *Nightline* on the television in the suite next door, but long after the people next door had turned the television off and there was nothing to be heard but silence, she was still wide awake.

She thought about how hateful and selfish she'd been, never being available to Nathan, then she worried about the possibility that Nina and Neetie were having a terrible time together, then she worried about the possibility that they were having a great time together. She ordered up a sandwich from the twenty-four-hour room service, and even though she wasn't hungry she sat eating it and every last potato chip they sent with it, thinking about the fact that it was in a hotel suite in Miami Beach a lot less grand than this one where the breakup of her marriage had happened, a lifetime ago. And how in the lobby of the same hotel from which John had made his exit, after a long, bitter estrangement she and Bertie had been reunited.

And what a reunion. Cee Cee was playing the showroom at the Carillon, and Bertie arrived in Miami Beach to sit by the bedside of her dying mother. It was one of those bizarre twists of fate that Cee Cee was certain was part of a predestined plot written on the day of everyone's birth, and she remembered how when she first walked into the lobby of the Carillon that day with those dogs she used to have yapping at her heels, and saw Bertie standing there after not seeing her for so long, she thought she was hallucinating.

"I forgive you," Bertie had said to her, and just remembering that haughty look Bert always got on her face when she thought she was so right about something, Cee Cee bristled. "Yeah, well thanks a whole fuckin' lot, Bert," she had said, "but I *don't* forgive you, and I never will." Of course that night she'd felt like a total schmuck for walking away from her, so in her usual fashion of overdoing it, she had gone to the hotel kitchen and picked up a bunch of dinners, then schlepped them over to the intensive care unit to feed all the relatives of the sick and the dying. Saint Cee Cee. Yeah, sure. Mother Teresa wasn't losing any sleep over the competition.

Anyway, Bertie did forgive her and they had gone on. Started sending their letters to one another again. And it was a few weeks later when Bertie sent her a poem in the mail. Cee Cee couldn't remember now who had written it.

> Friendship is the comfort
> The inexpressible comfort
> Of feeling safe with a person
> Having neither to weigh thoughts nor measure words
> But pouring all right out

Just as they are, chaff and grain together,
Certain that a friendly faithful hand
Will take and sift them
Keep what is worth keeping
And with a breath of comfort
Blow the rest away.

The poem had stayed in her mind forever. After all, pouring it all out was definitely her M.O., and for all their lives Bertie had managed to sift them out. Yeah, she thought now, it's good that Nina's visiting Neetie. The frostily air-conditioned living room of the suite was getting colder every minute, and she wished she remembered what the bellman told her about how to turn the air off. Even if Cee Cee personally hated that old bitch Neetie, it didn't matter because it was good for Nina to make a connection with somebody who gave her a sense of her own history, let her know that she had one, that once there was her grandmother Rosie who loved her daughter Bertie and that she was beautiful and fun and called her daughter "Puss" the same way Bertie did with Nina.

And it was good that Cee Cee was here in Miami for the same reason. To connect with her father and the part of herself that had come from him, a man who could make someone laugh by putting a dishtowel on his head and singing the words "Without a pair of pants" had definitely to be related to her by blood. And that was worth a lot. Finally after taking the room service tray out into the deserted hotel corridor, she fell asleep on the sofa in the living room of the suite, dreaming some vague dream about her mother, and eventually she woke with a pounding headache, dressed, and called down to the front desk and asked if the bellman would please get her a taxi, and soon she was back walking down the corridor of the convalescent home.

Nathan was arguing with a nurse about his breakfast.

"Daddy," Cee Cee said, "you're going into the hospital. Today. So put on your paisley robe or whatever you have to put on because I'm taking you over there now."

"Like hell you are," Nathan said.

"Doctor Feiffer told me you won't go to the hospital because you think you've lived enough. Well, you know what? You may have lived enough for you, but you haven't lived enough for me. I made a mistake, I stayed away from you for too long, and now I want you to stick around for a while so I can get to know you. Purely selfish, I'll admit, but I want to make up for some of those years, so Nina can get to know you, and I want to hear stories about my grandparents and what Leona was like when you were dating, and what you said the night you asked her to marry you."

"*She* asked *me.*"

"Well, I want to hear about that too. And about what I looked like the first time you saw me in the hospital nursery."

"A big mouth just like now."

She was pulling a little suitcase out of one of the closets, not sure if it was her father's or Marty Elman's, and packing toiletries in it and pajamas and a clean seersucker robe.

"I remember there were a lot of stories I used to ignore like about how smart I was and what my first words were, stories nobody else knows about me but you."

"I can tell you all that stuff in one day and you can go home," Nathan said, but he was turning on the bed now and putting his feet on the floor.

"I'm not going home until I get a date from you of when you're coming to Los Angeles to visit."

Nathan gave her a dismissing wave and a grunt, but he walked across the room to the bathroom unassisted.

Nina had never eaten in a cafeteria and the food looked great. The plates piled with squares of red Jell-O on lettuce, the pineapple rings on beds of cottage cheese, with a little strawberry half on the top. "Live it up," Neetie told her. "Have the Jell-O and the cottage cheese and a cream puff too. There are cream puffs at the end of the line."

While Uncle Herb stayed home, "the two girls," as Neetie called them, had gone to the movies to see *Hannah and Her Sisters* and then for an early dinner, and they got dressed up to do it. Neetie wore a white-and-yellow-flowered dress that made her dark skin look even darker, and Nina, whose hours in the sun had brought out every freckle on her face, wore a dress Cee Cee bought her, which was a pale yellow pinafore.

Cee Cee had called her from the hospital. She sounded nervous, and she told Nina that it was good that they were in Florida to be with their respective families and that even though she may not have acted like it sometimes, she thought people should be good to their families and try to take those relationships to their hearts. The things she said were really corny like from a greeting card, and probably she was feeling sentimental because she was calling from a hospital where she told Nina her father was going to have surgery immediately, which meant she and Nina might have to stay a day or two longer.

Nina said that was okay with her, and it was. She was getting used to the *burp burp* of Uncle Herbie, who was kind and smiled at her a lot and knew how to play twenty-one and gin rummy too. She had been relieved to find out that his surgery had removed his larynx, where he spoke, not his esophagus, where he ate, so no food fell out of the little hole. He also explained to her that though some others who had the same surgery sometimes used an amplifying device, he had chosen to learn, from another man who had the surgery years earlier, how to speak with his breath. Nina admired that.

The only tiresome part of her stay was Neetie's endless tirade against everyone in the world, but that was actually starting to be funny. Nina made a game out of trying to see if Neetie could get through any fifteen-minute period without either talking badly about somebody else or complaining about her own life.

"I never even got a cent out of the deal," she was saying now, as Nina held a red Jell-O square in her mouth, loving the way it dribbled down her throat as it melted, "because when my sister Rose died she left everything to your mother. Not that she had a fortune or anything as far as I know, but she didn't leave me so much as an earring. Remember that emerald ring she used to wear? I would have liked that. No, she gave it all to your mother, so then your mother dies and what happens? She leaves everything to you, naturally, and again I'm out in the cold, which is a figure of speech, since I'm living in Miami Beach," she said and laughed at what she was sure was her own wit. A busboy poured more coffee in her cup when she gestured for him with a snapping finger.

"You mean *this* emerald ring?" Nina asked and reached under the pinafore where the emerald ring, which she only wore when she got very dressed up, was hanging from the chain around her neck, and she held it out toward Neetie.

Neetie leaned forward, raising an eyebrow, then reached across and fingered the dangling ring hungrily.

"My sister Rosie's ring," she said, her eyes full of longing. "I'll never forget how much she loved it. I can picture it on her hand. God, I miss her. You know, she didn't leave me so much as a bobby pin because she was always so worried about your mother. Of course at the time I was hurt, but now in my old age I got smart. I mean there's no telling why people do things. Right? But that ring." She was still gazing at it and touching it, and Nina politely leaned forward to make it easier for her. "I remember when our mother gave it to her," Neetie said, and then her eyes fogged up as if that thought was an upsetting one. Finally she let go of the ring and dug her fork into the turkey pot pie she had chosen from the hot foods section, as Nina slid another cold square of red Jell-O onto her fork.

"Want to try it on?" she asked, hoping Aunt Neetie would say no but think what a nice girl she was for offering, except she'd barely finished the question when Neetie was standing behind her unclasping the chain, which she pulled away from the ring and placed on the table, and then she slid the ring onto her bony brown hand, and held her arm out stiff in front of her with her hand flexed as she gazed at the gleaming green stone.

"My sister's ring," she said, and then she wiped her eyes with her paper napkin.

As Cee Cee sat in the hospital watching Nathan's condition improve by the hour, measured by the number and volume of his complaints, she realized that the last time she'd been in a hospital was when Nina was born, and while Nathan was asleep she found a pay telephone in the hall and called Neetie's number.

"Hello?"

"Anita, this is Cee Cee Bloom."

"Oh, hello, Cee Cee."

Cee Cee knew she should ask about Neetie's husband, or maybe make small talk to be polite, but she couldn't think of any.

"How's Nina?" she asked.

"Why, she's a perfect angel," Neetie said, and without another word she handed the phone to Nina.

"H'lo?"

"Neen, we can go home tomorrow. I called my office and they made us reservations on Pan Am at two. The car will pick you up at noon."

"Okay."

"Neen."

"Yes?"

"Are you glad to be going home?"

"Um . . . yes."

Cee Cee had the limousine pick her up first and then to Neetie's to pick up Nina. She'd considered having the car pick Nina up first in order to avoid Neetie completely, but she knew that was wrong and that she had to be adult about this. Now as the long black car pulled up outside the Versailles and she saw Neetie and her husband waiting with Nina, she braced herself for the first meeting with the woman in more years than she wanted to count. Looked at her and remembered seeing her just before Bertie's mother died, in the same hospital where Nathan had just been signed off on by his doctor as "strong as an ox."

The poor old uncle croaked out a hello to Cee Cee and Nina gave her a welcoming hug, and as the driver opened the trunk of the limousine and put Nina's bag inside, Uncle Herb gave Nina a little pat and excused himself to go upstairs, and Cee Cee stood face-to-face with Neetie on the curb with the Miami Beach sun beating down on them and she could feel Neetie's dark eyes burning a hole right through her face. Stay even, Cee Cee told herself. In two minutes you and Nina will be out of here. If you can pull this one encounter off like a lady for Nina's sake, you'll have moved up in your own eyes and in hers.

"She was very, very well behaved," Neetie said.

"She always is," Cee Cee said.

"And your father is okay now?" Nice of her.

"Recovering comfortably from the surgery, thanks for asking."

"Well, Herb and I enjoyed her. Unfortunately he's under the weather."

"Sorry to hear it."

The driver closed the trunk. Almost out of here, Cee Cee said to herself, almost the fuck out of here. Neetie pulled a pack of cigarettes out of her purse and lit one. She's nervous, Cee Cee thought. More nervous about this confrontation than I am. Hah! But when Neetie put the hand holding the cigarette up to her face again, and Cee Cee saw the green flash of light on her hand, her heart lurched and all bets were off.

"Neetie, what are you doing wearing that ring?" She couldn't stop the words from tumbling out, and for a second thinking maybe it was Neetie's own ring and that she'd said something dumb.

"Nina gave it to me," Neetie answered with her head up just a little too high so as to look defensive, but she looked worried. Cee Cee glanced over at Nina, who nodded to confirm that what Neetie said was true, but the little girl's face told the whole story.

"What did you say to make her give it to you?" Cee Cee asked, straining to keep her voice under control.

"Nina, what did I say?" Neetie asked shrilly.

"Nothing. I wanted her to have it," Nina said. A lie.

"Why?" Cee Cee demanded.

"Because she doesn't have any memento of her sister."

"No," Cee Cee said, able to imagine the coercing that must have taken place over the last few days. "Neetie, Bertie left that ring to Nina, and I want you to give it back to her."

"You're nuts," Neetie said. "Who in the hell do you think you're talking to? You can't come here and tell me and my flesh and blood what to do about things that don't concern you."

A well-dressed older couple walked out of the front door of the Versailles. Cee Cee spoke quietly but with great clarity. "Neetie, give the kid the ring back right now, because if you don't I promise you I'll cause a scene out here in front of the Versailles that'll make Louis the Fourteenth spin in his grave like a chicken on a spit. I know you conned this child out of something her mother wanted her to have forever and she's so goodhearted she gave it to you. She's a soft touch, which is why she came to see you in the first place, but I can tell you as sure as I'm alive that I'm not so soft and she's not leaving here and I'm not either without her mother's ring. Now hand it over."

There was an expression of hatred on Neetie's face that made Cee Cee's heart race. She could feel her blood moving angrily through her body and she knew she would gladly miss her flight to Los Angeles and the next week's worth of flights if that's what it would take to get the ring back for Nina.

"Very dramatic, Cee Cee," Neetie said, now trying the soft-voice technique herself. "Is that little speech from one of your movies?"

Good shot, you nasty cunt, Cee Cee thought, but what she said a little louder this time was, "You want to see my movies? Tell you what. If you don't give me the ring, I'll get in and drive the limo through the plate-glass window of the building the way I did in the bar scene in *Jilted*." Out of the corner of her eye Cee Cee looked at Nina, who had a tight-lipped look on her face which after their years together Cee Cee knew very well was holding in a smile. "Or I'll stand in the street with a bullhorn the way I did in *The Long Walk* when I played the prison guard. Remember that one, Neetie? Only instead of barking orders I'll tell your nice neighbors that you steal from kids."

Neetie's tan faded and her horrified face was a pasty color of beige now. "You Hollywood trash," she said, "I could have gone to court a hundred times and taken this child away from you and maybe I still will if you don't mind your own business and get your trampy little self out of my —" But before she could finish her sentence, out of the building in a burst of gold lamé and rhinestones came Mrs. Altschuler and Mrs. Haber, the ladies from the pool.

"It's Cee Cee," they both squealed, and they were each carrying writing pads and pens, which they proffered in a request for autographs, and Nina watched as Neetie tried to regain her composure and Cee Cee instantly turned into the charming gracious star she always was for her fans. Fussing over the women as much as they fussed over her.

"Hi, girls," she said. "Is it hot enough for you? Oh, honey, I love your necklace."

"Anita keeps us posted on everything you do," Mrs. Haber said. "We think it's so nice that you and Nina make such an effort to be close to her."

Cee Cee looked into Neetie's black, angry, frustrated-by-the-intrusion eyes, and saw a flash of embarrassment.

"Oh, don't be silly," Cee Cee said, "Neetie is Nina's family, which naturally makes her *my* family. In fact, just as you came out the door, she was about to give Nina a ring that belonged to her sister Rose. Nina's grandmother. Isn't that generous of her?"

"Ooh, let's see. Gorgeous! You're giving *that* to her, Anita?"

As the women waited, Neetie slowly and reluctantly pulled the ring from her finger and placed it into Nina's outstretched hand.

"Thank you, Aunt Neet," Nina said, giving her a little hug.

"Ahhh," Mrs. Altschuler said. "That's adorable."

"Listen," Mrs. Haber said, "my mother, rest her soul, always told me, 'If you don't have your family, who *do* you have?'"

Cee Cee and Nina rode for a long time in the air-conditioned hiss of the limousine, each of them thinking over the last few days, before Nina, who had been looking out the window at the causeway, said quietly, "I thought you told me we should be nice and loving to our families, but you were pretty mean to Neetie."

"You know what?" Cee Cee said. "In her case I'll make an exception."

They were almost at the airport when Cee Cee looked down at the seat and noticed Nina's hand there, realizing for the first time it was actually big enough to wear the emerald ring. Not quite big enough for it to fit on her ring finger, so she had put it on her index finger. Cee Cee placed her hand over Nina's and patted it gently.

For the next few weeks she spoke with Nathan several times a day. He grumbled and railed about everything from the medication and the nurses to the bad reception on his hospital television. One day when she called him the doctor was in the room, and Nathan put him on the phone. "Cee Cee," Doctor Feiffer said, as if he was greeting an old friend, "he's doing so well, I recommended he take a trip out West. Think you can handle that?"

Cee Cee heard Nathan in the background saying something like, "Hey! You're the doctor, for chrissake. Don't *ask* her, tell her." Two weeks later when he arrived in Los Angeles he made it clear, even on the ride from the airport, that he was only staying for a short time because a Harriet Goldstein "from Philly" was already counting the days until his return to Miami Beach because when he did they were probably going to "shack up."

On the first night as he sat at dinner Cee Cee watched him talking with his mouth full and getting so much spaghetti sauce on his face and then his napkin, that when Nina asked to be excused to go to the kitchen to get herself more milk, she gentled the napkin away from him and took it to the kitchen with her to replace it.

"She likes me," Nathan said, looking at the still-swinging door to the kitchen. "And it's a good thing too."

"Why is that?" Cee Cee asked, knowing she was taking the bait.

"Because at this stage of the game, she's my only real chance at being a grandpa."

Cee Cee smiled, then felt a wistful pang. "Yeah, I guess I *am* getting a little past the time when I can give you a grandchild."

"Hey, listen," Nathan said, "on the wall of the occupational therapy room at the convalescent home, they had a sign with a quote from Satchell Paige. A colored baseball player, before your time, a great man. It said 'How old would you be, if you didn't know how old you was?'"

Cee Cee laughed. "So what's the answer for you?" she asked.

"Two months ago, eighty-five. Today, twenty-five. How 'bout you?"

"Some mornings twenty-six, other mornings a hundred and twenty-six."

"So on one of the mornings when you're twenty-six, grab some guy and make a baby," he said, laughing a funny snorting laugh Cee Cee knew she sometimes used herself. "I'm a *modern* guy. A free thinker," he said.

Nina came out of the kitchen with a glass of milk and a fresh white cloth napkin, which she slid onto Nathan's lap with what looked like the expertise of a headwaiter. Nathan smiled a thank-you, then looked at Cee Cee. "See? What'd I tell you?" he asked.

On the weekend he took Nina to Disneyland. It was the first visit for each of them and when they came home at ten at night, sunburned, exhausted, each wearing mouse ears with their names embroidered on the front, and both of them farther off the ground than the half a dozen Mylar helium balloons they were carrying, Cee Cee, who opened the front door to let them in, wasn't sure which of them she envied more.

Every night Nathan would call his girlfriend in Miami Beach and when she answered, Cee Cee could overhear him open the conversation by saying, "Hiya, hot stuff." He had the twinkle of the sheik of Araby every day now, and she felt tied to him, close to him, saw Nina blossom by having his attention, and she felt sad thinking about how overbearing her mother must have been with him to have kept this kind of spirit down.

One night when she got home, Nina and Nathan were throwing a Frisbee back and forth on the beach. It was already dark, so they were playing by the floodlights from the deck of the house. Nathan was showing off and catching the Frisbee behind his back, and Nina was shrieking loudly and diving for the Frisbee onto the sand. Cee Cee just stood on the deck and watched them for a long time before she called out to announce that she was home.

After a few days, Nina was able to tell Cee Cee lots of things she'd discovered about Nathan that Cee Cee had never known or imagined. Things that, when Nina told them to her, made Cee Cee laugh out loud. That Nathan liked his corned beef lean and his women fat. That he did a very funny imitation of a character named Rochester, who he told her used to be on the Jack Benny radio show, and that he loved to sing. Sing! Cee Cee couldn't believe it. The only song she'd ever heard him sing was "The Sheik of Araby."

That night while she brushed Nina's hair, a before-bed custom that had started in Carmel, Nina excitedly told her that she and Nathan had a surprise for her. "Great," Cee Cee said, tugging at a tangle.

"Ouch."

"Sorry."

"And after I get my nightgown on we want you to sit in the living room so we can show it to you. It's a duet, like when I sang 'Ballin' the Jack' with you when I was little, except that this one has a little harmony to it, so sometimes I have to hold my ears so I don't get mixed up and sing his part instead of mine."

"What's the song?" If it's "The Sheik of Araby," I'll kill him, Cee Cee thought.

"You'll see," Nina said, sliding her nightgown on over her head and running down the hall to the guest room to get Nathan.

As Cee Cee sat on the living-room sofa getting ready to be the audience, Nathan came bounding into the living room as excited as a child, followed by Nina who whispered some conspiratorial words into his ear, then hid behind the drapes as Nathan stepped up onto the brick hearth, held his hand up to his face as if he had a microphone, and said, "And now, direct from the Sands Hotel in Las Vegas, Nevada, that famous singing team of Nathan and Ninotchka." Ninotchka was his pet name for Nina.

"No, Nina Barron," came Nina's whispered voice from behind the drapes. Her bare feet were sticking out.

"Excuse me, Nathan Bloom and Nina Barron."

Nina emerged, blushing and all smiles, the braces on her teeth gleaming as they caught the light from a living-room table lamp, her bangs hanging in her eyes, and she looked nervously at Nathan, who gave her a nod, then she began to sing in some barely recognizable minor key, "I really can't stay."

"But, baby, it's cold outside," Nathan sang, and his voice by contrast was nothing short of great. Right on key, belting out the song as if all the world could hear him.

This is hysterical, Cee Cee thought, and she had to bite her lip to keep from laughing out loud.

"I've got to go 'way."

"But, baby, it's cold outside." Nathan was rocking back and forth snapping his fingers as if he was Stubby Kaye in *Guys and Dolls*.

"This evening has been so very nice . . ."

Her father. She had always assumed that her talent had come from Leona, only because she had spent her whole life having no idea who this man was. And he had tried to tell her so long ago that he was the one who carried the musical genes, but Leona had always shut him up.

"My mother will start to worry."

"Been hoping that you'd drop in . . ."

Her father and Nina each had a faraway look in their eyes, as if they weren't a short fat man and an eleven-year-old girl standing in a living room, but two stars, playing to an audience of thousands, except that Nina was holding her fingers in her ears as promised, in order to block out Nathan's big voice.

"Ahh, but it's coooold outside!!!!" When they were finished they took hands and bowed a deep bow they had obviously rehearsed, and Cee Cee stood to give them a big ovation. Then the two of them hurried over to the sofa where she stood and all three of them hugged.

A family hug. Because that's what we are, she thought. A silly little family of three lost souls. And it *was* cold outside.

Nathan's last night in Los Angeles was a night on which Cee Cee had a taping of her show. Nathan and Nina were coming to sit in the front row of the bleachers to watch. The house in Malibu was filled with the scent of Old Spice as Nathan dressed carefully in gray trousers, a light blue shirt, and a madras blazer, and then plastered down the wisps of remaining hair on the top of his head. Later at the studio, after the page led them to their taped-off seats, he lifted the back flaps of the jacket to sit as if he was wearing tails.

After Cee Cee sang her opening number and the audience applauded, while she waited for the next take to be set up, she came down to the bleachers to talk to the studio audience. It was what she did every week, usually asking for questions. Tonight after she sat on the edge of the runway she said, "Ladies and gentlemen, a very special man is sitting out there with you. If it wasn't for this man, I wouldn't be here tonight. He fed me, he clothed me, and I got my singing voice from him. Please welcome someone who has known me for more years than I'll ever admit, my wonderful daddy, Nathan Bloom."

The audience cheered, applauded, whistled, stomped, and craned their necks to see Nathan, who stood to greet their welcome with such aplomb it was as if he'd been rehearsing for this moment all his life. He bowed a little bow, nodding his bald head this way and that, and then waved an open-handed wave after which he blew a kiss. And when he did, both Cee Cee and Nina recognized the gesture. It was the one Cee Cee always made when the show was over and she took her last bow to say goodbye for now to her fans.

Harriet Goldstein

and

Nathan Bloom

are pleased to announce

their marriage

in Miami Beach, Florida

October 1st, 1986

Michael,

Just a note to ask if you ever received any of my earlier notes mentioning how I believe it would mean a lot to Nina to know you, even if it was just for a short visit.

Will you let me know?

Cee Cee

PEOPLE MAGAZINE
December 1986

Old-fashioned variety shows disappeared for good reason. They were dumb. With skits that wouldn't cut it in the high-school play, awkward cross talk, Muzak-like music, and too many costume changes. The production values of one musical number on MTV have made the smoke-filled special effects, or the Vaseline-covered screen which suddenly appears when a singer performs a love song on network television, look downright silly. The current proliferation of talk shows, and the intimate glimpses they offer into the personal lives of stars, make the banal chitchat on variety TV seem archaic.

Somehow, Cee Cee Bloom has kept her own variety show going and in the top ten, in spite of an abundance of the elements mentioned above. Cee Cee is a dinosaur in that she's one of the few existing comediennes who can really belt out a song as well as dance her feet off, but soon, despite her extraordinary gifts and Herculean effort to keep it all afloat, even the invincible Bloom won't be able to keep the dying form from expiring. Like its predecessor and most traceable influence, vaudeville, the variety show is soon to bid us a fond adieu, and in the future our glimpses of it will pass by us only as a part of those "Remember When" collections of the good old days.

Not to worry for Cee Cee Bloom, however. A talent like hers will always find greener and more up-to-date pastures.

LOS ANGELES, CALIFORNIA
August 1990

HAL LOOKED BETTER than Cee Cee had ever seen him as he emerged from the baggage claim area. When he spotted her driver Jake he waved a friendly wave, and when Jake, who had been chatting with an airport security guard, saw Hal walking toward the car, he hurried to relieve him of his luggage.

"Careful," Hal warned, "there are lots of goodies in those bags." When he opened the back door of the car to get in, he was surprised to see Cee Cee waiting for him. "Hey!!!" he shouted, sliding in close to her in the backseat and giving her a big bear hug. "You didn't have to make this trip," he said, but Cee Cee could tell how completely delighted he was that she had.

"Yes I did," she said, "because you're not the only one I'm picking up here." She looked at her watch and then back at Hal. "Zero minus two hours," she said.

"You're not going to fall apart on me are you?" he asked.

"Why would I do that? It's only the biggest, most important day of my life."

The front door of the car opened and Jake stuck his head in. "Think I ought to go up to the gate and see what's happening?" he asked Cee Cee. "According to the monitor, the flight's in."

"Maybe you should," Cee Cee said, and after a word with the airport security guard about not ticketing the VIP car, Jake was gone through the doors into the terminal.

"Do you think it's too late?" Cee Cee asked Hal. "Do you think it still means something?"

"I think it means the world," Hal said as she put her head against his shoulder, "more than anything you've ever done."

The airport doors opened again and a stream of people emerged, and at the end of the stream was Jake, and when Cee Cee saw who he had in tow she sat forward, opened the car door, and with a happy welcoming smile got out of the car, knowing that her appearance was causing its usual excitement, but she didn't care. "Have I got a hug for you," she said, moving forward with tears in her eyes. "Thank you for being here."

Nathan Bloom and Mrs. Nathan Bloom, the former Harriet Goldstein, stood arms-around-one-another as smiling and pudgy as Twee-dle-Dee and Tweedle-Dum. "Please," the little sweet-faced lady said, "are you kidding? For our children we'll go anywhere. After all, now you're *my* daughter too, right?"

"You bet," Cee Cee said, wondering what Leona would have thought of this woman, Cee Cee's stepmother. The idea of Nathan in love was too delicious to believe. And he was. She could tell by the glow on his cheeks.

"Listen, for us it's another honeymoon. From here we go on to San Diego," Nathan said, and Cee Cee recognized that sexy little twinkle in his eyes she had seen there only fleetingly years ago. Jake loaded their bags into the trunk of the limo and Cee Cee made the introductions to Hal.

"Not bad for two old kokkers, right?" Harriet asked Hal as she slid onto one of the rumble seats across from Nathan. "I hate to say it, but the only time I was in a limousine before this was to my late husband's, may he rest in peace, funeral. Pooh, pooh, pooh. So life is full of surprises."

"It sure is," Hal said, sitting close to Cee Cee and patting her on the leg.

Jake got into the driver's seat, pulled the rearview mirror down, and looked at all of them in the backseat.

"All in?" he asked.

"Only one more stop, Jakie," Cee Cee said.

"You got it," Jake told her, and they were on their way.

CABO SAN LUCAS

1987

THE INCIDENT in Cabo San Lucas came right on the heels of Nina's dancing school recital, which was probably what made Cee Cee handle it the way she did. Still, it was inexcusable and it wasn't until she looked back on it that she realized the way she behaved was a page torn from the worst part of her life with Leona. Only this time instead of Leona, it was Cee Cee standing out there during Nina's rehearsal in the auditorium at the Elks Club, mouthing the words of the song and poking her fingers into the corners of her own lips, pushing them up to make a smile so that when Nina glanced out there she would see her and be reminded to smile at the audience. Now *that* was life with Leona to a frigging "T."

As if it was yesterday Cee Cee remembered the way her fat, unhappy mother used to sit in a chair by the wall during all of Cee Cee's sweaty tap and ballet and jazz classes. And while the other mothers went outside to have a cigarette and gossip, Leona would listen to every word the dance teacher said to the kids, and write the names of the steps in the dance routine into a little spiral notebook that she would pull out later at home, so she could drill Cee Cee relentlessly. In fact, all these years later when Cee Cee was rehearsing a tap number for her show, in the back of her head she could still hear Leona's voice calling the steps out to her. *Step shuffle ball change, step shuffle ball change, step brush hop, step brush hop.*

Today she had canceled some meetings after Nina asked her to please come to a rehearsal of the recital because, she confided to Cee Cee, she was afraid at the performance she would be so nervous she might "mess up," and she wanted Cee Cee to see her dance while she was relatively calm. All year long the dance classes had been closed, so Cee Cee had never been able to come and watch, and now when the girls came running out on the stage to the blasting music, what Cee Cee had imagined would be an amateurish exercise looked surprisingly professional. But the most extraordinary surprise of all was the way Nina, ordinarily so low-key in the presentation of herself, now pushed back her shoulders and held her chin high and danced with a confident presence Cee Cee had never seen in her.

The girls were performing to a recording of Irene Cara singing "Fame," and their little voices belted out the lyrics along with the record as they moved across the stage at the Elks Club, as Cee Cee found herself covered with goose bumps while she watched, wondering if it was seeing Nina so transformed or the message of the song that was getting to her.

> I'm gonna live forever
> I'm gonna learn to fly high
> I feel it comin' together
> People will see me and die.

When Nina looked out into the semidarkness at Cee Cee, it was with an expression hungry for approval. Cee Cee knew it instantly and lifted a hand with thumb and forefinger circled as a high sign, the same one Leona had given her at every recital, and when Nina saw the gesture, her pretty little chin rose and her eyes flashed.

> I'm gonna make it to heaven
> Light up the sky like a flame
> I'm gonna live forever
> Baby, remember my name.

The sentiment in those lyrics! How that feeling had burned in Cee Cee every day of her life, stronger than any other need, until it compelled her to spend all of her energy moving toward the single-minded goal of success in her career. The success she now had. Once, years ago, during the long hungry times when she was getting nowhere as a performer, she had walked onto the location of a film on a New York street where they were casting extras.

"Please," she begged the second assistant director, "just let me walk by in a crowd."

"We're not casting uglies today, honey," the guy had said, and turned away to talk to someone else, and the rejection had burned into Cee Cee's chest, but still she pressed him, going after him and tugging on his arm.

"Hey, listen, I'll wear a hat with a veil. Nobody will see what I look like. Please let me get a movie credit on my résumé."

"Get lost," the son-of-a-bitch, rude with his own little piece of power, said without even looking at her.

Stung and hot-faced with rage, Cee Cee stood on that New York street, ringing with unyielding resolve, and just as the director was about to shoot a scene, in fact they were already on a bell and rolling, she shouted at the top of her lungs, "One of these days you assholes are gonna be beggin' *me* for a job." A few people on the set had laughed, and the irate director had yelled, "Cut," and had to get everybody settled down again while two burly guys on a signal from the A.D. picked Cee Cee up by the elbows and walked her a block away.

She had long ago forgotten who that director was and what the picture was they were making on the New York street, but just a few weeks ago a woman who was an extra on Cee Cee's show in the French Café sketch told her she had been in New York working on that shoot and had never forgotten that determined little girl. "I guess," the woman, who was a professional extra, said, "that's the kind of belief you have to have in yourself in order to survive in this fucking business."

And the woman was right. The day after Nina's recital Cee Cee and Nina would fly down to Cabo San Lucas, where Cee Cee was starring in a new picture. It was her first feature film in years. It had taken all those seasons of slaving away on television to become so hot again that the movie studios finally believed in her renewed potential to sell tickets. She was looking forward to it. Martin Kane, the director, was good at getting strong emotional work out of actors, and she knew he would lean on her to get her best. And she'd managed to wangle the job of unit still photographer for her latest flame, Scott Becker, the young, adorable guy she'd met at Goldie Hawn's party.

So he was a few years younger, like seven or eight, maybe nine, but he was a hot little honey, and she needed that now.

Nina's dance teacher was rehearsing the curtain call, and she was having a hard time getting everybody lined up on the stage. The girls fussed and took forever coming from one side of the wings, where they'd been crowded, since the Elks Club wasn't exactly the Hollywood Bowl, waiting for a turn to enter and take an individual bow. Each time the teacher tried to get them out onstage it was an endless struggle with bad timing, giggles, improper spacing, so she'd stop the music and send them off to try their entrances again from the beginning. Cee Cee looked at her watch. It was five o'clock. She was supposed to have a conference call with Martin Kane and the producer of the new film at six. If the rehearsal kept going like this, she'd never make it. Maybe she could help move things along here so they could all go home.

"Excuse me," she said, walking down to the front row of folding chairs and tapping the dance teacher on the shoulder. The teacher turned quickly and Cee Cee could tell by the woman's expression that she was harassed and tense. She now had the entire cast, thirty girls between the ages of ten and fourteen, up on the stage.

"Yes?" she said to Cee Cee.

"Well, I wanted to tell you that I know a little bit about this kind of thing and maybe if I could just explain how we did . . ."

The teacher's look stopped her. She was a long-necked long-waisted, regal-looking woman in her fifties with white hair pulled back in a severe bun. She was wearing a long-sleeved black leotard under a rehearsal skirt, which made her look like one of those modern dancers in an old Jules Feiffer cartoon who leap and dance to poetry.

"Mothers in the back row, or wait in the car, please," she said tense-jawed to Cee Cee.

This woman's got to be kidding, Cee Cee thought. She obviously has no idea who she's talking to. "Hey," she said, "I understand you're under pressure, but I've been in a lot of Broadway musicals. I've worked with every choreographer from Jerome Robbins to Jeffrey Hornaday and I'm telling you if you start with half of the girls on one side and the other half on the other, you're going to move them faster and get the feel of a bigger production number." There, she thought, that ought to do it.

The teacher's face was stone. "I never have them enter from both sides," she said in measured tones.

"Yeah, well maybe not, but if you try it you're gonna see that it takes half the time."

"Will you please sit down?" the teacher said. Obviously she wasn't understanding Cee Cee's point.

"Actually you could have the two groups cross one another. That's how we did it in the revival of *High Button Shoes*."

Miss Olivia snapped her head away from Cee Cee, looked at the girls on the stage, and said loudly to them, "All right, one more time. Clear the stage." Some of the girls straggled slowly in the direction of the wings, a few didn't move. This woman is crazy, Cee Cee thought. Here I am offering her the highest-priced help around for free. About to teach her and the girls Jerome Robbins's choreography, and she's ignoring me? Oh I get it! She probably thinks I'm one of the regular women who come here all the time. Those mothers who have nothing else to do but sit and drive her crazy all year round. She figures I'm one of them. Doesn't know who I am. Of course once I explain, she'll know it's a matter of one professional talking to another.

"Uh . . . Miss Olivia," Cee Cee said, and the teacher turned to her with narrowed eyes. "You realize of course who I —"

But before Cee Cee could tell her exactly which credentials she had that gave her the right to interrupt the rehearsal, the teacher leaned toward her and spoke so close into her face Cee Cee could smell the Dynamint she had in her mouth. "In *this* room," she said, "you are Nina's mother." Without looking, Cee Cee could feel that the girls who had been standing upstage and the ones who had started to walk away were now all in one clump downstage listening to the exchange between the two women.

She could hear the rustling of the net tutus as they brushed against one another and the whirr of the overworked air conditioner while she looked into the huge Keane painting eyes of the stone-faced Miss Olivia and realized there was no getting around the fact that this woman, who had knocked herself out all year to get these girls this far, was ten thousand percent right, and Cee Cee had been a total jackass to intrude.

In fact, not only did she know that, but so did every kid on that stage, including Nina at whom Cee Cee couldn't look, because she was afraid to see one of *those* expressions the kid had been giving her lately, expressions that according to the books were just what to expect from kids her age.

> Children in this stage of their lives crave a lot of attention, but on the other hand they don't want to stand out from the crowd. Nothing is more devastating than to be singled out for punishment or even praise in the classroom, or to be considered different in any way. If mother has the nerve to appear at school, daughter is mortified for days afterwards.

Nina had invited her to the rehearsal, but she hadn't counted on Cee Cee behaving like an egomaniac in front of the entire dancing class. Now Cee Cee felt so dumb she thought that if life was fair, the ceiling would fall in on her head and everyone would feel so sorry for her they'd forget what a schmuck she'd been. And now they all were waiting in this eternity of a moment for her to say something.

"I hear you," she said to the teacher, "and I'm sorry."

"What was that?" Miss Olivia asked, with the clear implication that she wanted Cee Cee to repeat her apology loud enough for the benefit of the girls.

"I said," Cee Cee said, obligingly louder, "I'm sorry, Miss Olivia," and as the rehearsal resumed, she moved to the back row where she sat for a long time trying to calm her feelings of despising herself, and eventually she became so caught up in watching the girls that she forgot all about the conference call she was expecting at home. In fact, by the end of the rehearsal she had to admit grudgingly the finale looked great, and so did every other number in the show.

Nina seemed actually to have talent, and her budding beauty was so mesmerizing that half the battle was won the minute she appeared onstage because you didn't want to look at anyone else. At least Cee Cee didn't. She sat watching her as dopey with admiration as any stage mother alive. So maybe the kid wasn't a fireball, crazed and driven and needy for the audience's love the way Cee Cee had always been, but there was a genuine spark there. Cee Cee wasn't making it up, and it wasn't just because Nina was hers that she thought that either. The kid was really good. Which was why she let what happened in Cabo San Lucas happen, and that was a mistake she wished she could erase.

The night the plane landed bringing the two of them to the Los Cabos location, it was pouring rain. The airplane stood on the field far away from the terminal until finally around the building through the teeming rain came the lights of a car. After the pilot opened an umbrella and walked Cee Cee and Nina down the steps of the studio's private jet and the driver made sure they were safe in the backseat of the limo, Nina settled comfortably into the seat and wanted to know all about the movie Cee Cee was here to make.

Over the last few years she had spent a great deal of time on the set of Cee Cee's television show, but this would be her first time on location for a film, and the idea of spending a few weeks in a pretty place she'd seen in the brochures seemed to please her. They would be staying and shooting at the Palmilla Hotel. As the car moved along on the bumpy dark road toward the hotel, Cee Cee told her the story of the film, which was about a family who was vacationing together as the marriage of the parents was falling apart.

"You mean there're kids in this?" Nina asked.

"Two kids," Cee Cee told her. "Stacy and Sammy are the names of the characters, the daughter and the son. Chelsea Bain plays Stacy. You'll like her. She's an amazing little actress."

In the morning, in the dining room of the hotel, Nina was introduced to dozens of people involved with the production — the hairdresser, the makeup man, the assistant directors — and all of them fussed over her, and then looked at Cee Cee and said things like, "She's so beautiful," as if Nina wasn't even sitting there, and Cee Cee would say, "Thank you," as if she had something to do with it.

When Chelsea Bain and her mother walked into the beam-ceilinged, tile-floored room and Nina spotted her, her heart pounded and she felt a feeling in her throat she didn't want to admit to herself was jealousy. And when the child actress who had obviously been chosen because of her close resemblance to Cee Cee was introduced to Cee Cee and told her, "You're my idol," and Cee Cee answered, "Aren't you a doll!" Nina wanted to leave the table. And Chelsea was from New York, so she even had that little New York toughness in her speech that Cee Cee had. As the two of them talked about the script for the film, Nina definitely felt wounded, left out, more than she ever did when Cee Cee paid attention to other adults.

While Chelsea's mother took a seat at a distant table and Cee Cee moved to another table to talk to the producer, Chelsea remained, looking Nina over, sizing her up, then said, "You're her daughter? Are you kidding? *I* look more like her than you do! Oh, yeah. That's 'cause you're not her *real* daughter. Right?"

Nina didn't answer.

"My mom told me about you and her, and your real mom is dead. Right?"

Nina nodded.

"Tough break," Chelsea said, only it wasn't at all sympathetic, and then she walked away and Nina hated her. And she hated her even more when Cee Cee came back to the table and after ordering breakfast for them in her version of Spanish, which sounded to Nina like Speedy Gonzalez talking to Daffy Duck, she told Nina, with a gesture toward the table where Chelsea and her mother sat, "I saw that kid's screen test. She was so good she jumped right off the screen. Wait till you see her work." She also told Nina for the hundredth time to drink only the bottled water.

The atmosphere on the set was loud and friendly, and Nina couldn't decide which member of the crew was the cutest. All of the men were handsome and flirted with her, and when they were together buzzing around the set, the abundance of maleness made her think of the way she imagined a band of pirates to behave, muscular and sweaty and sexy. But the process of making a movie was so slow and painstaking, that after a few days she realized that watching it was extraordinarily dull.

The amount of time it took so many people to move so many cables so few feet seemed ridiculously long to her, and finally she dropped out and spent most of her time under a beach umbrella near the water reading. At night she would have dinner with Cee Cee and the cast and crew from a big Mexican buffet and watch Scott, the young still photographer, flirt with Cee Cee and Cee Cee flirt back. And she suspected that when she was asleep Cee Cee was probably slipping away to be alone with him.

The tropical muggy evenings after dinner were spent in the large bar off the lobby, overlooking the sea, where the grating sound of the blender mixing the margaritas was a counterpoint to the three-piece combo. One night there was a band in the lounge after dinner, and while everyone from the film sat being cooled by the breeze from the sea, Cee Cee went up on the little bandstand and sang, "Here's That Rainy Day," and "My Funny Valentine" and some other really old songs. And afterward while the crew was cheering and stomping for her singing and Scott handed her a bottle of beer, Nina heard her say to him, "Bet you never even heard of those songs, kid," and he laughed and put his arm around her waist, and when the band played some other moony love song, he tugged Cee Cee by the arm and pulled her out on the dance floor.

"I think if we dance any closer than this we get thrown in a Mexican prison," Nina heard Scott say, and Cee Cee laughed.

"Looks like Cee Cee's mushing out," Nina heard a voice say, and it was Chelsea Bain, whose mom was drinking a margarita at the bar and smoking a cigarette and talking to one of the cameramen. And it was true, Cee Cee was definitely looking with goo-goo eyes at Scott, who Nina had to admit was really cool, but still she felt weird about it. As if she should maybe run over there and stand in front of them so nobody else could see.

"My mom's single too, so I understand," Chelsea told her. "They get horny." Nina felt her own face and body fill with an uncomfortable heat at that thought. "Afterward they always hate themselves, but at the moment if you try and warn them, they make you go to your room and play with your Barbies." Nina knew Cee Cee hadn't had any real boyfriend in a long while, maybe since John Perry left her for the second time. There were dates, guys who came over, took her to a screening at the studio, even some who sent her flowers, but the ones she liked, the men she got all dolled up to be with, talked to in her "other voice" on the phone, were always the ones who didn't seem to stay around too long, and the ones who were crazy about her, like sweet and wonderful Hal Lieberman, she didn't even consider as boy friends.

"Wanna come over to my room?" Chelsea asked. Nina looked into Chelsea's eyes. There was something she had learned to look for in the eyes of kids who made overtures of friendship to her over the last few years, a subtle, indescribable, too-eager look which meant they had no real interest in *her* but were longing somehow to be connected to Cee Cee. At home in Los Angeles it came in the form of invitations to birthday parties of kids she hardly knew, kids who, probably encouraged by their parents, would invite Nina in the hope that Cee

Cee would drive her to the party or pick her up at the party so the parents could meet Cee Cee and tell their friends that they had.

More than once on the playground at school Nina would suddenly spot two or three kids looking her over, saying, "No she's not. Her last name is Barron, not Bloom. Let's ask her. You ask her. Are you Cee Cee Bloom's daughter?" When her answer was affirmative, sometimes they would just giggle and walk away, sometimes they would ask lots of none-of-their-business questions, and sometimes they would be mean and say things about Cee Cee like, "I think she's dopey looking."

In Chelsea Bain's invitation to leave the bar there was none of that stuff going on, so Nina said yes. Leaving unnoticed, they walked silently through the tropical night, up the stone path to the suite Chelsea shared with her mother.

"I'm shooting tomorrow afternoon," Chelsea said, taking a Coke out of the refrigerator in the bar area and pouring it over a glassful of ice. "Want some?"

"No thanks."

"I'm doing my real big scene where I beg my father not to get a divorce. It's the one I did in the test. My acting coach got me ready and we worked real hard on my emotional memory. Know what that means?" Nina didn't. "It's like, when you're acting a scene, you just work off of things that have happened to you in your own real life that are like the ones you're acting. So I'm gonna just use the way I felt when my real mom and dad split up. Only in real life my dad left my mom for this slut named Karly at his office, and in the movie it's different. You get it? I just say the lines and think about the day my dad left us and I get so sad about that, that I cry and it looks like I'm crying over the characters Cee Cee and Michael Nouri play who are splitting up in the movie."

Nina thought emotional memory sounded really interesting, and also that she had such a storehouse of emotional memories herself, she could probably be a really good actress too.

"Want to run lines?" Chelsea asked her.

"Huh?"

"You know. Hold book for me. I'll give you the script and you can follow along with the words while I say them and make sure I have 'em right."

"Okay." Nina was excited. She was being included. Not just watching the way she did at the taping of Cee Cee's show, but now she had a job, running lines with one of the actresses in the movie. Chelsea handed her a dog-eared script and opened it to a page on which the dialogue and action for the character of Stacy had been highlighted in yellow.

"Ready?" she asked Nina.

"Yes," Nina said, feeling very important.

"You give me my cues, read the lines before Stacy's, and I'll give you back my lines. Go."

First came a speech from the character of Mitch, the father. "I guess you know what's going on, don't you, baby?" Nina read, and when she looked up at Chelsea she could see that the girl was throwing herself into the character, right there in the hotel room dressed in her white OP shorts and a peach La Coste shirt — her little eyes filled with tears and her funny Cee Cee–like face seemed to crumble and she said, "Yes, Dad, and I want you to love Mommy, and I want you to come home."

"I do love her, but I can't live with her anymore. There are problems. Insurmountable problems that someday you'll understand . . ."

"Understand. No. I won't ever understand how you can love Linda more than my mom. We were a family, we were like on television, me and you and Mom and Sammy," Chelsea said, and real tears were coming down her face. By the end of the scene she was sobbing so hard with her head in her hands that Nina set the script on the floor and reached out to comfort her, but before she could touch her, Chelsea's head bobbed up and she was wiping away the tears and laughing. "So? Are we talkin' Oscar time here, my friend, or what?" she asked. Nina was dazzled, amazed that someone her own age could be so in control that she could pull those tears out when she needed them and then just make them go away.

The knock on the door was Cee Cee coming to find Nina and take her back to their suite. Her hair was messy and her makeup was smeared and she had a glassy look in her eyes that made Nina think she and Scott had probably been "making out," or maybe even more. Before the two of them left to go to their suite, Chelsea's mom came in and said, "Into bed, girl. Big day tomorrow." Then Cee Cee hugged Chelsea and they talked about how exciting it was that tomorrow was

Chelsea's big shooting day, and about how tough it was to shoot scenes out of sequence, since her emotional scene was being shot long before the introductory scenes, and while they talked their actressy talk, Nina felt out of it again.

That night she couldn't get the scene she and Chelsea had read out of her mind, and the way Chelsea had been able just to call those tears up out of nowhere. "I want you to love Mommy. And I want you to come home." She fell asleep with the scene replaying itself over and over in her head. It was so early in the morning that it was still dark when she heard the phone ring in Cee Cee's room, but it wasn't just a wake-up call. It was a conversation of which Nina could hear bits and pieces, starting with "What? Oh no. What do they *think* it is? I thought we warned her about that."

Nina fell back to sleep, and a few hours later when she woke and dressed and strolled over to the dining room where the film was supposed to be shooting that day, none of the cast and crew were there. "They're in the lobby," one of the waiters told her, so she walked downstairs to the lobby where the company was all spread out, their big thick cables, lights, and cameras everywhere as they shot a scene where Cee Cee and the little boy who played the son have a fight while they're checking into the hotel.

"Quiet down, people, we're rolling."

After the shot Cee Cee noticed Nina sitting just behind the cameras and hurried over with a concerned look on her face. "Do you feel okay?" she asked Nina.

"Fine," Nina said.

Cee Cee looked relieved. "Chelsea was rushed to the hospital early this morning," Cee Cee told her. "Montezuma's revenge. Already. And on top of that she was up all night puking her guts out."

"Thanks for sharing that, Cee," Nina said, feeling a little queasy herself at the image of poor Chelsea about whose poor health she wouldn't have felt nearly as bad before last night as she did now that the girl had become her friend.

"So we're shooting around her for now," Cee Cee told her, while her makeup lady powdered her face with a powder brush. "That's why we're doing these scenes down here so we can put her stuff off for a day or two."

But a long hot day or two of shooting passed and Chelsea, confined to her hotel room, was still so sick she didn't even want to talk to anyone but Nina who came by and taught her some card games and card tricks, and just to make sure Chelsea would stay fresh for the day when she was well enough to go back to work, they ran lines over and over again. Finally, by the fourth day she said she was feeling better and they were scheduling her first shooting day for Thursday, but that morning when she stood up to walk to the bathroom she collapsed to the floor.

She was so depleted and weak there was no chance she was going to be able to get on a set within the next few days and play the demanding emotional part. Everyone on the crew was saying that maybe the worse the child looked, the better it was for the story, but nobody believed that, and Martin, the director, spent a lot of time frantically talking on the only telephone the hotel had, which was at a makeshift desk in a little glass cubicle right near the registration desk. Nina pretended to be playing with the big squawking parrot in the cage nearby just to overhear his conversation.

"The child can barely stand up," she heard him say angrily, as if it was Chelsea's own fault she was sick. "What about the girl who came in second? The pudgy one who dyed her hair red for the audition? Well, see if we can get her *off* the sitcom. Just for ten days of shooting in a major motion picture. Tell the agent her success will be good for the sitcom. I don't give a shit what you tell him. Just get me somebody fast."

That night an ambulance came to the hotel to pick up Chelsea and take her to the studio airplane, which was rushing her back to Los Angeles to see a specialist. Everyone from the film crew was there and they all watched as Cee Cee walked over to the stretcher while they carried Chelsea out, and hugged her frail little body, and then hugged her worried-looking mother who followed behind. Nina walked over too and squeezed Chelsea's hand and got a weak smile in return.

It was just as the ambulance pulled out of sight that Cee Cee stood next to Nina and said softly, so no one else in the crowd could hear, and so softly Nina was certain she had to be hearing wrong, "How would you like to play the part of Stacy?"

"Huh?"

"I mean, I know you don't look like my daughter, but you do look as if you could be Michael Nouri's daughter, and if I coached you I'll bet you could play those scenes. Don't you think? I mean if I hadn't seen you steal the show at the dancing school recital, I wouldn't even mention it, but you did."

Play the part of Stacy in a movie, with Cee Cee? For an instant Nina's heart sank with fear, then the idea started to excite her. The idea was so heady it didn't seem possible. Especially because Cee Cee seemed to really want her to do it. Seemed to think she could handle it. "I mean, what do you think?" Cee Cee asked her, and Nina was embarrassed because she knew her face was flushed with too much need.

"Um . . . I could try," was all she could say, and Cee Cee slapped her a congratulatory slap on the back and said, "Good for you, kiddo. I'll tell Martin."

Late in the day when the sun was starting to set, Cee Cee brought Martin, who smelled of too much cologne, over to the suite where they sat with Nina in the living room going over the part of Stacy scene by scene. Nina felt afraid, but she relaxed a little when she realized how many of the scenes she already knew by heart just from going over them with Chelsea. It felt funny now being the one who was saying the lines while Cee Cee and Martin gave her the cues, encouraging her, praising her, never taking their eyes from her. And all of the line readings were the ones she had heard Chelsea give over and over while Nina was next to her sickbed.

Cee Cee played the scenes with her, treating her the way Nina had always seen her treat the other people she worked with, gently and with a professional respect. And Martin, who had only nodded at Nina perfunctorily at meals and looked at her every time she had been around where they were shooting as if she was a necessary annoyance, was now calling her "darling" and asking her opinion about whether or not she thought a girl her age would say the words as written in the script, or if there was some other way she wanted to say those words that would feel more comfortable to her.

That night Michael Nouri came over to the suite and he and Nina worked on the big crying scene, the one Chelsea was supposed to shoot the morning she got sick. Martin stayed in the room and worked with them, but Cee Cee said she had some things to do and discreetly slipped out. Nina felt a little afraid, but she remembered Chelsea rehearsing the scene and just copied what she had seen her do, and when she finished she actually had a few tears on her face, and both Martin and Michael Nouri said, "Nice work."

"Tomorrow we'll shoot the big scene. After that, it'll be a breeze for you," Martin told her, and he left. For hours Nina laid on the bed in her room, her head spinning wildly. She knew the truth about all this was that they were desperate. That's why they were giving her the chance to play the part. She had seen them running videos of various kids that casting directors back in Los Angeles had rushed to them, and none of the girls they looked at seemed to interest them. From bits and pieces of things she overheard Martin say to other people, it was clear that Cee Cee had somehow convinced him to take a chance on using Nina in the part. "Cee Cee says she'll be able to get her through it," she overheard Martin say to the producer. "I think her genuine closeness with Cee Cee will play through and work for them both in the mother-daughter stuff."

Up until the dance recital and all the fuss that went with it, like the flowers Cee Cee gave her and the raves for her hard work from Miss Olivia and the other parents, Nina had never wanted to be in show business. Thought just the way her mother always did, that it was dumb and brassy and full of showoffs, and the only reason she began taking dancing classes was because it was good for her posture and great exercise. In Sarasota, when she was little, she went to dancing school and the recitals were simply a necessary evil insisted on by the teachers, who wanted to prove to the parents that the money they'd invested in all of those lessons wasn't being wasted, although in most cases it was.

But now Nina was getting the chance that other people only dreamed about and she knew it. "Are we talkin' Oscar time here, my friend, or what?" she remembered Chelsea saying to her that night. Oscar time. What if *she* was nominated for an Oscar? The Oscars were a subject that could send Cee Cee up a wall. They had snubbed her repeatedly in the early part of her career, and she never failed to look like a wounded puppy anytime anyone talked about them. In fact Nina was sure that the biggest attraction to the part of Jeannie, the wife in this film, was that she was such a sympathetic character, Cee Cee had to get a nomination for playing the part.

But what if she didn't and Nina got one for playing Stacy? Or what if they both did? Didn't that happen one year? Two actresses had to share the Oscar? Cee Cee and Nina would share it. Take turns keeping the statue in their rooms at home. "I'd like to thank the cast and crew, and most of all Cee Cee, who always believed in me," she would say. And Cee Cee would say, "And I'd like to thank Nina." By the time Cee Cee got back to the room, it was late and Nina was sound asleep on top of the bed with the script lying open on her chest.

In the early morning the wardrobe lady went through Nina's own clothes and picked a few that would be right for her to wear in the film, and Frank the makeup man gently dabbed some makeup base on her face and a lot of powder and then some blusher and used an eyelash curler which he held very close to her eye while she tried not to blink, and then he closed it lightly and asked her, "Do I have any skin?" and when she told him no he squeezed the eyelash curler hard and curled the lashes of her right eye, then did the same to the lashes of her left. While the hairdresser was brushing her hair, Nina looked in the mirror and saw her very pretty self looking back at her.

Cee Cee flitted in and out of the makeup trailer to see how Nina was, and she seemed much more nervous than Nina had ever seen her when she was going to shoot a scene herself. "You okay?" she kept asking Nina, but not waiting for the answer. Nina was glad her first scenes weren't with Cee Cee so Cee Cee could watch and tell her how good they were. Just as the hairdresser had the last stray hair sprayed down, Martin's cologne wafted into the trailer followed by Martin, who looked a little shaky when he took Nina's hand.

"How do you feel?" he asked her.

"Great," she said. "How do *you* feel?" That made him laugh a funny little laugh and relax a little. People made too much of a big deal about acting. Probably to make themselves think they deserved all the zillions of dollars actors got paid, because this was a snap. All she had to do now was go out there, sit at that table with handsome Michael Nouri, and say the words she knew so well she could say them backwards if she had to, and then the worst part of this would be over. And soon the summer would be over and she could go back to school and wait for the picture to be released. And everyone in her school would come to the premiere and faint at how good she was. In fact, maybe she would get an agent and get jobs in other pictures, or maybe just be in ones that Cee Cee made.

"All right, people, we're going to have a rehearsal," Martin said, and he sat next to Nina in the seat where Michael Nouri would sit when they started shooting, and he took Nina's hand. The crew was moving around quietly, and Martin spoke softly to her in what was nearly a whisper. "Nina, I want you to remember all the things we talked about, how deeply this girl is feeling her pain, how enormous a loss it is for her to have her father leave the family." Then he took a deep breath and moved forward in his chair so he could be closer to her and spoke confidentially, "Now," he said, "you probably remember some of your own losses," then he paused as if he was summoning the next part of his speech and said, "Like when your mother died. I know that you were there with her when she did, so you remember what it felt like to suddenly be left alone in the world, to know that you would never see your mother again. To feel her being ripped away from you, don't you?"

The crew was turning the lights on now, trying different ones and moving them around, and overlaid on the already humid morning, it was blasting hot where Nina sat unable to look at Martin's face, so she stared at the gold chain around his suntanned neck and chest, through his open Hawaiian flowered shirt. She knew that he was trying to get her to feel sad so that she would be able to cry. Trying to get her to use an emotional memory, that was what Chelsea had called it, because his words were cutting into her chest and making her feel sick. Up until this minute she had forgotten about emotional memory, and what she had done at all of the rehearsals was just to imitate the way Chelsea looked when she did it. But Martin was telling her now to use her own life.

"Remember the specifics. How she looked lying in that bed on that last day, feelings of fear and rage and need that you had, because that's what Stacy is feeling when she talks to her father and begs him to keep the family together. He's abandoning them just the way you must have felt your mother was abandoning you, and she's longing for a family the way you probably had your whole life." He was still whispering, and she knew that the usual noisy crew were tiptoeing around at his request so that he could do what he was doing, getting her in the mood, the saddest possible mood so that when he slid out of the seat and Michael Nouri slid into it, she would be hurting and sad.

Martin kept talking to her in his whisper, but she wasn't listening anymore. She was thinking about her mother in that bed in Carmel, how it felt to walk into that room and see her there, the searing pain of her mother's last day on earth when she lay there so gray on the bed, tubes coming from every part of her, not even looking human anymore. And then Martin was no longer next to her, he had slipped away and Michael Nouri was sitting in his place, and Nina's mind was in the sickroom with Bertie, and she sunk low in the chair as there was a bell, a clacker, and from very far away she heard Martin say, "Action!"

"You know what's going on, don't you, baby?" Michael Nouri said to Nina.

My turn. It's my turn, Nina thought, so hot that she was sure her face was sweating, because her upper lip felt wet. Medicine bottles, hypodermic needles, the intravenous being pumped into her mother.

"Yes, Dad, I know, and I want you to love Mommy." There. She said it. But Michael Nouri looked different to her now as she looked into his eyes. Worried or something.

"I do love her, but I can't live with her anymore. There are problems. Insurmountable problems that someday you'll understand when you're old enough to have a relationship of your own and when you're an adult and . . ."

Something was wrong. That wasn't the cue she remembered, and her mind was racing trying to figure out why not. Oh, God. She was supposed to have interrupted him after he said "someday you'll" only she had forgotten, so he went on and now she wasn't sure if she should . . .

"Cut." Mercifully a fan came on and a few of the lights were turned off and Martin was back at the table now, leaning over the two of them whispering directions Nina could barely hear; she knew her crying line was coming up and then she was going to have to use her emotional memory and she was afraid because remembering the details the way Martin wanted her to didn't work for her the way it worked for Chelsea. These were memories she had spent years trying to shake off. Memories she wished he hadn't made her think about again.

"You're doing fine," Martin told her. "We have lots of time, Nina. Don't worry about that. You just concentrate on all the things that are going through your mind and Stacy's mind, and we'll go again." Then he squeezed her hand and backed away into that other land on the far side of the cameras and again the fan went off and the lights were shining so hot and bright on her they made it impossible to see.

"All right, people, we're rolling."

"Action." The way Martin said that word, leaning hard on both syllables, made it almost sound like a sneeze, and for months after this day Nina would hear it over and over in her dreams.

"I guess you know what's going on, don't you, baby?" Michael Nouri said to her again.

"Yes, Dad, and I want you to love Mommy."

"I do love her, but I can't live with her anymore. There are problems. Insurmountable grown-up problems that someday you'll —"

"Understand?" Nina said, dredging into her mind a picture of Bertie lying on her deathbed, trying to remember those mornings when she would open the door to the room where Bertie lay dying and see Cee Cee fat and pale and drained sitting there holding Bertie's lifeless bony hand, trying to put on a face for Nina's benefit that said, "It's okay, honey. You can come in," when she saw Nina at the door. An emotional memory. But it didn't bring tears. It brought a frozen numbness, which was how Nina always reacted to emotion, the way she knew her mother had and her grandmother too, and according to everything she knew about her father, the man had never shed a tear in his life. And there was no way she was going to cry.

Her body felt weak and her mind was a blank, and she had no idea what to do next, so she stood. "I can't," she said standing, and it wasn't a line from the script. "I can't."

"Cut." Fans went on, people started moving around.

"I can't do this."

The hot lights were turned out and Michael Nouri put an arm around Nina, and now she could see beyond the camera where Cee Cee who must have just arrived stood with a look of unmistakable disappointment on her face, hesitant to come forward. But after a moment she did, only Martin was ahead of her, and when he got to Nina he started whispering again, his director's whisper. Telling her that now she was in the exactly right frame of mind. That if she could take the frustration she was feeling about not being able to play the part and bring it to the character, it would take her in exactly the right direction, and as he spoke he tried to gentle her back into the chair, but she wouldn't move.

"Martin," Nina managed to tell him, "I really can't do this. I won't do it. We all made a mistake thinking I could and I'm sorry. No, I can't, and I'm sorry."

Then she walked off the set past him, past Cee Cee, past the handsome crew members, careful not to trip on any of the cables, out of the hotel dining room and back to the suite where she sat in the air-conditioned living room on the sofa, hurting so badly she couldn't move.

I'm gonna make it to heaven
Light up the sky like a flame
I'm gonna live forever
Baby, remember my name.

In a matter of minutes she felt Cee Cee come in and sit on the sofa next to her. "It's my fault," Cee Cee said. "I thought you wanted it, so I pushed it, and I'm sorry. I'm really sorry."

"You told him about me and my mother and what to use, didn't you?" Nina asked.

Cee Cee felt sick with guilt. "Yes, and I hate myself for it."

"It's okay," Nina said her face a mask of pain and shame.

"Martin says he's willing to take the whole day just to work with you on this hard scene, because he thinks you have a nice quality and maybe you could —"

"No. I don't know how. And I don't want to. No," Nina said, never raising her voice.

Cee Cee sat with her for a long time, during which neither of them said anything. The phone rang several times but neither of them moved to answer it. Nina was about to walk into her own room to get away from Cee Cee when Cee Cee said, "Neen, remember that story I've told you a million times about the day your mother and I met? We were kids in Atlantic City and there was a guy there who —"

"I know," Nina said, weary of the story she'd heard a million times. "A guy from Hollywood. And my mother came with you and you auditioned for a part and so did some other girl and the guy picked the other girl to get the part."

"Exactly. But the reason I'm reminding you about it again is that on that day I thought my life was over. Destroyed. But now *I'm* a big star, and nobody's ever heard of that girl. Even though she beat me for the part. So you get my point?"

"No."

"The point is that you're like I was then. Thinking it's over, but you're wrong."

"No, I'm not, Cee Cee," Nina said looking at her. It was an uncomfortable moment because they both knew Cee Cee was vamping, saying anything she could think of to ease her own guilt and to save Nina's shattered ego.

"I'm not like you in that story, and I'm not like you in real life either. The person I'm like in that story is my mother, who sat backstage and watched you out there, and was happy doing that. You see, you may not believe it, Cee Cee, but some people are actually *happy* doing that."

For the next few days Nina rarely left the suite. She was too embarrassed to look at anyone from the cast or crew of the film. When she heard from Cee Cee that Chelsea Bain was back, she thought about going over to the set, but she was afraid that if she went over and watched Chelsea doing the scene she had blown, it would make her feel horrible, so she didn't.

That afternoon when she opened the door in answer to a knock, she didn't bother to ask who it was because she was sure it was room service bringing the club sandwich she had ordered earlier, but it was Chelsea, looking fattened up and healthy though the rosy cheeks were due to Frank the makeup man's blusher.

"Hey, girl," she said. "I finished working for the day. Want to go body surfing?"

Nina felt as if the sun had just come up, even though she was sure Cee Cee had sent Chelsea over to help lure her out of the hotel room. "I just ordered lunch," she said. Now she could see behind Chelsea the room service waiter who was coming up the steps carrying a tray.

"Excuse me," the waiter passing Chelsea asked Nina, "do you want this on the table outside on the terrace?"

"She does," Chelsea said, and she walked ahead of him into the suite and held the door to the terrace for him, then both girls followed him out to the tile patio overlooking the placid aqua sea beyond the pale beige sand beach. After Nina signed the check, the waiter left, and both girls sat, Nina with the large sandwich in front of her.

"C'n I have half?" Chelsea asked her.

"Sure," Nina said, putting one half of the sandwich and half the potato chips, half the cole slaw, and the entire dill pickle on an empty bread dish and pushing the dish toward Chelsea.

"You can have the whole pickle. I hate pickles."

"My mom says after this picture we're probably gonna hafta move to L.A.," Chelsea said, picking up the pickle and biting into it, then wincing a little from the sour taste. "Only I'm scared, because I don't want to leave my friends and my school."

"Oh, don't worry," Nina said, "you can call me and I'll show you around." A warm breeze picked up a paper coaster from the tray and blew it to the tile floor. Nina picked it up and put it on the tray and put her water glass on it. "Oh, and Chels," she said grinning. "This time remember not to drink the water."

Chelsea laughed a blush of a laugh, and the two girls sat back to eat their lunch.

Michael Barron
Barron, Malamud and Stern
1600 Golden Triangle Way
Pittsburgh, Pennsylvania 15213

Michael,

This is letter number I don't know how many, but
the time has come for me to cut the crap and get
directly to the chase. After your daughter was born I
swore to high heaven if you ever tried to see her, I'd
personally take her out of the country and go into hiding forever.

As you know, since Bertie's death I have been her
guardian and since she has come to live with me I have
gotten to know her very well. Now what I feel has
changed. I am writing this to tell you that I will do
whatever it takes to get you to see her even for a day.
Not for me, because as far as I'm concerned my feelings
remain the same, but because this girl who is coming
into her womanhood needs it. She knows you're out
there and I can tell it would help her to see you and to
ask you questions and just look at your face and get
some idea of where she comes from.

I have heard that you're sometimes in Los Angeles
on business, and I am asking if you, on one of those
trips, would spend one or two hours with her. It won't
hurt you and it could change her life.

Please, Michael, please. Meet her. I swear to
God, nobody wants your money, nobody wants to trap you
into anything, all we ask, or I should say I ask because
I would never tell her I am trying for this, so she
won't be disappointed if you should refuse, is for you
to give her a few hours of your time. Michael, this is
just a personal appeal. Not legal or business or anything like that. If you can only find it in your heart.

Cee Cee

MATTHERS, KENDALL AND SIVITZ

Ms. Cecilia Bloom
29 Malibu Colony Road
Malibu, California 90265

Dear Ms. Bloom,

    I am in receipt of your recent letter to Michael
Barron. Please be advised that this office represents
all of Mr. Barron's legal interests, and that in the
future, any questions you have regarding Mr. Barron's
paternal obligations, i.e., child support, should be
addressed to me.

Sincerely,

Ronald J. Sivitz
attorney to Michael Barron

MAUI, HAWAII

1989

A SMALL PLANE flying very low over the water takes you from the Maui airport to the airport at Hana, and the hotel sends what they call a limousine, which is really a van, to pick you up. Cee Cee was so glad to be out of Los Angeles on a vacation with Nina she didn't care what they sent, or even that two other families were being herded into the van behind them. One of the families consisted of an older couple with a daughter in her thirties who had the same sour expression on her face as her mother. The other family was a tanned, blond, robust preppy-looking couple with three towheaded children all under the age of ten.

As the van took off through the rich green tropical foliage, Cee Cee watched Nina watching the family with children wistfully. Their togetherness had a brochure dazzle, and an unreality about it that was made even more pronounced by the fact that all five of them were dressed exactly alike in white shorts, yellow-and-navy-striped rugby shirts, and brown Topsiders. Later at the beach they all wore matching red bathing suits and ran out of the surf holding hands with the water splashing symmetrically on either side of them as if the scene of their emerging from the water had been staged for a commercial.

The hotel suite where Cee Cee and Nina were staying was a two-bedroom cottage overlooking the ocean. It was furnished with tan wicker-and-bamboo chairs and couches and headboards, and bright floral-printed fabrics on the pillows, bleached wood floors, white walls, and a ceiling fan that made clanking noises, but neither Cee Cee or Nina could locate the switch to turn it off. Nina searched around in her suitcase, looking for one of her bathing suits, finally pulling one out and putting it on before she unpacked, which was unusually spontaneous for her. When she walked into the living room of the suite and Cee Cee looked at her, she was startled for a minute by her slim perfect legs and long-waisted body with high perfect round breasts poking their nipples forth under the bright blue nylon of the top, and astonished at how adult she looked.

So many times these days she found herself surprised by Nina's growth. A pair of shoes left in the living room couldn't possibly be little Nina's, she would think in amazement. The shoes were bigger than Cee Cee's now. In fact it was probably Nina's hurtling toward womanhood that prompted Cee Cee to call her producer and insist on a few weeks' vacation so she and Nina could take this trip during a school break. The time was moving fast and this person who was a little girl a minute ago was teetering on the edge of an age when her friends' approval meant everything and, if the profusion of recent expressions of mouth turned down and eyes rolled heavenward meant anything, everything Cee Cee had to offer was worthless.

> Junior high offspring spend a lot of time in their rooms, usually behind closed doors, wondering why their parents don't understand them. And yet they give us little to go on, few chatty intimate revelations which could make the muddle clearer for everyone. When they do talk, it tends to come in an unexpected rush, a sort of hurrying to get everything said before the next secretive mood descends. And even during these moments, few personal thoughts are revealed.

That was true of Nina most of the time now. But occasionally if Cee Cee got her alone someplace where it was just the two of them, it was possible to get her to talk. To break through the wall she had always put up, even as a tiny child, and which adolescence had made more impenetrable.

Once over a dinner on trays in Cee Cee's room in the Malibu house, the two of them gabbed while they ate and watched the sunset, and when the room became dark and they were deep in conversation, neither of them moved to turn on a light, as if the cover of the falling night was just what they needed to give them each license to tell the other what she felt. It was after Cee Cee had done some reminiscing about Bertie that Nina told her, "I'm starting to get to the point where I don't even remember my mother. Sometimes I try but nothing comes. Just a vague picture of a lady with pretty hair who was always hovering over me."

"Really?" Cee Cee asked, shaking her head in disbelief, as feelings of guilt and inadequacy rose in her chest. She had been sure that her efforts over the years to tell Nina stories about her mother and to have photos of Bert around were enough to keep the memories alive, and if that hadn't worked then she hadn't done her job or kept her promise. "I can't *believe* you don't remember. It hasn't been that long."

"Maybe for *you* it seems as if it hasn't. But six years for me is a big part of my life."

"Do you want to look at some old movies of her? I had all her eight-millimeter movies of the two of you when you were a baby transferred to tape. Of course some of them are nearly impossible to watch because *I* was the one who shot them and believe me —"

"No," Nina said, and it was unequivocal. "It doesn't matter."

"Of course it matters."

"Why should I set up a situation that makes me feel sad? To look at a picture of someone I'll never be able to see or talk to or be with again?"

"So you can get who she was, and know where you come from."

Nina shrugged. "If I wanted to know more about that I would have gone looking for my dad, who's alive. But I don't care. Life goes on. I'm me. Knowing why doesn't change that."

"You really don't ever want to meet your father?" Cee Cee asked, worried now because she had written many letters to Michael trying to convince him to see Nina, thinking it was big of her to be right out of the King Solomon story, the one who really loves the child is willing to share her and all that kind of bullshit. Michael's response had come from a lawyer telling Cee Cee to fuck off. But somehow Cee Cee still harbored the hope that he would change his mind. Prayed secretly that somewhere along the line he would get a pang of conscience and want to know what his daughter had become.

"No. I really don't care," Nina said, running her finger around the rim of an empty glass on her tray.

If the father never comes to see the children and they ask you why, I advocate that you tell the truth. If you dream up some cover story for him and the children find out later that you have lied, you will have destroyed your credibility with them.

After Cee Cee had found that advice in one of her books years ago, any time Michael's name came up, she called on the speech she'd practiced in her head about him. *You're a fabulous girl. But your father's screwed up. So badly he can't let himself see you. The poor guy doesn't know what he's missing.* By now she had said those things to Nina many times, and the response was always a kind of absent "uh-huh," which made Cee Cee back off, thinking the "uh-huh" meant the subject was too painful. Now Nina was telling her it was genuine lack of interest. Cee Cee wasn't sure she believed her, but she was surprised at the enormous relief she felt hearing it, because in spite of her efforts to reach out to Michael, the fear that sometimes woke her at four in the morning and other times kept her from falling asleep to begin with was that some day he would show up at her door, push past her, and before she could get to the stairs he'd be on his way out of the house arm in arm with a willing Nina, leaving Cee Cee to that lonely abyss she had called a life before Nina was in it.

"There are a few beaches at this place," Nina said reading from a pamphlet on the coffee table. "One of them is a few blocks down, and the closest one, the Red Sand Beach, is just on the other side of that cliff," she said, pointing out the window.

"Cliff?" Cee Cee said. "That's a word I usually put in the same column as rope-tow and hang-glider. The heading on the column is 'Things to Stay Away From.'" Nina, who knew enough about Cee Cee by now to ignore her protests, handed her her tennis shoes, slipped a pair of rubber thongs on her own feet, and they were out the door to the Red Sand Beach. Over the path past a few other bungalows like theirs, to the cliff above the cove.

Nina walked in front down the steep path, reaching back to hold Cee Cee's hand, and Cee Cee, who managed even with her rubber-soled shoes to slip twice, crept along trying to keep her eyes closed so she didn't have to look over the steep drop at the crashing surf on her right, letting Nina's hand guide her until they reached the bottom and stood on the Red Sand Beach.

The sand was a burnt rust color, and after Nina spread her towel out, she sat on it and opened a bottle of Hawaiian Tropic oil, which smelled so powerfully of coconut and pineapple it made Cee Cee's stomach rumble, while she squirted her own white number-fifteen sun protection cream on to her hand and spread it everywhere on herself, then lay back on the big white towel. She loved the sun, even though she'd read all the articles that said it was dangerous and aging, but she didn't care. With a sigh of satisfaction over her wise choice to take a vacation, she stretched out on her back and welcomed the rays of heat, grinning as if the warmth was from the heated body of a lover moving on top of her.

Nina stayed arched up on her elbows watching the waves, then looking at the clusters of people gathered in various spots on the beach. Far off in a cove she could see a tan, lean couple wearing very tiny bathing suits and oiling one another's bodies, and her eyes lingered on them for a long curious time, then moved to the young family from the airport van having a picnic lunch, then to four ladies who had big bellies and varying shades of frizzy hair and who sat on a blanket playing a four-handed game of cards.

"I'm going in the water," Nina said after a while to Cee Cee's inert body, then stood, brushed some sand from her legs, and ran down to the shore, her long curly hair flying behind her.

Cee Cee dozed and woke every few minutes to look out at the water to be sure she could spot Nina bobbing among the waves. Nina was swimming vigorously with a powerful stroke Cee Cee had seen her use in the pool at home, and confident that all was well, she was about to turn on her stomach again when she caught a glimpse of the family who was now coming down the path to the beach.

What must have stopped her eye was the resemblance the woman had to Bertie, something about her that reminded Cee Cee of her instantly. Not feature for feature, in fact the woman was a blond and Bertie's hair had been a chestnut brown, but she definitely had Bertie's carriage, her style. In the last few years Cee Cee's nearsightedness had worsened decidedly so she could never really trust what she saw from a distance, but this woman really was a Bertie-type, holding on to her little girl's hand in the same no-nonsense grip Cee Cee remembered Bertie using with Nina.

Nina was still stroking away in the water, splashing and jumping

up out of the waves every now and then as sleekly as a dolphin. Cee
Cee wondered if when Nina saw the woman who looked like Bertie,
it would evoke the memories she said she no longer had. Behind the
woman trotted a little boy who was whining about something as they
passed and behind the boy came a thick-waisted husband who wore
mirrored sunglasses and a baseball cap with the letter "P" on it. The
father was reprimanding the boy as they passed, and Cee Cee caught
the words "*I* decide what this family is doing and not you, and if you
don't get that . . ."

She turned on her stomach now and after a few minutes fell into a
sweet warm sleep, which was interrupted by the drops of cold water
falling all over her from Nina, who was shaking herself like a dog to
dry off, and laughing. "The waves are awesome," she said when she
sat, the water beading on her oiled body. "You should go in." She had
brought *A Tale of Two Cities* with her because she was reading it for
school. After she dried her hands, she opened the book to the page
she had turned down on the flight to Maui from Los Angeles. For a
while she read quietly to herself, and when she looked up, something
she saw startled her. "Oh, my God," she said with such drama in her
voice that Cee Cee, who had been trying to drift back to sleep, opened
her eyes thinking Nina must have spotted the woman who looked like
Bertie.

But that wasn't where she was looking at all. Her eyes were wide
at the sight of a long-haired bony-looking woman a few yards away
from them who had removed her muumuu and was jaybird naked
underneath it, and now was unselfconsciously spreading her blanket
on the beach. Next to her, holding a baby, was her muscular, golden-
brown husband, who was also stark naked. Cee Cee noticed now that
the couple who had been oiling one another down the beach had both
removed their suits too. Nina giggled. "Oh my God," she said again,
with an openmouthed, outraged grin.

"They didn't mention this in the brochure," Cee Cee said, as the
naked man handed the woman the baby, then took off in a run down
the beach to the water.

"Or *you* would have been here sooner," Nina said with the perfect
timing of a girl who had spent the last six years of her life listening to
jokes being delivered by the best comics in the business. Then she
stood. "Well . . . I'm going up to the room," she said.

"Is this making you uncomfortable, honey?" Cee Cee asked, looking up at her seriously and shielding her own eyes, which even behind her dark glasses felt scorched by the blazing sun.

"Oh no," Nina said with a wave of dismissal. "Does it bother you?"

"I don't even notice it," Cee Cee said.

Nina slid a T-shirt on over her still-wet suit. "I'm just running up to get myself a Coke. What can I get you?"

"How 'bout a penis colada?" Cee Cee said, heard herself, and let out a burst of laughter, and Nina looked at her the same way Bertie used to when she said something funny but too outrageous to laugh at, without first giving her a sideways glance of disapproval. Then she broke up, laughing so hard too that she had to sit back down on the towel for a minute to recover, and Cee Cee laughed to see her reaction, and their laughter continued to set one another off until Cee Cee said, "And hold the colada," and Nina, still giggling, was off up the hill to the room.

Cee Cee sat up, squeezed the suntan lotion bottle, and felt the hot cream squirt into her hand, then spread another coat of cream all over herself and decided that maybe she should at least dip a toe or two in the water. She was, after all, in Hawaii, and the water wouldn't be like the freeze-your-toes-off water in Malibu. So she stood and moved down toward the shore, passing the naked woman who was now nursing the baby at her breast, and the four fat card-playing women, two of whom reminded her of the De John Sisters, an act she'd worked with in the Catskills. "Thank God *they're* not naked," she mused.

In spite of the layers of protective lotion, her face was stinging from the heat, with the cream feeling as if it was bubbling. I should have worn a hat, she thought, as she passed the blanket of the family with the wife who looked like Bertie. What reminded her of the hat was seeing the father remove the baseball hat with the "P" on it, revealing his partly bald head with gray and brown hair surrounding it like a fuzzy cloud, and this time she heard him say to his son, who was whimpering softly, "You keep whining, pal, and you'll spend the rest of the day in the room without food."

God, she hated anyone who could talk to a poor child that way. With a stony, unsympathetic delivery that was so unfeeling it reminded her of someone in her past for whom she'd felt this same kind of heart-tearing anger, but she couldn't think who. And when she realized, she stopped right there on the sand that was burning her feet, and standing on that fiery-hot beach where there was not even a whisper of a breeze, she was covered with goose bumps because she knew now the "P" on the cap stood for Pirates. Pittsburgh Pirates, and the balding man whose second wife looked ironically like Bertie was Michael Barron. Nina's father, whom the child had never seen.

It had been years since Cee Cee had seen him, but there was no mistaking him. She turned to face the ocean, trying to collect herself, feeling simultaneously sickened and thrilled. She peeked once back over her shoulder at Michael and his second family, hoping none of them would look up and catch her staring. The baldness that had been promised even by the time Michael was in his early twenties had arrived. In fact, Cee Cee watched him pour some Coppertone into his hand and rub it into his bare scalp. When his little girl picked up his baseball hat and put it on her own head, he grabbed it away and put it back on himself. That's him all right, Cee Cee thought. Still Mister Nice Guy.

When the wife looked right at her, Cee Cee turned quickly and waded into the water, which for the first few minutes felt icy cold on her feet as she walked farther in, trying to decide what to do. Well, how about that? It looked as if Michael was married and had two kids. Jesus. No one ever told her that, or told Nina. I must finally have grown up, Cee Cee thought. Because the old me would have reeled around the minute I realized it was him, run over, grabbed the son-of-a-bitch by the face and shrieked into it, "How can a man abandon a beautiful child and never have the guts to look her in the face and tell her why?" But now I'm acting like a big girl, weighing my choices. The grown-up Cee Cee Bloom is actually giving it thought. Oh God, stop me from going over and kicking the stinking little slimy bastard right in the balls.

Thank God he didn't recognize me, she thought, but that can't last. Everywhere she went, once people realized she was there they ran up and asked for autographs, surrounded her, spread the word. And this was a small hotel; soon the news would be around that she was there, and the people who were her fans would be looking for her in the lobby, in the gift shop, or out here on the beach. Now the water was up to her knees and she tried to tell herself to be calm. To get clear-headed about what to do. Soon the water was up to her waist and her shoulders were sizzling from the sun reflecting off the water as she watched Michael-that-asshole-Barron sitting in the sand still griping at his poor children, while their mother spread oil on their little bodies.

Cee Cee stood feeling the waves push against her back, watching the members of the Barron family, their oiling tasks complete, lying down across their blanket like a line of gingerbread cookies ready to bake. When they seemed to be at rest, she waded slowly out of the water up onto the beach and then close to their blanket, where she stopped quietly and looked at their closed-eyed faces as they sunbathed.

The wife was sweet-looking and pretty with that same Audrey Hepburn elegance for which Michael clearly had a taste, but at closer range she was not as pretty as Bertie had been. The tiny girl looked alarmingly the way Nina had when she was that age. The boy was on his stomach so Cee Cee couldn't see what he looked like, and Michael, you dirty dog, Cee Cee thought, when she looked down at his wedding band. Filigreed gold, it was the one Bertie had given him. The cheap schmuck.

When she noticed that the little girl's eyes were open and looking at her curiously, Cee Cee turned and walked back to her towel. From a distance she glanced over at them a few times, unsure how she was going to handle their horribly coincidental presence here with Nina, feeling relieved that the girl was taking so long back at the cottage. But when nearly an hour had passed and she wasn't back and the Barron family was hitting a beach ball back and forth, Cee Cee gathered up her towel and Nina's, and the sunscreen and Nina's book, and navigated up the narrow hillside path as though there was no frightening drop-off next to it at all. A mission, she thought as she got to the top, realizing she'd been so afraid of the same walk earlier. That's me. Not much on the everyday stuff, but when there's a mission, I put my boots on and jump into the trenches.

In the cool living room of the cottage Nina was lying on the sofa reading a copy of *Vogue* Cee Cee had bought at the Los Angeles airport. "Oh, hi," she said, without looking at Cee Cee. "I felt nauseated from the sun so I figured I'd stay in here for a while."

" 'T'sokay," Cee Cee said, wondering if she could make up some kind of excuse for them to have to check out of the hotel. She could call Larry Gold and have him call her back when she knew Nina would answer. He could say they had to be back in L.A. in a hurry. Or she could tell Nina the truth. Oh, Nina, there's something I think you should know. The little jerk in the baseball hat is your father. And the "P" stands for prick. No. She'd say, By a very odd coincidence your father happens to be at this hotel. It would give Nina the choice to either watch him from far away or approach him. But how could she do that to Nina? Wasn't it too heavy a responsibility for a child suddenly to come across her father and his new family at a resort and have to figure out how to behave?

"Want lunch?" Cee Cee asked.

"Okay."

The rich green odor of the tropical growth all around the hotel dining room drifted gently in through the open doors as Cee Cee and Nina followed the muumuu-clad hostess to a table in the front of the room where they could get the best view of the panorama of the lawn and the beach and the sea. Cee Cee wore a big straw hat pulled down over her ears and large sunglasses covering the rest of her face and she was relieved that her disguise, which usually didn't fool anyone, seemed to be working. A quick scan of the restaurant told her the Barron family wasn't around, and she thought with a sad laugh to herself that maybe Michael had punished all of them and banished the entire family to the hotel room without food. The schmuck.

Nina looked over the menu, then out at the view, and Cee Cee saw a calm on her face she had rarely seen there at home. Certainly not recently.

"This place is great," Nina said. "So peaceful."

You should only know, Cee Cee thought, as if Michael Barron hadn't done enough damage to the life of this child, now he was here to ruin her vacation, and Cee Cee couldn't get rid of that clutching feeling in her chest of impending doom. Nina knew what Michael looked like, or at least what he used to look like, from old photographs of his wedding to Bertie, snapshots and films of trips Bertie and Michael had taken together. She hadn't looked at them in years and Michael looked different now, older and chubbier, but there might be a chance she could recognize him. Instinct counted for a lot, and Nina was a sensitive girl.

"I'm going to sign up for a massage later," Cee Cee said. "You interested in having one?"

"No way," Nina answered and Cee Cee realized by the slight blush accompanying the reply that the intimacy and sensuality of a massage was probably too much for a girl her age to handle. She continued nervously to watch the door to the dining room, thinking how ironic it was that she had brought Nina there so that the two of them could have a rest, and now she would spend their vacation feeling panicky and afraid. That was no good, she thought, knowing she would have to do something. Say something.

Nina ordered a hamburger and Cee Cee ordered the grilled mahi-mahi and passed the time waiting for their lunch to arrive with small talk about the naked people on the beach and the beauty of the hotel. Just as the waitress emerged from the kitchen carrying the tray with their lunch, Cee Cee's heart sank when she spotted the Barrons entering the dining room. Michael was wearing a colorful Hawaiian shirt, and a Panama hat with a black band. The children came next, more quiet and reserved than children should be, and the elegant wife, cool in white Bermuda shorts and a white blouse, was last.

"Booster seats," Cee Cee overheard Michael's wife say, and her stomach lurched when she saw Nina look over at the four of them being seated. But it was a brief glance with no significance, after which she dug immediately into her lunch, chattering about a bathing suit she'd seen in the hotel shop, and Cee Cee found herself jumping in and yakking inanely about clothes too, hoping to hold Nina's interest so she wouldn't look back at the table where the Barrons were seated.

"No coffee." Cee Cee waved off the busboy and signed the check immediately. Then instead of exiting the restaurant the way they came in, which would have taken them by Michael's table, Cee Cee steered Nina out onto the front terrace and onto the flower-filled hotel grounds for a walk. The early afternoon heat was thick and heavy and Cee Cee wished she had some idea, any idea, about how to handle this. Maybe it would all go away. Maybe Michael and his family would check out after lunch and Nina would never have to know they were there.

Back at the bungalow, Nina sat on the deck outside reading *A Tale of Two Cities*, and eventually she drifted off to sleep. When she had been asleep for a long time, Cee Cee went inside to her room and called Hal in New York.

"Truth is stranger than fiction," she said after telling him the story.

"Pack up immediately and go to another island," he said.

"And what do I tell Nina about why we're leaving?"

"Further adventure. I don't know. But you can't confront the guy. He obviously doesn't want them to know about her, and vice versa. This is one of those situations if you saw it in a movie you'd say, 'Oh yeah, sure. In the whole world these people end up in the same hotel?' I'd get out of there, Cee. Especially since she's already told you she doesn't want to see him. Pack up and hit the road."

"You're right. I'll call the Mauna Kea Hotel or the Kahala Hilton. We'll move. I'll tell her we're island-hopping."

"There you go," he said. "And, Cee, don't get too much sun. It's bad for you. Makes you think you're seeing people out of your past."

"Harold," she said softly because she thought she might have heard Nina stirring on the lounge outside, "isn't this too fucking weird? I'm such a nonviolent type. I can't even swat a fly. But I tell you as sure as I'm sitting here in this overpriced room, I could cheerfully put my hands around that weasel's neck and choke."

"Don't do it. Remember what happened to Claudine Longet?"

"What *did* happen to Claudine Longet?"

"I rest my case. On the other hand, everyone remembers Gandhi. Try being like him."

"Okay," Cee Cee said, "I'll skip dinner."

When she emerged from her room Nina was still asleep on the deck, so Cee Cee slipped into a muumuu and thongs and wrote her a note on a piece of hotel stationery.

> *WENT FOR MY MASSAGE*
> *BE BACK SOON.*   C.

She listened to the sound of her thongs as they flip-flopped across the gravel path toward the main hotel building, thinking how good it was going to feel to have the strong hands of a masseuse kneading her muscles. Sometimes in the past when the educated fingers of a masseuse pushed on just the right painfully knotted places in her shoulders and back and thighs, the release of tension was so powerful it could make her cry.

It was dark by the time she arrived at the lobby, and on bamboo based tables, fat white candles flickered inside of thick glass hurricane lamps, and people in colorful tropical clothes were meeting to go into the dining room.

A pretty oriental girl in a white coat approached and asked "Bloom?" when she saw Cee Cee at the front desk, and Cee Cee allowed herself to be led down a long hallway adjacent to the lobby, into a quiet, dimly lit eucalyptus-scented room with only a massage table and a hook on the wall for her clothes. After the masseuse discreetly slipped out of the room to give her the privacy to undress, Cee Cee removed her thongs, her clothes, and her watch, climbed on to the table and put her face into the hole of the face rest and was about to let herself relax when she heard Michael Barron's voice.

He was just outside the door of the room, and Cee Cee sat up alert, listening carefully, hoping to hear him better. He was talking loudly with one of the masseuses, and it sounded from what he was saying that he was just finished having a massage himself, and was signing the tab. Cee Cee grabbed the towel from under her and wrapped it around herself. The timing was perfect. He was alone, and so was she. She could go out there now to talk to him and not worry about his wife's hearing her, or Nina's knowing about it. Tell him she was here with his daughter and see how he handled it. Her heart felt as if someone had reached inside her chest and was squeezing it. This was the fight or flight moment and in an instant she would have to seize it, or let the opportunity of a lifetime pass her by.

Holding her towel together tightly at the top, she kicked the shuttered door open and stood face to face for the first time in many long years with Michael Barron, certain he was going to gasp with surprise when he saw her, but instead he smiled as if he'd been expecting her.

"Hello, Cecilia," he said. "I thought that was you on the beach today. And I've got to tell you, I noticed you've put on quite a bit of weight."

If her rage hadn't made her speechless, just seeing him this close would have. He was such a colossal asshole, he had to open with an insult. Collecting herself as best she could she said, "Michael, I'm here with —"

But before she could finish the sentence, he put his hand on her arm, the hand wearing Bertie's ring, and she could smell that same disgusting cologne she remembered him wearing. Royal Lyme or something like that, and her worst memory of him rushed into her mind. That night at the Kahala Hilton in 1967 when her husband was sleeping in his own hotel room and Bertie was in the next room sleeping and he'd put the full court press on Cee Cee, trying to get into her pants.

"I've wanted to fuck you since I saw you," he had said. "And you've wanted it, too, so what are we waiting for?" The sick slime.

"This was a bad coincidence," he said to her softly and calmly, as if it was cocktail party chitchat, "because Helen and the kids don't know a thing. But the good news is that *we've* been here for a week, so we're on our way home in the morning."

"No, Michael," Cee Cee said, trying to sound menacing, but having a hard time feeling as if she could intimidate anyone as she stood there wrapped in a towel. "It was not a bad coincidence, it was a good coincidence because I'm going to tell Nina you're here and let her have the chance to sit down with you in my suite, or in the location of your choice, and take one half hour to see your face."

"Not a chance," he said.

"Michael, you're the lowest, sickest, worst piece of garbage in this world," Cee Cee said, knowing this wasn't the smoothest way to handle the situation and feeling the pressure of tears against the inside of her eyes, but willing them to stay in with everything she had. "Unless you make some kind of peace with this girl."

"Don't fight me, Cee Cee," he said in a confidential voice. "I can have her taken away from you. I can call up shit from your past you can't even remember. You did a lot of drugs in your day, and fucked an awful lot of men. The court would probably want to know about that. Not to mention that 'family entertainment' company that puts out your movies. So you just go back to your room and order room service for you and Nina, and just for old times' sake you can put it on my tab. By tomorrow I'll be gone and you can pretend you never saw me. So come on now, do what I say."

"Don't threaten me," she said, hearing her voice sound shaky and childlike. "I'm not afraid of my past. You tell me you'll give this child one half hour. Tell me yes and I'll leave you alone for the rest of all of our lives."

Michael's jaw was set and he actually seemed to be considering doing what Cee Cee asked, and Cee Cee, who knew this toughness she was putting on was the biggest bluff of her life, held her breath while he did. Please, she thought, make him agree to this and you don't ever have to answer another one of my prayers.

"In the morning," he said. "I'll meet her down in the social hall on the far side of the pool. Early, say seven thirty. Tell her I'll meet her there for half an hour. We can talk there and then I'm leaving. If she doesn't want to come, I'll just stay there for fifteen minutes or so and if she doesn't show up, I'll leave."

Cee Cee felt a rush of triumph, and heroism on top of it for finally making this evil snake succumb and agree to see his child at long last. It was so heady, for a moment she even felt grateful to the little piece of pond scum.

"Oh, bless you, Michael," she said. "Thank you for doing this. You won't regret it. I promise you this girl is so special, and so good, and maybe someday you can find it in your heart to tell your family and get them to know her because she is such a joy." And while she rambled she already knew this was a mistake, but if it wasn't, and it could create some kind of a positive relationship between Nina and her father, it was worth it. After Michael turned and left, his Royal Lyme still in the air where Cee Cee stood, she moved, exhausted, into the massage room and lay on the table planning what she would say to Nina.

"Nina, the strangest thing has happened. Today when we were on the beach I saw a man who looked very familiar to me and I realized after I looked closely that it was your father."

"What?"

"He's here. Michael Barron is in this hotel with his family. A wife and two children, and I confronted him. He told me that they don't know about you, and I asked if he would see and talk to you alone, and that I would ask you if under the circumstances you wanted to talk to him."

"And what did he say?" Nina's eyes were defensive and her posture was stiff as she waited for the answer.

"He said he would. He's checking out tomorrow but told me that he'd meet you down at the rec room near the pool early in the morning. At seven thirty. He said if you weren't there in about fifteen minutes he would leave. That's how he would know that I asked you and you said no."

"Two kids," she said with no intonation at all. "How old are they?"

"Maybe six and four."

She sighed and looked down, clearly hurting, and instantly Cee Cee was awash with regret. Hal was right, why hadn't she left it alone? Packed Nina up and run away from this place instead of dragging her through the agony of this meeting. What in the hell would she get out of it anyway? Probably she would say no, now. Tell Cee Cee to forget it, sleep late in the morning, and let the son-of-a-bitch go back to Pittsburgh without seeing her. But then there was something in her eyes. A flicker of hope when she said, "I'll do it," looking at Cee Cee. "Did you bring a travel clock? I'll set it for five so I can have some time to work on my hair."

They played Scrabble and had a room service dinner and though each of them yawned sleepily before they parted to go to her bedroom, Cee Cee didn't sleep at all and she could hear Nina moving around all night too, knowing the girl must simultaneously be looking forward to and dreading the dawn. Finally Cee Cee must have drifted off, because before it was daylight she sensed someone in the room and looked up to see Nina, an apparition at the foot of her bed. She looked as if she had spent the entire night working on her hairstyle. It was waved perfectly and she wore light blusher on her cheeks and a new outfit of silk turquoise shorts and a camp shirt, and she looked as elegant to Cee Cee as if she'd just stepped out of the pages of *Town & Country* magazine.

"I'm going down there," she said. "See you when it's over."

"It's only six forty-five," Cee Cee said, her voice husky with sleep as she looked at the digital clock on the dresser.

"I know. I want to just sit there for a while and think about things."

"Okay, honey," Cee Cee said, and watched her go with her own heart so fearful it pinned her to the bed, where she lay for a long time watching the numbers on the digital clock, watching it minute by minute until it became seven thirty, trying to imagine how the meeting between them was going. What Michael was saying to Nina, and how Nina was feeling, certain that Michael couldn't be anything but smitten with her and her extraordinary beauty. At eight o'clock she got out of bed and took a shower, shampooing her hair with the creamy coconut-smelling shampoo the hotel placed there. And at eight thirty-five, she was glad Nina wasn't back yet, assumed it was a good sign that she wasn't rushing back in tears. Decided that maybe it meant they had really gotten into it, talked about the past, maybe even planned to see one another again.

At eight fifty she slipped into shorts and a T-shirt and some thongs, then put on a big hat and dark glasses and decided to stroll down toward the social hall and tiptoe by to see if she could see any sign of them. A brown-skinned beachboy nodded to her as she passed the pool and made her way across a large grassy area leading to the rec room. Probably Nina and Michael weren't there anymore. Maybe Michael had decided the timing was perfect and took her to the dining room to have breakfast with his family. Right. The rec room was empty, and a hopeful Cee Cee turned and headed back toward the dining room, but before she got to the top of the hill she spotted Nina, sitting tailor-fashion on a chaise lounge she had moved away from the pool area, under a tree to face the ocean.

Cee Cee hurried to the spot. "Neen?" she said as she approached.

"Hello, Cee Cee," the girl said, looking up at her with vacant eyes. The look from Nina stopped Cee Cee from saying anything back; something had gone wrong. Very wrong. She stood there silently as a morning breeze blew the buttery odor of macadamia nut pancakes from the dining room past her, making her feel suddenly ravenous with hunger. "He didn't show," Nina told her, looking back at the ocean.

He didn't show. Cee Cee sat on the grass next to the lounge chair and put her hand on the girl's arm, and they stayed there watching the surf crash on the rocks below, deciding how to spend the second day of their vacation.

HOLLYWOOD
REPORTER

CEE CEE BLOOM
CALLS IT QUITS

Cee Cee Bloom will not be back as star of her network TV series next season, choosing to exit after seven years of her variety skein. Bloom's decision was announced by her agent, Larry Gold of the William Morris Agency. The network has asked her to reconsider but she has remained firm.

Bloom explained that after the demands of six years and one hundred fifty-six shows, she wanted to be free for a while from the demands of a weekly show.

She is now in discussions with Hemisphere Studios. The final episode of *The Cee Cee Bloom Show* will air May 16.

BLOOM INKS FEATURE FILM PACT

Cee Cee Bloom's "Bloom Off the Rose" Productions has signed an open-ended development deal with Hemisphere Studios. Bloom will both star in and produce feature film projects developed by her company.

NEWPORT BEACH, CALIFORNIA

February 1990

SOMETIMES Cee Cee felt like the guy she used to watch on *The Hollywood Palace* years ago. The one who kept plates twirling in the air on the tops of big long sticks, and whose entire act was based on making sure all the plates were in constant motion at the same time. Under her deal at the studio there were countless projects, each one needing all of her attention to keep it going, and there were days when she felt as if any minute they could all come crashing down on her head.

When it all got to be too much, it helped to glance over at one of the many photographs of Nina she had scattered around her office. So many, in fact, that some of the people who worked for her referred to her office as "the shrine." In the middle of a meeting or while she was on the phone, she would look at the pictures and be warmed by them, finding herself almost unable to remember Nina at some of the early stages captured by those shots, many of them taken by Cee Cee with a camera so automatic she called it her P.H.D. camera, for Push Here, Dummy. The array of pictures told stories of the seven years the two of them had survived, and the actual Nina, who was so grown up and beautiful now, was hard to connect to the funny, pouty little girl in the early photos.

There was no doubt she had been, as Bertie promised on her death-bed, good for Cee Cee. An anchor in an insane world, and despite the many errors Cee Cee knew she had made along the way, she could tell the reverse was also true. This was a child whose own mother had said about her when she was only six, "I feel lucky she's not wearing a tweed suit and carrying a briefcase." Well, that had to be because

Nina had spent her early years being as straitlaced as her stick-up-the-ass father, and more selfconscious about propriety than her lovable but working-too-hard-to-be-gracious mother. Now she laughed with a peal of a giggle so heartfelt it made Cee Cee laugh to hear it, and she talked on the phone too much, and rushed off to the mall after school, and fell asleep over her homework, and pined over certain boys in her class, and went gaga at the sight of certain movie stars, and seemed to have as normal a teenager's life as anybody could.

She had a crowd of friends from school who came exploding into their house, rushing past Cee Cee and up to Nina's room where they slammed the door behind them, then jabbered in shrill rapid-fire voices punctuated by outbursts of laughter with just enough hysteria in them to tell Cee Cee they had to be talking about boys. And eventually when their curfews dictated, they would brush past Cee Cee as they ran the other way, and the house would fall silent. Normal, of course, but Cee Cee hated to admit how left out she felt, knowing those girls had access to a part of Nina that, except for a moment here and there, had slipped away from their relationship completely.

The plop-down-with-snacks-together-on-the-couch-by-the-television days were over. The "stay and let's talk before lights out" requests, and "tell me more about my mother" sessions, which always served to make them feel closer to one another, were a part of a little-girl phase that was no more. And saddest of all was the absence of those admiring looks Nina used to give her, the ones with just a little bit of awe in them, that had lately been replaced by new expressions, which alternated between impatient tolerance and exasperated disdain.

> Fifteen seeks liberation, yet she still finds many roads closed to her because of her age. So she compromises by pulling away from her family, manifested in sparse conversation, a locked bedroom door or meals eaten separately.

Ain't that the truth, Cee Cee thought, always relieved to learn from the books she read that others had gone through this before her.

This morning she looked at the most recent picture of Nina, which sat on the antique breakfront the studio had left in Cee Cee's office from the previous tenant, a director who had moved on to another studio after three failed films in a row at this one. The photo was an eight-by-ten taken by one of those photographers who comes around to the schools, sets up a makeshift studio where he shoots portraits of each of the students, then charges the parents some whopping amount of money to buy them. And Cee Cee, who frequently referred to herself as "the queen of overkill," had naturally ordered the jazziest package the guy was selling, including a key ring with Nina's picture inside a tiny frame. Then she sent one of the photos off to Hal, one to her father and his wife, and even broke down and sent one to Nina's aunt, Anita-the-jewel-thief-Bennet.

There was something in Nina's eyes in that particular picture that maybe only someone as close to her as Cee Cee would notice, and the only way to describe it, the word that floated through Cee Cee's mind every time she looked at it, was *haunted*. There was an unmistakable pain Cee Cee sensed there behind the forced smile she knew the photographer must have insisted on before he would snap the shutter, and no matter where she was in the large executive office at the studio, no matter from what angle or at what distance, she could feel the pain: when she sat at her desk talking on the phone, wheeling and dealing and arguing with the big bosses about what she thought worked and didn't work for the films her production company was developing; and when she sat tailor-fashion on the sofa instead of stiffly behind the desk, trying to communicate with the screenwriters so they would feel she was working with them and wouldn't be intimidated by all the stardom heaped on her after the success of her last few films.

Lately she would find herself looking long at that one school picture, certain in some mother's inner knowing spot that the hollow-eyed girl looking back was more troubled than she let on. Okay, maybe it wasn't such big intuition on her part. Maybe her worries had more to do with the recent outbursts of anger she'd seen from Nina. The anger toward Cee Cee seemed to come from nowhere and Cee Cee couldn't shrug it off. Instead, Nina's anger could light a fire in Cee Cee's stomach that flared into her chest where she would carry it all day, unable to concentrate completely on anything.

"You look gross in that dress," Nina would say, and even if Cee Cee had thought when she put the dress on that she looked great in it, she would instantly pull it off and change to another one. "You're too old for those shorts." "Would you go to my school meeting looking like a parent instead of some weirdo?" "You really bombed on Letterman last night." "Why would they want *you* to host *Saturday Night Live*? Are they desperate?"

Any of those comments taken alone was hurtful, but accompanied by Nina's venomous reading, they could make Cee Cee have to sit quietly and remind herself that *she* was the grown-up, the parent, and had to stay in control, and remember how much the kid must be hurting herself to lash out like that. To try to stay composed and not to do what she would if those remarks had come from anyone else, which was to let loose with a big "Fuuuuck You!!!"

It seemed funny now that in anticipation of Nina's teens, Cee Cee had told herself the legendary mother-and-daughter bloodlettings were reserved for the genetically related. Certain that all the qualities she had detested in Leona were the same ones she saw and hated in herself. Therefore, she concluded, she and Nina would be spared that ritual separation dance. After all, there was precious little if anything of Cee Cee that Nina had taken on. And that was the faulty thinking she had used to lull herself into believing they would beat the odds. But the war between them was escalating, genes or no genes, and Cee Cee was afraid she wouldn't be able to handle much more of it. Last week there had been a big stab in the gut when both of them happened to find themselves in the kitchen foraging for snacks.

"Some girl at school who doesn't know who I am was talking about going to the movies and seeing this really great actress who she wants to be just like?" she said. She was starting to pick up that California speech rhythm, where statements ended as questions, from the kids at school. "And you're not going to believe who the actress was?"

Cee Cee knew the girl at school was probably talking about her. Her new picture was in wide release and was doing great business.

"Meryl Streep," she joked.

"No, you!" Nina said, ignoring the joke and devouring her fourth chocolate chip cookie while Cee Cee, who prudently cut an apple in half and then ate only one of the halves, looked on in envy.

"Well, did you thank her?" Cee Cee asked.

"Why would *I* thank her?" Nina asked, a black cloud of anger filling her eyes. "She wasn't talking about *me*." And in a huff she wrapped a few more cookies in a paper napkin, shoved them into the pocket of her robe, and left the room.

"Well, didn't you tell her that I'm your . . ." The unfinished sentence hung in the air. I'm your what? Her guardian, Cee Cee would think. It sounds like a matron in a prison. Looking back, she remembered a million reasons she had given herself over the last seven years for not going through with a legal adoption of Nina. Sometimes the reason was her certainty the kid would never go for it, wouldn't want to change her name, and would never really think of Cee Cee as a parent no matter what Cee Cee did, so the idea of going through a ceremony to get a piece of paper saying she was the parent seemed false and unnecessary. After all, she had made a will leaving everything to her father and Nina anyway, so she didn't have to adopt the kid to make her her heir.

And then there had always been Cee Cee's fear that starting adoption proceedings might rock their precarious boat, stir up the ire of that prick Michael Barron, who could rear his ugly head and do God knows what. Or, worse yet, Bertie's Aunt Neetie could come crawling out of the woodwork to use the whole issue as a way to extort money to buy herself some jewelry. Of course, now Cee Cee knew the truth about both of those people after meeting up with them, which was that neither really gave a shit about the kid and would probably agree to let Cee Cee adopt her. But still she didn't call her lawyers and tell them to ready the adoption papers.

Now she decided she wasn't doing anything about it because they were past it. Nina was a woman, for God's sake, and at this stage going through some legal ceremony to say she was Cee Cee's daughter was completely after the fact. Nina would probably laugh if Cee Cee even brought it up, and think it was dumb. She doesn't want to be related to me anyway, Cee Cee thought. Related to me, hah! She doesn't even want to have a *meal* with me.

That night when Cee Cee walked in the front door carrying a briefcase filled with scripts in one hand and some costume designer's renderings in another, she heard the telephone ringing insistently, so she put everything she was holding down in a heap on the kitchen counter and grabbed the receiver. The call was for Nina. A boy. When boys had first started calling, Cee Cee would run into Nina's room and do a little dance and sing, "A boy! A boy! Thank heaven it's a boy!" And Nina would laugh. But the adolescent hormones were flying and these days even a smile from Cee Cee when she told her who was waiting on the phone was a reason for a flare-up.

"Neen?" Cee Cee hollered, but there was no answer, and Antonia must have been in the laundry room because the answering machine wasn't on, and the housekeeper usually answered the phone if Nina didn't. "Neen?" Nothing. "Hold on," Cee Cee said into the phone to the boy whose name she didn't ask, not wishing to risk, under the new rules, seeming too nosy, then she pushed the hold button and hurried upstairs. She could hear the shower in Nina's bathroom, which was probably why Nina hadn't heard the phone.

"Neen?" Cee Cee knocked on Nina's bathroom door, but the running water made it impossible for Nina to hear her, so she tried the door. It was unlocked and she pushed it open. Through the glass shower she could see steam rising around the back of Nina's long naked body, and Nina with her head thrown back appearing to love the water as it flowed down her. She was slim and long-waisted, Cee Cee noted with guilt about what she always thought of as her own weight problem. Skinnier than Cee Cee remembered. Of course she hadn't seen her without clothes on in ages. Unlike some of her friends who sometimes wore shorts and halter tops, Nina was modest about her developing body, and most of the time dressed in clothes to conceal it.

Maybe, Cee Cee thought, she should just close the door unnoticed, and go back to the phone and take a message. The boy could call Nina back. But then she reconsidered. Teenaged boys were as weird as teenaged girls. The boy might think it was a rejection if Nina didn't take his call. "Nina!" This time Nina heard her and she turned, and when she saw Cee Cee standing in the open door of her bathroom, the horrible rage that filled her face was so fierce, for a split second Cee Cee thought it had to be a joke. It was no joke.

"Get out of here. Get the fuck out of here. Can't I have a minute of privacy? What do you *want?*" She was shaking as she opened the shower door and steam poured into the room, and she reached for a giant bath towel, which she threw around her shoulders as if it was a long cape, and now she stood there, wet hair matted against her head, her skinny body trembling, her eyes red with tears.

"Jeez, I'm sorry," Cee Cee said, feeling stunned and helpless. "I came to tell you you had a phone call," and she left the bathroom, walked into her own room, and sat on her bed feeling stunned. Now it was going too far. Now she felt as if Nina really did hate her in that

same narrow-eyed and blood-boiling way she remembered hating
Leona, and being flesh and blood had nothing to do with it. Maybe
every teenager hated every parent in that same way until they separated, until they had their own identity, and then the crisis would
pass. That's what it said in all the books.

Trying to communicate with a teen can be a weary two-step. Forward
to closeness, retreat to confrontation. Treat them like a child, they feel
patronized; treat them like an adult, they feel anxious. A good way to
handle this forward/backward motion is to see it for what it is: part of
the long haul to adulthood. Intense though these times are, they will
soon pass unless you get all snarled up in them.

For a few minutes after reading the paragraphs of advice in those
books, Cee Cee would feel relief. Then her own anger would rise and
all reason would spill away, because to be on the receiving end of the
kind of wrath Nina had just shown was like getting a kick in the gut,
and the pain of rejection it created inside Cee Cee was worse than any
desperation she ever felt when a man walked out on her. Certainly far
more hurtful than reading some scathing review of her work, because
this one hit her so deep inside that, until she started raising a kid, she
hadn't even known that place existed. It was hard to believe someone
could open you up and twist your vital organs until they ached
because you cared about them so much.

She was tired and tense herself, and working too hard, and she
always felt apologetic for thinking that thought, because it seemed to
be what Hal would call "a high-class problem," since it was great to
be a successful star after so many years of what a recent *New York
Times* article called "the vicissitudes of La Bloom's career." Somehow
those studio boys in suits expected her to move from picture to picture
without a pause in between, convincing her that this time if she built
up "a body of work" she would "never slide back" again. Slide back.
That meant doing television, or worse yet Vegas or Atlantic City.

And even though she realized what they were telling her was just
a way to scare her into doing what they wanted her to do, knew that
they were manipulating her by using the terror most performers have
of waking up one day and finding themselves out in the cold, still she
bought into it. Because it had been so hard-won, because she never
quite believed it was really happening for her. And because as much

as she hated even to say the words to herself, as hard as she tried to keep it from showing, the truth was she was starting to feel it was harder to keep running on the kind of energy she once had, because she was getting older. Aging. Shit.

In her own bathroom she pulled her sweater over her head, then slid her jeans down to the floor, unhooked her bra, which had left the mark of the too-tight elastic around her, and, dressed only in her black lace panties, looked at herself in the full-length mirror on the door. After just seeing Nina's body, every lump and bump on her own looked even worse than she remembered. Her middle was a little too round, but the legs were still great for her age. And the tits, well the size was perfect, but gravity was definitely having its way with them.

She laughed to herself, remembering Marlon Brando's line in *The Last Tango in Paris*, where he told the young girl that someday she'd be playing soccer with her own tits. Now she cupped a hand around each of hers, lifted them a little higher to where they used to be, and for a fleeting instant entertained the thought of calling a plastic surgeon and getting a tit job. A bra tuck they called it, pull them up a little just like this. "Get serious, Bloom," she said, as the thought passed. Why would anyone in her right mind let someone touch her with a knife unless it was to remove something that might kill her? Then she moved her hands to the sides of her breasts, squeezed them together so the nipples pointed straight at the mirror, and said, "Reach for the sky," to her reflection. The tits were still okay.

"Besides, there ain't nobody beating my door down to look at them anyway," she said, shrugging, and ran the water into the bathtub where she sat for an hour replaying that moment of Nina's rage, wondering how and when and if they would ever get back to laughing together, reading together, gabbing away like buddies. Missing her as much as if she'd gone far away, because the Nina she knew had done just that.

The next morning Nina made herself a fast breakfast and her eyes avoided Cee Cee's as she moved to the front door with relief when she heard the honking car horn of one of her friends who had come to take her to school. Today was Valentine's Day, Cee Cee noticed by the date in the newspaper, which she lingered over, reading everything she might ordinarily skip like "Dear Abby" and "Peanuts" while she sipped some lukewarm coffee. Then she read the "Astrological Forecast," feeling foolish every morning when she checked the View section of the *L.A. Times* for it, hating the fact that even though she really believed it was bullshit, she was irresistibly attracted to it. *"Refuse to be intimidated by family member's anger."* Hah! Everybody who read this asshole thing must have a teenager at home. The rest of the message said, *"Phone call brings long-awaited gratification."* "Sure, sure," she said, not letting herself think about what that could possibly mean, as she poured more hot coffee and headed upstairs, carrying the cup with her. Maybe she would stop and shop for some Valentine goodies on her way in to the office this morning, and later she could leave them on Nina's bed. Then at least for a minute or two while Nina's eyes lit up at the sight of yet another stuffed animal to add to the huge collection she already had, there would be a truce, and maybe the two of them would share even a brief moment of warmth. A moment Cee Cee craved so powerfully she didn't even care if it took bribery to get it.

She pulled some fresh towels out of the linen closet, and just as she passed through her bedroom the phone rang and she picked it up.

"H'lo."

"Hey there! Cee Cee Bloom." It was Larry Gold. There was an excited edge in his voice, which always meant he had some good news. "Hold on to your hat, lady." Cee Cee's insides were shaking because she knew what it was he could be about to tell her. Something she had tried hard not to hope for, to think about, or to need, superstitious that the hope would make it go away. "Best actress nomination for the Oscar! How about that for the kid from the Bronx, ladies and gentlemen? Is that a good way to start your day?"

Cee Cee sat on the bed so suddenly that the hot coffee from the newly filled cup she was holding splashed on her robe, but she didn't care. "It sure is, Larry. It sure as hell is."

"The official letter will be coming in a day or two with the date of the ceremony, I think it's the twenty-sixth of March, and all the info will be in that. Meantime, congratulations, kiddo. We made it."

When she put the phone down she lay back among the pillows on her unmade bed, enjoying the quiet feeling of elation combined with disbelief. Feeling what it meant finally to be where she had been heading every day of her life. Well, *almost* there. To *really* be there would be to stand on that stage hanging on to that gorgeous gold statue, looking out at America and spouting one of the many speeches she'd rehearsed every night of her life since she could remember. *I'd like to thank my director* . . .

With a sensation of lightness she hadn't felt in years, maybe since John Perry proposed to her when she was nineteen, she showered, dressed, and gathered up the papers she needed to take into her office for her ten o'clock meeting. When she got into the car and reached her foot out toward the gas pedal, she realized the front seat had been pushed back, as if someone taller had driven it. But nobody else ever drove her car. Antonia had her own little Plymouth Fury and Nina was too young to drive. She pulled the lever under the seat and moved the seat closer to the dashboard, turned the key in the ignition and the radio came blasting on, but not to her station, 105.1 KKGO. This was some jarring heavy metal station. So she pushed the button until she found KKGO and pulled out of the driveway to go to the studio.

When Nina called her at the office from the Santa Monica Mall to ask if she could buy herself a new pair of stretch Levi's, it was as if nothing bad had happened between them at all. Hormones, Cee Cee thought, knowing that her own could sometimes make her feel as if she needed an exorcist. Fair was fair and Nina was entitled to her bad times too. "Yes, you can buy the Levi's," Cee Cee told her. "Oh, and Neen . . . I got the nomination."

"Cee Cee!" Nina squealed. "That is so cool. That is awesome." It was genuine excitement. And when she added, "You deserve it," she sounded just like Bertie used to, and Cee Cee felt a pang of nostalgia. Then Nina rattled on about how she hoped Tom Cruise, her new favorite heartthrob, was nominated so they could sit near him at the ceremony, and while they talked Cee Cee looked over at the shelf across from her desk at the huge white stuffed rabbit she had just bought Nina for Valentine's Day. The rabbit held a red heart which read SOME BUNNY THINKS YOU'RE GREAT. There were other little goodies for her: a heart-shaped bud vase and some heart-shaped soap, and a charm bracelet with tiny heart charms dangling from it, and she'd even found some of those old-fashioned heart-shaped candies that had YOU'RE CUTE and BE MINE printed on them.

All the way home from work that night she thought about the best way for them to celebrate the nomination. Maybe the excitement would carry them along and after Nina opened all of the Valentine's Day gifts they would go to a movie in Westwood or order dinner in from the Chinese restaurant or pack a picnic and take it out on the sand and watch the sunset.

When she walked in the door of the Malibu house, which usually had a slight mildew scent, this time she was engulfed by the sweet thick smell of flowers, and she was astonished by the number of baskets and vases that filled the living room. Roses in bright yellows and deep reds, rich purple irises, and pink peonies with open lettucey faces by the dozens everywhere. One by one she collected and read each card, one from her business manager, Wayne, one from Larry Gold and another from the entire William Morris office, a massive basket from Hal, another from the studio executives, another from the producer of the film. And every card held some variation of the message that an Oscar nomination for Cee Cee had been a long time in coming. High with joy, she picked up one of the baskets and carried it upstairs to her bedroom, where she put it on her dresser, then took all of the goodies she had bought for Nina and went into Nina's room to leave them for her.

The room was neat. Cee had to give the girl that. Nina was like Bertie in that way. Not a slob like Cee Cee, who always had everything so out of place she never knew where to find it. Sometimes she could waste an hour trying to find some sweater she wanted to wear and thought she'd mislaid, then remember she'd sent it to the cleaners. But not Nina; even when there was no cleaning lady around, her room was perfect. And despite her protests of womanhood, the room still looked very much like the room of a little girl, with stuffed animals all over the bed and on every shelf.

Stuffed dogs and lions and elephants on the bookshelves, the windowsills, the desk, and the bed. Winnie-the-Pooh and Tigger and Eeyore, and a giant Minnie Mouse in the corner. Some of the animals Cee Cee could remember buying for her, but most of them had been gifts from or traded for with her friends. Alone in the girl's silent room, Cee Cee put the new Valentine's Day bunny in the middle of the bed, placed the other gifts on the night table, reached across the bed and stroked a furry white toy cat gently, then picked up the mama kangaroo, sat on the bed, and held it on her lap.

Nina, she thought, we will get through this. As soon as I finish the next picture we'll go away somewhere and have time to talk. Guiltily she remembered how she'd said that before, planned other trips with Nina that had fallen through. Since that painful trip to Hawaii, quite a few of their vacation plans had gone awry. The first because of an urgent business problem, and a few months ago because Nina had come down with a violent stomach flu, and by the time she was well enough to reschedule, Cee Cee was too caught up in some project she couldn't interrupt. Well, this time they would do it. Of course it would have to be after the Oscars because between now and then she had to concentrate on getting into shape, work out with her trainer every day for hours, and decide what dress she was wearing to the ceremony and get fitted for it.

The mama kangaroo had big eyes and a funny round nose, and Cee Cee could see that the baby stuffed kangaroo, which should have been sitting in the mama's pouch, was sitting on Nina's dresser instead. As she stood to leave the room, she picked up the baby and was going to slide it into the mama's pouch, but it wouldn't fit, couldn't slide in. As she tried to force it, it felt as if something was at the bottom of the pouch taking up the space. Absently she slid two fingers into the soft belly of the kangaroo to feel what it was, and when she pulled her fingers out, between them was a small plastic Ziploc bag filled with an unmistakable powdery white substance Cee Cee recognized immediately as cocaine. Dear God, no. With a snap in her chest everything fell into place. The moods, the skinniness, the seat in the car being pushed so far back. Probably even the mysterious stomach troubles a few months ago. No, please don't let this be happening. Not to this kid who's had so much to fight through already. Nausea overwhelmed her and she sat back down on the pristine bed to pull herself together and decide what to do.

There was a certain detached expression Bertie used to get on her face when she couldn't or didn't want to handle something. Cee Cee still remembered very clearly how that expression became more and more closed in direct proportion to how emotional the situation was. Like the time Cee Cee screamed bloody murder at her in the lobby of that hotel in Miami Beach, and Bertie just stood there, not even blinking. And then there was that year in Malibu right after Bertie found out

Michael Barron was on a business trip in Los Angeles at the same time she and Nina were visiting Cee Cee in Malibu, and Bertie rushed out the door to find him and beg him to see his daughter. Naturally the lowlife cocksucker had refused, and Cee Cee would never forget the way Bertie had come back to the house wearing that stoic nothing-can-get-me expression, which was how Cee Cee knew the minute she saw her what Michael's answer had been.

Now Nina had that expression on *her* face, while she looked at Cee Cee who was waving the Ziploc bag of drugs in the air, and Cee Cee knew as she heard herself say every out-of-control word that came into her head that she was doing every wrong thing imaginable in this situation, if in fact there was a situation, which she prayed that there wasn't. Even as she shrieked in anger, she held on to the hope there would be a reason, an excuse, an explanation for drugs being in the room of this child.

"Who the fuck do you think you're talking to?" she railed at Nina. "I know what this is and I want to know why you have it and where you got it, and I want to know right now, goddammit, or you're never walking out that door again, except to go to school. Do you hear me? And don't give me any bullshit either because I've been around the block more times than the ice cream man and I'm not some naïve housewife you can con."

"Cee Cee," Nina said, without a trace of emotion, "I already told you, I don't have any idea where that came from. I don't even know if the kangaroo used to belong to Jody or Lindsay or Beth or Allison. It's been sitting in my room for at least a year. Why are you doing this?"

Please, Cee Cee thought, please let that be true, and that I'm getting crazy for no reason at all here. "Nina, tell me you don't do drugs and that you never have."

"I don't do drugs and I never have," she said without a flicker of any emotion on her face.

"You swear?"

"I swear."

"I don't believe you."

Nina shrugged, but it wasn't a hostile shrug, it was an indifferent one.

"If I walked into your room with a knife and cut open every stuffed animal, would I find more dope?"

"Not that I know of," Nina said. Her coolness was remarkable. Even if she wasn't guilty, it would be impossible for a kid to be so undaunted by the red-faced out-of-control carrying-on Cee Cee was doing, about which she was beginning to feel really foolish. Dumb. A kid this cool had to be innocent, didn't she?

They were standing in the kitchen, and Cee Cee walked to the sink and, without taking her eyes from Nina's, emptied the bag of white powder into the garbage disposal, ran the water, and then ran the disposal for a long noisy time. Nina watched, with the same stoic expression she'd had on her face since the confrontation began when she walked in. Outside a car horn honked.

"Who's out there?" Cee Cee asked.

"Melissa."

"What does she want?"

"We're going over to Allison's. May I go now?"

"We're not finished here."

"Okay, then she'll wait."

"Nina, where did the drugs come from?"

"I don't know."

The car horn honked again.

Maybe she didn't know. Maybe she was telling the absolute truth. And if she wasn't, she was the one who ought to be nominated for a frigging Oscar for this performance here, because there wasn't a blush, an extra blink, even a trace of defiance in her expression that would give her away. Cocaine. Imfuckingpossible. But which one of those other girls would have had it?

"May I please go?" Nina asked, again without impatience.

"Yeah," Cee Cee said, "sure, go on."

When she got to the door Nina turned back again.

"Thanks for the Valentine's Day presents," she said, and Cee Cee watched her leave. The house was quiet, but in her head she could still hear the echoes of her own hysterical accusations as she walked back upstairs, picturing what the whole scene would have looked like to an outsider. Nina was taller than she was, and there Cee Cee had stood, looking up at her, screaming like some irrational idiot. Like

Mammy Yokum wagging her bossy little finger at Li'l Abner. For a while she sat on her bed leafing through copies of *Rolling Stone* and *Ms.*, but she couldn't shake the way she felt, when she'd looked at that little bag of cocaine.

It had to be a mistake. Maybe she should call each of those girls and confront them, or better still call their parents and try to get an answer out of them. Obviously the drugs had been left in the kangaroo pouch by someone else. Had to be. There was no way Nina could afford to buy drugs. Her allowance was so limited and so carefully doled out to her, it would take her forever to be able to afford even what was in that one little bag. In spite of the fact that Cee Cee bought her nice clothes and they lived in a big fancy house, the girl's personal cash situation was practically nil. Anytime she wanted to buy something, she had to call Cee Cee and get her permission. Okay, so maybe Cee Cee gave the permission a little too often, but there was never any cash involved. There wasn't a way in the world she could have paid for drugs like that.

"Nina, Cee Cee brought you here because she's afraid you might be using drugs and that maybe we could talk about it."

"Well, there's nothing to talk about, because I'm not," Nina said in a small voice. "So there's no more to say." The girl was neatly dressed as always and the light makeup she wore was carefully and tastefully applied. She looked more like a photograph in a teen magazine than someone who had been coerced into the room by an adult suspecting her of drug use.

"If I were you I wouldn't want to talk either. Cee Cee drops you here into the office of some adult you don't even know and expects you to trust me. Why should you? You don't even know me, but maybe you could tell me why Cee Cee was so panicked on the phone."

"I don't know."

"Is she always that way?"

Nina didn't react.

"What's it like for you when she gets that way?"

Nina looked over at the door to the waiting room.

"She can't hear us out there, these walls are soundproof, and I told her she could come in to our private session only when you felt comfortable about it. So even though she's waiting out there, we don't have to let her in at all if we need the time for ourselves."

Nina shrugged. "It doesn't matter to me." Again there was silence.

"When Cee Cee acts that way at home, how do you deal with it?"

"I don't."

"Do you hide?"

"Well, I wouldn't call it hiding, but I try to stay away from her."

"And what do you do the other times? The times when you can't stay away?"

"The other times . . . I guess I tell her what I know she wants to hear."

"Good heavens!" Florrie Kagan, the family therapist Cee Cee had tracked down after frantic phone calls all over town, sat back in her chair, and Nina saw a pleased-with-herself expression on the woman's face that meant she thought she'd found an inroad. "You must have to play a role all the time. What role do you play with her?"

Nina took a long look at her. The woman was about Cee Cee's age, but much prettier with pouffy blond hair and giant piercing blue eyes. She wore a sweater that came down past her narrow hips over a long skirt and boots. "Is it the role of the people-pleaser, or the role of the good daughter? Tell me who you play." Nina wasn't sure where this was going or even what she was going to answer, until she heard it come out of herself as she said it.

"I play my mother."

"What does that mean?"

"It means I guess I act like I'm her friend who thinks she's great. Her loyal, perfect friend."

"And that's who you think your mother was to Cee Cee?"

"I *know* that's who she was."

"What happened to your mother?"

Nina looked down at her lap.

"You know what, Nina? I just saw a wall come down. This must be so hard for you. How did your mom die?"

Nina didn't look up.

"Nina. I know this must be tough. Can you tell me what happened to your mom?"

"She died of cancer."

"How old were you?"

"Eight."

"How long was the process of dying?"

"She was sick off and on for two years."

"Did you realize what was happening?"

Nina spoke but didn't look up. "At the end . . . she had this plan? To go off to Carmel? So I wouldn't have to see her the way she was when she was real bad at the end. But Cee Cee went to Carmel to be with her and Cee Cee told her she had to send for me. So she did and I got to be with her for the last few months."

"And how was that for you?"

"Well, you can trust me, it wasn't the prom," she said, and as her answer rang through the office she thought how much she sounded like Cee Cee.

"Did you have a chance to say goodbye?"

"At the time I didn't even know what that meant. I guess I always thought she was going to come back."

"And now?"

Nina's eyes looked up, but far away and not at the doctor. "Now I know she's not."

"Nina, these are tough times for kids your age in terms of the availability of drugs and the peer pressure to use. Cee Cee called me because she found cocaine in your room, which you said you didn't know was there. Do you know of any of your friends who are using?"

"No."

"Do you know any kids at your school who are?"

"I'm sure it's around," she said, "but . . ." She shrugged as an end to the sentence.

"You and Cee Cee have been through quite a few painful experiences together. Your mother's death, your father's abandonment, Cee Cee's personal problems and career problems. All very heavy for a girl your age. Can you talk about any of that?"

"No."

Cee Cee sat in the waiting room staring at the same page in *Better Homes and Gardens* she'd been staring at for the last fifteen minutes, her insides throbbing with fear, knowing this could be a turning point from which she and Nina might never come back. A break between them that could never be repaired. She remembered the way it happened with Leona. How one day in 1956 or '57 she had looked at her mother and said to herself, I'll tolerate my life with her until I can get the fuck out, but that's it. I'll never tell her one more thing about me. Never let myself care about her, never. Never confide in her or let her know who I am. And now she had the agonizing certainty that Nina was not only having those feelings about her, but was taking drugs to dull the pain.

When after nearly an hour had passed and the door from the inner office opened, Cee Cee jumped to her feet, and after Florrie gestured gently for her to come in, she walked slowly toward the inner office wondering what had transpired while she'd been sitting out there imagining the worst.

"Cee Cee, Nina says she thinks you're overreacting. She says she doesn't use drugs and has even agreed to be tested to prove it. What do you think of that?"

I think she's lying through her perfectly straight teeth, Cee Cee thought, then thought, Thank you, God, then wasn't sure what she thought. "What do *you* think of that?" she asked the lady shrink.

"Well, I suggested that even though there may not be drugs involved, the two of you might want to continue to come in here together a few times just to work on your relationship, and she agreed to that."

"She did?" Cee Cee's heart jumped with hope. Nina's face was expressionless.

"How about if we set a time in a week or so for the two of you to come back?" Florrie asked.

Nina nodded. Florrie opened a calendar book and mentioned some possible appointment times. None of them were good for Cee Cee, who was scheduled up to her ears at work, but she didn't say that. "Whichever one is good for Nina is good for me." Nina picked a Friday appointment in a week at three thirty.

That week was crazy busy for Cee Cee. The Oscar nomination had created a flurry of events in her career, offers to field, magazine layouts to do, phone calls from Barbara Walters wanting her to tape a show in a few days which would run on Oscar night. Thankfully, and unusually, everything at home was so calm and almost back to pleasant, she didn't even mention the idea of drug testing for fear of stirring up an argument.

In fact, she was starting to feel as if maybe the whole drug thing had been her paranoia, another example of her going too far, and that finding the drugs one of those bratty little girls had hidden in Nina's room had been God's way of getting the two of them to counseling so their mother-daughter problems could get fixed. On the morning of the appointment with Doctor Kagan, the shrink, Cee Cee told Nina she would pick her up at school at three o'clock.

She was early so she was able to get a parking spot right in front of the school where she sat for a while thinking about what the two of them might say to one another in today's session, feeling hopeful that things between them were on the mend. It was hot in the car, so after a while she got out and leaned against the door and watched the kids pouring out of the building. For a long time her eyes followed one particular group of girls who were a little older than Nina, walking along laughing and talking, and she was impressed with how womanly and sophisticated they seemed. More sophisticated than she had ever been at that age. At *any* age, she thought to herself, and wondered how those girls got along with *their* parents. In another passing group she noticed a tall straight-haired blond girl dressed in a plaid skirt and green sweater who was clearly the focal point of her friends. The girl was talking away and gesturing, and as she did, Cee Cee noticed that on the third finger of her right hand was Bertie's emerald ring.

The answer, the cash. That's how she got it. Goddammit. Goddamn her. I won't fucking have it. A crashing rush of adrenaline flooded through her. Stop it, she told herself. You're imagining things. The girl had walked by pretty fast, so she could be mistaken. There were a lot of emerald rings in the world. In fact the emerald was the birthstone for the month of May, so maybe the girl's birthday was in May and it was her own ring, which just happened to resemble Bertie's from a distance. But instead of staying by her parked car where she had promised Nina she'd meet her, Cee Cee moved quickly after the girl and her friends who were now about a half a block away. You're crazy, she told herself, you're going to make an asshole of yourself and of Nina because you're a certifiable lock-up case.

"Hi, Nance," she heard a boy's voice yell from across the street, and Cee Cee saw the girl who was wearing the ring raise a hand high to wave at the boy. The wave gave Cee Cee another look at the ring, and this time, even from the distance, she was sure it was Bertie's ring. Nina's ring. Now she moved faster, and when she was a few feet behind the girls who had now turned the corner she shouted, "Nancy!" The girl turned around to look at her and so did her three friends. Cee Cee noticed the friends exchange looks when they saw who had stopped them. When they realized it was Cee Cee Bloom, not just anybody's mother but a movie star, they looked nervous. That gave Cee Cee enough of a feeling of power to move closer to the girl with the ring, who, she could now see, looked as guilty as sin.

"I need to talk to you," Cee Cee said.

"Okay," the girl replied and gave one of those nods to the others that a gangleader in a bad crime movie gives to the gang to tell them "It's okay to leave, but don't go too far away, just in case."

Cee Cee braced herself as the girl walked farther down the block next to her, with a brash confident walk that only a girl who looks that good can, and the minute the other girls were out of earshot she said, "She told me it belonged to her, not you. That she needed the money. She said that her real mother left it to her when she died so she could do whatever she wanted with it."

"She told you the truth," Cee Cee said, looking down at the girl's perfect hand holding on to a history book, and there was the ring, looking just the way it had once looked on Bertie. Cee Cee flashed on that time in Miami when she'd spotted the ring on Neetie's hand and had gone bananas over it, and how that night when they had arrived at home in Malibu and Nina put the ring back into her musical pink ballerina jewelry box that plunked out "Love Makes the World Go 'Round" she had thanked Cee Cee gratefully for retrieving it.

For so many years Nina's hand had been too small to wear the beautiful piece of jewelry on her ring finger, even with ring guards, but last year she tried it on and came running in to Cee Cee's room to show her that it fit her on the same finger where Bertie had always worn it, and it was like a rite of passage. Coincidentally, two days later she got her first menstrual period. Since then she'd worn the ring for special occasions, always when she did stopping frequently to look down at her hand to admire it.

"It did belong to her. But her mother was my best friend, and it belonged to her grandmother first, and it would mean a lot if you would sell it back to me."

The girl sighed a sigh which said, I don't want to do what you're asking, but you're an adult and if I don't you'll probably start a big stink about it.

"How much did you pay for it?" Cee Cee pressed.

"Seven hundred dollars." The goddamned ring was worth a hell of a lot more than that.

"I'll give you nine hundred." The girl was pouting and looked as if she was thinking about giving Cee Cee a hard time. "I don't have that much cash on me," Cee Cee apologized, knowing the girl might just get up and storm away if she didn't handle her properly. "But if you give me the ring now, I'll have my secretary meet you here tomorrow at this time on this spot with the money."

As if she was ending an engagement, the girl reluctantly slid the ring from her finger and handed it over to Cee Cee. "Tomorrow at this time on this spot," she said looking into Cee Cee's eyes.

"You got it," Cee Cee said, and turned to go when the girl's voice stopped her.

"She threw this into the deal too."

Cee Cee turned back. In the girl's hand was a compact. It had fake rhinestones on the lid, and had been a gift from someone at the studio to Cee Cee for Christmas. Kept in her room, in her own jewelry box. The kind of glitzy item teenagers liked, and Nina had taken it to sweeten the deal when she sold the ring. Stole it from Cee Cee and sold it. It was hard for Cee Cee to think those words. When she got back to her car, stinging with the ugly truth, Nina was sitting in the passenger seat, waiting for her.

"Where'd you go?" Nina asked.

"Down the street," Cee Cee answered and got into the car.

In Doctor Kagan's waiting room, Cee Cee, too numb to even think about what she was going to say when they got inside the office with the cool I've-seen-it-all lady doctor, watched through a veil of fear as Nina paged through some schoolbook, a legitimate way to avoid conversation with Cee Cee. She was wearing a nearly angelic look on her face, and looking at her sitting there, Cee Cee remembered when she was a kid and Leona took her to see Patty McCormack in *The Bad Seed* on Broadway. When the mother in the play realized her child was a murderer passing herself off as an innocent, the look Nancy Kelly who played the part wore on her face had to be the same one Cee Cee wore now. Stiff, pained, shocked, hurt.

"Well, now," Florrie said, leading them into her office, and Cee Cee felt a terror of what would happen next, because she knew she was about to break open the blister of lies that would have to release the poison into their lives. Had to tell Nina now that she knew her secret. And after she did there was no outcome she could imagine that wouldn't be painful. Every ending for the scene she had played in her mind as she drove blindly to Brentwood and parked and rode up in the elevator to this office was horrible.

"Well, how have you two been doing this week?" the doctor asked.

Nina shrugged and made a noise which sounded like "N'kay," and Cee Cee said nothing. She thought seriously about grabbing Nina by the neck and shaking her hard enough to scare the shit out of her, and to maybe scare out a confession, too, knowing that the shrink would pull her off before she really hurt her.

"Did you have a drug test, Nina?" Florrie asked matter-of-factly.

"No," Nina said. "Why *would* I?" As though a drug test had never been discussed in this office.

Florrie looked at Cee Cee as if to ask her why anybody who had been as crazily convinced one week ago that her kid was taking drugs wouldn't have pushed her to take the promised test, but Cee Cee looked away from her at Nina.

"Nina," Cee Cee said, pausing before she asked the next, wishing she didn't have to. "Where's the emerald ring?"

"What?"

"Your mother's emerald ring. The one Neetie tried to take from you. Remember how excited we were when it finally fit your finger? And you wore it a few times to parties. Where is it?" There was a long pause, during which the silence drummed away in Cee Cee's ears.

"I lost it."

"When?"

"A while ago."

"Why didn't you tell me? You knew it was insured. In fact that was why we decided it was okay for you to wear it every now and then. I could have reported it and you could have had the money to replace it. Do you remember where you lost it?"

"If I remembered where I lost it, I could go there and get it and it wouldn't be lost, would it?" The bitchiness in her voice helped Cee Cee to proceed, and ask a question to which sadly she knew the answer.

"Are you lying?"

"I forgot about the insurance," Nina said, looking hurt and slumping into the chair, "and I know how emotional you get and I thought you'd go crazy. Besides, it was *my* ring. My mother left it to *me*. So why should I have to answer to you? I lost it."

"Well, I found it," Cee Cee said and pulled the ring from her pocket, where she had been holding it tightly in her fist all the way to the doctor's office from the school, and which she now held up as the three of them looked at its deep green glow catching the overhead light. "I stopped Nancy at school today and bought it back for you. And my compact too."

"Oh, shit!" Nina cried with an embarrassed agonized howl. "I hate you so much," and she covered her face with her hands.

"So you've been conning us, Nina. Conning Cee Cee for a long time. Covering your tracks very well. That must have been a hard job," Florrie said quietly.

"Did you take my car out at night?" Cee Cee asked.

From behind her hands, Nina nodded a slight nod. "When you were sleeping. A lot of times."

Cee Cee felt cold all over. "Nina, what did I do? Where did I screw it all up? Why didn't you tell me what I was doing wrong?"

Nina took her hands away from her face now and got to her feet. All her coolness was gone and her face was splotchy with anger and her hair askew. "Guess what?" she said, glaring into Cee Cee's face. "This time it isn't about you, Cee Cee. For once in our lives, something isn't about you, it's about me! Me! I am sick of you trying to make everything in the world about you." And she rushed to the door and with a grunt pulled the inner door toward her, then forced herself against the outer door, ran through the waiting room, and with a slam of that door was gone.

*   *   *

When she wasn't home by ten that night, Cee Cee sat with the high
school roster and called the home of every girl she ever remembered
being in her home. Some were asleep and their sympathetic-voiced
parents said they had no idea where Nina was. Some phones didn't
answer. Soon in her anguish Cee Cee wasn't sure which ones she had
called and which ones she hadn't. She thought about calling Kevin
Myers, but over the past year, probably because hanging around with
him hadn't been considered cool, Nina had pretty much phased him
out of her life.

At two in the morning she still sat with her hand on the phone,
trembling with exhaustion, not sure if she should call the police or
drive the streets and look for Nina herself. *Runaways.* She had skipped
over that chapter in the book about parents and teenagers, not even
imagining it would ever be necessary to read it. Now she read it.

> Running is almost always a cry for help, and you must face these needs
> and learn to deal with them. Over a million teenagers choose this solu-
> tion every year and the average runner is a fifteen-year-old girl. Usually
> within a few days your child will be back at home.

Please God. As the sun came up, Cee Cee walked upstairs with a
blinding headache and a heart that felt ripped in half and called Doctor Kagan. When she got the answering service, she begged them to
let her hold on while they tracked her down.

"Cee Cee, what news?" the doctor said within minutes.

"What should I do?" she asked. "Tell me what to do. Should I drive
all over town looking in alleys? Should I hire a detective? Should I
call the hospitals and the morgue? Please tell me what I'm supposed
to do, because I can't stand not knowing where she is. What if she
needs food? What if she thinks I won't *take* her back? I have to tell
her that I'm going to help her through this."

"Cee Cee, what I'm going to tell you will be the hardest thing for
you, but I think you need to wait, to give it another day or two, let
her play this out, because I believe she wants to come home and that
you'll hear from her very soon."

Barbara Walters and her crew would be arriving in a few hours to
tape an interview with her, and Cee Cee knew she looked as horrible
as she felt. So what if I look like shit, she thought. Dear God, bring
me my kid back safe and I'll turn in all the fame, all the nominations,

and every fucking ticket anybody ever bought to come and see me anywhere. But the phone didn't ring with any word of Nina, and after a blazing hot shower, which Cee Cee took with the shower door open and the phone pulled across the bathroom so she could hear it in case it rang while she was in there, and three cups of coffee she brewed so strong they could wake the dead, she answered the door to her makeup lady by saying, "I think you've got your work cut out for you today, girl."

She could hear Barbara Walters's crew arriving as the base coat and concealer and blusher were being applied, and while her face was being powdered in place, and her hair was teased, combed, and sprayed into obedience, she tried desperately from some reserve tank of wherewithal to dredge up some enthusiasm for the interview she had made a commitment to give. Finally with a face painted on that magically brightened her own pale-with-fatigue one, she dressed in a soft pink jersey shirt and pants and went into her living room, which was now filled with cameras and technicians and lights, to chat with Barbara Walters. And as she passed the assistant producer, she thought she heard the young woman doing a last-minute check on details before they started to shoot.

"Telephone bells turned off?" Cee Cee heard her ask.

"No!" Cee Cee whirled around and shouted. "You can't shut the phones off, I'm expecting an urgent call!"

"But we —"

"No! You can't shut the phones off and that's final!"

The young woman looked over Cee Cee's head at the producer, who gave an everybody-has-their-own-craziness nod back to say it was okay to leave the phone bells alone, and Cee Cee went in to meet Barbara Walters. But the phone didn't ring at all.

"You're a busy lady. A movie star, a producer, a single mother. Tell me about your daughter."

The lights were hot and Cee Cee held tightly to the arm of the sofa. She was trembling and weak and so sick inside she was sure it had to show, but she fixed her face into the Cee Cee Bloom position and answered. "She's sensational," she said. "A joy and a gem and the light of my life."

The interview seemed to take all day. Questions about her past, her marriage, her television show, her films, her future plans, but later when the lights were turned off and Barbara Walters left after thanking her for a great interview and the crew had cleared out, she sat by the telephone again, and all she could remember about the interview was what she had said about Nina.

There was no word that night either, and the next morning, after about an hour's sleep, she went to have her dress for the Oscars fitted at Bob Mackie's studio. The dress was long and slinky and covered with bugle beads, and when it was finished it would fit her like a glove. Cee Cee stood still as Bob Mackie circled her, congratulating her for the nomination with his sweet boyish smile, amazed at how thin she was these days. And that was when she realized she hadn't eaten anything in nearly two days.

When the fitting was over, she went into the three-way-mirrored dressing room to slip the dress off carefully to avoid the pins, but before she did, she leaned against the center mirror and watched as an infinite number of Cee Cees in all directions covered their faces and wept.

Three days had passed. It was a Monday afternoon and Cee Cee was in her office, in a meeting for her next film. The director, the writer, the two producers, and all of the development people, Cee Cee's and the studio's, sat spread around the room, on chairs, on the sofas, and on the floor, talking about the script and some of the last-minute changes, when the door opened.

"Cee Cee," her secretary said, "it's Nina." Her face looked alarmed. Cee Cee left the meeting, walked to her secretary's desk in the outer office, and took the phone.

"Hello?"

The voice on the other end of the line was Nina's but in a panic that made it sound shrill and eerie. "Cee Cee, you have to help me. I can't breathe and my face is swollen and I . . . I'm sorry, but I snorted something at Lisa's and I . . ."

"Where's Lisa's house?" Cee Cee asked her.

"On Tigers Trail. Six four one."

"Hang on, I'm coming," Cee Cee said and hung up.

She drove like a maniac over the canyon, running stop signs and red lights, and when she reached Lisa's house she double-parked and ran up the steps, tried the door, and barged into the house. There were dozens of crumpled tissues all over the floor and the chairs, and Lisa sat crying on the sofa, holding bunched-up tissues to her face.

"I'm okay," she said, "but she's really bad."

Cee Cee heard a loud moan, which she recognized as Nina's, and followed the sound to a little chintz and ruffled powder room where Nina crouched over the toilet retching and vomiting. Cee Cee put an arm around her, brushed her hair from her face, and held her head.

"Sorry, Cee, I'm sorry," Nina said.

Cee Cee wet a washcloth with cold water to wash Nina's face, which, now that the girl turned to her, she could see was swollen and distorted. And when Nina looked up and caught sight of herself in the mirror, she wailed, "Oh God," and Cee Cee could hear by the gurgled sound of the wail that her throat was closing.

The doctor in the emergency room told Cee Cee they had to intubate Nina because her vocal chords were swollen and her airway was in jeopardy of obstructing, which could have killed her if they'd been a few minutes later. The swollen face was an angioneurotic edema, caused by the drug. It was crank, a mixture of speed and God knows what else that had been used to cut it. Lisa had been put into a separate hospital room from Nina with only a dripping nose, and by the time her parents, a curly haired conservative-looking man in a gray suit, and a pretty blond mother, arrived at the hospital, Cee Cee was standing beaten and drained in the waiting room, placing her fourth phone call to Florrie, but still getting only the answering service. The parents didn't see her as they passed, but Cee Cee, who recognized them from school meetings, heard the father say to the mother, "I told you Nina probably got drugs from that piece of garbage Cee Cee Bloom and then gave them to Lisa. But you'd never listen, would you?"

"Shut up, Frank," she heard the woman answer.

Cee Cee's first impulse was to run after the guy, grab him by the throat, and scream obscenities into his face. To tell him it was *his* kid who got the dope, not her kid, and she started out the door to go after him, but stopped when she saw Florrie walking briskly down the corridor toward her.

"I got your message and came immediately. Is she all right?"

"The doctor said she will be," Cee Cee said.

"Can I see her?"

"I'll take you in."

Nina had a tube in her nose that was draining and a tube coming out of her mouth, and though Cee Cee had already seen her, each time she looked at her this way she had to hold on to the footboard of the bed to keep her knees from buckling under her. Nina narrowed her eyes when she looked at Florrie and realized who it was, and she wouldn't even look at Cee Cee.

"Nina," Florrie said, "it must feel pretty horrible being in that bed with all of those tubes in you, knowing that you came very close to dying. And I think it's significant that you called Cee Cee to come and save you instead of calling an ambulance yourself. Does that just mean you were afraid the police would find out about the drugs? Or does it mean that you're finally ready to accept Cee Cee's help with your drug problem?"

Nina stared at the ceiling. Cee Cee's face and body hurt with anxiety and pain, looking at this baby, this young child, so disfigured and destroyed by the abuse she'd brought on herself in this horrible way. *God give me strength,* she used to hear her own mother utter every day of her life. And now it was what she found herself asking, *God give me the strength to get through this one. Leona,* she thought, *I'm using your prayer because I finally get it, I finally understand you, and I'm sorry for every time I ever made you worry about me. For every time I shrieked at you, hated you, wanted to hurt you and didn't know why. Because now, at last, I understand how you felt. How a mother feels. And I wish you were around to say you told me so.*

"Dear girl," Florrie said to Nina, "perhaps now we can begin our treatment, because I'm sure that after this you'll be willing to make a commitment to stop using drugs. Won't you?"

Nina's response to Florrie's question was to turn her face back to the ceiling with an expression that, despite the helpless state and her supine position, still managed to look defiant. Florrie took Cee Cee by the elbow and moved her out of the room into the hospital corridor.

"What do I do?" Cee Cee asked.

"You put her into detox and then a rehab program. I know an excellent one in Newport Beach. You take her there, you leave her there, you do whatever you can to find out why she uses and try to change that, which can be a long and painful process. But Cee Cee, mostly . . ." Florrie put her hand on Cee Cee's arm. "Mostly you pray."

The sky was a muddy brown as Cee Cee drove south on the San Diego Freeway. Nina was asleep in the passenger seat; her face, though still puffy around the eyelids, was almost back to it's normal size. That morning at St. Johns Hospital she had stared out the window, sullen and pouting while Cee Cee packed the few toiletries she had used in the last few days and was allowed to take with her to the rehabilitation clinic. Her clothes were packed and waiting in the car per Florrie's instructions that Cee Cee take her directly to the drug clinic, because a stop at home could be disruptive to the process.

"Many times parents have said, 'We're just stopping off to pick up some clothes,' and when they got home, they were manipulated into changing their minds."

For a few minutes before they checked out, Florrie sat with the two of them in the cold, metallic, stripped-bare hospital room. A nurse came by pushing a wheelchair as standard hospital procedure to take Nina down to the car, but Cee Cee waved her off.

"Nina," Florrie said very softly, "can you connect with the specific pain you're feeling when you use?"

Nina didn't answer.

"What does being high give you that you can't get on your own?" It looked as if Nina wasn't going to answer, because she continued to stare out the window at the hospital wing opposite, but then she said, "Because my outsides don't match my insides. Outside I'm this nice quiet, okay-looking girl, but inside I want to be something else."

"What kind of something else?"

Again she thought for a while, then said, "I want to be able to be funny and tell jokes and have people like me because I have guts, and wear something with rhinestones in it . . . and unless I'm high I'm too scared."

Cee Cee couldn't believe what she was hearing. The kid was gorgeous; so many times she had looked at her in awe of her burgeoning beauty, thinking that she looked like all the beautiful girls Cee Cee had envied all her life. And with a brain and a sense of humor to match that beauty. How could she not know that about herself? "So I get high to go to school, because otherwise I'm nobody, and if I have to be nobody, I'd rather be dead."

"Nina, when you're high, who's your behavior model?" Florrie asked her.

The answer was so obvious Cee Cee wanted to blurt it out and would have if Florrie hadn't raised a hand to stop her. When Nina replied, there was amazement in her voice, because she spoke the answer just as she realized what the answer was.

"When I'm high, I act like Cee Cee does all the time. Gutsy, saying anything I feel like and cracking people up."

Dear God, Cee Cee thought, why would anyone want to act like that? I do it because it's all I know how to do.

"Has it been hard over the last seven years to keep up with whatever it means to belong to Cee Cee Bloom?"

There was a silence, then Nina smiled, a smile that looked eerie on her bright red face, and said in a voice that sounded odd coming from her, "You bet your ass," and all three of them laughed a laugh of recognition.

Now as Cee Cee pulled up to the admitting entrance of the hospital in Newport Beach, what at another time might have brought rage simply caused a blanket of weariness to fall over her, because standing in wait, festooned with their cameras, was an army of fan-magazine photographers. Somehow the sons-of-bitches knew everything, maybe from someone who worked at the other hospital, maybe from someone on Cee Cee's own staff who was selling the information about her troubles. And there they stood, waiting to take shots of Nina's entry into the hospital so that they could sell the pictures to the tabloids.

Instead of pulling into the portico where they stood, Cee Cee stopped and with a screech of tires backed up and found herself waking Nina and walking her into the hospital through an obscure entrance she found, just behind the linen service man who was making a delivery.

A nurse frisked her. Cee Cee stood and watched a big black nurse, wearing a plastic pin that said that her name was Marvel, actually frisking Nina for drugs, while Cee Cee stood there feeling as guilty as if she had been caught red-handed killing the very person she cared about the most.

While the nurse patted Nina down Cee Cee noticed Nina hung her head in a way that looked so tough, she must have seen it in some old "women in prison" movie on television. It was almost as if she was relishing the role of the beaten-down bad kid because it was so unlike the perfect girl she'd been, or pretended to be, up until so recently. Cee Cee's stomach was cramped and twisted, and she could feel every touch of the nurse's hands on Nina as if she was living through the humiliation herself. Marvel handed Nina a plastic specimen cup and was ushering her toward a door marked RESTROOM.

"You can leave any time now, honey," Marvel said to Cee Cee, with more than a little hint of I'm-running-the-show-here. "She's starting detox right after her shower, and after that you're not allowed to even talk to her for about three weeks."

Cee Cee made a noise in her throat to indicate that what the woman had just told her was absurd. "You mean I can't *see* her. But it's okay to call her on the phone. Right?"

"You can call *me*," the nurse said. "I'll be glad to let you know how she's doing," and she gave Cee Cee a little wave of dismissal. "But, no you can't call her, and she can't call you. Not till the doctor says so." When Cee Cee looked as if she was about to give her an argument, Marvel looked at her closely and said, "Why don't you stop by Doctor Pappas's office and get the packet we give out to the parents. The rules are all in there real clear."

Nina was in the bathroom now and Marvel was using her own foot, wearing white Nike tennis shoes, as a doorstop to hold the door partially open, until Cee Cee saw Nina's hand pass the urine specimen out to her. Marvel looked down just long enough to mark *BARRON* with a grease pencil on the side of the plastic cup and then looked back at Cee Cee. "You go on now," she said. Nina emerged from the bathroom, and Cee Cee walked closer to her, hoping to give her a parting hug, but before she could, Nina shook her off. "I'm leaving," Cee Cee said.

"Bye," Nina said, and walked with Marvel down the hospital hall.

"You've got to be joking about the three weeks," she said to the doctor. "I'm not gonna make it through that. Anyway, why keep *me* out? I'm not going to bring her any drugs." Doctor Pappas was in his late fifties, handsome in an Anthony Quinn sort of way, olive skinned with white hair and a slight Greek accent.

"No, but you might perhaps be a reminder to her of why she's been using them."

"I don't get it. You mean *I'm* the reason? Hey, I know I'm a pain in the ass, but Doctor Kagan sent you her records. Her mother died a grisly death when she was eight years old, and her father is the worst prick that ever lived. You *know* what her life has been like. And what about peer pressure? That's what pushes kids to use, isn't it?"

"Ms. Bloom, it would be too easy to blame any and all of those things. The reasons for adolescent addiction are mixed and complicated. The sad fact is that today thirty percent of the addicted population are adolescents. They're a perfect target for the drug sellers, as is anyone who is fearful, feeling rebellious, anxious to be attractive to the opposite sex. And it's also classic for the child of an overbearing and famous parent to seek independence from that parent, and solace in substance abuse from the sad fact that he or she will never be equal to that parent. Maybe since you caught Nina so early in life, by working together we can find out what her particular reasons are and infuse her with enough confidence in herself to make her want to get and remain sober."

"What can I do? Tell me and I'll do it."

"After she's been detoxed, I want to put her in a private rehab program not far from here which I facilitate. You can go home, and come to a family meeting there when I think she's ready to have you. At least three weeks. In the meantime," he said, handing her half a dozen small paper booklets, "it would be good if you would attend some of these."

Cee Cee looked down at what he had given her. Brochures from Alanon, Naranon, AA, Cocaine Anonymous, CODA, Adult Children of Alcoholics. "Those are lists of meetings of Twelve Step programs of various types. Programs that will help you to understand what we do here better than my explaining it to you. Go to them, find one or find several where you're comfortable, and go every day, at least once. We like to say ninety meetings in ninety days, but going to more than that won't hurt you. Because if you sit there long enough, eventually the commonality of the situations hits home and you learn through the pain of others how to overcome your own."

"I don't have . . ." She started to say she didn't have time to go to a bunch of meetings. To explain she had work to do, the Oscars to prepare for, but she stopped herself. "Look, it's not my pain that worries me. I'm okay. It's the kid's pain we're talking about here. This is a kid who could have O.D.'d on crank. Who told me she had to toot up just to make it through a schoolday. And I don't remember the last time I saw her arms. She could be mainlining for all I know."

"You seem to have the lingo down already," the doctor said, looking long at her, and she felt herself flush.

"I'm in show business," she said.

"I'm very aware of that fact," Pappas said, "but I'm in the reality business. So now we're going to deal in Nina's reality. As unpleasant as that may turn out to be."

"I'll go to meetings," Cee Cee said, "and I'll see you" — she looked at Pappas for an answer but he had none for her. ". . . when I see you," she said, and she left his office and walked through the quiet corridors of the hospital, feeling cold and tired and not sure what day or time it was. When she got to the delivery entrance where her car was parked, she noticed for the first time that it was dark, and she got into the car and drove into the night alone. Somewhere along the freeway her stomach growled. She was hungry, so she pulled off at the next exit and into the drive-through entrance of a McDonald's.

"Next, please," said a disembodied voice.

"Big Mac, side of fries, and a Coke."

After she picked up her food, she pulled the car into a parking space in the brightly lit parking lot, looking through the windows at the families inside McDonald's enjoying their dinners, and she envied them.

"God grant me the serenity to accept the things I cannot change, the courage to change the things I can, and the wisdom to know the difference."

The next morning she stood on the beach in Santa Monica before sunrise, holding the hands of two people she'd never seen before in her life. In fact, she was part of a large circle made up of dozens of people she'd never seen before. She was wearing her disguise, the hat and the sunglasses, and it seemed to be working. So far not one person there had asked if she was Cee Cee Bloom. The Serenity Prayer, she thought. That ought to be called the mother's prayer.

As the meeting began she sat on the blanket she'd brought, holding a Styrofoam cup of hot coffee and four cookies, which she ate in rapid succession, not caring if they were going to make her look fat in her Oscar dress, and she watched carefully and listened to the welcomes and to someone reading the Twelve Steps, and then she realized they were going around the group and everyone was saying his or her name. Just the first name, after which everybody said "Hi" to them by name, but Cee Cee was such a funny name that if she said it and they took a good look at her, everyone would know who she was.

"I'm Pat," she said when it was her turn.

"Hi, Pat," everyone said, and she felt relieved when they went on to the next person and nobody seemed the wiser that she wasn't Pat, but she hated herself for lying at the same time. Mostly what happened at these meetings, she was figuring out now, was that people got up and told their stories. One young girl in her twenties said that her husband was so physically abusive she had to move out on him, because it was one thing for him to hit her before, but now she was pregnant, and she thanked all of them for being there for her because, she said, "Without you people I would have nobody."

Then a very straight-looking, handsome, gray-haired man said that last week was his birthday, and he was trying to figure out why that depressed him, and then he remembered that when he was a kid he always hated his birthdays because he had to have his birthday dinner at a restaurant that had a bar in it, so his father could leave the rest of the family and sit at the bar and drink, and how his father still ran his life, and he wanted to stop wishing his father would die already.

One girl said she spent the money her parents sent her to buy books and clothes at college on drugs, so she had to go to the college bookstore and steal the books, and then to the clothing stores and steal clothes. And now that she was sober and working her program, she was up to Step Nine, which said, "We will try to make direct amends to people we have harmed, where amends are possible to make," so she had gone back to those stores she had stolen from years before and offered to pay them back for the merchandise.

An older woman said she used the twelve noon, twelve midnight plan. "I never ask myself how I'm gonna get through the day. When

I wake up I tell myself I'll just try to get to twelve noon, and at twelve noon I say, I'll just try to make it to twelve midnight. It's how I survive my husband's drinking." Cee Cee reached into her purse and took out a pen, and the only paper she could find was an old envelope, so on the back of it she wrote herself a note that said, TWELVE NOON. TWELVE MIDNIGHT. She would try that.

Maybe these meetings worked, or maybe they were just a bunch of slogans and coffee. But she needed something, anything, so she sat tailor-seat on her blanket on the sand listening to it all, taking it in, hearing the way other people lived with their problems. These little bits of people's lives are better, sadder, more human, and much more moving than any of the stories the writers who come in to meet with me at the studio ever bring, she thought. These people are spilling their real beans all over the place, and feeling better for it, and even getting applause after they do. She could never do that in front of strangers. When a character she played was in pain, that was okay. She could cry and scream and writhe and suffer publicly as someone else, but not as Cee Cee Bloom, who thankfully no one at this meeting seemed to realize she was.

When the meeting on the beach was over, she helped some of the others pick up coffee stirrers and half-empty Styrofoam cups, and put them in a trash can, then walked to where she'd parked the BMW in the lot, slid in, and picked the pile of lists of meetings up from the passenger seat. At nine o'clock she was at a rolls-and-coffee breakfast meeting in the basement of a church in Woodland Hills.

> Our Father
> Who art in Heaven,
> Hallowed be thy name.
> Thy kingdom come
> Thy will be done . . .

"Well, don't *you* look familiar," she heard a woman's voice say very loud at the break, and she cringed, wondering what she was going to say to some fan, how she was going to explain why she was here, but then realized the person who had said that wasn't talking to her, but to another woman, and the two women hugged and went off to find two seats together so they could chat until the break was over. Cee Cee sat in the back, close to the exit door so when it got boring she could leave early. But she was never bored and she never left early. Not from that meeting or from the candlelight meeting in Hollywood she attended that night, or the meeting that was conducted while the group took a walk on the Venice bike path. Or even at the meeting of gay men and transvestites she went to by mistake, where a short bald man came over and said to her, "Jim Dale does a great Cee Cee Bloom, but you know what? I think yours is better."

She went to a Cocaine Anonymous meeting in the north valley and a guy wearing a pin that said THERE IS NO PROBLEM WHICH CAN'T BE SOLVED BY THE DIRECT APPLICATION OF EXPLOSIVES asked if she would give him her phone number. She declined politely, hoping he wouldn't apply the explosives to her face. In that meeting she looked around and decided she was probably the only person in the room who didn't have a tattoo. In fact, when she first walked in and saw the people who were showing up, she was so unnerved by how tough they all looked it made her want to leave, but as they stood one by one to tell their stories, they looked different to her.

A recovering drug dealer–user who had his first honest job, working for a cold storage company, told everyone how the minute there was some quiet time at work, he sat in his seat high atop the hydraulic lift, read his Twelve Step study book, and meditated. Then there was a recovering heroin addict whose wife had committed suicide three months and one day earlier, who received a ninety-day chip at the meeting as his reward for being sober for three months. He had started on his road to sobriety the day after her death. They were all filled with gratitude for the safety of "these rooms" as they called the places they came to meet with one another, and support one another, and get each other through the difficulty of becoming and staying sober.

At a meeting in Brentwood, Cee Cee stopped on her way in the door because inside she saw a few people she knew. One of them was a woman studio executive, very high up in the Hollywood hierarchy, and when the woman saw Cee Cee she came right over to her. "If there's anything I can do" was all she said, and she squeezed Cee Cee's hand warmly. Cee Cee decided not to go back to that meeting, or to any other one where there was a chance they would go around the room and give their names. In those, she always allowed herself to lie and say she was someone else. Until she understood by the end of day ten, by which point she had been to more than thirty meetings, the queen of overkill, that nearly everyone had known all along she was Cee Cee Bloom and that it didn't matter.

One by one she had canceled the fitness-training sessions she had booked after she'd heard about the Oscar nomination, canceled her firming facials and a photo session with *People* magazine because she wanted to spend the time at meetings. She postponed two of her new projects and didn't go in to the office, just went to these meetings, day after day, night after night, trying to get it. And she had some private sessions with Florrie too.

"Why the compulsion to work so much, so hard, so constantly?"

"I don't know. Because it feels good, and makes me feel powerful, important. Sometimes I think I need it to feel alive."

"What happens when you stop?"

"Well . . . I'm okay for a little while and then . . ."

"And then?"

"If I stop . . ." She paused and then laughed an embarrassed laugh and admitted, "I guess it's my drug of choice."

Florrie nodded as the two women's eyes met.

"When she gets out of rehab she's going to need you. I think you should take a long look at your future schedule and make it one that gives you a lot of time for her, even if that means cutting back on your own productivity. Will you do that?"

"I want to be able to do it."

"But will you do it?"

"I can probably do that."

"Cee Cee, will you do it?"

Cee Cee didn't speak.

"Answer the question for yourself, not for me," the doctor said.

On day twelve, at her thirty-sixth Twelve Step meeting, she felt herself standing and wanted to sit down, but was called on by the leader before she could change her mind, and with the rapidly beating heart of a first-time performer with stage fright said, "Hi, I'm Cee Cee." Then wondered what in the hell she was going to say.

"Hi, Cee Cee," everyone said back to her. Then she waited a beat to listen for snickers or for people saying "Don't we know it," but nobody did, and she went on. "I'm raising a teenager, thought I was doing pretty good at it, but recently I found out she's into drugs. So

I've been trying to learn about my part in that by coming to these meetings. About the times I've given her things instead of giving her me, and the times I've looked the other way when she walked out of the house with friends I wasn't sure about. And the times I said to myself I have no right to control her, because I'm not her real mother, and even if I was, I hated my mother for controlling me and I don't want my kid to hate me that way so I'll back off.

"And if kids learn by example, my own life hasn't exactly been a shining one. I'm disorganized and sloppy, I'm moody and unpredictable. I used to do drugs myself, a lot, and though I stopped, I have an addiction of my own. You see, the reason I was able to stop using drugs was because they were hurting my performing, which means the drugs were getting in the way of my bigger addiction, because I have one and it took me all this time to realize what it is.

"I'm hooked on the high I get from performing and stardom, and some version of success I made up when I was a little kid and never bothered to change. But even though that's not what I think success is about anymore, I don't think, I mean, I'm not so sure I can kick the habit of scoring that high again and again, because it was how I turned on for so long. And because of that, I've pushed aside my personal life over and over again to get the phony synthetic kind of love that comes from an audience, instead of taking in the real blast that comes from being loved by the people I love.

"I don't mean to knock my career. It's wonderful that I'm good at what I do and that people like it, and that when they see me up there in the movies they laugh and cry with me, but over the last seven years, *that* was never what really did it for me . . . gave me unending joy, filled me up. That was done by my little girl. Being with her was what made me glad to be alive. When that little face told me she thought I was funny or brave or important . . . that was when I got the real goods.

"And the horrible thing is, you never figure when you watch that little pink person come into the world, so cute and scrawny and helpless, that one day she'll be taking your car while you're asleep and going out to score drugs with money that she got by selling her belongings and yours too, and you tell yourself, even when you look right into the jewelry box and things are gone, that you probably left them somewhere or maybe the plumber took them on his way past the closet to fix the bathroom faucets. But now I know that I just kept denying and denying, and thinking when I looked at her that she couldn't need anything more grown-up than her teddy bears.

"And because I took her innocence and her goodness and her love for granted, and didn't pay close enough attention, she started using drugs. The kid had to get high just to go to school, to be with friends, to feel okay about herself. And now I'm afraid that I let the most valuable person in my life slide away, and that I'll never be able to . . . I have to make this right. Have to get her to know she's more important to me than . . . oh my God, oh my God."

The man next to her, who was big and beefy looking, wearing a baseball cap with a short ponytail sticking out of the adjustable part in the back, stood and held her in his arms, and she stayed there for a while with her face against his shirt that smelled of starch and sweat. Then, finally when she was able to, she said, "Thank you for letting me share," and everyone applauded for her, as she sat down wondering what she had accomplished, but some of it was starting to sink in, as she sat with the Twelve Step literature, the Alanon day-by-day messages, and the Blue Book, and read and thought and wrote and took stock of the past seven years.

It was a Sunday afternoon when she got the word from the doctor telling her that next week Nina would be ready to have her come to a family meeting with the other boys and girls in rehab and the members of their families, and she was jubilant. She was in her room when the phone rang, so she scribbled the date and the time and the directions down on the pad next to her bed, and as she did she thought excitedly about what she would say, and how good it was going to be to see Nina's face, ready to have her there. Maybe Nina would rush to her and hug her, maybe . . . As she looked at what her hand had written on the page, she realized that the family group in Newport Beach at the rehab center was being held on Monday night, March 26, at eight o'clock, which would be halfway through the Oscar ceremony.

"Thank you for calling," she said into the phone. "I'll be there."

The small row of dormitory houses belonging to Seaside Sobriety where Nina had now lived for nearly three weeks sat on a narrow street across from a wide expanse of a beautiful off-white sandy beach, in what was in other parts of the neighborhood a pricey vacation home community in Newport Beach. The neighborhood reminded Cee Cee of the way it had looked in Beach Haven, New Jersey, when she was in summer stock. In fact, the accommodations reminded her of the place where the cast had lived, but it was clear by looking at the faces of the young people who filed into the living room where tonight's meeting was being held that they weren't here to be in a musical play.

When Cee Cee saw Nina walk in among a group of girls, she felt afraid that the girl would be embarrassed by her and wish she wasn't there. Maybe she would do her usual and say the wrong thing in front of the other kids, who, she could see by the laughing and the elbowing and wisecracking among them, had become Nina's new group of friends. Nina waved a little wave to her, but stayed with the friends, none of whom moved to speak to any of their parents, who were forming a group right near where Cee Cee stood. It wasn't until the door to the living room was pushed open with a flourish, and handsome Doctor Pappas moved through the parent group and pulled a big frayed armchair for himself to one end of the room, that the others began pulling chairs into a circle.

Now Cee Cee noticed how each of the kids carried a pillow. As she moved into the group, she saw the other family members sit on their chairs in an outside circle, and the kids put their pillows on the floor in the center of the circle, then sit on them. A few of the kids positioned themselves directly in front of their mothers. Cee Cee saw Nina notice that and then plop her own pillow in front of Cee Cee and sit facing into the circle. According to the rules, the only treat parents could bring their kids was sugarless gum. Cee Cee saw one of the mothers offer some to her own daughter, so she offered some to Nina, who shook her head to decline.

"Okay," Pappas said, "let's have a feelings round. Say who you are and how you're feeling. Bobby, why don't you begin?"

"Hi, I'm Bobby, I'm an alcoholic, addict."

"Hi, Bobby."

"I'm feeling scared because my dad's here for the first time."

"I'm Gary. Addict."

"Hi, Gary."

"I'm feeling glad because next week's my graduation from this place and I get to go home, which is cool since I haven't seen my dog in three months."

Everyone laughed, especially Gary's mother whom he resembled, who said, "Thanks, pal."

"I'm Jenna, I'm an alcoholic." This girl looked as if she was nine years old. Tiny and dark skinned, with giant brown eyes.

"Hi, Jenna."

"I'm three weeks sober, and I'm feeling bummed out because neither one of my parents is here tonight, and last week they hardly came to any meetings either, and I hate their fucking guts."

"Hi, I'm Nina. I'm an addict." Cee Cee hoped no one noticed how she flinched when she heard those words.

"Hi, Nina."

And all the way around the circle. Addicts, alcoholics, many of the kids said they were both, and not one of them was over the age of seventeen. Cee Cee had to stop herself from shaking her head in disbelief at the straightforward way these kids spoke in front of their parents with no holds barred. Now the focus moved to the outside of the circle, to the parents. Cee Cee had been looking them all over carefully. One of the mothers sat behind her daughter and tenderly brushed the girl's hair. A father massaged his son's shoulders. One couple sat far away from their son and clutched each other's hands so tightly that their knuckles were white.

"I'm Harv, Bobby's dad. I'm an adult child of an alcoholic, an alcoholic, a co-dependent, and a sick son-of-a-bitch for not coming to any of these meetings before tonight. I'm feeling glad I'm here."

"Hi, Harv."

"I'm Edith, Gary's mother."

"Hi, Edith."

"I'm feeling glad Gary's coming home soon, too, because I'm sick of taking care of the goddamned dog."

"I'm Cee Cee. I'm with Nina, and I'm feeling fine," she said.

A chorus of kids' voices rang out, and because they were trying to top one another in volume it was hard to make out exactly what they were saying at first, but they repeated it at her a few times. "Fucked up, insecure, neurotic emotion."

"What?" Cee Cee asked, looking around nervously.

Doctor Pappas was smiling. "The group has an aversion to the word *fine*," he explained. "They think it's a catchall, a cover-up for real feelings. They say it's an acronym for fucked-up, insecure, neurotic emotion. A way to conceal how you really feel."

Cee Cee had to laugh a little laugh. After all the meetings she'd attended, she should have known these kids would have an instant bullshit detector. "They're right," she said. "I feel real scared."

"I'm Joanne, I'm Danny's mother."

"Hi, Joanne."

"And I've got to say what I'm feeling, which I'll bet is what a lot of people here would like to say, which is that I'm feeling uncomfortable because Cee Cee Bloom is here, and knowing she was coming tonight had everyone around here gossiping for the last few days, and I don't know if I can be myself with some movie star in our group. I don't feel like she's one of us."

Cee Cee's heart sank, and all eyes went to Doctor Pappas. "Joanne, when Cee Cee is in this group, she is a mother just like you, except for the fact that she has . . ."

"Several million dollars in the bank," someone quipped, and a few people laughed, but Cee Cee felt tense now because she saw by Nina's back that her body was tensing up.

". . . a higher profile," Pappas went on. "She hurts over her family's problems just like you do. She cries when her child is suffering just like you do. So let's go on."

The next parent and the next and the next said their names, but Cee Cee didn't hear them. She watched Nina's body language as the girl pulled her knees to her chest and put her head forward so her chin rested in the space between them, trying to make herself small enough to be unnoticeable.

"Nina, you look particularly unhappy," Pappas said. "Can you say why?" Cee Cee would have bet that Nina, in a group this size, would never talk about what was going on with her, but the weeks in this place must have had their effect because she spoke right up.

"Because here I am trying to get over the worst thing in my life, and just like always it gets to be about Cee Cee Bloom, and I'm sick of that. All I ever wanted even with my real mother was to be in a regular family, ordinary, you know? Where the mother cleans the oven, and the father comes home and says, 'What's for dinner?' And

instead I went from a bad situation as the daughter of a single mother
to living with Cee Cee and being the . . ." And then she said a few
words that were unintelligible, after which she stopped short and
everyone was uncomfortably quiet until Pappas asked:

"The what, Nina?"

Nina shook her head no. She was refusing to finish the sentence.

"Come on, Nina," one of the kids said, "you told all of *us*."

"Living with Cee Cee and being . . ." Pappas said, leading her.

"The nobody to a star."

"Why a nobody?" Pappas asked quietly, and no one moved while
they waited for her answer.

By the time Nina spoke, it was in a tortured voice that would have
been painful to hear no matter what it said, but the words delivered
the killing blow. "Because I'm not her daughter. Sometimes I lie and
tell people I am, but that's what it is. A lie. I'm nobody's daughter,
not my mother's, my father's, or Cee Cee's. She never cared enough
to make me her daughter or she would have adopted me when my
mother died. And I've thought about that every day of my life for the
last eight years. Sometimes Cee Cee would come home and say, 'I
have a surprise for you,' and I would always think, 'This is it. Today's
the day she's going to say she'll adopt me, and that will be the surprise.' But it never was. It was always a stuffed animal or a sweater
or tickets to a play, and I was always afraid to say, 'Don't you get it,
that's not what I want. I want *you*. To belong to *you*, to belong *with*
you. Because I'm a person who doesn't belong to anyone.' But I never
said that because I was afraid she'd say no."

Pappas gave Nina what looked to Cee Cee like a conspiratorial congratulations for being able to say what she had in front of Cee Cee.
Obviously it was information she had shared with Pappas, with the
whole group of kids before this. Then the doctor looked at Cee Cee
as if to ask her if she wanted to respond. *How can I do it?* she thought.
*How will I ever be able to tell her what I should have told her every day for
the last eight years?* Then she cleared her throat, which had become
clogged with nervousness, and spoke.

"For a big part of my life I thought the same thing about myself
that Joanne over there said about me. That I was different than other
people. But over the last eight years of living with Nina, and now
after coming to these meeting rooms for even this little while, what I

know for absolute certain is that what Doctor Pappas said was true. I'm the same as everybody else. In spades. I'm raising a child and I want the best life has to offer for her just like all of you want for your kids. I work hard at what I do and I want it to go well, just like all of you feel about your work. I want to be loved and respected the same as everyone in this room does. And just like every parent here, because it's all trial and error, I raised my kid making a lot of mistakes. Like being in her face too much when she doesn't want me around, and being out to lunch too often when she does want me to be around, and I wish I could turn back the clock to that first day and do everything right but I can't so . . ."

"Cee Cee," Doctor Pappas interrupted, "may I suggest that you talk directly to Nina." Then he made a little gesture to Nina to move inside the circle so she could turn around and look at Cee Cee, and she did. Her pretty but pale face turned up at her, her eyes blinking fast in a way Cee Cee knew she always used to hold in her tears.

"Nina," Cee Cee said, "it took your mother's death to make me think I grew up, because taking care of her when she was dying was the only unselfish thing I've ever done in my life. By the end, I guess she knew it, so that even though it was pretty obvious I was the candidate least likely to succeed at the job, she must have figured, from the way I finally set everything aside but her, that I had the potential to be a caring person and it would be okay for her to appoint me as your guardian.

"At the time it made me happy, but I didn't even have a clue that first day you and I were together what it was gonna mean. In my wildest dreams I didn't imagine that the job description of motherhood was that one day you start feeling so close to another person that when she hurts even the least little bit, it kills you, and that without even thinking about it, you get so attached to that person and need her love so much, that even if she looks at you crooked, you want to cry. And maybe I never told you up till now, but what being with you taught me that I never knew was that it was possible to love another person more than I love myself. I know I don't always show it, doing dumb things, making wrong choices, but believe me, it's true."

She paused for a moment, and when she did Dr. Pappas spoke. "But after saying all that you still haven't said the words."

"Huh?" Cee Cee asked looking at him.

"You still haven't simply stated what it is I believe you want to tell Nina."

"You mean . . . ?"

Pappas nodded and Cee Cee looked into Nina's pathetically ringed and bloodshot eyes and said, "Neen, I love you. I love you as if I was the one who gave birth to you in that delivery room myself, instead of the one who fainted. I couldn't love you any more if you were born from my body. But I have to admit there hasn't been one day that we've been together when I didn't fear I wasn't good enough, smart enough, understanding enough, loving enough to live up to being as good as your real mother would have been for you. And that was the biggest reason I was afraid to adopt you. Because of what *I'm* not."

Nina looked down into her lap now with what seemed to Cee Cee to be a look of relief.

"And believe me when I tell you, your mother wasn't perfect. Sometimes she could be a cold, judgmental pain in the kiester. Holding feelings inside, being too rigid about how things were supposed to be. But she had other stuff about her that I loved, and her best quality, at least for my money, and the thing that I know made her a great mother, was the way she'd stand up with an opinion about things I did that she didn't like, even if the risk was rejection or me mouthing off at her, which I did a lot. And on the other side of that coin, she was just as unafraid to say, 'Goddammit, you did something great and I'm proud of you,' and never thought that saying that meant she was putting herself in second position by getting out of the way and making me feel appreciated."

Now there was a little smile on Nina's face as if she was remembering those aspects of Bertie too.

"I hope it's not too late for me to say I want to try harder to be that way for you. Not scared to point out what I think is wrong for fear you'll hate me if I do, and thoughtful enough to pat you on the back as often as I can. I have lots of fears that have plagued me and run me for too long, and one of those is what's kept me from admitting to you what I'm about to tell you now, which is not what I planned to say here tonight, but I have to.

"For a big part of my life I was a user too. A heavy user. It was one of the reasons your mother was planning at first to give you to your Aunt Neetie instead of to me. I smoked grass and sometimes hash to go to sleep and for the longest time I tooted up to go to work, and then used some more to get me through the work day . . . and to get me through the fact that I felt fat, or unattractive, or different than everybody else. Your mother once screamed her head off at me, trying to get me to stop. And the reason I never told you or anybody that about me is because I was afraid if it came out, it would somehow be what separated us, that you would think I was garbage for having that in my past. It's also part of the reason I never tried to adopt you, though I've thought about it every day for the last eight years too, and wanted to but was always afraid if I started the process and social workers came and checked on me, they would find out I once did drugs and say what I feared. That I didn't deserve to be your mother.

"Having you in my life has made me a human being, given me a reason to wake up on mornings when I was too depressed to move. I couldn't believe it when you said that you did drugs so you could be like me. Because I've spent a lifetime wishing *I* could be like *you*. Beautiful and dignified, smart and classy. Knowing just how to behave, and being in enough control to pull it off. I admire you so much, and if I never told you I loved you all these years, I realize now that the reason was probably that I was afraid to, since I've lost everyone I've ever loved."

Nina nodded knowingly, then spoke softly. "Me too."

"And you know what else?" Cee Cee said. "Not that this makes it okay, but you've never said you love me either."

Again there was silence, interrupted only by the cracking of one of the kid's chewing gum and what sounded to Cee Cee like a floor polisher somewhere off in the distance in the hospital corridor.

"Nina," Doctor Pappas asked, "*do* you love Cee Cee?"

Nina didn't answer, and the silence was killing to Cee Cee, who figured it could go either way now and the kid could say no, and that would be the worst thing she could ever hear, but then Nina's lower lip trembled and her face collapsed, and she cried, that kind of cry where no sound comes out and the crier seems to be inhaling all of the tears and can't say a word. Then she nodded, a very slow nod, and took in a huge breath, and Doctor Pappas asked softly, "Well, why don't you tell her?"

Nina took a few breaths and tried to gain control, as Cee Cee sat forward in her chair expectantly. "I love you, Cee Cee," Nina said, punctuated by intakes of breath. "I really do love you a lot."

Thank you, God, oh thank you for that, thank you, Cee Cee thought.

"I love the way you always stick up for yourself and for me. And I think it's so cool the way you try to be so nice to your fans even when they bug you, and the way you try to act real tough but inside you're really full of mush." That caused a light giggle to ripple through the group, and brought a smile that started inside Cee Cee's chest and moved to her face, and her smile seemed to buoy Nina to continue.

"You're what some of the kids in this group call 'truly awesome.' But, see, one of the things I've been finding out about me is that I can't always handle awesome too well? Because what I really need is real? And I don't know if you and I will ever get there. To being real. Because you're still always going to be you, Cee Cee Bloom, and I'm still going to be me, wishing for a real life with real parents. And that's the kind of stuff that all the meetings and groups in the world can't change."

Doctor Pappas handed Nina a wad of Kleenex, and she wiped her eyes and blew her nose and went on. "What I'm saying is, I think I'm scared that talking about not using won't make me not want to get out of here and use again. But yes . . . I love you, and I've been super-afraid to tell you that before tonight. Before I knew that you love me . . . and that I wasn't someone you got stuck with because your friend died." She bit her lip and looked straight and hard at Cee Cee, waiting to see what would happen next, and Cee Cee moved to the middle of the circle, took Nina's hands, lifted her to her feet, and pulled her into her arms where they wept, and Doctor Pappas passed a box of Kleenex around to many of the other people in the group who needed it too.

The moon lit the narrow beach street as Cee Cee and Nina walked toward Cee Cee's car, arms around one another's waists. Some of the tiny, funky, one-story houses they passed had wind chimes, which hung quietly in the still night. A few of the houses just beyond the row of Seaside Sobriety houses were lit only by the flickering lights of televisions.

"Doctor Pappas said he thinks you'll be able to come home in a few weeks," Cee Cee said as they reached the car, which was parked just opposite the open sliding glass door of a house inside of which Cee Cee spotted an older couple, watching the Academy Awards.

"I'll come back on Wednesday for the next family meeting," she said, taking Nina's hand, "and for every meeting after that. I promise. I'm going to do everything I can to get us through this." Nina squeezed her hand gratefully, then looked past her at the television in the little house, and when Cee Cee followed her gaze back to the small set she saw Billy Crystal introducing Gregory Peck, who strode handsome and elegant up to the podium, and when the applause ended he said something about five gifted women. And then he named them, and as he did a piece of each of their films rolled by. Isabelle Adjani, *Camille Claudel*. Jessica Lange, *Music Box*. Cee Cee Bloom, *Lives of Sophie West*. Cee Cee, who never liked the way she looked on film, was relieved that the clips were so short.

When Gregory Peck had announced all the nominations, he opened the envelope and announced, "And the Oscar goes to Jessica Tandy for *Driving Miss Daisy*." In an instant the audience rose to their feet and Cee Cee took a long deep breath as Nina put a supporting arm around her shoulder and held on tight, and they both watched as Jessica Tandy took the stage. The old couple in the house were applauding along with the television audience.

"I never expected in a million years that I'd be in this position, and I thank my lucky stars . . ." Jessica Tandy said, "and Richard and Lily Zanuck, and that forgotten man Bruce Beresford. I'm on cloud nine."

Cee Cee turned away from the television and looked at Nina. She could hear the old woman in the house they were standing next to saying, "Well, it's about time she won one of those things."

"Do you feel awful that you're not the winner?" Nina asked her.

"Oh, kiddo," Cee Cee said. "That's where you're wrong. I have you. And that makes me the biggest and luckiest winner I know."

They hugged again, and Cee Cee got into the car and Nina waved goodbye as the car pulled away, and then she walked slowly back to the small house where some of the group were waiting for her.

LOS ANGELES, CALIFORNIA

August 1990

IT WAS seven years exactly from the day of Bertie's death, one of those eerie coincidences Cee Cee remembered thinking when she entered today's event into her appointment calendar. Now it crossed her mind again while she sat in the back of the limousine, which snaked with funereal slowness through the relentless freeway traffic. Her father, Harriet, and Hal sat with her, staring out of the darkened windows, lost in their respective thoughts, and as the oddly mixed architecture of the downtown skyline came into view signaling their imminent arrival, Hal reached over and took Cee Cee's hand.

"How're you holding up, old girl?"

She answered with a fervent squeeze of his hand.

Within minutes the limo slowed and Cee Cee leaned forward to look out the window in amazement at the size of the group waiting for them at the curb. So many of Nina's friends were there, all of them wearing what were for them somber clothes, and every one of them was serious-faced. Particularly Kevin, who stood in the front of the group and nodded a nod of encouragement to Cee Cee as she opened the door for herself and emerged from the car.

And then Jake, looking very official today in a uniform, including the rarely worn chauffeur's cap, opened his own door and walked around to the front door on the passenger side, opened that one with a flourish, and out stepped Nina. A cheer rose from the group, as all of the friends ran to greet her, to encircle her, hugging and congratulating her noisily, and finally they nearly lifted her off her feet to usher her along the sidewalk and up the steps to the courthouse.

Cee Cee took a deep breath and stopped at the bottom of the steps just to watch, filled with a grateful, joyous ache at seeing Nina getting the demonstration of love she needed so much now. Then, needing some support herself, she put an arm around her father and one around Hal, and with Harriet hanging onto Nathan's arm, the four of them bounced excitedly up the steps like the quartet from *The Wizard of Oz.*

Jim Andrews, Cee Cee's bespectacled, handsome, tweedy-looking lawyer, who was waiting in the marble hallway, smiled when he saw the size of the group. "I don't know if the judge's chambers are big enough to seat this many people," he said.

"So we'll stand," Nathan Bloom told him.

The last months had been a grueling series of painful sessions for Nina and Cee Cee. Sometimes Cee Cee would have stomachaches before going to a group meeting or an hour of therapy with Nina in anticipation of what she would hear next. Once, sitting on the far end of Doctor Pappas's sofa, as far as she could get from Cee Cee who sat on the other end, Nina confessed, "For a long time I blamed you for killing my mother. I thought if you had taken better care of her, if you hadn't sent away the nurse, she would have lived. So I hated you." Then she turned and put her face against the back of the sofa and cried silently. There was no way Cee Cee could respond to that. Another time, in a rage, Nina cried out, "It's not fair that someone as wonderful as my mother died and someone as horrible as you is still alive."

Then, immediately regretting it, she stood and went to Cee Cee and held her, saying, "I'm sorry. I'm so sorry."

And there were lighter times.

"Cee Cee, how did you learn to parent?" Doctor Pappas asked.

"Are you kidding? From my lunatic mother. I vowed I was never gonna be like that. She was loud and crass and when she showed up at school to take me to an audition I used to die of embarrassment. Everywhere I went, before I got into the room there was Leona, talking too much and talking too loud and saying all the wrong things. It made me nuts so I . . ." She stopped because the doctor and Nina were both grinning at her. "Oh yeah," she said. "I guess that's where I learned."

They celebrated on the day Cee Cee filed for adoption, and on the day when the phone call came from the lawyer telling them Michael

Barron had signed the release of abandonment, so the only possible impediment to setting the court date would be an investigation by a social worker.

"Both Doctor Pappas and Doctor Kagan say that despite all that's happened, you've worked hard to be a good mother to Nina," the social worker said. "Do you think that's right?" He was a young man of about thirty dressed in a suit and tie, unawed by Cee Cee's stardom, and that was the last question he asked her during a long and exhaustive interview.

"I can only tell you I've had moments I could kick myself for, but I've also had some moments I think I've been more mother than Harriet Nelson and Donna Reed rolled into one. Of course, the bottom line about being somebody's parent is what you learn. And for me, raising another human being has been the most important, most creative, most humbling experience I've ever had, and that's why it would mean so much to me and to Nina if we could . . ." That was when she had lost it for a second, but she stopped until she was able to talk again and said, "If we could, if I could . . . make it legal."

Now Hal and Nathan sat on a marble bench talking about the stock market, and Richie Charles entered, greeted by a very surprised squeal and a hug from Nina, and Florrie Kagan bustled in at the last second moving quietly to Cee Cee to give her a warm and approving embrace just as the door from the courtroom opened and a guard in a khaki uniform poked his head out and gestured to Jim Andrews, who said, "Okay, people, here we go." Then the guard opened the door to the tiny courtroom wider and ushered them through, walking single file to a large dark wood door at the back, upon which he knocked, and after a moment he gestured for all of them to follow him into the judge's chambers.

The judge was a pretty, page-boyed woman in her fifties, and she smiled a big smile and stood as she watched the gang of people troop in and find places to sit, or stand, to watch what was going to happen next.

"Looks to me like a party," she said.

"That's what it is," Harriet said.

The emotion in the room was palpable, the joy and the hope and the wonder, and the relief brought a giddiness to each person there, as Cee Cee's lawyer spoke. "Good morning, Your Honor, James R. Andrews appearing on behalf of petitioner Cee Cee Bloom and the extended family."

A court reporter took everything down as the judge said, "This is the matter of Cee Cee Bloom. The petitioner is present as well as the minor and their attorney, Mr. Andrews. The report from the County Bureau of Adoptions is admitted into evidence by reference. Please raise your right hand."

Cee Cee did. "Do you solemnly swear before this court that the information you have given is the truth, the whole truth, and nothing but the truth, so help you God?"

"I do," Cee Cee said.

"I assume you are here because you want to go ahead with the adoption?"

"That's right," Cee Cee said, and, continuing to look at the judge, she reached out her hand in Nina's direction and felt Nina take it.

The judge looked at Nina now and spoke gently. "Nina, when a child your age is being adopted, it is required of the state to ask that child if she can wholeheartedly say she consents to the adoption of her own free will. Do you want Cee Cee Bloom to adopt you, to be your legal parent forever?"

All eyes were on Nina now. She knew it, and she was flushed and bright-eyed. "Yes I do," she said, and it was forthcoming and clear.

"And, Cee Cee? Do you promise you will treat her in all respects as your lawful child? To make the child your own, to care for her and treat her as your rightful heir forever?"

"I sure do," Cee Cee said emphatically.

"I have a consent form I would like you to read, and if you approve, sign it."

Cee Cee bent over and shuffled around in her purse to find a pair of reading glasses. "This is what happens when you have an older mother, dear," she joked to Nina, and everyone laughed as she put the glasses on to read the form the judge had given her. When she'd read it, she nodded to Jim Andrews, who said, "Let the record reflect that the petitioner has read the consent in the open court."

"Since you have read it, if you approve, please sign your full name in black ink. According to the court the report is approved and filed." There was a lot of stamping of papers, and Cee Cee relaxed against the back of her chair for the first time.

The judge now looked at Cee Cee and Nina standing together, and smiled a very warm unjudgelike smile. "The court finds that it's in the best interest of the minor that the petition be granted. The petition is therefore granted, and hereafter you have the relationship of mother and daughter. All the responsibilities of that relationship and the duties thereof. I'm signing the decree." And she did. "Congratulations," she said.

Cee Cee would always remember that nobody moved for what seemed like a long time, then Nina came to her and looked at her and put her arms around her neck, and Nathan said, "Somebody take a picture," and a few flashbulbs went off. "Take one with the judge," somebody else said, and Cee Cee and Nina stood with the judge, and more flashbulbs went off. One of the kids had a camera, and Hal pulled one out of his pocket too. Everyone was carrying on and laughing now, and Nathan called out, "I want another picture. Let's have another picture," and Nina called out, "Come on, Hal, give your camera to someone else to take a picture of us. I want you to be in the picture with me and my mother."

Cee Cee beamed when she heard those words, and as Hal handed the lawyer his camera to take their picture, he put a loving arm around both Cee Cee and Nina.

"Smile, ladies," Nathan said, and each of them was glad to oblige.

After they moved out of the courtroom and back into the corridor, it seemed as if nobody from their group wanted to leave. The kids' voices and laughter echoed down the high-ceilinged hall, and the high spirits of the morning made everyone feel friendly and talkative. Richie and Hal were reliving old times, and Florrie was getting to know Nathan and his wife. Cee Cee looked over at Nina, who was at the edge of the group talking animatedly with Kevin, and watched as she touched his arm, said, "Excuse me," and slipped away from the group down the corridor toward the ladies room.

"Remember that time we worked that club in Pittsburgh?" Richie asked Cee Cee, and he launched into some story about a guy who owned a club they'd all worked in years ago, as Hal laughed along remembering the character Richie was describing. But Cee Cee wasn't listening. Her eyes were glued to the ladies room door, and after what seemed like an eternity she started away from the circle of people nervously, and made her way down the hall with what she hoped looked like a casual gait. Something was wrong. She heard her heels tap-tapping against the marble floor, or maybe it was the sound of her heart pounding as she pushed the door to the ladies room open hard, and when she didn't see anyone she shouted.

"Nina!"

The silence was long, and then there was a flush, after which the door to one of the stalls opened and Nina emerged.

"Are you okay?" Cee Cee asked, walking to her and looking up into the girl's eyes. Thank God. They looked normal.

Nina held her gaze knowingly. "I am okay," she said. "For now. But I had to get away from everybody for a minute because my stomach felt funny. I think it was just butterflies from all the excitement." Then she went to the sink and washed her hands, pulled a paper towel from the holder and dried them. She was wearing the emerald ring. She was a beautiful young woman, even prettier than Bertie had been, but it was clear by the way she glanced at herself in the mirror that, for her, the beauty still hadn't begun to reflect.

"I guess I'll always worry when I see you slip away. Even if it's just to go to the ladies room," Cee Cee said now, looking at their two faces together in the mirror over the sinks, thinking how changed they both were since this same day in 1983.

Nina turned away from the mirror now, looked at Cee Cee, then lovingly took her arm. "I guess you will," she said, and the two of them turned, their arms linked just the way they used to be long ago when they walked on the beach in Carmel, and together they walked across the wide hall of the courthouse to join the others.